GREAT TALES OF

THE AMERICAN WEST

Great Tales

OF THE

American West

EDITED, AND WITH AN INTRODUCTION

BY HARRY E. MAULE

THE
MODERN LIBRARY
NEW YORK

THE MODERN LIBRARY
is published by RANDOM HOUSE, INC.

Manufactured in the United States of America by H. Wolff

CONTENTS

ACKNOWLEDGMENTS

For permission to reprint copyrighted material the following acknowledgments are gratefully made to:

Houghton Mifflin Co., for the story "The Outcasts of Poker Flat" by Bret Harte, published in various editions of the writings of Bret Harte by Houghton Mifflin Co.

Harper & Brothers, for the story "Buck Fanshaw's Funeral" (Buck Fanshaw's death—preparations for his burial—Scotty Briggs and the minister) from Volume II of *Roughing It*, Hillcrest edition. Copyright, 1899 by The American Publishing Co. Copyright, 1899 by Samuel L. Clemens.

Harper & Brothers, for the story "The Winning of the Biscuit-Shooter" by Owen Wister from the book *Lin McLean*, published by Harper & Brothers. Copyright, 1897 by Harper & Brothers. Copyright, 1925 by Owen Wister.

Doubleday, Doran & Co., for the story "Hearts and Crosses" by O. Henry from *Heart of the West*, published by Doubleday, Doran & Co. Copyright, 1903-1904-1905-1906-1907 by Doubleday, Doran & Co.

Stewart Edward White, for the story "A Corner in Horses" from *Arizona Nights*, published by Doubleday, Page & Co., 1913. Copyright, 1907 by The Outing Publishing Co. Copyright, 1907 by The McClure Co.

Mrs. Eugene Manlove Rhodes, for the story "Beyond the Desert," first published in *McClure's Magazine*, February, 1914. Copyright, *McClure's Magazine*, 1914. From the book *West Is West*, copyright, 1917 by The H. K. Fly Co.

Zane Grey, Inc., and Lina Elise Grey, President, for the story "Tappan's Burro," published by Harper & Brothers. Copyright, 1923 by Zane Grey.

Short Stories Magazine and William MacLeod Raine, for the story "Last Warning," published in *Short Stories*,

January 10, 1943. Copyright, 1942 by Short Stories, Inc.

Short Stories Magazine and Clarence E. Mulford, for the story "Hopalong Sits In," published in *Short Stories,* 1929. Copyright, 1929 by Doubleday, Doran & Co. Copyright, 1933 by Clarence E. Mulford.

Short Stories Magazine and W. C. Tuttle, for the story "Sunset," published in *Short Stories,* February 10, 1934. Copyright, 1934 by Doubleday, Doran & Co.

James B. Hendryx and *Western Story Magazine,* for the story "Routine Patrol," copyright, 1938 by Street & Smith Publications, Inc.

Henry Herbert Knibbs, for the story "A Shot in the Dark," copyright by Henry Herbert Knibbs.

George R. Miller, Trustee U/W of Nancy C. Russell, for the story "Dog Eater" by Charles M. Russell from *More Rawhides,* published by the Montana Newspaper Association, copyright, 1925 by C. M. Russell. Also published in *Trails Plowed Under,* copyright, 1927 by Doubleday, Page & Co.

Marguerite Harper and Luke Short, for the story "Court Day" by Luke Short, originally published in *Collier's Magazine,* May 20, 1939. Copyright, 1939 by Crowell Publishing Co. Copyright, 1939 by Luke Short.

Sydney A. Sanders and Ernest Haycox, for the story "Stage to Lordsburg" by Ernest Haycox, originally published in *Collier's Magazine,* 1937. Copyright, 1937 by Ernest Haycox.

Brandt & Brandt, for the story "Wine on the Desert" by Max Brand from *Wine on the Desert and Other Stories,* published by Dodd, Mead & Co. Copyright, 1936 by Frederick Faust.

Random House, Inc. for the story *The Indian Well* by Walter Van Tilburg Clark. Copyright 1943 by Walter Van Tilburg Clark.

Brandt & Brandt, for the story "To Find a Place" by Robert Easton from *The Happy Man,* published by The Viking Press, Inc. Copyright, 1942-1943 by Robert Easton.

INTRODUCTION

THE Western story has a long and distinguished genealogy, and it springs, as all good stories must, from a natural affinity of the author for his material. No one in this line of ancestors ever sat down and said to himself, "Now I'll write a Western." On the contrary, he saw material which was grist to his mill and wrote the best story he could, regardless of background. The result captured the fancy of the whole reading world and set a literary fashion which has lasted for fifty years.

The progenitors of the type, Bret Harte, Mark Twain, Owen Wister, O. Henry, Stewart Edward White, and long before any of them, Washington Irving, all wrote what deeply interested them, without any idea that they were pointing the way for countless writers who followed in their footsteps. No matter what the author's geographical background was or how much time he spent in the West, if the drama of the country got into his blood and if he steeped himself in his subject matter enough, either by first-hand experience or by study, then the West became a part of him and he a part of it. Out of that affinity of the author for material that engages his bone-deep interest spring stories that will last, and so it was with the leaders in the field of the Western story. They created an authentic picture of one of the most thrilling periods in all history.

It has been my aim to present in this book the best and most representative work of such men and to trace roughly the growth of the Western story over the years. It is not ivory-tower stuff. The Western story, dealing as it invariably does with events, action, strife, portrays the conflict inevitable in the settlement of a raw land, in the crowding of several hundred years of history into a half century.

So, there were no "Western stories" as such in the beginning, just good stories about vastly interesting events in an unknown wilderness. It would be impossible to list all the early writers who used the West as a setting. Certainly James Fenimore Cooper and Washington Irving pointed the way long before the tide of emigration turned westward. In 1832 Irving wrote his *Western Journals* as the result of a trip to the then scarcely explored country which is now Missouri, Kansas and Oklahoma. In 1836 came his *Astoria*, a novel of the fur empire of the Northwest, and in 1837 *The Adventures of Captain Bonneville, U.S.A.* and *A Tour of the Prairies.* The world had to wait until after the war between the States, when the movement of expansion took on its real momentum, for the Western story to assume its true identity. Bret Harte and Mark Twain, the first steady producers of the form, were both in California, having gone there to make their fortunes after the Civil War. Both worked as printers and as newspaper reporters. They met in San Francisco in the late 1860's but so far as is known established no close or enduring contact. Indeed, Samuel L. Clemens at this time had not adopted writing as his vocation. He was recently out of an abortive military career but the memories of his life as a Mississippi River pilot were still fresh. Locating in Nevada he became a prospector and later a reporter in Virginia City. "The Jumping Frog of Calaveras County" was his first writing to attract attention. It was a few years later that he began producing the stories later gathered together and published in 1872 under the title of *Roughing It*, from which I have selected the tale "Buck Fanshaw's Funeral." These stories, it will be noted, were done long before his classic novels *Tom Sawyer* and *Huckleberry Finn.*

Similarly Bret Harte, an Easterner working for a newspaper in Northern California, drew the material for his best work from his experiences in the mining country. He had done two small books of poems and sketches and the short novel *M'Liss*, but in "The Luck of Roaring Camp" and "The Outcasts of Poker Flat," published in 1868 and 1869 respectively, in the *Overland Monthly Magazine* of which he was the first editor, he struck his real stride. They appeared in book form the next year with other stories of California of that time—and a great literary reputation was made.

Despite the unfortunate tone of patronage for the rude civilization they were reporting and the authors' lack of perspective on what this life meant to America as a whole, the Western stories of Mark Twain and Bret Harte stand up today and read as excitingly as they did when they first delighted the English-speaking world. Moreover, allowing for a heightening of effect, they stand as sound, authentic reports of what life was like in those days.

In the twenty years following there were few writers of Western fiction whose work survived the stultifying literary mores of the time. True, there were many books of non-fiction, diaries of the explorers, notably those of Lewis and Clark, published and republished from 1814 on; the multi-volume Parkman history of early America, issued between 1865 and 1898; the pictures of Currier and Ives, which illustrated the life of the expanding frontier; the old *Leslie's Weekly*, which year after year reported in articles and pictures the land west of the Mississippi which was being forged to the United States by rude men who had gone west to find a way of life after the Civil War. But we are here thinking of fiction and probably the Western scene was too raw, too crude for the desiccated taste of our literate East.

More than anyone else, I venture to say, did Theodore Roosevelt in his book *The Winning of the West* make the meaning of the land beyond the Mississippi clear to the whole country when it was published in four volumes from 1889 to 1896. The man who was later to be one of our most idolized Presidents knew and liked the Philadelphian, Owen Wister, whom he met in Wyoming. Though Wister was a dude (not an entirely uncomplimentary term in the Western vocabulary) he loved and understood the West, and its residents took him to their bosom.

Wister generally has been credited with being the father of the Western story and *The Virginian* has been called the first of its kind. Our fiction public was not willing to read of the West on even terms until they had been educated by fifteen or twenty years' diet of Mark Twain, Bret Harte and the non-fiction writers. "Teddy" was responsible for a lot of things in this country and he will have to accept his share of the glory for preparing the public for *The Virginian* ("when you say that, smile") which appeared in 1902. Shortly after came Wister's collection of short stories published under the title *Lin McLean* and it is from this volume that I have selected the incomparable "The Winning of the Biscuit-Shooter."

The ground was broken. A young man named William Sydney Porter in 1882 left his home in North Carolina to regain his health in Texas. He also was trying to find himself as a writer and in due course took the nom de plume of O. Henry. Among his early stories was the collection later published in 1907 under the title *The Heart of the West*. But even O. Henry could not eliminate entirely the slightly supercilious tone dictated by the East for the crudities of the West. Owen Wister concealed it better than most writers of his time, but the inherent snobbishness of that state of being we have come to know as the Main Line is, nevertheless, there in Wister's work for the discerning.

It took Stewart Edward White to shake off the last vestiges of this patronizing attitude of authors of the

90's and to write of the West on its own terms from its own point of view. White understood the significance of this surging life more clearly than any writer up to then, except Theodore Roosevelt. A native of Michigan, he developed an interest in the drama of the westward march of civilization and followed it in person. He preferred to write non-fiction, but when he set himself to putting the drama of Western life into a story he could do a thriller to rank with the best of them. His first book, *The Westerners* appeared in 1901. The total body of White's work on frontier America, fiction and non-fiction, in my opinion, will last as the best and fullest presentation of American pioneering in all its phases that we have had or will have. He has given us the lumber camps of Michigan and Wisconsin, the plains, mountains, deserts, forests, Indian fighting, cattle ranching, the early explorers and trappers, the prospectors and miners, gold rushes and land booms, bad men and outlaws. White perhaps knew more parts of the West really well than most writers of his time. Moreover, his books show the author's consciousness of the historical process and accentuate the meaning for posterity of each phase of the epic. I chose a story from his *Arizona Nights*, "A Corner in Horses," as being appropriate for this book, even though it may be a bit hilarious to be typical of the author's grave informativeness. Most of his fiction runs to novel or novelette length, too long for this book.

After *The Virginian* the Western story was in full swing and no magazine was complete without several of them, nor any publishing list without a Western book or two. Those were the days when Zane Grey, William McLeod Raine and a few others achieved sales in the hundreds of thousands. However, in the 1900's we were not commercially so quick on the trigger as we are now and up to 1914 there were only three or four pulp magazines heavily angled on Western stories. Along with the popular illustrated magazines they did a conscientious job and helped in the development of a generation of Western writers who took their art seriously and, as we said then, who knew their stuff.

It is out of the group of writers who developed in the twenty-odd years after 1900 that many of the stories in this book are selected, because they represent the cream of the crop of those excellent vintage years. Since, say, around 1935, the Western story has gone into still another phase which I would like to mention shortly.

I will not labor the point of literary finish of the writers who developed in the two decades before 1930. These men, conscientious craftsmen all, some of them artists, were above all natural *story-tellers* and for the most part wrote out of experience and direct observation. In the 1900's the West was still the West. There was plenty of pioneer life going on and the violence of sudden change even then took its toll of human life. Moreover, most of these writers grew up with the legend of what had gone before. Indian fighting, bad men, the great cattle drives, were a part of their inherited folk knowledge. True, some of them later correlated and checked their childhood recollections by historical research.

The beloved Eugene Manlove Rhodes, whom many connoisseurs call the best of them all, was a cowboy himself in New Mexico and Arizona when the land was young. In later years when he was studying and writing, his melancholy nostalgia for the old days crept into much of his output.

William McLeod Raine, English born but Western reared, saw plenty of the wild West from the early 90's on, and traveled over most of the country. He rode with rangers and rustlers; he bunked with nesters and gamblers. He has known the country for forty years and in his stories has given a picture of its conflict as he saw it.

Zane Grey, whose astronomic sales have brought forth the gibes of the envious, for all his intolerable overwriting, knew the country and its people and for as long as he was doing Western stories kept his memories fresh by association. He took long and arduous pack trips in wild and inaccessible country. In campfire talks with his companions or guides, he soaked in his material.

So with W. C. Tuttle, who did a certain amount of cowpunching himself and whose father was a Western sheriff of the traditional sort. So with James B. Hendryx, who quit his job as a cowboy to join the Klondike gold rush and who, in that experience, absorbed the material for his stories of the North. There he met the prototype of his Corporal Downey of the Mounted. Henry Herbert Knibbs, friend and co-worker of Gene Rhodes, spent his life in the Southwest and to him authenticity of detail was akin to a religion. Although the Tonto Kid does not appear in his story "A Shot in the Dark," readers will recognize the country and the Mebbyso mine. It is placed in Tonto Kid territory and his presence is implicit. Charles M. Russell, the internationally known painter whose story "Dog Eater" can be taken literally or not, as the mood of the reader directs, was called throughout the world of art the "cowboy artist." Having gone West as a youth, he did just about all the jobs there were on a cattle ranch. But his real interest lay in painting and his Western pictures rank in the esteem of collectors with those of Frederic Remington. He had no formal education, either in art or letters, and his only books, other than a volume of reproductions of some of his most famous paintings under the title of *Trails Plowed Under* and a collection of his illustrated letters entitled *Good Medicine*, were *Rawhide Rawlins* and *More Rawhides*, two little volumes of tall tales published locally in Montana. These stories, told in the inimitable idiom of the cowboy, are perfect examples of the robust humor and dead-pan manner characteristic of the time.

Clarence E. Mulford is a New Yorker, now resident in Maine, but his encyclopedic knowledge of Western history would put many native sons to shame. On a visit to the site of old Bent's Fort, for example, he conducted his guide when the latter confessed he really didn't know where it was, and traced the exact outlines of the fort and its approaches on the prairie. Later he built a scale model of it which checked with the best historical accounts. A man of many hobbies, Mr. Mulford has made the history, folklore, customs, etc., of the West his consuming interest. He has, for example, a collection of frontier firearms worthy of a museum and every piece has been repaired and conditioned by Mr. Mulford so that it will shoot as well as ever it did at Deadwood or Dodge. Out of such knowledge came his well-beloved character, Hopalong Cassidy.

Bridging the gap between the leaders of the Western story in the early 1900's and the present was the fabulous Max Brand, who was commonly reported to have written *and sold* a little matter of a million words a year for twenty-five years. His name in private life was Frederick Faust and he was killed in action in Italy where he had gone as a war correspondent considerably over the usual age. He would have had no regrets. He died doing the job he was best fitted to do for a cause in which he passionately believed. His output in the two decades between the wars included every type of popular fiction, with a fair share of Westerns. Perhaps his best-known book in this field was the still popular *Destry Rides Again,* originally published in 1930. As an indication of his versatility we must mention that he created the Dr. Kildare stories which became so popular in the movies. The point, for our purposes, is that his story "Wine on the Desert," chosen for this volume, blazes the trail toward the best of the Western stories as we know them today—stories in which attention to character study and literary finish replaced the old emphasis on action.

Among the newer voices represented here are the stories by Luke Short and Ernest Haycox, men who won their spurs in the free-for-all of the 20's but who have steadily developed their technique without sacrifice of drama or the common touch.

We come then to the modern refinement of the Western story as practiced by Walter Van Tilburg Clark, whose book *The Ox-Bow Incident* thrilled the reading public in 1940 by proving that a Western could also be a psychological study of literary significance. Not all of Mr. Clark's short stories are of the sort that make the big-circulation magazines with their multitudinous taboos. "The Indian Well," which I have chosen for his entry here, was first published in one of the "little" magazines. Obviously, it is not of the slick-paper type. It is, however, one of the most beautiful evocations of the Southwestern desert that I have ever read.

Similarly representative of the writer's approach to the West today are Robert Easton's stories of an ultra-modern ranch in the California hills; not that the cattle business is run so much like a factory everywhere today. There are many regions where methods and conditions are pretty much as they were thirty or forty years ago. What Mr. Easton shows us, however, is that, regardless of methods, most of the people, even on the headquarters ranch of the streamlined El Dorado Investment Company, have the stamp of the old West on them. Tradition dies hard.

The standard of selection for the stories which follow has been primarily interest—the best story of its kind available. I have shunned the synthetic and the tongue-in-cheek product. Every writer represented here is a sincere craftsman who respected his material. Secondarily, I have chosen stories to show examples of the development of the form. I have tried to give a panorama of the conflict which afforded writers so rich a field for drama. Lastly, as far as possible, I have tried to include stories which would mark the fascinating scenic and geographical variety of the land west of the Mississippi. Regrettably, space limitations prohibit the use of many excellent tales by accomplished story-tellers whose work, because of its intrinsic interest, deserves a place in a book of this kind. These writers, like those here included, made original contributions to the development of the Western story instead of simply following lines already laid down. In any event, here are the leaders, the trailblazers in the Western story, of whatever period.

Many of the writers represented here are friends of long standing with whose work I have been associated as editor and publisher. To them and to others who have helped in the difficult task of locating long out-of-print material and in arranging for authorization to reprint I render my thanks.

Harry E. Maule

New York—
February 15, 1945.

GREAT TALES
OF THE
AMERICAN WEST

THE OUTCASTS OF POKER FLAT

by Bret Harte

As Mr. John Oakhurst, gambler, stepped into the main street of Poker Flat on the morning of the 23rd of November, 1850, he was conscious of a change in its moral atmosphere since the preceding night. Two or three men, conversing earnestly together, ceased as he approached, and exchanged significant glances. There was a Sabbath lull in the air, which, in a settlement unused to Sabbath influences, looked ominous.

Mr. Oakhurst's calm, handsome face betrayed small concern in these indications. Whether he was conscious of any predisposing cause was another question. "I reckon they're after somebody," he reflected; "likely it's me." He returned to his pocket the handkerchief with which he had been whipping away the red dust of Poker Flat from his neat boots, and quietly discharged his mind of any further conjecture.

In point of fact, Poker Flat was "after somebody." It had lately suffered the loss of several thousand dollars, two valuable horses, and a prominent citizen. It was experiencing a spasm of virtuous reaction, quite as lawless and ungovernable as any of the acts that had provoked it. A secret committee had determined to rid the town of all improper persons. This was done permanently in regard of two men who were then hanging from the boughs of a sycamore in the gulch, and temporarily in the banishment of certain other objectionable characters. I re-

3

gret to say that some of these were ladies. It is but due
to the sex, however, to state that their impropriety was
professional, and it was only in such easily established
standards of evil that Poker Flat ventured to sit in judgment.

Mr. Oakhurst was right in supposing that he was included in this category. A few of the committee had
urged hanging him as a possible example and a sure
method of reimbursing themselves from his pockets of
the sums he had won from them. "It's agin justice," said
Jim Wheeler, "to let this yer young man from Roaring
Camp—an entire stranger—carry away our money." But
a crude sentiment of equity residing in the breasts of
those who had been fortunate enough to win from Mr.
Oakhurst overruled this narrower local prejudice.

Mr. Oakhurst received his sentence with philosophic
calmness, none the less coolly that he was aware of the
hesitation of his judges. He was too much of a gambler
not to accept fate. With him life was at best an uncertain
game, and he recognized the usual percentage in favor
of the dealer.

A body of armed men accompanied the deported wickedness of Poker Flat to the outskirts of the settlement.
Besides Mr. Oakhurst, who was known to be a coolly
desperate man, and for whose intimidation the armed
escort was intended, the expatriated party consisted of a
young woman familiarly known as "The Duchess"; another who had won the title of "Mother Shipton"; and
"Uncle Billy," a suspected sluice-robber and confirmed
drunkard. The cavalcade provoked no comments from
the spectators, nor was any word uttered by the escort.
Only when the gulch which marked the uttermost limit
of Poker Flat was reached, the leader spoke briefly and
to the point. The exiles were forbidden to return at the
peril of their lives.

As the escort disappeared, their pent-up feelings found
vent in a few hysterical tears from the Duchess, some
had language from Mother Shipton, and a Parthian vol-

ley of expletives from Uncle Billy. The philosophic Oakhurst alone remained silent. He listened calmly to Mother Shipton's desire to cut somebody's heart out, to the repeated statements of the Duchess that she would die in the road, and to the alarming oaths that seemed to be bumped out of Uncle Billy as he rode forward. With the easy good humor characteristic of his class, he insisted upon exchanging his own riding-horse, "Five-Spot," for the sorry mule which the Duchess rode. But even this act did not draw the party into any closer sympathy. The young woman readjusted her somewhat draggled plumes with a feeble, faded coquetry; Mother Shipton eyed the possessor of "Five-Spot" with malevolence, and Uncle Billy included the whole party in one sweeping anathema.

The road to Sandy Bar—a camp that, not having as yet experienced the regenerating influences of Poker Flat, consequently seemed to offer some invitation to the emigrants—lay over a steep mountain range. It was distant a day's severe travel. In that advanced season the party soon passed out of the moist, temperate regions of the foothills into the dry, cold, bracing air of the Sierras. The trail was narrow and difficult. At noon the Duchess, rolling out of her saddle upon the ground, declared her intention of going no farther, and the party halted.

The spot was singularly wild and impressive. A wooded amphitheatre, surrounded on three sides by precipitous cliffs of naked granite, sloped gently toward the crest of another precipice that overlooked the valley. It was, undoubtedly, the most suitable spot for a camp, had camping been advisable. But Mr. Oakhurst knew that scarcely half the journey to Sandy Bar was accomplished, and the party were not equipped or provisioned for delay. This fact he pointed out to his companions curtly, with a philosophic commentary on the folly of "throwing up their hand before the game was played out." But they were furnished with liquor, which in this emergency stood them in place of food, fuel, rest, and prescience. In spite of his remonstrances, it was not long before they were more or less under its influence. Uncle Billy passed rapidly from a bellicose state into one of stupor, the Duchess became maudlin, and Mother Shipton snored. Mr. Oakhurst alone remained erect, leaning against a rock, calmly surveying them.

Mr. Oakhurst did not drink. It interfered with a profession which required coolness, impassiveness, and presence of mind, and, in his own language, he "couldn't afford it." As he gazed at his recumbent fellow exiles, the loneliness begotten of his pariah trade, his habits of life, his very vices, for the first time seriously oppressed him. He bestirred himself in dusting his black clothes, washing his hands and face, and other acts characteristic of his studiously neat habits, and for a moment forgot his annoyance. The thought of deserting his weaker and more pitiable companions never perhaps occurred to him. Yet he could not help feeling the want of that excitement which, singularly enough, was most conducive to that calm equanimity for which he was notorious. He looked at the gloomy walls that rose a thousand feet sheer above the circling pines around him, at the sky ominously clouded, at the valley below, already deepening into shadow; and, doing so, suddenly he heard his own name called.

A horseman slowly ascended the trail. In the fresh, open face of the newcomer Mr. Oakhurst recognized Tom Simson, otherwise known as "The Innocent," of Sandy Bar. He had met him some months before over a "little game," and had, with perfect equanimity, won the entire fortune—amounting to some forty dollars—of that guileless youth. After the game was finished, Mr. Oakhurst drew the youthful speculator behind the door and thus addressed him: "Tommy, you're a good little man, but you can't gamble worth a cent. Don't try it over again." He then handed him his money back, pushed him gently from the room, and so made a devoted slave of Tom Simson.

There was a remembrance of this in his boyish and enthusiastic greeting of Mr. Oakhurst. He had started, he said, to go to Poker Flat to seek his fortune. "Alone?" No, not exactly alone; in fact (a giggle), he had run away with Piney Woods. Didn't Mr. Oakhurst remember Piney? She that used to wait on the table at the Temperance House? They had been engaged a long time, but old Jake Woods had objected, and so they had run away, and were going to Poker Flat to be married, and here they were. And they were tired out, and how lucky it was they had found a place to camp, and company. All this the Innocent delivered rapidly, while Piney, a stout, comely damsel of fifteen, emerged from behind the pine-tree, where she had been blushing unseen, and rode to the side of her lover.

Mr. Oakhurst seldom troubled himself with sentiment, still less with propriety; but he had a vague idea that the situation was not fortunate. He retained, however, his presence of mind sufficiently to kick Uncle Billy, who was about to say something, and Uncle Billy was sober enough to recognize in Mr. Oakhurst's kick a superior power that would not bear trifling. He then endeavored to dissuade Tom Simson from delaying further, but in vain. He even pointed out the fact that there was no provision, nor means of making a camp. But, unluckily, the Innocent met this objection by assuring the party that he was provided with an extra mule loaded with provisions, and by the discovery of a rude attempt at a log house near the trail. "Piney can stay with Mrs. Oakhurst," said the Innocent, pointing to the Duchess, "and I can shift for myself."

Nothing but Mr. Oakhurst's admonishing foot saved Uncle Billy from bursting into a roar of laughter. As it was, he felt compelled to retire up the cañon until he could recover his gravity. There he confided the joke to the tall pine-trees, with many slaps of his leg, contortions of his face, and the usual profanity. But when he returned to the party, he found them seated by a fire—for

the air had grown strangely chill and the sky overcast—
in apparently amicable conversation. Piney was actually
talking in an impulsive girlish fashion to the Duchess,
who was listening with an interest and animation she had
not shown for many days. The Innocent was holding
forth, apparently with equal effect, to Mr. Oakhurst and
Mother Shipton, who was actually relaxing into amiabil-
ity. "Is this yer a d—d picnic?" said Uncle Billy, with
inward scorn, as he surveyed the sylvan group, the glancing firelight, and the tethered animals in the foreground.
Suddenly an idea mingled with the alcoholic fumes that
disturbed his brain. It was apparently of a jocular nature, for he felt impelled to slap his leg again and cram
his fist into his mouth.

As the shadows crept slowly up the mountain, a slight
breeze rocked the tops of the pine-trees and moaned
through their long and gloomy aisles. The ruined cabin,
patched and covered with pine boughs, was set apart for
the ladies. As the lovers parted, they unaffectedly exchanged a kiss, so honest and sincere that it might have
been heard above the swaying pines. The frail Duchess
and the malevolent Mother Shipton were probably too
stunned to remark upon this last evidence of simplicity,
and so turned without a word to the hut. The fire was replenished, the men lay down before the door, and in a
few minutes were asleep.

Mr. Oakhurst was a light sleeper. Toward morning he
awoke benumbed and cold. As he stirred the dying fire,
the wind, which was now blowing strongly, brought to
his cheek that which caused the blood to leave it,—
snow!

He started to his feet with the intention of awakening
the sleepers, for there was no time to lose. But turning to
where Uncle Billy had been lying, he found him gone. A
suspicion leaped to his brain, and a curse to his lips. He
ran to the spot where the mules had been tethered—they
were no longer there. The tracks were already rapidly
disappearing in the snow.

The momentary excitement brought Mr. Oakhurst back to the fire with his usual calm. He did not waken the sleepers. The Innocent slumbered peacefully, with a smile on his good-humored, freckled face; the virgin Piney slept beside her frailer sisters as sweetly as though attended by celestial guardians; and Mr. Oakhurst, drawing his blanket over his shoulders, stroked his mustaches and waited for the dawn. It came slowly in a whirling mist of snowflakes that dazzled and confused the eye. What could be seen of the landscape appeared magically changed. He looked over the valley, and summed up the present and future in two words, "Snowed in!"

A careful inventory of the provisions, which, fortunately for the party, had been stored within the hut, and so escaped the felonious fingers of Uncle Billy, disclosed the fact that with care and prudence they might last ten days longer. "That is," said Mr. Oakhurst sotto voce to the Innocent, "if you're willing to board us. If you ain't —and perhaps you'd better not—you can wait till Uncle Billy gets back with provisions." For some occult reason, Mr. Oakhurst could not bring himself to disclose Uncle Billy's rascality, and so offered the hypothesis that he had wandered from the camp and had accidentally stampeded the animals. He dropped a warning to the Duchess and Mother Shipton, who of course knew the facts of their associate's defection. "They'll find out the truth about us all when they find out anything," he added significantly, "and there's no good frightening them now."

Tom Simson not only put all his worldly store at the disposal of Mr. Oakhurst, but seemed to enjoy the prospect of their enforced seclusion. "We'll have a good camp for a week, and then the snow'll melt, and we'll all go back together." The cheerful gayety of the young man and Mr. Oakhurst's calm infected the others. The Innocent, with the aid of pine boughs, extemporized a thatch for the roofless cabin, and the Duchess directed

Piney in the rearrangement of the interior with a taste
and tact that opened the blue eyes of that provincial
maiden to their fullest extent. "I reckon now you're used
to fine things at Poker Flat," said Piney. The Duchess
turned away sharply to conceal something that reddened
her cheeks through their professional tint, and Mother
Shipton requested Piney not to "chatter." But when Mr.
Oakhurst returned from a weary search for the trail, he
heard the sound of happy laughter echoed from the
rocks. He stopped in some alarm, and his thoughts first
naturally reverted to the whiskey, which he had pru-
dently cached. "And yet it don't somehow sound like
whiskey," said the gambler. It was not until he caught
sight of the blazing fire through the still blinding storm,
and the group around it, that he settled to the conviction
that it was "square fun."

Whether Mr. Oakhurst had cached his cards with the
whiskey as something debarred the free access of the
community, I cannot say. It was certain that, in Mother
Shipton's words, he "didn't say 'cards' once" during that
evening. Haply the time was beguiled by an accordion,
produced somewhat ostentatiously by Tom Simson from
his pack. Notwithstanding some difficulties attending the
manipulation of this instrument, Piney Woods managed
to pluck several reluctant melodies from its keys, to an
accompaniment by the Innocent on a pair of bone castanets. But the crowning festivity of the evening was
reached in a rude camp-meeting hymn, which the lovers,
joining hands, sang with great earnestness and vocifera-
tion. I fear that a certain defiant tone and Covenanter's
swing to its chorus rather than any devotional quality,
caused it speedily to infect the others, who at last joined
in the refrain:—

> "*I'm proud to live in the service of the Lord,*
> *And I'm bound to die in His army.*"

The pines rocked, the storm eddied and whirled above

the miserable group, and the flames of their altar leaped
heavenward, as if in token of the vow.

At midnight the storm abated, the rolling clouds
parted, and the stars glittered keenly above the sleeping
camp. Mr. Oakhurst, whose professional habits had enabled him to live on the smallest possible amount of
sleep, in dividing the watch with Tom Simson somehow
managed to take upon himself the greater part of that
duty. He excused himself to the Innocent by saying that
he had "often been a week without sleep." "Doing
what?" asked Tom. "Poker!" replied Oakhurst senten-
tiously. "When a man gets a streak of luck,—nigger-
luck,—he don't get tired. The luck gives in first. Luck,"
continued the gambler reflectively, "is a mighty queer
thing. All you know about it for certain is that it's bound
to change. And it's finding out when it's going to change
that makes you. We've had a streak of bad luck since we
left Poker Flat,—you come along, and slap you get into
it, too. If you can hold your cards right along you're all
right. For," added the gambler, with cheerful irrele-
vance—

" 'I'm proud to live in the service of the Lord,
And I'm bound to die in His army.' "

The third day came, and the sun, looking through the
white-curtained valley, saw the outcasts divide their
slowly decreasing store of provisions for the morning
meal. It was one of the peculiarities of that mountain climate that its rays diffused a kindly warmth over the win-
try landscape, as if in regretful commiseration of the
past. But it revealed drift on drift of snow piled high
around the hut,—a hopeless, uncharted trackless sea of
white lying below the rocky shores to which the casta-
ways still clung. Through the marvelously clear air the
smoke of the pastoral village of Poker Flat rose miles
away. Mother Shipton saw it, and from a remote pinnacle of her rocky fastness hurled in that direction a final

malediction. It was her last vituperative attempt, and
perhaps for that reason was invested with a certain degree of sublimity. It did her good, she privately informed
the Duchess. "Just you go out there and cuss, and see."
She then set herself to the task of amusing "the child," as
she and the Duchess were pleased to call Piney. Piney
was no chicken, but it was a soothing and original theory
of the pair thus to account for the fact that she didn't
swear and wasn't improper.

When night crept up again through the gorges, the
reedy notes of the accordion rose and fell in fitful spasms
and long-drawn gasps by the flickering campfire. But
music failed to fill entirely the aching void left by insuffi-
cient food, and a new diversion was proposed by Piney,
—story-telling. Neither Mr. Oakhurst nor his female
companions caring to relate their personal experiences,
this plan would have failed too, but for the Innocent.
Some months before he had chanced upon a stray copy
of Mr. Pope's ingenious translation of the Iliad. He now
proposed to narrate the principal incidents of that poem
—having thoroughly mastered the argument and fairly
forgotten the words—in the current vernacular of Sandy
Bar. And so for the rest of that night the Homeric demi-
gods again walked the earth. Trojan bully and wily
Greek wrestled in the winds, and the great pines in the
cañon seemed to bow to the wrath of the son of Peleus.
Mr. Oakhurst listened with quiet satisfaction. Most especially was he interested in the fate of "Ash-heels," as
the Innocent persisted in denominating the "swift-footed
Achilles."

So, with small food and much of Homer and the accordion, a week passed over the heads of the outcasts. The
sun again forsook them, and again from leaden skies the
snowflakes were sifted over the land. Day by day closer
around them drew the snowy circle, until at last they
looked from their prison over drifted walls of dazzling
white, that towered twenty feet above their heads. It be-

came more and more difficult to replenish their fires even from the fallen trees beside them, now half hidden in the drifts. And yet no one complained. The lovers turned from the dreary prospect and looked into each other's eyes, and were happy. Mr. Oakhurst settled himself coolly to the losing game before him. The Duchess, more cheerful than she had been, assumed the care of Piney. Only Mother Shipton—once the strongest of the party—seemed to sicken and fade. At midnight on the tenth day she called Oakhurst to her side. "I'm going," she said, in a voice of querulous weakness, "but don't say anything about it. Don't waken the kids. Take the bundle from under my head, and open it." Mr. Oakhurst did so. It contained Mother Shipton's rations for the last week, untouched. "Give 'em to the child," she said, pointing to the sleeping Piney. "You've starved yourself," said the gambler. "That's what they call it," said the woman querulously, as she lay down again, and, turning her face to the wall, passed quietly away.

The accordion and the bones were put aside that day, and Homer was forgotten. When the body of Mother Shipton had been committed to the snow, Mr. Oakhurst took the Innocent aside, and showed him a pair of snowshoes, which he had fashioned from the old pack-saddle. "There's one chance in a hundred to save her yet," he said, pointing to Piney; "but it's there," he added, pointing toward Poker Flat. "If you can reach there in two days she's safe." "And you?" asked Tom Simson. "I'll stay here," was the curt reply.

The lovers parted with a long embrace. "You are not going, too?" said the Duchess, as she saw Mr. Oakhurst apparently waiting to accompany him. "As far as the cañon," he replied. He turned suddenly and kissed the Duchess, leaving her pallid face aflame, and her trembling limbs rigid with amazement.

Night came, but not Mr. Oakhurst. It brought the storm again and the whirling snow. Then the Duchess, feeding the fire, found that some one had quietly piled beside the hut enough fuel to last a few days longer. The tears rose to her eyes, but she hid them from Piney.

The women slept but little. In the morning, looking into each other's faces, they read their fate. Neither spoke, but Piney, accepting the position of the stronger, drew near and placed her arm around the Duchess's waist. They kept this attitude for the rest of the day. That night the storm reached its greatest fury, and, rending asunder the protecting pines, invaded the very hut.

Toward morning they found themselves unable to feed the fire, which gradually died away. As the embers slowly blackened, the Duchess crept closer to Piney, and broke the silence of many hours: "Piney, can you pray?" "No, dear," said Piney simply. The Duchess, without knowing exactly why, felt relieved, and, putting her head upon Piney's shoulder, spoke no more. And so reclining, the younger and purer pillowing the head of her soiled sister upon her virgin breast they fell asleep.

The wind lulled as if it feared to waken them. Feathery drifts of snow, shaken from the long pine boughs, flew like white winged birds, and settled about them as they slept. The moon through the rifted clouds looked down upon what had been the camp. But all human stain, all trace of earthly travail, was hidden beneath the spotless mantle mercifully flung from above.

They slept all that day and the next, nor did they waken when voices and footsteps broke the silence of the camp. And when pitying fingers brushed the snow from their wan faces, you could scarcely have told from the equal peace that dwelt upon them which was she that had sinned. Even the law of Poker Flat recognized this, and turned away, leaving them still locked in each other's arms.

But at the head of the gulch, on one of the largest pine-trees, they found the deuce of clubs pinned to the bark with a bowie-knife. It bore the following, written in pencil in a firm hand:—

†

BENEATH THIS TREE
LIES THE BODY
OF
JOHN OAKHURST,
WHO STRUCK A STREAK OF BAD LUCK
ON THE 23D OF NOVEMBER, 1850,
AND
HANDED IN HIS CHECKS
ON THE 7TH DECEMBER, 1850.

†

And pulseless and cold, with a Derringer by his side and a bullet in his heart, though still calm as in life, beneath the snow lay he who was at once the strongest and yet the weakest of the outcasts of Poker Flat.

BUCK FANSHAW'S FUNERAL

by MARK TWAIN

SOMEBODY has said that in order to know a community, one must observe the style of its funerals and know what manner of men they bury with most ceremony. I cannot say which class we buried with most éclat in our "flush times," the distinguished public benefactor or the distinguished rough—possibly the two chief grades or grand divisions of society honored their illustrious dead about equally; and hence, no doubt, the philosopher I have quoted from would have needed to see two representative funerals in Virginia* before forming his estimate of the people.

There was a grand time over Buck Fanshaw when he

* Refers, of course, to Virginia City, Nevada. Ed.

died. He was a representative citizen. He had "killed his man"—not in his own quarrel, it is true, but in defense of a stranger unfairly beset by numbers. He had kept a sumptuous saloon. He had been the proprietor of a dashing helpmeet whom he could have discarded without the formality of a divorce. He had held a high position in the fire department and been a very Warwick in politics. When he died there was great lamentation throughout the town, but especially in the vast bottom-stratum of society.

On the inquest it was shown that Buck Fanshaw, in the delirium of a wasting typhoid fever, had taken arsenic, shot himself through the body, cut his throat, and jumped out of a four-story window and broken his neck —and after due deliberation, the jury, sad and tearful, but with intelligence unblinded by its sorrow, brought in a verdict of death "by the visitation of God." What could the world do without juries?

Prodigious preparations were made for the funeral. All the vehicles in town were hired, all the saloons put in mourning, all the municipal and fire-company flags hung at half-mast, and all the firemen ordered to muster in uniform and bring their machines duly draped in black. Now—let us remark in parenthesis—as all the peoples of the earth had representative adventurers in the Silverland, and as each adventurer had brought the slang of his nation or his locality with him, the combination made the slang of Nevada the richest and the most infinitely varied and copious that had ever existed anywhere in the world, perhaps, except in the mines of California in the "early days." Slang was the language of Nevada. It was hard to preach a sermon without it, and be understood. Such phrases as "You bet!" "Oh, no, I reckon not!" "No Irish need apply," and a hundred others, became so common as to fall from the lips of a speaker unconsciously— and very often when they did not touch the subject under discussion and consequently failed to mean anything.

After Buck Fanshaw's inquest, a meeting of the short-haired brotherhood was held, for nothing can be done on the Pacific coast without a public meeting and an expression of sentiment. Regretful resolutions were passed and various committees appointed; among others, a committee of one was deputed to call on the minister, a fragile, gentle, spiritual new fledgling from an Eastern theological seminary, and as yet unacquainted with the ways of the mines. The committeeman, "Scotty" Briggs, made his visit; and in after days it was worth something to hear the minister tell about it. Scotty was a stalwart rough, whose customary suit, when on weighty official business, like committee work, was a fire helmet, flaming red flannel shirt, patent leather belt with spanner and revolver attached, coat hung over arm, and pants stuffed into boot tops. He formed something of a contrast to the pale theological student. It is fair to say of Scotty, however, in passing, that he had a warm heart, and a strong love for his friends, and never entered into a quarrel when he could reasonably keep out of it. Indeed, it was commonly said that whenever one of Scotty's fights was investigated, it always turned out that it had originally been no affair of his, but that out of native goodheartedness he had dropped in of his own accord to help the man who was getting the worst of it. He and Buck Fanshaw were bosom friends, for years, and had often taken adventurous "pot-luck" together. On one occasion, they had thrown off their coats and taken the weaker side in a fight among strangers, and after gaining a hard-earned victory, turned and found that the men they were helping had deserted early, and not only that, but had stolen their coats and made off with them! But to return to Scotty's visit to the minister. He was on a sorrowful mission, now, and his face was the picture of woe. Being admitted to the presence he sat down before the clergyman, placed his fire-hat on an unfinished manuscript sermon under the minister's nose, took from it a red silk handkerchief, wiped his brow and heaved a sigh of dismal impressiveness, explanatory of his business. He choked, and even shed tears; but with an effort he mastered his voice and said in lugubrious tones:

"Are you the duck that runs the gospel-mill next door?"

"Am I the—pardon me, I believe I do not understand."

With another sigh and a half-sob, Scotty rejoined:

"Why you see we are in a bit of trouble, and the boys thought maybe you would give us a lift, if we'd tackle you—that is, if I've got the rights of it and you are the head clerk of the doxology-works next door."

"I am the shepherd in charge of the flock whose fold is next door."

"The which?"

"The spiritual adviser of the little company of believers whose sanctuary adjoins these premises."

Scotty scratched his head, reflected a moment, and then said:

"You ruther hold over me, pard. I reckon I can't call that hand. Ante and pass the buck."

"How? I beg pardon. What did I understand you to say?"

"Well, you've ruther got the bulge on me. Or maybe we've both got the bulge, somehow. You don't smoke me and I don't smoke you. You see, one of the boys has passed in his checks, and we want to give him a good send-off, and so the thing I'm on now is to roust out somebody to jerk a little chin-music for us and waltz him through handsome."

"My friend, I seem to grow more and more bewildered. Your observations are wholly incomprehensible to me. Cannot you simplify them in some way? At first I thought perhaps I understood you, but I grope now. Would it not expedite matters if you restricted yourself to categorical statements of fact unencumbered with obstructing accumulations of metaphor and allegory?"

Another pause, and more reflection. Then, said Scotty:

"I'll have to pass, I judge."

"How?"

"You've raised me out, pard."

"I still fail to catch your meaning."

"Why, that last lead of yourn is too many for me—that's the idea. I can't neither trump nor follow suit."

The clergyman sank back in his chair perplexed. Scotty leaned his head on his hand and gave himself up to thought. Presently his face came up, sorrowful but confident.

"I've got it now, so's you can savvy," he said. "What we want is a gospel-sharp. See?"

"A what?"

"Gospel-sharp. Parson."

"Oh! Why did you not say so before? I am a clergyman—a parson."

"Now you talk! You see my blind and straddle it like a man. Put it there!"—extending a brawny paw, which closed over the minister's small hand and gave it a shake indicative of fraternal sympathy and fervent gratification.

"Now we're all right, pard. Let's start fresh. Don't you mind my snuffling a little—becuz we're in a power of trouble. You see, one of the boys has gone up the flume—"

"Gone where?"

"Up the flume—throwed up the sponge, you understand."

"Thrown up the sponge?"

"Yes—kicked the bucket—"

"Ah—has departed to that mysterious country from whose bourn no traveler returns."

"Return! I reckon not. Why, pard, he's *dead!*"

"Yes, I understand."

"Oh, you do? Well I thought maybe you might be getting tangled some more. Yes, you see he's dead again—"

"*Again!* Why, has he ever been dead before?"

"Dead before? No! Do you reckon a man has got as many lives as a cat? But you bet you he's awful dead now, poor old boy, and I wish I'd never seen this day. I don't want no better friend than Buck Fanshaw. I knowed him by the back; and when I know a man and like him, I freeze to him—you hear *me*. Take him all round, pard, there never was a bullier man in the mines. No man ever knowed Buck Fanshaw to go back on a friend. But it's all up, you know, it's all up. It ain't no use. They've scooped him."

"Scooped him?"

"Yes—death has. Well, well, well, we've got to give him up. Yes, indeed. It's a kind of a hard world, after all, *ain't* it? But pard, he was a rustler! You ought to seen him get started once. He was a bully boy with a glass eye! Just spit in his face and give him room according to his strength, and it was just beautiful to see him peel and go in. He was the worst son of a thief that ever drawed breath. Pard, he was *on* it! He was on it bigger than an Injun!"

"On it? On what?"

"On the shoot. On the shoulder. On the fight, you understand. *He* didn't give a continental for *any*body. *Beg* your pardon, friend, for coming so near saying a cuss-word—but you see I'm on an awful strain, in this palaver, on account of having to cramp down and draw everything so mild. But we've got to give him up. There ain't any getting around that, I don't reckon. Now if we can get you to help plant him—"

"Preach the funeral discourse? Assist at the obsequies?"

"Obs'quies is good. Yes. That's it—that's our little game. We are going to get the thing up regardless, you know. He was always nifty himself, and so you bet you his funeral ain't going to be no slouch—solid silver doorplate on his coffin, six plumes on the hearse, and a nigger on the box in a biled shirt and a plug hat—how's that for high? And we'll take care of *you*, pard. We'll fix you all right. There'll be a kerridge for you; and whatever you want, you just 'scape out and we'll 'tend to it. We've got a shebang fixed up for you to stand behind, in No. 1's house, and don't you be afraid. Just go in and toot your horn, if you don't sell a clam. Put Buck through as bully as you can, pard, for anybody that knows him will tell you that he was one of the whitest men that was ever in the mines. You can't draw it too strong. He never could stand it to see things going wrong. He's done more to make this town quiet and peaceable than any man in it. I've seen him lick four Greasers in eleven minutes, myself. If a thing wanted regulating, *he* warn't a man to go browsing around after somebody to do it, but he would prance in and regulate it himself. He warn't a Catholic. Scasely. He was down on 'em. His word was, 'No Irish need apply!' But it didn't make no difference about that when it came down to what a man's rights was—and so, when some roughs jumped the Catholic boneyard and started in to stake out town-lots in it he *went* for 'em! And he *cleaned* 'em, too! I was there, pard, and I seen it myself."

"That was very well indeed—at least the impulse was —whether the act was strictly defensible or not. Had deceased any religious convictions? That is to say, did he feel a dependence upon, or acknowledge allegiance to a higher power?"

More reflection.

"I reckon you've stumped me again, pard. Could you say it over once more, and say it slow?"

"Well, to simplify it somewhat, was he, or rather had he ever been connected with any organization sequestered from secular concerns and devoted to self-sacrifice in the interests of morality?"

"All down but nine—set 'em up on the other alley, pard."

"What did I understand you to say?"

"Why, you're most too many for me, you know. When you get in with your left I hunt grass every time. Every time you draw, you fill; but I don't seem to have any luck. Let's have a new deal."

"How? Begin again?"

"That's it."

"Very well. Was he a good man, and—"

"There—I see that; don't put up another chip till I look at my hand. A good man, says you? Pard, it ain't no name for it. He was the best man that ever—pard, you would have doted on that man. He could lam any galoot of his inches in America. It was him that put down the riot last election before it got a start; and everybody said he was the only man that could have done it. He waltzed in with a spanner in one hand and a trumpet in the other, and sent fourteen men home on a shutter in less than three minutes. He had that riot all broke up and prevented nice before anybody ever got a chance to strike a blow. He was always for peace, and he would *have* peace—he could not stand disturbances. Pard, he was a great loss to this town. It would please the boys if you could chip in something like that and do him justice. Here once when the Micks got to throwing stones through the Methodis' Sunday-school windows, Buck Fanshaw, all of his own notion, shut up his saloon and took a couple of six-shooters and mounted guard over the Sunday-school. Says he, 'No Irish need apply!' And they didn't. He was the bulliest man in the mountains, pard! He could run faster, jump higher, hit harder, and hold more tanglefoot whisky without spilling it than any man in seventeen counties. Put that in, pard—it'll please the boys more than anything you could say. And you can say, pard, that he never shook his mother."

"Never shook his mother?"

"That's it—any of the boys will tell you so."

"Well, but why *should* he shake her?"

"That's what *I* say—but some people does."

"Not people of any repute?"

"Well, some that averages pretty so-so."

"In my opinion the man that would offer personal violence to his own mother, ought to—"

"Cheese it, pard; you've banked your ball clean outside the string. What I was a drivin' at, was, that he never *throwed off* on his mother—don't you see? No indeedy. He give her a house to live in, and town lots, and plenty of money; and he looked after her and took care of her all the time; and when she was down with the smallpox I'm d—d if he didn't set up nights and nuss her himself! *Beg* your pardon for saying it, but it hopped out too quick for yours truly. You've treated me like a gentleman, pard, and I ain't the man to hurt your feelings intentional. I think you're white. I think you're a square man, pard. I like you, and I'll lick any man that don't. I'll lick him till he can't tell himself from a last year's corpse! Put it *there!*" (Another fraternal handshake—and exit.)

The obsequies were all that "the boys" could desire. Such a marvel of funeral pomp had never been seen in Virginia. The plumed hearse, the dirge-breathing brass bands, the closed marts of business, the flags drooping at half-mast, the long, plodding procession of uniformed secret societies, military battalions and fire companies, draped engines, carriages of officials, and citizens in vehicles and on foot, attracted multitudes of spectators to the sidewalks, roofs, and windows; and for years afterward, the degree of grandeur attained by any civic display in Virginia was determined by comparison with Buck Fanshaw's funeral.

Scotty Briggs, as a pall-bearer and a mourner, occupied a prominent place at the funeral, and when the sermon was finished and the last sentence of the prayer for the dead man's soul ascended, he responded, in a low voice, but with feeling:

"AMEN. No Irish need apply."

As the bulk of the response was without apparent relevancy, it was probably nothing more than a humble tribute to the memory of the friend that was gone; for, as Scotty had once said, it was "his word."

Scotty Briggs, in after days, achieved the distinction of becoming the only convert to religion that was ever gathered from the Virginia roughs; and it transpired that the man who had it in him to espouse the quarrel of the weak out of inborn nobility of spirit was no mean timber whereof to construct a Christian. The making him one did not warp his generosity or diminish his courage; on the contrary it gave intelligent direction to the one and a broader field to the other. If his Sunday-school class progressed faster than the other classes, was it matter for wonder? I think not. He talked to his pioneer small-fry in a language they understood! It was my large privilege, a month before he died, to hear him tell the beautiful story of Joseph and his brethren to his class "without looking at the book." I leave it to the reader to fancy what it was like, as it fell, riddled with slang, from the lips of that grave, earnest teacher, and was listened to by his little learners with a consuming interest that showed that they were as unconscious as he was that any violence was being done to the sacred proprieties!

THE WINNING OF THE BISCUIT-SHOOTER

by OWEN WISTER

IT was quite clear to me that Mr. McLean could not know the news. Meeting him to-day had been unforeseen —unforeseen and so pleasant that the thing had never come into my head until just now, after both of us had talked and dined our fill, and were torpid with satisfaction.

I had found Lin here at Riverside in the morning. At my horse's approach to the cabin, it was he and not the postmaster who had come precipitately out of the door.

"I'm turruble pleased to see yu'," he had said, immediately.

"What's happened?" said I, in some concern at his appearance.

And he piteously explained: "Why, I've been here all alone since yesterday!"

This was indeed all; and my hasty impressions of shooting and a corpse gave way to mirth over the child and his innocent grievance that he had blurted out before I could get off my horse.

Since when, I inquired of him, had his own company become such a shock to him?

"As to that," replied Mr. McLean, a thought ruffled, "when a man expects lonesomeness he stands it like he stands anything else, of course. But when he has figured on finding company—say—" he broke off (and vindictiveness sparkled in his eye)—"when you're lucky enough to catch yourself alone, why, I suppose yu' just take a chair and chat to yourself for hours.—You've not seen anything of Tommy?" he pursued, with interest.

I had not; and forthwith Lin poured out to me the pent-up complaints and sociability with which he was bursting. The foreman had sent him over here with a sackful of letters for the post, and to bring back the week's mail for the ranch. A day was gone now, and nothing for a man to do but sit and sit. Tommy was overdue fifteen hours. Well, you could have endured that, but the neighbors had all locked their cabins and gone to Buffalo. It was circus week in Buffalo. Had I ever considered the money there must be in the circus business? Tommy had taken the outgoing letters early yesterday. Nobody had kept him waiting. By all rules he should have been back again last night. Maybe the stage was late reaching Powder River, and Tommy had had to lay over for it. Well, that would justify him. Far more likely he had gone to the circus himself and taken the mail with him. Tommy was no type of man for postmaster.

Except drawing the allowance his mother in the East gave him first of every month, he had never shown punctuality, that Lin could remember. Never had any second thoughts, and awful few first ones. Told bigger lies than a small man ought, also.

"Has successes, though," said I, wickedly.

"Huh!" went on Mr. McLean. "Successes! One ice-cream-soda success. And she"—Lin's still wounded male pride made him plaintive—"why, even that girl quit him, once she got the chance to appreciate how insignificant he was compared with the size of his words. No, sir. Not one of 'em retains interest in Tommy."

Lin was unsaddling and looking after my horse, just because he was glad to see me. Since our first acquaintance, that memorable summer of Pitchstone Canon when he had taken such good care of me and such bad care of himself, I had learned pretty well about horses and camp craft in general. He was an entire boy then. But he had been East since, East by a route of his own discovering —and from his account of that journey it had proved, I think, a sort of spiritual experience. And then the years of our friendship were beginning to roll up. Manhood of the body he had always richly possessed; and now, whenever we met after a season's absence and spoke those invariable words which all old friends upon this earth use to each other at meeting—"You haven't changed, you haven't changed at all!"—I would wonder if manhood had arrived in Lin's boy soul. And so to-day, while he attended to my horse and explained the nature of Tommy (a subject he dearly loved just now), I looked at him and took an intimate, superior pride in feeling how much more mature I was than he, after all.

There's nothing like a sense of merit for making one feel aggrieved, and on our return to the cabin Mr. McLean pointed with disgust to some firewood.

"Look at those sorrowful toothpicks," said he; "Tommy's work."

So Lin, the excellent hearted, had angrily busied himself, and chopped a pile of real logs that would last a week. He had also cleaned the stove, and nailed up the bed, the pillow-end of which was on the floor. It appeared the master of the house had been sleeping in it the reverse way on account of the slant. Thus had Lin cooked and dined alone, supped alone, and sat over some old newspapers until bed-time alone with his sense of virtue. And now here it was long after breakfast, and no Tommy yet.

"It's good yu' come this forenoon," Lin said to me. "I'd not have had the heart to get up another dinner just for myself. Let's eat rich!"

Accordingly, we had richly eaten, Lin and I. He had gone out among the sheds and caught some eggs (that is how he spoke of it), we had opened a number of things in cans, and I had made my famous dish of evaporated apricots, in which I managed to fling a suspicion of caramel throughout the stew.

"Tommy'll be hot about these," said Lin, joyfully, as we ate the eggs. "He don't mind what yu' use of his canned goods—pickled salmon and truck. He is hospitable all right enough till it comes to an egg. Then he'll tell any lie. But shucks! Yu' can read Tommy right through his clothing. 'Make yourself at home, Lin,' says he, yesterday. And he showed me his fresh milk and his stuff. 'Here's a new ham,' says he; 'too bad my damned hens 'ain't been layin'. The sons-o'-guns have quit on me ever since Christmas.' And away he goes to Powder River for the mail. 'You swore too heavy about them hens,' thinks I. Well, I expect he may have traveled half a mile by the time I'd found four nests."

I am fond of eggs, and eat them constantly—and in Wyoming they were always a luxury. But I never forget those that day, and how Lin and I enjoyed them thinking of Tommy. Perhaps manhood was not quite established in my own soul at that time—and perhaps that is the reason why it is the only time I have ever known which I would live over again, those years when people

said, "You are old enough to know better"—and one
didn't care!

Salmon, apricots, eggs, we dealt with them all prop-
erly, and I had some cigars. It was now that the news
came back into my head.

"What do you think of—" I began, and stopped.

I spoke out of a long silence, the slack, luxurious silence of digestion. I got no answer, naturally, from the
torpid Lin, and then it occurred to me that he would
have asked me what I thought, long before this, had he
known. So, observing how comfortable he was, I began
differently.

"What is the most important event that can happen in
this country?" said I.

Mr. McLean heard me where he lay along the floor of
the cabin on his back, dozing by the fire; but his eyes
remained closed. He waggled one limp, open hand
slightly at me, and torpor resumed her dominion over
him.

"I want to know what you consider the most important event that can happen in this country," said I,
again, enunciating each word with slow clearness.

The throat and lips of Mr. McLean moved, and a
sulky sound came forth that I recognized to be meant
for the word "War." Then he rolled over so that his face
was away from me, and put an arm over his eyes.

"I don't mean country in the sense of United States,"
said I. "I mean this country here, and Bear Creek, and—
well, the ranches southward for fifty miles, say. Important to this section."

"Mosquitoes'll be due in about three weeks," said Lin.
"Yu' might leave a man rest till then."

"I want your opinion," said I.

"Oh, misery! Well, a raise in the price of steers."

"No."

"Yu' said yu' wanted my opinion," said Lin. "Seems
like yu' merely figure on givin' me yours."

"Very well," said I. "Very well, then."

I took up a copy of the Cheyenne *Sun*. It was five weeks old, and I soon perceived that I had read it three weeks ago; but I read it again for some minutes now.

"I expect a railroad would be more important," said Mr. McLean, persuasively, from the floor.

"Than a rise in steers?" said I, occupied with the Cheyenne *Sun*. "Oh, yes. Yes, a railroad certainly would."

"It's got to be money, anyhow," stated Lin, thoroughly wakened. "Money in some shape."

"How little you understand the real wants of the country!" said I, coming to the point. "It's a girl."

Mr. McLean lay quite still on the floor.

"A girl," I repeated. "A new girl coming to this starved country."

The cow-puncher took a long, gradual stretch and began to smile. "Well," said he, "yu' caught me—if that's much to do when a man is half-witted with dinner and sleep." He closed his eyes again and lay with a specious expression of indifference. But that sort of thing is a solitary entertainment, and palls. "Starved," he presently muttered. "We are kind o' starved that way, I'll admit. More dollars than girls to the square mile. And to think of all of us nice, healthy, young—bet yu' I know who she is!" he triumphantly cried. He had sat up and leveled a finger at me with the throw-down jerk of a marksman. "Sidney, Nebraska."

I nodded. This was not the lady's name—he could not recall her name—but his geography of her was accurate.

One day in February my friend, Mrs. Taylor, over on Bear Creek, had received a letter—no common event for her. Therefore, during several days she had all callers read it just as naturally as she had them all see the new baby; and baby and letter had both been brought out for me. The letter was signed,

"Ever your afectionite frend

"Katie Peck."

and was not easy to read, here and there. But you could

piece out the drift of it, and there was Mrs. Taylor by
your side, eager to help you when you stumbled. Miss
Peck wrote that she was overworked in Sidney, Nebraska, and needed a holiday. When the weather grew
warm she should like to come to Bear Creek and be like
old times. "Like to come and be like old times" filled
Mrs. Taylor with sentiment and the cow-punchers with
expectation. But it is a long way from February to warm
weather on Bear Creek, and even cow-punchers will forget about a new girl if she does not come. For several
weeks I had not heard Miss Peck mentioned, and old
girls had to do. Yesterday, however, when I paid a visit
to Miss Molly Wood (the Bear Creek school-mistress),
I found her keeping in order the cabin and the children
of the Taylors, while they were gone forty-five miles to
the stage station to meet their guest.

"Well," said Lin, judicially, "Miss Wood is a lady."

"Yes," said I, with deep gravity. For I was thinking of
an occasion when Mr. McLean had discovered that truth
somewhat abruptly.

Lin thoughtfully continued. "She is—she's—she's—
what are you laughin' at?"

"Oh, nothing. You don't see quite so much of Miss
Wood as you used to, do you?"

"Huh! So that's got around. Well, o' course I'd ought
t've knowed better, I suppose. All the same, there's lots
and lots of girls do like gettin' kissed against their wishes
—and you know it."

"But the point would rather seem to be that she—"

"Would rather seem! Don't yu' start that professor
style o' yours, or I'll—I'll talk more wickedness in worse
language than ever yu've heard me do yet."

"Impossible!" I murmured, sweetly, and Master Lin
went on.

"As to point—that don't need to be explained to me.
She's a lady all right." He ruminated for a moment. "She
has about scared all the boys off, though," he continued.
"And that's what you get by being refined," he con-

cluded, as if Providence had at length spoken in this matter.

"She has not scared off a boy from Virginia, I notice," said I. "He was there yesterday afternoon again. Ridden all the way over from Sunk Creek. Didn't seem particularly frightened."

"Oh, well, nothin' alarms him—not even refinement," said Mr. McLean, with his grin. "And she'll fool your Virginian like she done the balance of us. You wait. Shucks! If all the girls were that chilly, why, what would us poor punchers do?"

"You have me cornered," said I, and we sat in a philosophical silence, Lin on the floor still, and I at the window. There I looked out upon a scene my eyes never tired of then, nor can my memory now. Spring had passed over it with its first, lightest steps. The pastured levels undulated in emerald. Through the many-changing sage, that just this moment of to-day was lilac, shone greens scarce a week old in the dimples of the foot-hills; and greens new-born beneath today's sun melted among them. Around the doublings of the creek in the willow thickets glimmered skeined veils of yellow and delicate crimson. The stream poured turbulently away from the snows of the mountains behind us. It went winding in many folds across the meadows into distance and smallness, and so vanished round the great red battlement of wall beyond. Upon this were falling the deep hues of afternoon—violet, rose, and saffron, swimming and meeting as if some prism had dissolved and flowed over the turrets and crevices of the sandstone. Far over there I saw a dot move.

"At last!" said I.

Lin looked out of the window. "It's more than Tommy," said he, at once; and his eyes made it out before mine could. "It's a wagon. That's Tommy's bald-faced horse alongside. He's fooling to the finish," Lin severely commented, as if, after all this delay, there should at least be a homestretch.

Presently, however, a homestretch seemed likely to occur. The bald-faced horse executed some lively maneuvers, and Tommy's voice reached us faintly through the light spring air. He was evidently howling the remarkable strain of yells that the cow-punchers invented as the speech best understood by cows—"Oi-ee, yah, whoop-yah-ye-ee, oooo-oop, oop, oop-oop-oop-oop-yah-hee!" But that gives you no idea of it. Alphabets are worse than photographs. It is not the lungs of every man that can produce these effects, nor even from armies, eagles, or mules were such sounds ever heard on earth. The cow-puncher invented them. And when the last cow-puncher is laid to rest (if that, alas! have not already befallen) the yells will be forever gone. Singularly enough, the cattle appeared to appreciate them. Tommy always did them very badly, and that was plain even at this distance. Nor did he give us a homestretch, after all. The bald-faced horse made a number of evolutions and returned beside the wagon.

"Showin' off," remarked Lin. "Tommy's showin' off." Suspicion crossed his face, and then certainty. "Why, we might have knowed that!" he exclaimed, in dudgeon. "It's her." He hastened outside for a better look, and I came to the door myself. "That's what it is," said he. "It's the girl. Oh yes. That's Taylor's buckskin pair he traded Balaam for. She come by the stage all right yesterday, yu' see, but she has been too tired to travel, yu' see, or else, maybe, Taylor wanted to rest his buckskins —they're four-year-olds. Or else—anyway, they laid over last night at Powder River, and Tommy he has just laid over too, yu' see, holdin' the mail back on us twenty-four hours—and that's your postmaster!"

It was our postmaster, and this he had done, quite as the virtuously indignant McLean surmised. Had I taken the same interest in the new girl, I suppose that I, too, should have felt virtuously indignant.

Lin and I stood outside to receive the travelers. As their cavalcade drew near, Mr. McLean grew silent and watchful, his whole attention focused upon the Taylors' vehicle. Its approach was joyous. Its gear made a cheerful clanking, Taylor cracked his whip and encouragingly chirruped to his buckskins, and Tommy's apparatus jingled musically. For Tommy wore upon himself and his saddle all the things you can wear in the Wild West. Except that his hair was not long, our postmaster might have conducted a show and minted gold by exhibiting his romantic person before the eyes of princes. He began with a black-and-yellow rattlesnake skin for a hat-band, he continued with a fringed and beaded shirt of buckskin, and concluded with large, tinkling spurs. Of course, there were things between his shirt and his heels, but all leather and deadly weapons. He had also a riata, a cuerta, and tapaderos, and frequently employed these Spanish names for the objects. I wish that I had not lost Tommy's photograph in Rocky Mountain costume. You must understand that he was really pretty, with blue eyes, ruddy cheeks, and a graceful figure; and besides, he had twenty-four hours' start of poor dusty Lin, whose best clothes were elsewhere.

You might have supposed that it would be Mrs. Taylor who should present us to her friend from Sidney, Nebraska; but Tommy on his horse undertook the office before the wagon had well come to a standstill. "Good friends of mine, and gentlemen, both," said he to Miss Peck; and to us, "A lady whose acquaintance will prove a treat to our section."

We all bowed at each other beneath the florid expanse of these recommendations, and I was proceeding to murmur something about its being a long journey and a fine day when Miss Peck cut me short, gayly:

"Well," she exclaimed to Tommy, "I guess I'm pretty near ready for them eggs you've spoke so much about."

I have not often seen Mr. McLean lose his presence of mind. He needed merely to exclaim, "Why, Tommy, you told me your hens had not been laying since Christmas!" and we could have sat quiet and let Tommy try to find all the eggs that he could. But the new girl was a sore embarrassment to the cow-puncher's wits. Poor Lin stood by the wheels of the wagon. He looked up at Miss Peck, he looked over at Tommy, his features assumed a rueful expression, and he wretchedly blurted:

"Why, Tommy, I've been and eat 'em!"

"Well, if that ain't!" cried Miss Peck. She stared with interest at Lin as he now assisted her to descend.

"All?" faltered Tommy. "Not the four nests?"

"I've had three meals, yu' know," Lin reminded him, deprecatingly.

"I helped him," said I. "Ten innocent, fresh eggs. But we have left some ham. Forgive us, please."

"I declare!" said Miss Peck, abruptly, and rolled her sluggish, inviting eyes upon me. "You're a case, too, I expect."

But she took only brief note of me, although it was from head to foot. In her stare the dull shine of familiarity grew vacant, and she turned back to Lin McLean. "You carry that," said she, and gave the pleased cow-puncher a hand valise.

"I'll look after your things, Miss Peck!" called Tommy, now springing down from his horse. The egg tragedy had momentarily stunned him.

"You'll attend to the mail first, Mr. Postmaster!" said the lady, but favoring him with a look from her large eyes. "There's plenty of gentlemen here." With that her glance favored Lin. She went into the cabin, he following her close, with the Taylors and myself in the rear. "Well, I guess I'm about collapsed!" said she, vigorously, and sank upon one of Tommy's chairs.

The fragile article fell into sticks beneath her, and Lin leaped to her assistance. He placed her upon a firmer foundation. Mrs. Taylor brought a basin and towel to bathe the dust from her face, Mr. Taylor produced whiskey, and I found sugar and hot water. Tommy would doubtless have done something in the way of assistance or restoratives, but he was gone to the stable with the horses.

"Shall I get your medicine from the valise, deary?" inquired Mrs. Taylor.

"Not now," her visitor answered; and I wondered why she should take such a quick look at me.

"We'll soon have yu' independent of medicine," said Lin, gallantly. "Our climate and scenery here has frequently raised the dead."

"You're a case, anyway!" exclaimed the sick lady, with rich conviction.

The cow-puncher now sat himself on the edge of Tommy's bed, and, throwing one leg across the other, began to raise her spirits with cheerful talk. She steadily watched him—his face sometimes, sometimes his lounging, masculine figure. While he thus devoted his attentions to her, Taylor departed to help Tommy at the stable, and good Mrs. Taylor, busy with supper for all of us in the kitchen, expressed her joy at having her old friend of childhood for a visit after so many years.

"Sickness has changed poor Katie some," said she. "But I'm hoping she'll get back her looks on Bear Creek."

"She seems less feeble than I had understood," I remarked.

"Yes, indeed! I do believe she's feeling stronger. She was that tired and down yesterday with the long stage-ride, and it is so lonesome! But Taylor and I heartened her up, and Tommy came with the mail, and to-day she's real spruced-up like, feeling she's among friends."

"How long will she stay?" I inquired.

"Just as long as ever she wants! Me and Katie hasn't met since we was young girls in Dubuque, for I left home when I married Taylor, and he brought me to this country right soon; and it ain't been like Dubuque much, though if I had it to do over again I'd do just the same, as Taylor knows. Katie and me hasn't wrote even,

not till this February, for you always mean to and you
don't. Well, it'll be like old times. Katie'll be most thirty-
four, I expect. Yes. I was seventeen and she was sixteen
the very month I was married. Poor thing! She ought to
have got some good man for a husband, but I expect she
didn't have any chance, for there was a big fam'ly o'
them girls, and old Peck used to act real scandalous, getting drunk so folks didn't visit there evenings scarcely at
all. And so she quit home, it seems, and got a position in
the railroad eating-house at Sidney, and now she has
poor health with feeding them big trains day and night."

"A biscuit-shooter!" said I.

Loyal Mrs. Taylor stirred some batter in silence.
"Well," said she then, "I'm told that's what the yard-
hands of the railroad call them poor waiter-girls. You
might hear it around the switches at them division stations."

I had heard it in higher places also, but meekly accepted the reproof.

If you have made your trans-Missouri journeys only
since the new era of dining-cars, there is a quantity of
things you have come too late for, and will never know.
Three times a day in the brave days of old you sprang
from your scarce-halted car at the summons of a gong.
You discerned by instinct the right direction, and, passing steadily through doorways, had taken, before you
knew it, one of some sixty chairs in a room of tables and
catsup bottles. Behind the chairs, standing attention, a
platoon of Amazons, thick-wristed, pink-and-blue, began
immediately a swift chant. It hymned the total bill-of-
fare at a blow. In this inexpressible ceremony the name
of every dish went hurtling into the next, telescoped to
shapelessness. Moreover, if you stopped your Amazon in
the middle, it dislocated her, and she merely went back
and took a fresh start. The chant was always the same,
but you never learned it. As soon as it began, your mind
snapped shut like the upper berth in a Pullman. You
must have uttered appropriate words—even a parrot will

—for next you were eating things—pie, ham, hot cakes—
as fast as you could. Twenty minutes of swallowing, and
all aboard for Ogden, with your pile-driven stomach
dumb with amazement. The Strasburg goose is not dieted
with greater velocity, and "biscuit-shooter" is a grand
word. Very likely some Homer of the railroad yards first
said it—for what men upon the present earth so speak
with imagination's tongue as we Americans?

If Miss Peck had been a biscuit-shooter, I could account readily for her conversation, her equipped deportment, the maturity in her round, blue, marble eye. Her
abrupt laugh, something beyond gay, was now sounding
in response to Mr. McLean's lively sallies, and I found
him fanning her into convalescence with his hat. She herself made but few remarks, but allowed the cow-puncher
to entertain her, merely exclaiming briefly now and then,
"I declare!" and "If you ain't!" Lin was most certainly
engaging, if that was the lady's meaning. His wide-open
eyes sparkled upon her, and he half closed them now and
then to look at her more effectively. I suppose she was
worth it to him. I have forgotten to say that she was
handsome in a large California-fruit style. They made a
good-looking pair of animals. But it was in the presence
of Tommy that Master Lin shone more energetically
than ever, and under such shining Tommy was transpar-
ently restless. He tried, and failed, to bring the conversation his way, and took to rearranging the mail and the
furniture.

"Supper's ready," he said, at length. "Come right in,
Miss Peck; right in here. This is your seat—this one,
please. Now you can see my fields out of the window."

"You sit here," said the biscuit-shooter to Lin; and
thus she was between them. "Them's elegant!" she presently exclaimed to Tommy. "Did you cook 'em?"

I explained that the apricots were of my preparation.

"Indeed!" said she, and returned to Tommy, who had
been telling her of his ranch, his potatoes, his horses.
"And do you punch cattle, too?" she inquired of him.

"Me?" said Tommy, slightingly; "gave it up years ago; too empty a life for me. I leave that to such as like it. When a man owns his own property"—Tommy swept his hand at the whole landscape—"he takes to more intellectual work."

"Lickin' postage-stamps," Mr. McLean suggested, sourly.

"You lick them and I cancel them," answered the postmaster; and it does not seem a powerful rejoinder. But Miss Peck uttered her laugh.

"That's one on you," she told Lin. And throughout this meal it was Tommy who had her favor. She partook of his generous supplies; she listened to his romantic inventions, the trails he had discovered, the bears he had slain; and after supper it was with Tommy, and not with Lin, that she went for a little walk.

"Katie was ever a tease," said Mrs. Taylor, of her childhood friend, and Mr. Taylor observed that there was always safety in numbers. "She'll get used to the ways of this country quicker than our little school-marm," said he.

Mr. McLean said very little, but read the newly arrived papers. It was only when bedtime dispersed us, the ladies in the cabin and the men choosing various spots outside, that he became talkative again for a while. We lay in the blankets we had spread on some soft, dry sand in preference to the stable, where Taylor and Tommy had gone. Under the contemplative influence of the stars, Lin fell into generalization.

"Ever notice," said he, "how whiskey and lyin' act the same on a man?"

I did not feel sure that I had.

"Just the same way. You keep either of 'em up long enough, and yu' get to require it. If Tommy didn't lie some every day, he'd get sick."

I was sleepy, but I murmured assent to this, and trusted he would not go on.

"Ever notice," said he, "how the victims of the whiskey and lyin' habit get to increasing the dose?"

"Yes," said I.

"Him roping six bears!" pursued Mr. McLean, after further contemplation. "Or any bear. Ever notice how the worser a man's lyin' the silenter other men'll get? Why's that, now?"

I believe that I made a faint sound to imply that I was following him.

"Men don't get took in. But ladies now, they—"

Here he paused again, and during the next interval of contemplation I sank beyond his reach.

In the morning I left Riverside for Buffalo, and there or thereabouts I remained for a number of weeks. Miss Peck did not enter my thoughts, nor did I meet anyone to remind me of her, until one day I stopped at the drug-store. It was not for drugs, but gossip, that I went. In the daytime there was no place like the apothecary's for meeting men and hearing the news. There I heard how things were going everywhere, including Bear Creek.

All the cow-punchers liked the new girl up there, said gossip. She was a great addition to society. Reported to be more companionable than the school-marm, Miss Molly Wood, who had been raised too far east, and showed it. Vermont, or some such dude place. Several had been in town buying presents for Miss Katie Peck. Tommy Postmaster had paid high for a necklace of elk-tushes the government scout at McKinney sold him. Too bad Miss Peck did not enjoy good health. Shorty had been in only yesterday to get her medicine again. Third bottle. Had I heard the big joke on Lin McLean? He had promised her the skin of a big bear he knew the location of, and Tommy got the bear.

Two days after this I joined one of the round-up camps at sunset. They had been working from Salt Creek to Bear Creek, and the Taylor ranch was in visiting distance from them again, after an interval of gathering and branding far across the country. The Virginian, the gentle-voiced Southerner, whom I had last seen lingering with Miss Wood, was in camp. Silent three-quarters of the time, as was his way, he sat gravely watching Lin McLean. That person seemed silent also, as was not his way quite so much.

"Lin," said the Southerner, "I reckon you're failin'."

Mr. McLean raised a somber eye, but did not trouble to answer further.

"A healthy man's laigs ought to fill his pants," pursued the Virginian.

The challenged puncher stretched out a limb and showed his muscles with young pride.

"And yu' cert'nly take no comfort in your food," his ingenious friend continued, slowly and gently.

"I'll eat you a match any day and place yu' name," said Lin.

"It ain't sca'cely hon'able," went on the Virginian, "to waste away durin' the round-up. A man owes his strength to them that hires it. If he is paid to rope stock he ought to rope stock, and not leave it dodge or pull away."

"It's not many dodge my rope," boasted Lin imprudently.

"Why, they tell me as how that heifer of the Sidney-Nebraska brand got plumb away from yu' and little Tommy had to chase afteh her."

Lin sat up angrily amid the laughter, but reclined again. "I'll improve," said he, "if yu' learn me how yu' rope that Vermont stock so handy. Has she promised to be your sister yet?" he added.

"Is that what they do?" inquired the Virginian, serenely. "I have never got related that way. Why, that'll make Tommy your brother-in-law, Lin!"

And now, indeed, the camp laughed a loud, merciless laugh.

But Lin was silent. Where everybody lives in a glass-house the victory is to him who throws the adroitest stone. Mr. McLean was readier witted than most, but the gentle, slow Virginian could be a master when he chose.

"Tommy has been recountin' his wars up at the Taylors'," he now told the camp. "He has frequently campaigned with General Crook, General Miles, and General Ruger, all at onced. He's an exciting fighter, in conversation, and kep' us all scared for mighty nigh an hour. Miss Peck appeared interested in his statements."

"What was you doing at the Taylors' yourself?" demanded Lin.

"Visitin' Miss Wood," answered the Virginian with entire ease. For he also knew when to employ the plain truth as a bluff. "You'd ought to write to Tommy's mother, Lin, and tell her what a dare-devil her son is gettin' to be. She would cut off his allowance and bring him home, and you would have the runnin' all to yourself."

"I'll fix him yet," muttered Mr. McLean. "Him and his wars."

With that he rose and left us.

The next afternoon he informed me that if I was riding up the creek to spend the night he would go for company. In that direction we started, therefore, without any mention of the Taylors or Miss Peck. I was puzzled. Never had I seen him thus disconcerted by woman. With him woman had been a transient disturbance. I had witnessed a series of flighty romances, where the cowpuncher had come, seen, often conquered, and moved on. Nor had his affairs been of the sort to teach a young man respect. I am putting it rather mildly.

For the first part of our way this afternoon he was moody, and after that began to speak with appalling wisdom about life. Life, he said, was a serious matter. Did I realize that? A man was liable to forget it. A man was liable to go sporting and helling around till he waked up some day and found all his best pleasures had become just a business. No interest, no surprise, no novelty left, and no cash in the bank. Shorty owed him fifty dollars. Shorty would be able to pay that after the round-up, and he, Lin, would get his time and rustle altogether some five hundred dollars. Then there was his homestead claim on Box Elder, and the surveyors were coming in this fall. No better location for a home in this country than Box Elder. Wood, water, fine land. All it needed was a house and ditches and buildings and fences, and to be planted with crops. Such chances and considerations should sober a man and make him careful what he did. "I'd take in Cheyenne on our wedding-trip, and after that I'd settle right down to improving Box Elder," concluded Mr. McLean, suddenly.

His real intentions flashed upon me for the first time. I had not remotely imagined such a step.

"*Marry* her!" I screeched in dismay. "Marry *her!*"

I don't know which word was the worse to emphasize at such a moment, but I emphasized both, thoroughly.

"I didn't expect yu'd act that way," said the lover. He dropped behind me fifty yards and spoke no more.

Not at once did I beg his pardon for the brutality I had been surprised into. It is one of those speeches that, once said, is said forever. But it was not that which withheld me. As I thought of the tone in which my friend had replied, it seemed to me sullen, rather than deeply angry or wounded—resentment at my opinion not of her character so much as of his choice! Then I began to be sorry for the fool, and schemed for a while how to intervene. But have you ever tried to intervene? I soon abandoned the idea, and took a way to be forgiven, and to learn more.

"Lin," I began, slowing my horse, "you must not think about what I said."

"I'm thinkin' of pleasanter subjects," said he, and slowed his own horse.

"Oh, look here!" I exclaimed.

"Well?" said he. He allowed his horse to come within about ten yards.

"Astonishment makes a man say anything," I proceeded. "And I'll say again you're too good for her—and

I'll say I don't generally believe in the wife being older than the husband."

"What's two years?" said Lin.

I was near screeching out again, but saved myself. He was not quite twenty-five, and I remembered Mrs. Taylor's unprejudiced computation of the biscuit-shooter's years. It is a lady's prerogative, however, to estimate her own age.

"She had her twenty-seventh birthday last month," said Lin, with sentiment, bringing his horse entirely abreast of mine. "I promised her a bear-skin."

"Yes," said I, "I heard about that in Buffalo."

Lin's face grew dusky with anger. "No doubt yu' heard about it!" said he. "I don't guess yu' heard much about anything else. I ain't told the truth to any of 'em—but her." He looked at me with a certain hesitation. "I think I will," he continued. "I don't mind tellin' you."

He began to speak in a strictly business tone, while he evened the coils of rope that hung on his saddle.

"She had spoke to me about her birthday, and I had spoke to her about something to give her. I had offered to buy her in town whatever she named, and I was figuring to borrow from Taylor. But she fancied the notion of a bearskin. I had mentioned about some cubs. I had found the cubs where the she-bear had them cached by the foot of a big boulder in the range over Ten Sleep, and I put back the leaves and stuff on top o' them little things as near as I could the way I found them, so that the bear would not suspicion me. For I was aiming to get her. And Miss Peck, she sure wanted the hide for her birthday. So I went back. The she-bear was off, and I clumb up inside the rock, and I waited a turrible long spell till the sun traveled clean around the canon. Mrs. Bear came home, though, a big cinnamon; and I raised my gun, but laid it down to see what she'd do. She scrapes around and snuffs, and the cubs start whining, and she talks back to 'em. Next she sits up awful big, and lifts up a cub and holds it to her close with both her

paws, same as a person. And she rubbed her ear agin the
cub, and the cub sort o' nipped her, and she cuffed the
cub, and the other cub came toddlin', and away they
starts rolling, all three of 'em! I watched that for a long
while. That big thing just nursed and played with them
little cubs, beatin' 'em for a change onced in a while, and
talkin', and onced in a while she'd sit up solemn and look
all around so life-like that I near busted. Why, how was
I goin' to spoil that? So I come away, very quiet, you
bet! for I'd have hated to have Mrs. Bear notice me.
Miss Peck, she laughed. She claimed I was scared to
shoot."

"After you had told her why it was?" said I.

"Before and after. I didn't tell her first, because I felt
kind of foolish. Then Tommy went and he killed the
bear all right, and she has the skin now. Of course the
boys joshed me a heap about gettin' beat by Tommy."

"But since she has taken you?" said I.

"She ain't said it. But she will when she understands
Tommy."

I fancied that the lady understood. The once I had
seen her she appeared to me as what might be termed an
expert in men, and one to understand also the reality of
Tommy's ranch and allowance, and how greatly these
differed from Box Elder. Probably the one thing she
could not understand was why Lin spared the mother and
her cubs. A deserted home in Dubuque, a career in a railroad eating-house, a somewhat vague past, and a present
lacking context—indeed, I hoped with all my heart that
Tommy would win!

"Lin," said I, "I'm backing him."

"Back away!" said he. "Tommy can please a woman
—him and his blue eyes—but he don't savvy how to
make a woman want him, not any better than he knows
about killin' Injuns."

"Did you hear about the Crows?" said I.

"About young bucks going on the war-path? Shucks!

That's put up by the papers of this section. They're aimin' to get Uncle Sam to order his troops out, and then folks can sell hay and stuff to 'em. If Tommy believed any Crows—" he stopped, and suddenly slapped his leg.

"What's the matter now?" I asked.

"Oh, nothing." He took to singing, and his face grew roguish to its full extent. "What made yu' say that to me?" he asked, presently.

"Say what?"

"About marrying. Yu' don't think I'd better."

"I don't."

"Onced in a while yu' tell me I'm flighty. Well, I am. Whoop-ya!"

"Colts ought not to marry," said I.

"Sure!" said he. And it was not until we came in sight of the Virginian's black horse tied in front of Miss Wood's cabin next the Taylors' that Lin changed the lively course of thought that was evidently filling his mind.

"Tell yu'," said he, touching my arm confidentially and pointing to the black horse, "for all her Vermont refinement she's a woman just the same. She likes him dangling round her so earnest—him that nobody ever saw dangle before. And he has quit spreein' with the boys. And what does he get by it? I am glad I was not raised good enough to appreciate the Miss Woods of this world," he added, defiantly—"except at long range."

At the Taylors' cabin we found Miss Wood sitting with her admirer, and Tommy from Riverside to admire Miss Peck. The biscuit-shooter might pass for twenty-seven, certainly. Something had agreed with her—whether the medicine, or the mountain air, or so much masculine company; whatever had done it, she had bloomed into brutal comeliness. Her hair looked curlier, her figure was shapelier, her teeth shone whiter, and her cheeks were a lusty, overbearing red. And there sat Molly Wood talking sweetly to her big, grave Virginian;

to look at them, there was no doubt that he had been "raised good enough" to appreciate her, no matter what had been his raising!

Lin greeted everyone jauntily. "How are yu', Miss Peck? How are yu', Tommy?" said he. "Hear the news, Tommy? Crow Injuns on the war-path."

"I declare!" said the biscuit-shooter.

The Virginian was about to say something, but his eye met Lin's, and then he looked at Tommy. Then what he did say was, "I hadn't been goin' to mention it to the ladies until it was right sure."

"You needn't to be afraid, Miss Peck," said Tommy. "There's lots of men here."

"Who's afraid?" said the biscuit-shooter.

"Oh," said Lin, "maybe it's like most news we get in this country. Two weeks stale and a lie when it was fresh."

"Of course," said Tommy.

"Hello, Tommy!" called Taylor from the lane. "Your horse has broke his rein and run down the field."

Tommy rose in disgust and sped after the animal.

"I must be cooking supper now," said Katie shortly.

"I'll stir for yu'," said Lin, grinning at her.

"Come along then," said she; and they departed to the adjacent kitchen.

Miss Wood's gray eyes brightened with mischief. She looked at her Virginian, and she looked at me.

"Do you know," she said, "I used to be afraid that when Bear Creek wasn't new any more it might become dull!"

"Miss Peck doesn't find it dull, either," said I.

Molly Wood immediately assumed a look of doubt. "But mightn't it become just—just a little trying to have two gentlemen so very—determined, you know?"

"Only one is determined," said the Virginian.

Molly looked inquiring.

"Lin is determined Tommy shall not beat him. That's all it amounts to."

"Dear me, what a notion!"

"No, ma'am, no notion. Tommy—well, Tommy is considered harmless, ma'am. A cow-puncher of reputation in this country would cert'nly never let Tommy get ahaid of him that way."

"It's pleasant to know sometimes how much we count!" exclaimed Molly.

"Why, ma'am," said the Virginian, surprised at her flash of indignation, "where is any countin' without some love?"

"Do you mean to say that Mr. McLean does not care for Miss Peck?"

"I reckon he thinks he does. But there is a mighty wide difference between thinkin' and feelin', ma'am."

I saw Molly's eyes drop from his, and I saw the rose deepen in her cheeks. But just then a loud voice came from the kitchen.

"You, Lin, if you try any of your foolin' with me, I'll histe yu's over the jiste!"

"All cow-punchers—" I attempted to resume.

"Quit now, Lin McLean," shouted the voice, "or I'll put yu's through that window, and it shut."

"Well, Miss Peck, I'm gettin' most a full dose o' this treatment. Ever since yu' come I've been doing my best. And yu' just cough in my face. And now I'm going to quit and cough back."

"Would you enjoy walkin' out till supper, ma'am?" inquired the Virginian as Molly rose. "You was speaking of gathering some flowers yondeh."

"Why, yes," said Molly, blithely. "And you'll come?" she added to me.

But I was on the Virginian's side. "I must look after my horse," said I, and went down to the corral.

Day was slowly going as I took my pony to the water. Corncliff Mesa, Crowheart Butte, these shone in the rays that came through the canon. The canon's sides lifted like tawny castles in the same light. Where I walked the odor of thousands of wild roses hung over the margin

where the thickets grew. High in the upper air, magpies
were sailing across the silent blue. Somewhere I could
hear Tommy explaining loudly how he and General
Crook had pumped lead into hundreds of Indians; and
when supper-time brought us all back to the door he was
finishing the account to Mrs. Taylor. Molly and the Virginian arrived bearing flowers, and he was saying that
few cow-punchers had any reason for saving their
money.

"But when you get old?" said she.

"We mostly don't live long enough to get old, ma'am,"
said he, simply. "But I have a reason, and I am saving."

"Give me the flowers," said Molly. And she left him to
arrange them on the table as Lin came hurrying out.

"I've told her," said he to the Southerner and me,
"that I've asked her twiced, and I'm going to let her
have one more chance. And I've told her that if it's a log
cabin she's marryin', why Tommy is a sure good wooden
piece of furniture to put inside it. And I guess she knows
there's not much wooden furniture about me. I want to
speak to you." He took the Virginian round the corner.
But though he would not confide in me, I began to dis-
cern something quite definite at supper.

"Cattle men will lose stock if the Crows get down as
far as this," he said, casually, and Mrs. Taylor suppressed a titter.

"Ain't it hawses they're repawted as running off?" said
the Virginian.

"Chap come into the round-up this afternoon," said
Lin. "But he was rattled, and told a heap o' facts that
wouldn't square."

"Of course they wouldn't," said Tommy, haughtily.

"Oh, there's nothing in it," said Lin, dismissing the
subject.

"Have yu' been to the opera since we went to Cheyenne, Mrs. Taylor?"

Mrs. Taylor had not.

"Lin," said the Virginian, "did yu' ever see that opera 'Cyarmen'?"

"You bet. Fellow's girl quits him for a bull-fighter. Gets him up in the mountains, and quits him. He wasn't much good—not in her class o' sports, smugglin' and such."

"I reckon she was doubtful of him from the start. Took him to the mount'ins to experiment, where they'd not have interruption," said the Virginian.

"Talking of mountains," said Tommy, "this range here used to be a great place for Indians till we ran 'em out with Terry. Pumped lead into the red sons-of-guns."

"You bet," said Lin. "Do yu' figure that girl tired of her bull-fighter and quit him, too?"

"I reckon," replied the Virginian, "that the bull-fighter wore better."

"Fans and taverns and gypsies and sportin'," said Lin. "My! but I'd like to see them countries with oranges and bull-fights! Only I expect Spain, maybe, ain't keepin' it up so gay as when 'Carmen' happened."

The table-talk soon left romance and turned upon steers and alfalfa, a grass but lately introduced in the country. No further mention was made of the hostile Crows, and from this I drew the false conclusion that Tommy had not come up to their hopes in the matter of reciting his campaigns. But when the hour came for those visitors who were not spending the night to take their leave, Taylor drew Tommy aside with me, and I noticed the Virginian speaking with Molly Wood, whose face showed diversion.

"Don't seem to make anything of it," whispered Taylor to Tommy, "but the ladies have got their minds on this Indian truck."

"Why, I'll just explain—" began Tommy.

"Don't," whispered Lin, joining us. "Yu' know how women are. Once they take a notion, why, the more yu' deny the surer they get. Now yu' see, him and me" (he

jerked his elbow towards the Virginian) "must go back
to camp, for we're on second relief."

"And the ladies would sleep better knowing there was
another man in the house," said Taylor.

"In that case," said Tommy, "I—"

"Yu' see," said Lin, "they've been told about Ten
Sleep being burned two nights ago."

"It ain't!" cried Tommy.

"Why, of course it ain't," drawled the ingenious Lin.
"But that's what I say. You and I know Ten Sleep's all
right, but we can't report from our own knowledge seeing
it all right, and there it is. They get these nervous no-
tions."

"Just don't appear to make anything special of not going back to Riverside," repeated Taylor, "but—"

"But just kind of stay here," said Lin.

"I will!" exclaimed Tommy. "Of course, I'm glad to
oblige."

I suppose I was slow-sighted. All this pains seemed to
me larger than its results. They had imposed upon
Tommy, yes. But what of that? He was to be kept from
going back to Riverside until morning. Unless they proposed to visit his empty cabin and play tricks—but that
would be too childish, even for Lin McLean, to say nothing of the Virginian, his occasional partner in mischief.

"In spite of the Crows," I satirically told the ladies, "I
shall sleep outside, as I intended. I've no use for houses
at this season."

The cinches of the horses were tightened, Lin and the
Virginian laid a hand on their saddle-horns, swung up,
and soon all sound of the galloping horses had ceased.
Molly Wood declined to be nervous, and crossed to her
little neighbor cabin; we all parted, and (as always in
that blessed country) deep sleep quickly came to me.

I don't know how long after it was that I sprang from
my blankets in half-doubting fright. But I had dreamed
nothing. A second long, wild yell now gave me (I must
own to it) a horrible chill. I had no pistol—nothing. In

the hateful brightness of the moon my single thought was "House! House!" and I fled across the lane in my underclothes to the cabin, when round the corner whirled the two cow-punchers, and I understood. I saw the Virginian catch sight of me in my shirt, and saw his teeth as he smiled. I hastened to my blankets, and returned more decent to stand and watch the two go shooting and yelling round the cabin, crazy with their youth. The door was opened, and Taylor courageously emerged, bearing a Winchester. He fired at the sky immediately.

"B'gosh!" he roared. "That's one." He fired again. "Out and at 'em. They're running."

At this, duly came Mrs. Taylor in white with a pistol, and Miss Peck in white, staring and stolid. But no Tommy. Noise prevailed without, shots by the stable and shots by the creek. The two cow-punchers dismounted and joined Taylor. Maniac delight seized me, and I, too, rushed about with them, helping the din.

"Oh, Mr. Taylor!" said a voice. "I didn't think it of you." It was Molly Wood, come from her cabin, very pretty in a hood-and-cloak arrangement. She stood by the fence, laughing, but more at us than with us.

"Stop, friends!" said Taylor, gasping. "She teaches my Bobbie his A B C. I'd hate to have Bobbie—"

"Speak to your papa," said Molly, and held her scholar up on the fence.

"Well, I'll be gol-darned," said Taylor, surveying his costume, "if Lin McLean hasn't made a fool of me tonight!"

"Where has Tommy got?" said Mrs. Taylor.

"Didn't yu' see him?" said the biscuit-shooter, speaking her first word in all this.

We followed her into the kitchen The table was covered with tin plates. Beneath it, wedged, knelt Tommy with a pistol firm in his hand; but the plates were rattling up and down like castanets.

There was a silence among us, and I wondered what we were going to do.

"Well," murmured the Virginian to himself, "if I could have foresaw, I'd not—it makes yu' feel humiliated yu'self."

He marched out, got on his horse, and rode away. Lin followed him, but perhaps less penitently. We all dispersed without saying anything, and presently from my blankets I saw poor Tommy come out of the silent cabin, mount, and slowly, very slowly, ride away. He would spend the night at Riverside, after all.

Of course we recovered from our unexpected shame, and the tale of the table and the dancing plates was not told as a sad one. But it is a sad one when you think of it.

I was not there to see Lin get his bride. I learned from the Virginian how the victorious puncher had ridden away across the sunny sagebrush, bearing the biscuit-shooter with him to the nearest justice of the peace. She was astride the horse he had brought for her.

"Yes, he beat Tommy," said the Virginian. "Some folks, anyway, get what they want in this hyeh world."

From which I inferred that Miss Molly Wood was harder to beat than Tommy.

HEARTS AND CROSSES

by O. HENRY

BALDY WOODS reached for the bottle, and got it. Whenever Baldy went for anything he usually—but this is not Baldy's story. He poured out a third drink that was larger by a finger than the first and second. Baldy was in consultation; and the consultee is worthy of his hire.

"I'd be king if I was you," said Baldy, so positively that his holster creaked and his spurs rattled.

Webb Yeager pushed back his flat-brimmed Stetson, and made further disorder in his straw-colored hair. The tonsorial recourse being without avail, he followed the liquid example of the more resourceful Baldy.

"If a man marries a queen, it oughtn't to make him a two-spot," declared Webb, epitomizing his grievances.

"Sure not," said Baldy, sympathetic, still thirsty, and genuinely solicitous concerning the relative value of the cards. "By rights you're a king. If I was you, I'd call for a new deal. The cards have been stacked on you—I'll tell you what you are, Webb Yeager."

"What?" asked Webb, with a hopeful look in his pale-blue eyes.

"You're a prince-consort."

"Go easy," said Webb. "I never black-guarded you none."

"It's a title," explained Baldy, "up among the picture-cards; but it don't take no tricks. I'll tell you, Webb. It's a brand they've got for certain animals in Europe. Say that you or me or one of them Dutch dukes marries in a royal family. Well, by and by our wife gets to be queen. Are we king? Not in a million years. At the coronation ceremonies we march between little casino and the Ninth Grand Custodian of the Royal Hall Bedchamber. The only use we are is to appear in photographs, and ac-cept the responsibility for the heir-apparent. That ain't any square deal. Yes, sir, Webb, you're a prince-consort; and if I was you, I'd start a interregnum or a habeas cor-pus or somethin'; and I'd be king if I had to turn from the bottom of the deck."

Baldy emptied his glass to the ratification of his War-wick pose.

"Baldy," said Webb, solemnly, "me and you punched cows in the same outfit for years. We been runnin' on the same range, and ridin' the same trails since we was boys. I wouldn't talk about my family affairs to nobody but you. You was line-rider on the Nopalito Ranch when I married Santa McAllister. I was foreman then; but what am I now? I don't amount to a knot in a stake rope."

"When old McAllister was the cattle king of West Texas," continued Baldy with Satanic sweetness, "you was some tallow. You had as much to say on the ranch as he did."

"I did," admitted Webb, "up to the time he found out I was tryin' to get my rope over Santa's head. Then he kept me out on the range as far from the ranch-house as he could. When the old man died they commenced to call Santa the 'cattle queen.' I'm boss of the cattle —that's all. She 'tends to all the business; she handles all the money; I can't sell even a beef-steer to a party of campers, myself. Santa's the 'queen'; and I'm Mr. Nobody."

"I'd be king if I was you," repeated Baldy Woods, the royalist. "When a man marries a queen he ought to grade up with her—on the hoof—dressed—dried—corned— any old way from the chaparral to the packing-house. Lots of folks thinks it's funny, Webb, that you don't have the say-so on the Nopalito. I ain't reflectin' none on Miz Yeager—she's the finest little lady between the Rio Grande and next Christmas—but a man ought to be boss of his own camp."

The smooth, brown face of Yeager lengthened to a mask of wounded melancholy. With that expression, and his rumpled yellow hair and guileless blue eyes, he might have been likened to a schoolboy whose leadership had been usurped by a youngster of superior strength. But his active and sinewy seventy-two inches and his girded revolvers forbade the comparison.

"What was that you called me, Baldy?" he asked. "What kind of a concert was it?"

"A 'consort,'" corrected Baldy—"'a prince-consort.' It's a kind of short-card pseudonym. You come in sort of between Jack-high and a four-card flush."

Webb Yeager sighed, and gathered the strap of his Winchester scabbard from the floor.

"I'm ridin' back to the ranch to-day," he said, half-heartedly. "I've got to start a bunch of beeves for San Antone in the morning."

"I'm your company as far as Dry Lake," announced Baldy. "I've got a round-up camp on the San Marcos cuttin' out two-year-olds."

The two *compañeros* mounted their ponies and trotted away from the little railroad settlement, where they had foregathered in the thirsty morning.

At Dry Lake, where their routes diverged, they reined up for a parting cigarette. For miles they had ridden in silence save for the soft drum of the ponies' hoofs on the matted mesquite grass, and the rattle of the chaparral against their wooden stirrups. But in Texas discourse is seldom continuous. You may fill in a mile, a meal, and a murder between your paragraphs without detriment to your thesis. So, without apology, Webb offered an addendum to the conversation that had begun ten miles away.

"You remember, yourself, Baldy, that there was a time when Santa wasn't quite so independent. You remember the days when old McAllister was keepin' us apart, and how she used to send me the sign that she wanted to see me? Old man Mac promised to make me look like a colander if I ever come in gun-shot of the ranch. You remember the sign she used to send, Baldy—the heart with a cross inside of it?"

"Me?" cried Baldy, with intoxicated archness. "You old sugar-stealing coyote! Don't I remember! Why, you dad-blamed old long-horned turtle-dove, the boys in camp was all cognoscious about them hieroglyphs. The 'gizzard-and-crossbones' we used to call it. We used to see 'em on truck that was sent out from the ranch. They was marked in charcoal on the sacks of flour and in lead-pencil on the newspapers. I see one of 'em once chalked on the back of a new cook that old man McAllister sent out from the ranch—danged if I didn't."

"Santa's father," exclaimed Webb gently, "got her to promise that she wouldn't write to me or send me any word. That heart-and-cross sign was her scheme. Whenever she wanted to see me in particular she managed to put that mark on somethin' at the ranch that she knew I'd see. And I never laid eyes on it but what I burnt the wind for the ranch the same night. I used to see her in that coma mott back of the little horse-corral."

"We knowed it," chanted Baldy; "but we never let on. We was all for you. We knowed why you always kept that fast paint in camp. And when we see that gizzard-and-crossbones figured out on the truck from the ranch we knowed old Pinto was goin' to eat up miles that night instead of grass. You remember Scurry—that educated horse-wrangler we had—the college fellow that tangle-foot drove to the range? Whenever Scurry saw that come-meet-your-honey brand on anything from the ranch, he'd wave his hand like that, and say, 'Our friend Lee Andrews will again swim the Hell's point to-night.'"

"The last time Santa sent me the sign," said Webb, "was once when she was sick. I noticed it as soon as I hit camp, and I galloped Pinto forty mile that night. She wasn't at the coma mott. I went to the house; and old McAllister met me at the door. 'Did you come here to get killed?' says he; 'I'll disoblige you for once. I just started a Mexican to bring you. Santa wants you. Go in that room and see her. And then come out here and see me.'"

"Santa was lyin' in bed pretty sick. But she gives out a kind of a smile, and her hand and mine lock horns, and I sets down by the bed—mud and spurs and chaps and all. 'I've heard you ridin' across the grass for hours, Webb,' she says. 'I was sure you'd come. You saw the sign?' she whispers. 'The minute I hit camp,' says I. ''Twas marked on the bag of potatoes and onions.' 'They're always together,' says she, soft like—'always together in life.' 'They go well together,' I says, 'in a stew.' 'I mean hearts and crosses,' says Santa. 'Our sign—to love and to suffer—that's what they mean.'

"And there was old Doc Musgrove amusin' himself

with whisky and a palm-leaf fan. And by and by Santa goes to sleep; and Doc feels her forehead; and he says to me: 'You're not such a bad febrifuge. But you'd better slide out now, for the diagnosis don't call for you in regular doses. The little lady'll be all right when she wakes up.'

"I seen old McAllister outside. 'She's asleep,' says I, 'And now you can start in with your colander-work. Take your time; for I left my gun on my saddle-horn.'

"Old Mac laughs, and he says to me: 'Pumpin' lead into the best ranch-boss in West Texas don't seem to me good business policy. I don't know where I could get as good a one. It's the son-in-law idea, Webb, that makes me admire for to use you as a target. You ain't my idea for a member of the family. But I can use you on the Nopalito if you'll keep outside of a radius with the ranch-house in the middle of it. You go upstairs and lay down on a cot, and when you get some sleep we'll talk it over.' "

Baldy Woods pulled down his hat, and uncurled his leg from his saddle-horn. Webb shortened his rein, and his pony danced, anxious to be off. The two men shook hands with Western ceremony.

"*Adiós*, Baldy," said Webb. "I'm glad I seen you and had this talk."

With a pounding rush that sounded like the rise of a covey of quail, the riders sped away toward different points of the compass. A hundred yards on his route Baldy reined in on the top of a bare knoll, and emitted a yell. He swayed on his horse; had he been on foot, the earth would have risen and conquered him; but in the saddle he was a master of equilibrium, and laughed at whisky, and despised the center of gravity.

Webb turned in his saddle at the signal.

"If I was you," came Baldy's strident and perverting tones, "I'd be king!"

At eight o'clock on the following morning Bud Turner rolled from his saddle in front of the Nopalito ranch-house, and stumbled with whizzing rowels toward the gallery. Bud was in charge of the bunch of beef-cattle that was to strike the trail that morning for San Antonio. Mrs. Yeager was on the gallery watering a cluster of hyacinths growing in a red earthenware jar.

"King" McAllister had bequeathed to his daughter many of his strong characteristics—his resolution, his gay courage, his contumacious self-reliance, his pride as a reigning monarch of hoofs and horns. *Allegro* and *fortissimo* had been McAllister's tempo and tone. In Santa they survived, transposed to the feminine key. Substantially, she preserved the image of the mother who had been summoned to wander in other and less finite green pastures long before the waxing herds of kine had conferred royalty upon the house. She had her mother's slim, strong figure and grave, soft prettiness that relieved in her the severity of the imperious McAllister eye and the McAllister air of royal independence.

Webb stood on one end of the gallery giving orders to two or three sub-bosses of various camps and outfits who had ridden in for instructions.

" 'Morning," said Bud, briefly. "Where do you want them beeves to go in town—to Barber's, as usual?"

Now, to answer that had been the prerogative of the queen. All the reins of business—buying, selling, and banking—had been held by her capable fingers. The handling of the cattle had been entrusted fully to her husband. In the days of "King" McAllister, Santa had been his secretary and helper; and she had continued her work with wisdom and profit. But before she could reply, the prince-consort spake up with calm decision:

"You drive that bunch to Zimmerman and Nesbit's pens. I spoke to Zimmerman about it some time ago."

Bud turned on his high boot-heels.

"Wait!" called Santa quickly. She looked at her husband with surprise in her steady gray eyes.

"Why, what do you mean, Webb?" she asked, with a small wrinkle gathering between her brows. "I never deal with Zimmerman and Nesbit. Barber has handled every head of stock from this ranch in that market for five years. I'm not going to take the business out of his hands." She faced Bud Turner. "Deliver those cattle to Barber," she concluded positively.

Bud gazed impartially at the water-jar hanging on the gallery, stood on his other leg, and chewed a mesquite-leaf.

"I want this bunch of beeves to go to Zimmerman and Nesbit," said Webb, with a frosty light in his blue eyes.

"Nonsense," said Santa impatiently. "You'd better start on, Bud, so as to noon at the Little Elm waterhole. Tell Barber we'll have another lot of culls ready in about a month."

Bud allowed a hesitating eye to steal upward and meet Webb's. Webb saw apology in his look, and fancied he saw commiseration.

"You deliver them cattle," he said grimly, "to—"

"Barber," finished Santa sharply. "Let that settle it. Is there anything else you are waiting for, Bud?"

"No, m'm," said Bud. But before going he lingered while a cow's tail could have switched thrice; for man is man's ally; and even the Philistines must have blushed when they took Samson in the way they did.

"You hear your boss!" cried Webb, sardonically. He took off his hat, and bowed until it touched the floor before his wife.

"Webb," said Santa rebukingly, "you're acting mighty foolish to-day."

"Court fool, your Majesty," said Webb, in his slow tones, which had changed their quality. "What else can you expect? Let me tell you. I was a man before I married a cattle queen. What am I now? The laughing-stock of the camps. I'll be a man again."

Santa looked at him closely.

"Don't be unreasonable, Webb," she said calmly. "You haven't been slighted in any way. Do I ever interfere in your management of the cattle? I know the business side

of the ranch much better than you do. I learned it from
Dad. Be sensible."

"Kingdoms and queendoms," said Webb, "don't suit
me unless I am in the pictures, too. I punch the cattle
and you wear the crown. All right. I'd rather be High
Lord Chancellor of a cow-camp than the eight-spot in a
queen-high flush. It's your ranch; and Barber gets the
beeves."

Webb's horse was tied to the rack. He walked into the
house and brought out his roll of blankets that he never
took with him except on long rides, and his "slicker,"
and his longest stake-rope of plaited raw-hide. These he
began to tie deliberately upon his saddle. Santa, a little
pale, followed him.

Webb swung up into the saddle. His serious, smooth
face was without expression except for a stubborn light
that smoldered in his eyes.

"There's a herd of cows and calves," said he, "near the
Hondo waterhole on the Frio that ought to be moved
away from timber. Lobos have killed three of the calves.
I forgot to leave orders. You'd better tell Simms to attend to it."

Santa laid a hand on the horse's bridle, and looked her
husband in the eye.

"Are you going to leave me, Webb?" she asked quietly.

"I am going to be a man again," he answered.

"I wish you success in a praiseworthy attempt," she
said, with a sudden coldness. She turned and walked directly into the house.

Webb Yeager rode to the southeast as straight as the
topography of West Texas permitted. And when he
reached the horizon he might have ridden on into blue
space as far as knowledge of him on the Nopalito went.
And the days, with Sundays at their head, formed into
hebdomadal squads; and the weeks, captained by the
full moon, closed ranks into menstrual companies carrying "Tempus fugit" on their banners; and the months
marched on toward the vast camp-ground of the years;

but Webb Yeager came no more to the dominions of his queen.

One day a being named Bartholomew, a sheep-man—and therefore of little account—from the lower Rio Grande country, rode in sight of the Nopalito ranch-house, and felt hunger assail him. *Ex consuetudine* he was soon seated at the mid-day dining-table of that hospitable kingdom. Talk like water gushed from him: he might have been smitten with Aaron's rod—that is your gentle shepherd when an audience is vouchsafed him whose ears are not overgrown with wool.

"Missis Yeager," he babbled, "I see a man the other day on the Rancho Seco down in Hidalgo County by your name—Webb Yeager was his. He'd just been engaged as manager. He was a tall, light-haired man, not saying much. Maybe he was some kin of yours, do you think?"

"A husband," said Santa cordially. "The Seco has done well. Mr. Yeager is one of the best stockmen in the West."

The dropping out of a prince-consort rarely disorganizes a monarchy. Queen Santa had appointed as *mayordomo* of the ranch, a trusty subject, named Ramsay, who had been one of her father's faithful vassals. And there was scarcely a ripple on the Nopalito ranch save when the gulf-breeze created undulations in the grass of its wide acres.

For several years the Nopalito had been making experiments with an English breed of cattle that looked down with aristocratic contempt upon the Texas long-horns. The experiments were found satisfactory; and a pasture had been set apart for the blue-bloods. The fame of them had gone forth into the chaparral and pear as far as men ride in saddles. Other ranches woke up, rubbed their eyes, and looked with new dissatisfaction upon the long-horns.

As a consequence, one day a sunburned, capable, silk-kerchiefed nonchalant youth, garnished with revolvers, and attended by three Mexican *vaqueros*, alighted at the Nopalito ranch and presented the following business-like epistle to the queen thereof.

Mrs. Yeager—The Nopalito Ranch:
DEAR MADAM:
I am instructed by the owners of the Rancho Seco to purchase 100 head of two and three-year-old cows of the Sussex breed owned by you. If you can fill the order please deliver the cattle to the bearer; and a check will be forwarded to you at once.

Respectfully,
WEBSTER YEAGER,
Manager of the Rancho Seco.

Business is business, even—very scantily did it escape being written "especially"—in a kingdom.

That night the 100 herd of cattle were driven up from the pasture and penned in a corral near the ranch-house for delivery in the morning.

When night closed down and the house was still, did Santa Yeager throw herself down, clasping that formal note to her bosom, weeping, and calling out a name that pride (either in one or the other) had kept from her lips many a day? Or did she file the letter, in her business way, retaining her royal balance and strength?

Wonder, if you will; but royalty is sacred; and there is a veil. But this much you shall learn.

At midnight Santa slipped softly out of the ranch-house, clothed in something dark and plain. She paused for a moment under the live-oak trees. The prairies were somewhat dim, and the moonlight was pale orange, diluted with particles of an impalpable, flying mist. But the mock-bird whistled on every bough of vantage; leagues of flowers scented the air; and a kindergarten of little shadowy rabbits leaped and played in an open space near by. Santa turned her face to the southeast and threw kisses thitherward; for there was none to see.

Then she sped silently to the blacksmith-shop, fifty

yards away; and what she did there can only be surmised. But the forge glowed red; and there was a faint
hammering such as Cupid might make when he sharpens
his arrowpoints.

Later she came forth with a queer-shaped, handled
thing in one hand, and a portable furnace, such as are
seen in branding-camps, in the other. To the corral where
the Sussex cattle were penned she sped with these things
swiftly in the moonlight.

She opened the gate and slipped inside the corral. The
Sussex cattle were mostly a dark red. But among this
bunch was one that was milky white—notable among the
others.

And now Santa shook from her shoulder something
that we had not seen before—a rope lasso. She freed the
loop of it, coiling the length in her left hand, and
plunged into the thick of the cattle.

The white cow was her object. She swung the lasso,
which caught one horn and slipped off. The next throw
encircled the forefeet and the animal fell heavily. Santa
made for it like a panther; but it scrambled up and
dashed against her, knocking her over like a blade of
grass.

Again she made the cast, while the aroused cattle
milled round the four sides of the corral in a plunging
mass. This throw was fair; the white cow came to earth
again; and before it could rise Santa had made the lasso
fast around a post of the corral with a swift and simple
knot, and had leaped upon the cow again with the rawhide hobbles.

In one minute the feet of the animal were tied (no rec-
ord-breaking deed) and Santa leaned against the corral
for the same space of time, panting and lax.

And then she ran swiftly to her furnace at the gate and
brought the branding-iron, queerly shaped and white-
hot.

The bellow of the outraged white cow, as the iron was
applied, should have stirred the slumbering auricular

nerves and consciences of the near-by subjects of the Nopalito, but it did not. And it was amid the deepest nocturnal silence that Santa ran like a lapwing back to the ranch-house and there fell upon a cot and sobbed— sobbed as though queens had hearts as simple ranchmen's wives have, and as though she would gladly make kings of prince-consorts, should they ride back again from over the hills and far away.

In the morning the capable, revolvered youth and his *vaqueros* set forth, driving the bunch of Sussex cattle across the prairies to the Rancho Seco. Ninety miles it was; a six days' journey, grazing and watering the animals on the way.

The beasts arrived at Rancho Seco one evening at dusk; and were received and counted by the foreman of the ranch.

The next morning at eight o'clock a horseman loped out of the brush to the Nopalito ranch-house. He dismounted stiffly, and strode, with whizzing spurs, to the house. His horse gave a great sigh and swayed foam-streaked, with down-drooping head and closed eyes.

But waste not your pity upon Belshazzar, the flea-bitten sorrel. To-day, in Nopalito horse-pasture he survives, pampered, beloved, unridden, cherished record-holder of long-distance rides.

The horseman stumbled into the house. Two arms fell around his neck and someone cried out in the voice of woman and queen alike: "Webb—oh, Webb!"

"I was a skunk," said Webb Yeager.

"Hush," said Santa, "did you see it?"

"I saw it," said Webb.

What they meant God knows; and you shall know, if you rightly read the primer of events.

"Be the cattle-queen," said Webb; "and overlook it if you can. I was a mangy, sheep-stealing coyote."

"Hush!" said Santa again, laying her fingers upon his mouth. "There's no queen here. Do you know who I am?

I am Santa Yeager, First Lady of the Bedchamber
Come here."

She dragged him from the gallery into the room to the
right. There stood a cradle with an infant in it—a red,
ribald, unintelligible, babbling, beautiful infant, sputter-
ing at life in an unseemly manner.

"There's no queen on this ranch," said Santa again.
"Look at the king. He's got your eyes, Webb. Down on
your knees and look at his Highness."

But jingling rowels sounded on the gallery, and Bud
Turner stumbled there again with the same query that
he had brought, lacking a few days, a year ago.

" 'Morning. Them beeves is just turned out on the
trail. Shall I drive 'em to Barber's, or—"

He saw Webb and stopped, open-mouthed.

"Ba-ba-ba-ba-ba-ba!" shrieked the king in his cradle,
beating the air with his fists.

"You hear your boss, Bud," said Webb Yeager, with a
broad grin—just as he had said a year ago.

And that is all, except that when old man Quinn,
owner of the Rancho Seco, went out to look over the
herd of Sussex cattle that he had bought from the Nopalito ranch, he asked his new manager:

"What's the Nopalito ranch brand, Wilson?"

"X Bar Y," said Wilson.

"I thought so," said Quinn. "But look at that white
heifer there; she's got another brand—a heart with a
cross inside of it. What brand is that?"

A CORNER IN HORSES

by STEWART EDWARD WHITE

IT was dark night. The stray-herd bellowed frantically from one of the big corrals; the cow-and-calf-herd from a second. Already the remuda, driven in from the open plains, scattered about the thousand acres of pasture. Away from the conveniences of fence and corral, men would have had to patrol all night. Now, however, everyone was gathered about the camp fire.

Probably forty cowboys were in the group, representing all types, from old John, who had been in the business forty years, and had punched from the Rio Grande to the Pacific, to the Kid, who would have given his chance of salvation if he could have been taken for ten years older than he was. At the moment Jed Parker was holding forth to his friend Johnny Stone in reference to another old crony who had that evening joined the round-up.

"Johnny," inquired Jed with elaborate gravity, and entirely ignoring the presence of the subject of conversation, "what is that thing just beyond the fire, and where did it come from?"

Johnny Stone squinted to make sure.

"That?" he replied. "Oh, this evenin' the dogs see something run down a hole, and they dug it out, and that's what they got."

The newcomer grinned.

"The trouble with you fellows," he proffered, "is that you're so plumb alkalied you don't know the real thing when you see it."

"That's right," supplemented Windy Bill drily. "*He* come from New York."

"No!" cried Jed. "You don't say so? Did he come in one box or in two?"

Under cover of the laugh, the newcomer made a raid on the Dutch ovens and pails. Having filled his plate, he squatted on his heels and fell to his belated meal. He was a tall, slab-sided individual, with a lean, leathery face, a sweeping white mustache, and a grave and sardonic eye. His leather chaps were plain and worn, and his hat had been fashioned by time and wear into much individuality. I was not surprised to hear him nicknamed Sacatone Bill.

"Just ask him how he got that game foot," suggested Johnny Stone to me in an undertone, so, of course, I did not.

Later someone told me that the lameness resulted from his refusal of an urgent invitation to return across a river. Mr. Sacatone Bill happened not to be riding his own horse at the time.

The Cattleman dropped down beside me a moment later.

"I wish," said he in a low voice, "we could get that fellow talking. He is a queer one. Pretty well educated apparently. Claims to be writing a book of memoirs. Sometimes he will open up in good shape, and sometimes he will not. It does no good to ask him direct, and he is as shy as an old crow when you try to lead him up to a subject. We must just lie low and trust to Providence."

A man was playing on the mouth organ. He played excellently well, with all sorts of variations and frills. We smoked in silence. The deep rumble of the cattle filled the air with its diapason. Always the shrill coyotes raved out in the mesquite. Sacatone Bill had finished his meal, and had gone to sit by Jed Parker, his old friend. They talked together low-voiced. The evening grew, and the eastern sky silvered over the mountains in anticipation of the moon.

Sacatone Bill suddenly threw back his head and laughed.

"Reminds me of the time I went to Colorado!" he cried.

"He's off!" whispered the Cattleman.

A dead silence fell on the circle. Everybody shifted position the better to listen to the story of Sacatone Bill.

About ten years ago I got plumb sick of punchin' cows around my part of the country. She hadn't rained since Noah, and I'd forgot what water outside a pail or a trough looked like. So I scouted around inside of me to see what part of the world I'd jump to, and as I seemed to know as little of Colorado and minin' as anything else, I made up the pint of bean soup I call my brains to go there. So I catches me a buyer at Benson and turns over my pore little bunch of cattle and prepared to fly. The last day I hauled up about twenty good buckets of water and threw her up against the cabin. My buyer was settin' his hoss waitin' for me to get ready. He didn't say nothin' until we'd got down about ten mile or so.

"Mr. Hicks," says he, hesitatin' like, "I find it a good rule in this country not to overlook other folks' plays, but I'd take it mighty kind if you'd explain those actions of yours with the pails of water."

"Mr. Jones," says I, "it's very simple. I built that shack five year ago, and it's never rained since. I just wanted to settle in my mind whether or not that damn roof leaked."

So I quit Arizona, and in about a week I see my reflection in the winders of a little place called Cyanide in the Colorado mountains.

Fellows, she was a bird. They wasn't a pony in sight, nor a squar' foot of land that wasn't either street or straight up. It made me plumb lonesome for a country where you could see a long ways even if you didn't see much. And this early in the evenin' they wasn't hardly anybody in the streets at all.

I took a look at them dark, gloomy old mountains, and a sniff at a breeze that would have frozen the whiskers or hope, and I made a dive for the nearest lit winder. They was a sign over it that just said:

THIS IS A SALOON

I was glad they labeled her. I'd never have known it. They had a fifteen-year-old kid tendin' bar, no games goin', and not a soul in the place.

"Sorry to disturb your repose, bub," says I, "but see if you can sort out any rye among them collections of sassapariller of yours."

I took a drink, and then another to keep it company— I was beginnin' to sympathize with anythin' lonesome. Then I kind of sauntered out to the back room where the hurdy-gurdy ought to be. Sure enough, there was a girl settin' on the pianner stool, another in a chair, and a nice shiny drummer danglin' his feet from a table. They looked up when they see me come in, and went right on talkin'.

"Hello, girls!" says I.

At that they stopped talkin' complete.

"How's tricks?" says I.

"Who's your woolly friend?" the drummer asks of the girls.

I looked at him a minute, but I see he'd been raised a pet, and then, too, I was so hungry for sassiety I was willin' to pass a bet or two.

"Don't you *admire* these cow gents?" snickers one of the girls.

"Play somethin', sister," says I to the one at the pianner.

She just grinned at me.

"Interdooce me," says the drummer in a kind of a way that made them all laugh a heap.

"Give us a tune," I begs, tryin' to be jolly, too.

"She don't know any pieces," says the salesman.

"Don't you?" I asks pretty sharp.

"No," says she.

"Well, I do," says I.

I walked up to her, jerked out my guns, and reached around both sides of her to the pianner. I ran the muzzles up and down the keyboard two or three times, and then shot out half a dozen keys.

"That's the piece I know," says I.

But the other girl and the drummer had punched the breeze.

The girl at the pianner just grinned, and pointed to the winder where they was some ragged glass hangin'. She was dead game.

"Say, Susie," says I, "you're all right, but your friends is tur'ble. I may be rough, and I ain't never been curried below the knees, but I'm better to tie to than them sons of guns."

"I believe it," says she.

So we had a drink at the bar, and started out to investigate the wonders of Cyanide.

Say, that night *was* a wonder. Susie faded after about three drinks, but I didn't seem to mind that. I hooked up to another saloon kept by a thin Dutchman. A fat Dutchman is stupid, but a thin one is all right.

In ten minutes I had more friends in Cyanide than they is fiddlers in hell. I begun to conclude Cyanide wasn't so lonesome. About four o'clock in comes a little Irishman about four foot high, with more upper lip than a muley cow, and enough red hair to make an artificial aurorer borealis. He had big red hands with freckles pasted onto them, and stiff red hairs standin' up separate and lonesome like signal stations. Also his legs was bowed.

He gets a drink at the bar, and stands back and yells:

"God bless the Irish and let the Dutch rustle!"

Now, this was none of my town, so I just stepped back of the end of the bar quick where I wouldn't stop no lead. The shootin' didn't begin.

"Probably Dutchy didn't take no note of what the locoed little dogie *did* say," thinks I to myself.

The Irishman bellied up to the bar again, and pounded on it with his fist.

"Look here!" he yells. "Listen to what I'm tellin' ye! God bless the Irish and let the Dutch rustle! Do ye hear me?"

"Sure, I hear ye," says Dutchy, and goes on swabbin' his bar with a towel.

At that my soul just grew sick. I asked the man next to me why Dutchy didn't kill the little fellow.

"Kill him!" says this man. "What for?"

"For insultin' of him, of course."

"Oh, he's drunk," says the man, as if that explained anythin'.

That settled it with me. I left that place, and went home, and it wasn't more than four o'clock, neither. No, I don't call four o'clock late. It may be a little late for night before last, but it's just the shank of the evenin' for to-night.

Well, it took me six weeks and two days to go broke. I didn't know sic 'em about minin'; and before long I *knew* that I didn't know sic 'em. Most all day I poked around them mountains—not like our'n—too much timber to be comfortable. At night I got to droppin' in at Dutchy's. He had a couple of quiet games goin', and they was one fellow among that lot of grubbin' prairie dogs that had heerd tell that cows had horns. He was the wisest of the bunch on the cattle business. So I stowed away my consolation, and made out to forget comparing Colorado with God's country.

About three times a week this Irishman I told you of —name O'Toole—comes bulgin' in. When he was sober he talked minin' high, wide, and handsome. When he was drunk he pounded both fists on the bar and yelled for action, tryin' to get Dutchy on the peck.

"God bless the Irish and let the Dutch rustle!" he yells about six times. "Say, do you hear?"

"Sure," says Dutchy, calm as a milk cow, "sure, I hear ye!"

I was plumb sorry for O'Toole. I'd like to have given him a run; but, of course, I couldn't take it up without makin' myself out a friend of this Dutchy party, and I couldn't stand for that. But I did tackle Dutchy about it one night when they wasn't nobody else there.

"Dutchy," says I, "what makes you let that bow-legged cross between a bulldog and a flamin' red sunset tromp on you so? It looks to me like you're plumb spirit-less."

Dutchy stopped wipin' glasses for a minute.

"Just you hold on," says he. "I ain't ready yet. Bimeby I make him sick; also those others who laugh with him."

He had a little gray flicker in his eye, and I thinks to myself that maybe they'd get Dutchy on the peck yet.

As I said, I went broke in just six weeks and two days. And I was broke a plenty. No hold-outs anywhere. It was a heap long ways to cows; and I'd be teetotally chawed up and spit out if I was goin' to join these minin' terra-pins defacin' the bosom of nature. It sure looked to me like hard work.

While I was figurin' what next, Dutchy came in. Which I was tur'ble surprised at that, but I said good-mornin' and would he rest his poor feet.

"You like to make some money?" he asks.

"That depends," says I, "on how easy it is."

"It is easy," says he. "I want you to buy hosses for me."

"Hosses! Sure!" I yells, jumpin' up. "You bet you! Why, hosses is where I live! What hosses do you want?"

"All hosses," says he, calm as a faro dealer.

"What?" says I. "Elucidate, my bucko. I don't take no such blanket order. Spread your cards."

"I mean just that," says he. "I want you to buy all the hosses in this camp, and in the mountains. Every one."

"Whew!" I whistles. "That's a large order. But I'm your meat."

"Come with me, then," says he. I hadn't but just got up, but I went with him to his little old poison factory. Of course, I hadn't had no breakfast; but he staked me to a Kentucky breakfast. What's a Kentucky breakfast? Why, a Kentucky breakfast is a three-pound steak, a bottle of whisky, and a setter dog. What's the dog for? Why, to eat the steak, of course.

We come to an agreement. I was to get two-fifty a head commission. So I started out. There wasn't many hosses in that country, and what there was the owners hadn't much use for unless it was to work a whim. I picked up about a hundred head quick enough, and reported to Dutchy.

"How about burros and mules?" I asks Dutchy.

"They goes," says he. "Mules same as hosses; burros four bits a head to you."

At the end of a week I had a remuda of probably two hundred animals. We kept them over the hills in some "parks," as these sots call meadows in that country. I rode into town and told Dutchy.

"Get them all?" he asks.

"All but a cross-eyed buckskin that's mean, and the bay mare that Noah bred to."

"Get them," says he.

"The bandits want too much," I explains.

"Get them anyway," says he.

I went away and got them. It was scand'lous; such prices.

When I hit Cyanide again I ran into scenes of wild excitement. The whole passel of them was on that one street of their'n, talkin' sixteen ounces to the pound. In the middle was Dutchy, drunk as a soldier—just plain foolish drunk.

"Good Lord!" thinks I to myself, "he ain't celebratin' gettin' that bunch of buzzards, is he?"

But I found he wasn't that bad. When he caught sight of me, he fell on me drivelin'.

"Look there!" he weeps, showin' me a letter.

I was the last to come in; so I kept that letter—here she is. I'll read her.

> Dear Dutchy:—I suppose you thought I'd flew the coop, but I haven't and this is to prove it. Pack up your outfit and hit the trail. I've made the biggest free gold strike you ever see. I'm sending you specimens. There's tons just like it, tons and tons. I got all the claims I can hold myself; but there's heaps more. I've writ to Johnny and Ed at Denver to come on. Don't give this away. Make tracks. Come in to Buck Cañon in the Whetstones and oblige.
>
> Yours truly,
>
> Henry Smith.

Somebody showed me a handful of white rock with yeller streaks in it. His eyes was bulgin' until you could have hung your hat on them. That O'Toole party was walkin' around, wettin' his lips with his tongue and swearin' soft.

"God bless the Irish and let the Dutch rustle!" says he. "And the fool had to get drunk and give it away!"

The excitement was just started, but it didn't last long. The crowd got the same notion at the same time, and it just melted. Me and Dutchy was left alone.

I went home. Pretty soon a fellow named Jimmy Tack come around a little out of breath.

"Say, you know that buckskin you bought off'n me?" says he, "I want to buy him back."

"Oh, you do," says I.

"Yes," says he. "I've got to leave town for a couple of days, and I got to have somethin' to pack."

"Wait and I'll see," says I.

Outside the door I met another fellow.

"Look here," he stops me with. "How about that bay mare I sold you? Can you call that sale off? I got to leave town for a day or two and—"

"Wait," says I. "I'll see."

By the gate was another hurryin' up.

"Oh, yes," says I when he opens his mouth. "I know all your troubles. You have to leave town for a couple of days, and you want back that lizard you sold me. Well, wait."

After that I had to quit the main street and dodge back of the hog ranch. They was all headed my way. I was as popular as a snake in a prohibition town.

I hit Dutchy's by the back door.

"Do you want to sell hosses?" I asks. "Everyone in town wants to buy."

Dutchy looked hurt.

"I wanted to keep them for the valley market," says he, "but . . . How much did you give Jimmy Tack for his buckskin?"

"Twenty," says I.

"Well, let him have it for eighty," says Dutchy; "and the others in proportion."

I lay back and breathed hard.

"Sell them all, but the one best hoss," says he—"no, the *two* best."

"Holy smoke!" says I, gettin' my breath. "If you mean that, Dutchy, you lend me another gun and give me a drink."

He done so, and I went back home to where the whole camp of Cyanide was waitin'.

I got up and made them a speech and told them I'd sell them hosses all right, and to come back. Then I got an Injin boy to help, and we rustled over the remuda and held them in a blind cañon. Then I called up these miners one at a time, and made bargains with them. Roar! Well, you could hear them at Denver, they tell me, and the weather reports said, "Thunder in the mountains." But it was cash on delivery, and they all paid up. They had seen that white quartz with the gold stickin' into it, and that's the same as a dose of loco to miner gents.

Why didn't I take a hoss and start first? I did think of

it—for about one second. I wouldn't stay in that country then for a million dollars a minute. I was plumb sick and loathin' it, and just waitin' to make high jumps back to Arizona. So I wasn't aimin' to join this stampede, and didn't have no vivid emotions.

They got to fightin' on which should get the first hoss; so I bent my gun on them and made them draw lots. They roared some more, but done so; and as fast as each one handed over his dust or dinero he made a rush for his cabin, piled on his saddle and pack, and pulled his freight in a cloud of dust. It was sure a grand stampede, and I enjoyed it no limit.

So by sundown I was alone with the Injin. Those two hundred head brought in about twenty thousand dollars. It was heavy, but I could carry it. I was about alone in the landscape; and there were the two best hosses I had saved out for Dutchy. I was sure some tempted. But I had enough to get home on anyway; and I never yet drank behind the bar, even if I might hold up the saloon from the floor. So I grieved some inside that I was so tur'ble conscientious, shouldered the sacks, and went down to find Dutchy.

I met him headed his way, and carryin' of a sheet of paper.

"Here's your dinero," says I, dumpin' the four big sacks on the ground.

He stooped over and hefted them. Then he passed one over to me.

"What's that for?" I asks.

"For you," says he.

"My commission ain't that much," I objects.

"You've earned it," says he, "and you might have skipped with the whole wad."

"How did you know I wouldn't?" I asks.

"Well," says he, and I noted that jag of his had flew. "You see, I was behind that rock up there, and I had you covered."

I saw; and I began to feel better about bein' so tur'-ble conscientious.

We walked a little ways without sayin' nothin'.

"But ain't you goin' to join the game?" I asks.

"Guess not," says he, jinglin' of his gold. "I'm satisfied."

"But if you don't get a wiggle on you, you are sure goin' to get left on those gold claims," says I.

"There ain't no gold claims," says he.

"But Henry Smith—" I cries.

"There ain't no Henry Smith," says he.

I let that soak in about six inches.

"But there's a Buck Cañon," I pleads. "Please say there's a Buck Cañon."

"Oh, yes, there's a Buck Cañon," he allows. "Nice limestone formation—makes good hard water."

"Well, you're a marvel," says I.

We walked on together down to Dutchy's saloon. We stopped outside.

"Now," says he, "I'm goin' to take one of those hosses and go somewheres else. Maybe you'd better do likewise on the other."

"You bet I will," says I.

He turned around and tacked up the paper he was carryin'. It was a sign. It read:

THE DUTCH HAS RUSTLED

"Nice sentiment," says I. "It will be appreciated when the crowd comes back from that little *pasear* into Buck Cañon. But why not tack her up where the trail hits the camp? Why on this particular door?"

"Well," said Dutchy, squintin' at the sign sideways, "you see I sold this place day before yesterday—to Mike O'Toole."

BEYOND THE DESERT

by Eugene Manlove Rhodes

MacGregor was in haste. He pressed forward in a close, fine rain. A huge and graceless hulk of a man, he rode craftily, a brisk jog, a brisk walk. Where the trail was steep, he slipped from the saddle and led the way to the next smooth bit.

Hard by the head of the pass, where the peaks of San Quentin frowned through fog and mist, he paused in a brief lull between showers. Far behind and below there was a glimpse of toiling horsemen, a wavering black line where the trail clung to the hillside.

MacGregor lifted the heavy brows that pent his piggy little red eyes. His face was a large red face, heavy, square, coarse-featured, stubbly. It now expressed no emotion. Unhurriedly, he took up a long thirty-forty from the sling below the stirrup-leather, raised the sights high, and dropped two bullets in the trail before the advancing party. They shrank back to a huddling clump.

Under shelter of his long slicker, he wiped the rifle carefully and returned it to the scabbard. "Persons of no experience," he grumbled. "They ride with small caution for a country of boulders and such-like cover. 'Tis plain I have naught to fear from them; for now they will think twice and again at each bend and rock-fall. Aweel—I hae seen worse days. Thanks to this good rain, I neednae fear the desert, whether for mysel' or the beastie. But beyant the desert? Ay, there's the kittle bit. There's a telephone line awa' to the south—and if the guid folk of Datil be at all of enterprising mind, 'tis like I shall hear tidings."

Dawn found him beyond the desert, breasting the long slow ridges beneath the wooded mountain of the Datils. The storm had passed away. The desert brimmed with a golden flood of light, a flood that rolled eastward across the level, to check and break and foam against the dense cool shadow of the Datil Range. So dense and so black was that shadow that the rambling building of the CLA ranch scarce bulked blacker, hardly to be seen, save for a thin wisp of wood smoke that feathered in the windless air.

"Ay," said the horseman. "Now the pot boils. Here comes one at a hard gallop—wrangling horses, belike. And now he sees me and swerves this way. Truly, I am very desirous that this man may be Mundy himself. I would ever like best to deal with principals. Be it Clay Mundy or another, yon bit wire has gien him word and warning to mark who comes this way. I must e'en call science to my own employ. Hullo, Central! . . . Hullo! Give me Spunk, please. . . . Hullo, Spunk. MacGregor speaking. Spunk, I am now come to a verra straight place, and I would be extremely blithe to hae your company. For, to deal plainly wi' you, my neck is set on the venture, no less. . . . I am obleegit to you. Ye hae aye been dependable. See if you canna bring Common-sense wi' you. Hullo, Central! Gimme Brains. . . . What's that? No answer? Try again, Central, gin ye please. The affair is verra urgent."

The oncoming rider slowed down. MacGregor turned to meet him, his two hands resting on the saddle-horn.

" 'Tis Mundy's self, thanks be," he muttered. "Now, do you twa walk cannily, Spunk and Common-sense. Here is the narrow bit. Aha, Brains! Are ye there at the last of it? That's weel! I shall need you!"

The riders drew abreast.

"Hands up, you!"

Mundy's gun was drawn and leveled with incredible swiftness. MacGregor's hands did not move from the saddle-horn.

"That is no just what ye might call a ceevil greeting, Mr. Mundy. Ye give me but a queer idea of your hospitality. And man, ye think puirly! Do ye see this rifle under my knee? Thirty-forty, smokeless—and, had I meant ye ill, it was but stepping behind a bit bush to tumble you from the saddle or e'er ye clapped eyes on me."

"You have my name, I see," said Mundy. "And there is certainly some truth in your last saying. Guess you didn't know we were expecting you. Unless all signs fail, you are fresh from the loot of Luna. Now, stick up those hands or I'll blow you into eternity!"

"And that is a foolish obsairve," said MacGregor composedly. " 'Into eternity!' says he. Man, I wonder at ye! We're in eternity now,—every minute of it,—as much as we e'er shall be. And I was well knowing to yon mischief-making telephone—but I took my chance of finding you a man of sense. For my hands, they are very well where they are. You have me covered—what more would you wish? I have conscientious scruples aboot this hands-up business. It is undeegnified in the highest degree."

"Very well. I am coming to get your gun. Keep your hands on the saddle-horn. If you crook a finger, I'll crook mine."

" 'Tis early yet in the day, Mr. Mundy." MacGregor held the same attitude. "Dinna be hasty in closing in upon me. I was thinking to propose a compromise."

"A compromise? And me with finger on trigger—me that could hit you blindfold?"

"Nae doot of it at all. Ye have the name of a man of speerit and of one skilly wi' his gun and unco' swift to the back o' that. Myself, I am slow on the draw—but, man! if I'm slow, I'm extraordinar' eefeecient! If you crook that finger you are speaking of, I am thinking the two of us may miss the breakfast cooking yonder."

"Fool! I can shoot you three times before you get to the gun."

"Nae doot, nae doot," said MacGregor pacifically. "It

has been done. But, come, Mr. Mundy. I must deal plainly wi' you. Understand me weel. I am laying no traps to tempt your eye to rove—so dinna look, but e'en take my word for it. Gin ye were free to look, ye wad see some ten-twelve black specks coming this way ahindt me on the plain, a long hour back, or near two—and ye may draw your ain conclusions thereby. To speak the plain truth, I doot they mean me nae guid at a'.''

"I should conclude that this was your unlucky day, Mr. Whatever-your-name-is. Quite aside from these gentlemen behind, or from myself, the whole country east of here is warned by telephone. Heavy, heavy hangs over your head!"

"I am a little struck wi' that circumstance myself," said MacGregor simply. "Ye see the seetuation wi' great clearness, Mr. Mundy. But I have seen worse days, and trust to come fairly off from this one yet. For, if you can eenstruct me in what way I should be any worse off to be shot by you just now than to be hanged in a tow from a pleasant juniper a little later, I shall be the more obleegit. For then I can plainly see my way to give myself up to you. If you cannae do this, then I shall expect ye, as a reasoning man yourself, to note that ye can have naught to gain by changing shots wi' one who has naught to lose, and to conseeder the proposeetion I make to you—as I should surely do and the cases were changed."

"You put it very attractively and I see your point," said Mundy. A slow smile lit up his face. He put his gun back in the scabbard. "Well, let's have it."

"And a verra guid choice, too. If it be not askin' too much, let us e'en be riding toward yon ranch gate while ye hear my offer. Yonder weary bodies gain on us while we stand here daffing."

They made a strange contrast: Mundy, smooth, slender, and graceful, black of hair and eye, poised, lithe, and tense; MacGregor, stiff, unwieldy, awkward, gross, year-bitten.

"For the first of it, ye should know that not one of

these gentry behind have seen my face, the which I kep'
streectly covered durin' my brief stay in Luna. Second,
though no great matter, ye may care to know that the bit
stroke I pulled off in Luna was even less than justice.
For within year and day a good friend of mine was there
begowked and cozened by that same partnership—yes,
and that wi' treachery and broken trust to the back of it
—of mair than I regained for him by plain and open
force at noonday. So much for that. Third, for your own
self, it is far known that you and the Wyandotte Company and Steelfoot Morgan are not agreeing verra
well—"

"You never heard that I've taken any the worst of it,
did you?"

"No, but that they keep you weel occupied. Also, that
hired warriors from the Tonto are to join wi' Webb of
the Wyandotte. So hear me now. I neednae ask if ye
have ony but discreet persons aboot ye?"

Mundy laughed. "Boys are floating in the hills with a
pack outfit. No one at the ranch to-day but Hurley, the
water-mason."

"Verra weel. Do you send him away betimes on that
beastie atween your knees, and I'll be water-mason to
you—the mair that I can run your steam-pump as well
as the best. The story will be that the outlaw-body
passed by night, unseen, liftin' your night-horse as he
flitted, and leavin' this sorrel of mine. Your man Hurley
can join your outfit and lose himself. And when they see
how it is, that their man has got cleanly away, these men
from Luna will know that the jig is definitely up, and
they will be all for the eating and sleeping."

"Very pretty, and it can be done—since they do not
know you," agreed Mundy. "But I do not see where I am
to gain anything."

"You are to hear, then," said the outlaw. "I will praise
the bridge that carried me over, but I will do more, too;
I will mend that bridge. I will fight your battles with

you against all comers. Not murder, you mind, but plain warfare against men fit for war."

"A fighting man, and slow on the draw?"

"I am that same, both the one and the other. Slow, I cannot deny it—slow in compare with the best. Someway, I dinna prosper verra weel as chief man—but as the next best there is none better rides leather."

"You come well recommended."

"By myself, you are meaning? And, just that you may know the worth of that recommend, I am telling ye that my name is no exactly Maxwell. I would have ye to observe, Mr. Mundy, that I keepit my name streectly to myself for such time as ye might have taken the sound of it as a threat, and give it to you now only when it comes mair as a promise. So now I offer you the naked choice, peace or war."

"I am decidedly inclined toward peace," said Clay Mundy, smiling again, "if only to hear you talk. And, after all, your late exploit at Luna is nothing to me. But as to your value in my little range war—you forgot to mention the name, you know."

"The name is MacGregor."

"Not Sandy MacGregor? Of Black Mountain?"

"That same. Plain shooting done neatly."

"You're on!" said Clay Mundy.

II

Mr. Maxwell had been given a mount, a rope, and a branding-iron, and so turned loose to learn the range. So far, his services had been confined to peaceful activities; for the bitter cattle war between Clay Mundy and his enemies, "Steelfoot" Morgan and Webb of the Wyandotte, had languished since the rains set in.

All day it had been cloudy. While Mr. Maxwell was branding his maverick, it began to rain. By the time he turned it loose, the rain had turned to a blinding storm, and he was glad to turn his back to its fury and ride his straightest for the nearest shelter, Pictured Rock, an overhanging cliff of limestone, whose walls and roof are covered with the weird picture-writing of Apache and Navaho.

As he turned the bend in the cañon, Maxwell saw a great light glowing under Pictured Rock, veiled by the driving rain. Another, storm-driven like himself, was before him. He paused at the hill-foot and shouted:

"Hullo, the house! Will your dog bite?"

"*Hi!*"—it was a startled voice. A slender figure in a yellow slicker appeared beside the fire. "Dog's dead, poor fellow—starved to death! Come on up!"

The C L A man rode up the short zigzag of the trail to the fire-lit level. He took but one glance and swept off his hat, for the face he saw beneath the turned-up sombrero was the bright and sparkling face of a girl.

"You will be Miss Bennie May Morgan? I saw you in Magdalena at the steer-shipping."

"Quite right. And you are Mr. Sandy Maxwell, the new warrior for Clay Mundy."

"Faces like ours are not easily forgot," said Maxwell.

Miss Bennie laughed. "I will give you a safe-conduct. Get down—unless you are afraid of hurting your reputation, that is." She sat upon her saddle blankets where they were spread before the fire, and leaned back against the saddle.

The C L A man climbed heavily down and strode to the fire.

"How about that lunch?" demanded Miss Bennie. "It's past noon."

"Sorry, Miss Morgan, but I have not so much as a crumb. And that is a bad thing, for you are far from home, and who knows when this weary storm will be by? But dootless they will be abroad to seek for you."

Miss Bennie laid aside the hat and shook her curly head decidedly. "Not for me. Dad thinks I'm visiting Effie at the XL and Effie thinks I'm home by this time.

But this storm won't last. The sun will be out by three. You'll see! And now, if you please, since you can't feed me, hadn't you better entertain me? Sit down, do!"

"It is like that I should prove entertaining for a young maid, too!" said Maxwell, carrying a flat stone to the fire to serve for a seat.

"Oh, you never can tell! Suppose, for a starter, you tell me what you are thinking so busily."

"I am thinking," said Maxwell slowly, "that you are a bonny lass and a merry one. And I was thinking one thing, too. The XL is awa' to the southeast and the Morgan home ranch as far to the southwest. Now, what may Miss Bennie Morgan need of so much northing, ten long miles aside from the straight way, and her friend Effie thinking she was safe home and all? And then I thought to myself, the folk of the San Quentin are very quiet now. It is to be thought that the season of great plenty has put them in better spunk with the world. And it is an ill thing that a way cannot be found to make an end of this brawling for good and all. And, thinks I, the bonny Earl of Murray himself was not more goodly to the eye than the man Clay Mundy—and it is a great peety for all concerned that Clay Mundy is not storm-bound this day at Pictured Rock, rather than I!"

"Well!" Miss Bennie gasped and laughed frankly, blush-red, neck and throat. "Oh, you men! And while you were making this up—"

"It is what I thought," said Maxwell stoutly. "Only I wasnae thinking words, d'ye see? I was just thinking thoughts. And it is no verra easy to put thoughts into words."

"Well, then—while you were thinking all those preposterous thoughts, I was seeing a wonderful picture, very much like this storm, and this cave, and this fire, and us. If I were a painter, this is what I would try to paint: a hillside like this—the black night and the wild storm: a red fire glowing in a cave-mouth, and by the fire a man straining into the night at some unseen danger—a cave-man, clad in skins, with long matted hair, broad-shouldered, long-armed, ferocious, brutal—but unafraid. He is half crouching, his knees bent to spring; a dog strains beside his foot, snarling against the night, teeth bared, neck bristling; behind them, half hid, shrinking in the shadow—a woman and a child. And the name of that picture would be 'Home!' "

Maxwell's heavy face lit up, his dull and little eye gleamed with an answering spark, his sluggish blood thrilled at the spirit and beauty of her. His voice rang with a heat of frank admiration:

"And that is a brave thought you have conjured up, too, and I will be warrant you would be unco' fine woman to a cave-man. I would have you observe that the thoughts of the two of us differed but verra little when all is said—forbye it ran in my mind that a much younger person was to be cave-man to you."

"Now you are trying to torment me," said Miss Bennie briskly. "I can't have that. Roll a smoke—I know you want to. The storm is slacking already—we will be going soon."

"A pipe, since you are so kind," said Maxwell, fumbling for it.

"Do you admire your friend Clay Mundy so much?" said Miss Bennie next, elbows on knees, chin in hands.

Maxwell rolled a slow eye on her, and blew out a cloud of smoke. "My employer. I did not say friend, though if I like him no worse it may come to that yet. He has the devil's own beauty—which thing calls the louder to me, misshapen as you see me. He is a gallant horseman, fame cries him brave and proven. But I am not calling him friend yet till I know the heart of him. Fifty-and-five I am, and I can count on the fingers of my twa hands the names of those I have been willing to call wholly friends. So you will not be taking Clay Mundy to your cave upon my say-so till I am better acquaint wi' him. But dootless you know him verra weel yourself."

Miss Bennie evaded this issue. She became suddenly gloomy. "It is plain that you are a stranger here, since you can talk so glibly of any lasting peace in San Quentin. A wicked, stiff-necked, unreasoning pack they are— dad and all! There has never been anything but wrong and hate here, outrage and revenge, and there never will be. It is enough to make one believe in the truth of original sin and total depravity!"

"No truth at all!" cried Maxwell warmly. "Oreeginal sin is just merely a fact—no truth at a'! Folks are aye graspin' at some puir haflin' fact and settin' it up to be the truth. But the storm is breaking. It will be clear as suddenly as it came on. I will be seeing that you get safe home—"

"No, you mustn't. It would only make you a hard ride for nothing. No need of it at all. There is time for me to get home while the sun is still an hour high."

"It doesn't seem right," protested Maxwell.

"Really, I'd rather you wouldn't," said Miss Bennie earnestly. "I don't want to be rude, but I am still"—she gave him her eyes and blushed to her hair—"I am still— north of where I should be, as you so shrewdly observed. And your camp lies farther yet to the north."

"Good-by, then, Miss Morgan."

"Good-by, Mr. MacGregor."

He stared after her as she rode clattering down the steep.

"MacGregor!" he repeated. "MacGregor, says she! And never a soul of the San Quentin kens aught of the late MacGregor save Clay Mundy's own self! Here is news! Is she so unco' chief wi' him as that, then? And who told her whaur my camp was? She was glib to say she had time enow to go home or sundown—but she was careful she didnae say she was gaun there! Little lady, it is in my mind that you are owre far north!"

She waved her hand gaily; her fresh young voice floated back to him, lingering, soft and slow:

"He was a braw gallant,
And he rid at the ring:
And the bonny Earl of Murray—
Oh! He might have been a king."

The girl passed from sight down the narrow cañon. MacGregor-Maxwell put foot to stirrup. When he came to the beaten trail again, he shook his great shoulders as if to throw off a weight. He held his cupped hand to his mouth. "Hullo, Central! Can you get Brains for me? . . . Try again, please. . . . Now, Brains, you are partly acquaint wi' this day's doings. But did you mark the bonny blush of her at the name of Clay Mundy—and her so far from the plain way, wi' no cause given? . . . Well, then, I am telling you of it—and what am I to do in such case as that? . . . Oh! I am to see where Clay Mundy rides this day—if it is any affair of mine—is that it? . . . Surely it is my business. Any man is natural protector to any woman against any man—except himself. . . . And if he means her naething but good? . . . It is what I will know."

III

"I thought it was you," said Miss Bennie May Morgan, "so I waited for you. Aren't you rather out of your own range, Mr. Maxwell? The Morgans'll get you if you don't watch out!"

With elaborate surprise, MacGregor took his bearings from the distant circling hills. "Why, so I am! I was on my way to Datil," he explained. "I see now"—he jerked a thumb back over his shoulder—"that I should have ridden east-like this morning instead of west."

"It is shorter that way—and dryer," she agreed.

"Shall I ride with you a bit on your way?" asked MacGregor. "I can still get back to my camp before sundown. Mind you, I am not saying at all that I shall go to my camp by that hour, but only that there is time enough."

Then Miss Bennie Morgan knew where she stood. She

flicked at her stirrup with a meditative quirt. "Why, I said something about like that to you last week at Pictured Rock, didn't I?"

"Very much like that."

She turned clear, unflinching eyes upon him. "Well, let's have it!"

"Er—why—uh!" said MacGregor, and swallowed hard. "I don't quite understand you."

"Oh, yes, you do!" said Miss Bennie cheerfully. "Don't squirm! What's on your mind?"

In her inmost heart Miss Bennie knew certainly—without reason, as women know these things—that this grim old man-at-arms liked her very well, and came as a friend.

"Blackmail? Oh, no—that is not in your line. And I do not take you for a telltale, either." She looked him over slowly and attentively—a cruel, contemplative glance. "I see!" She dropped the reins and clapped her hands together. "You were planning to take Clay Mundy's place with me—is that it?"

MacGregor plucked up spirit at the taunt. "And that was an unkind speech of you, Miss Morgan!"

Her eyes danced at him. "There is but one thing left, then. You have come to plead with me for your friend—your employer—to ask me to spare his youth and innocence—to demand of me, as the phrase goes, if my intentions are honorable."

"It is something verra like that, then, if I must brave your displeasure so far as to say it. It was in my mind to give you but the bare hint that your secret was stumbled upon. For what one has chanced upon this day another may chance upon tomorrow."

The girl dropped all pretense. "I think you meant kindly by me, Mr. MacGregor, and I thank you for it. And you must consider that our case is hard indeed. For where can we meet, if not secretly? Fifty miles each way, every ranch is lined up on one side or the other of this feud. One word to my father's ear will mean bloodshed and death—and then, whoever wins, Bennie Morgan must lose."

"Yet you must meet?" said MacGregor.

She met his eyes bravely. "Yet we must meet!" She said it proudly.

"You two should wed out of hand, then, and put the round world between you and this place," said Mac-Gregor.

Miss Bennie sighed. "That is what I tell Clay. It is the only way. Soon or late, if we live here, those two would meet, my father and my husband. If we go away, father may get over it in time. Clay doesn't want to go. He can't bear to have it said that he had to run away from San Quentin. But I will never marry him till he is ready to go."

"He is a fool for his pains, and I will be the one who will tell him that same!" declared MacGregor stoutly. "Him and his pride! He should be proud to run further and faster than ever man ran before, on such an argument."

"No; you mustn't say one word to him about me—please! He would be furious. He's as cross as a bear with a sore head now—so I think he is coming to my way of thinking, and doesn't like to own up. Don't you say anything. I'll tell him—not that you have seen me, but that we might so easily be seen, and that our meetings must be few and far between from now on. That will help him to make up his mind, too, if he feels—" She checked herself, with a startled shyness in her sudden drooping lids. She was only a young girl, for all her frank and boyish courage. "I will warn him, then—and yet I think there is no man who would not think twice before he whispered evil of Ben Morgan's daughter and"—she held her head proudly and lifted her brave eyes—"and Clay Mundy's sweetheart!"

MacGregor checked his horse, his poor, dull face for once lit up and uplifted. Whatever had been best of him

in all his wasted and misspent life stirred at the call of
her gallant girlhood.

"I think there will be few men so vile as to think an
evil thing of you," he said. "Miss Morgan, I was a puir
meddlin' fool to come here on such an errand—and yet I
am glad that I came, too. And now I shall go back and
trouble you nae mair. Yet there is one thing, too, before
I turn back."

She faced him where he stood, so that he carried with
him a memory of her dazzling youth against a dazzle of
sun.

"If ever you have any need of me—as is most unlike—
I shall be leal friend to you; I shall stick at nothing in
your service. It is so that I would have you think of old
MacGregor. Good-by!"

"I shall not forget," said Bennie.

"Good-by, then!" said MacGregor again. He bent over
her hand.

"Good-by!"

IV

A week later MacGregor was riding the cedar brakes
on the high flanks of the mountain, branding late calves.
As the day wore on he found himself well across in the
Wyandotte-Morgan country, prowling in the tangle of
hills, south of the Magdalena road, which was the accepted dividing line. And as he came down a ridge of
backbone from the upper bench, he saw a little curl of
smoke rising above the Skullspring bluff.

MacGregor remarked upon this fact to Neighbor, his
horse. "We are in a hostile country, Neighbor," said he.
"For all we are so quiet and peaceful these days, it will
be the part of prudence to have a look into this matter."

He tied Neighbor in a little hollow of the hill, and
went down with infinite precaution to the edge of the cliff
above Skullspring.

Three men were by the fire below, all strangers to MacGregor. That gentleman lay flat on the rock, peering through a bush, and looked them over. Two were cowboys: their saddled horses stood by. The third person, a tall man of about thirty, had the look of a town man. He wore a black suit and a "hard-boiled" hat. By the fire stood a buggy and a harnessed horse.

"I tell you," said the older cowboy, a sullen-faced young man, "I'll be good and glad a-plenty when this thing is over with. It's a shaky business."

"Don't get cold feet, Joe," advised the tall man. "You're getting big money—mighty big money—for a small risk."

"I notice there's none of these San Quentin *hombres* caring for any of it," grumbled Joe sulkily.

"Aw, now, be reasonable," said the tall man. "He wouldn't risk letting any of the home people know—too shaky! You get the chance just because you're a stranger."

Plainly, here was mischief afoot. It seemed likely to MacGregor that Clay Mundy was to be the object of it.

The younger man of the party spoke up: "I'm not only goin' to get away, but I'm goin' to keep on gettin' away! I'm after that dough all right, all right—but lemme tell you, Mr. Hamerick, this country'll be too hot for me when it's over."

MacGregor barely breathed. It appeared that the tall man was Hamerick, for he answered: "I'm going away myself—so far away, as the saying goes, that it'll take nine dollars to send me a postal card. But this is the chance of a life-time to make a big stake, and we don't want to make a hash of it. Keep your nerve. Your part is easy. You take the right-hand trail and drift south across that saddle-back pass yonder, so you'll get there before I do. You'll find the Bent ranch right under the pass. Nobody there. The Bents have all gone to Magdalena for supplies. If any one should come, it's all off, for today. If we see your fire, Mundy and me'll turn back. We'll pull it off to-morrow."

Mundy! MacGregor's heart leaped. Were the men to entice Mundy to the Bent ranch and murder him there, while he was off his guard, thinking himself among friends? MacGregor drew his gun, minded to fall upon the plotters without more ado: the vantage of ground more than made up for the odds of numbers. But he put back his gun. They were to separate. He would follow the man Hamerick and deal with him alone.

"I am to meet Mundy at that little sugar-loaf hill yonder, four or five miles out on the plain," said Hamerick. "Then I'll go on down the wagon road to Bent's with him. You boys'll have plenty of time to get settled down."

"If we don't run into a wasps' nest," said Joe sulkily.

Hamerick scowled. "I'm the one that's taking the biggest risk, with this damned buggy—but I have to have it, to play the part. I'll leave it, once I get safe back to my saddle."

"Yes—and we three want to ride in three different directions," said Joe.

MacGregor waited for no more. He rolled back from the bare rim with scarce more noise than a shadow would have made. He crawled to the nearest huddle of rocks and hid away. Presently there came the sound of wheels and a ringing of shod feet on rock. The two cowboys toiled up the trail beyond the cliff-end, paced slowly by, black against the sky-line, and dipped down into a dark hollow that twisted away toward Bent's Pass.

The tingling echoes died. MacGregor climbed back to Neighbor. The game was in his hands. Keeping to the ridge, he would gain a long mile on the wagon road, deep in the winding pass.

When he came into the wagon road the buggy was just before him. MacGregor struck into a gallop.

The stranger had been going at a brisk gait, but at

sight of the horseman he slowed to a prim and mincing little trot.

"A fine day, sir!" said MacGregor civilly, as he rode alongside.

"It certainly is," said the stranger. He was plainly ill at ease at this ill-timed meeting, but tried to carry it off. "How far is it to Old Fort Tularosa—can you tell me?"

MacGregor squinted across the plain. "Forty miles, I should say. Goin' across?"

The stranger shook his head. "Not today. I think I will camp here for the night and have a look in the hills for deer. You're not going to the fort yourself, are you?"

MacGregor grinned. "Well, no—not today. The fact is, sir,"—he bent over close and sank his voice to a confidential whisper,—"the fact is, if you're for camping here the night, I must even camp here too."

"What!"

"Just that. And, first of all, do you remark this little gun which I hold here in my hand? Then I will ask you to stop and to get out upon this side, holding to your lines verra carefully lest the beastie should run away, while I search you for any bit weapons of your ain. For you spoke very glibly of hunting a deer—and yet I do not see any rifle."

Hamerick groaned as he climbed out; he had not thought of that.

"I haven't any rifle. My revolver is under the cushion —but of course you can search me, if you think I've got another. What the devil do you want, anyway? If it's money you're after, you'll get most mighty little."

"All in good time, all in good time," said MacGregor cheerfully.

He went through Hamerick for arms, finding none; he went through the buggy, finding the gun under the cushion. He inspected this carefully, tried it, and stuck it in his waist-band.

"You see I have no money—you have my gun—what

more do you want of me?" spluttered Hamerick. "Let me go! I have an appointment—I'll be late now."

"With that deer, ye are meaning? Do you know, sir, that in my puir opeenion, if you knew how you are like to keep that appointment of yours, you would be little made up with it?"

Hamerick stammered. He had no idea of what his captor was driving at, but he had his own reasons for great uneasiness. He pulled himself together with an effort. "I —I don't know what you mean. I see now that you are not a robber, as I first thought. You are mistaking me for some other man. You can't be doing yourself any possible good by keeping me here. I tell you, I am waited for."

"Take my word for it, sir, if you knew my way of it, you would be less impatient for that tryst of yours."

"What—what the devil do you mean?"

"I will tell you, then, Mr. Hamerick." At this unexpected sound of his own name, Hamerick started and trembled. "If Clay Mundy is at all of my mind, this is what we shall do. We will set you on Clay Mundy's horse and put Clay Mundy's hat upon your head; and we two will get in your bit wagon and drive you before our guns —just at dusk, d'ye mind?—to the Bent ranch; and there, if I do not miss my guess, you will be shot to death by hands of your own hiring!"

Here MacGregor was extremely disconcerted by the behavior of his prospective victim. So far from being appalled, Hamerick was black with rage.

"You fool! You poor spy! Idiot! Bungler! Why couldn't you tell me you were Mundy's man?"

"Steady, there! Are you meaning to face it out that you did not plan to murder Clay Mundy? Because we are going on now to see him."

Hamerick gathered up the reins eagerly. "Come on, then, damn you—before it's too late." There was relief and triumph in his voice—and at the sound of it Mac-

Gregor sickened with a guess at the whole dreadful business. The bright day faded. "Me kill Clay Mundy? Why, you poor, pitiful bungler, Clay Mundy brought me here to play preacher for him!"

MacGregor drew back. His face flamed red to his hair; his eyes were terrible. He jerked out Hamerick's gun and threw it at Hamerick's feet. There was a dreadful break in his voice. "Protect yourself!" he said.

But Hamerick shrank back, white-lipped, cringing. "I won't! I won't touch it!"

"Cur!"

"Oh, don't kill me, don't murder me!" He was wringing his hands, almost screaming.

MacGregor turned shamed eyes away. He took up Hamerick's gun. "Strip the harness from that horse, then, take the bridle, and ride! And be quick, lest I think better of it. Go back the way you came, and keep on going! For I shall tell your name and errand, and there is no man of Morgan's men but will kill you at kirk or gallows-foot."

He watched in silence as Hamerick fled. Then he rode down the pass, sick-hearted, brooding, grieving. At the plain's edge he saw a horseman near by, coming swiftly. It was Clay Mundy.

MacGregor slowed up. The flush of burning wrath had died away; his face was set to a heavy, impassive mask. He thrust Hamerick's gun between his left knee and the stirrup-leather, and gripped it there. Then he rode on to meet Clay Mundy. As at their first meeting, he laid both hands on the saddle-horn as he halted.

Clay Mundy's face was dark with suspicion.

"Have you seen a fool in a buggy?" he demanded.

"I see a fool on a horse!" responded MacGregor calmly. "For the person you seek, I have put such a word in his ear that he will never stop this side of tide-water. What devil's work is this, Clay Mundy?"

"You meddler! Are you coward as well as meddler, that you dare not move your hands?"

"Put up your foolish gun, man—you cannae fricht me with it. The thing is done, and shooting will never undo it. There will be no mock-marriage this day, nor any day —and now shoot if you will, and damned to you! Man! have ye gone clean mad? Or did ye wish to proclaim it that ye were no match for the Morgans in war? And did ye think to live the week out? That had been a chance had you married her indeed, with book and bell—as whaur could ye find better mate? But after such black treachery as ye meant you couldnae hope—oh, man, ye are not in your right mind; the devil is at your ear!"

"It is hard to kill a man who will not defend himself," said Mundy thickly. "I spared your life once because you amused me—"

"And because it was a verra judeecious thing, too— and you are well knowing to that same. Think ye I value my life owre high, or that I fear ye at all, that I come seeking you? Take shame to yourself, man! Have a bet·· ter thought of it yet! Say you will marry the lassie be- fore my eyes, and I will go with you on that errand; or turn you back, and I will go with her back to the house of the Morgans—and for her sake I will keep your shame to mysel'."

"Fool!" said Mundy. "I can kill you before you can touch your gun."

"It is what I doubt," said MacGregor. "Please your- self. For me there is but the clean stab of death—but you must leave behind the name of a false traitor to be a hissing and a by-word in the mouths of men."

"I will say this much, that I was wrong to call you coward," said Mundy in a changed voice. "You are a bold and stubborn man, and I think there is a chance that you might get your gun—yes, and shoot straight, too! I will not marry the girl—but neither will I harm her. But I will not be driven further. I am not willing to skulk away while you tell her your way of the story. That would be too sorry a part. I will go on alone, and tell her, and send her home."

"You will say your man fled before the Morgans, or was taken by them, or some such lies, and lure her on to her ruin," said MacGregor. "I will not turn back."

"I will give you a minute to turn back," said Mundy.

"It is what I will never do."

"Then you will die here," said Mundy.

"Think of me as one dead an hour gone," said Mac-Gregor steadily. "My life is long since forfeit to every law of God or man. I am beyond the question. Think rather of yourself. You have the plain choice before you: a bonny wife to cherish, and bairns to your knee—life and love, peace and just dealing and quiet days—or, at the other hand, but dusty death and black shame to the back of that!"

As a snake strikes, Mundy's hand shot out. He jerked MacGregor's gun from the scabbard and threw it behind him. His face lit up with ferocious joy.

"You prating old wind-bag! How about it now? I am sorry for the girl myself—but she shall be the shame of the Morgans to-morrow. They have crowed over me for the last time."

"For the last time, Mundy, give it up! In the name of God!"

"Get off that horse! I will give you your life—you're not worth my killing. Never be seen on the San Quentin again!"

"Mundy—"

"Get off, I say!" Mundy spurred close, his cocked gun swung shoulder high.

"Aweel," said MacGregor. He began to slide off slowly, his right hand on the saddle-horn. His left hand went to the gun at his left knee; he thrust it up under Neighbor's neck and fired—once, twice, again! Crash of flames, roaring of gun-shots—he was on his back, Neighbor's feet were in his ribs—he fired once more, blindly.

Breathless, crushed, he struggled to his knees, the blood pumping from two bullet-holes in his great body.

A yard away, Clay Mundy lay on his face, crumpled and still, clutching a smoking gun.

"I didnae touch his face," said MacGregor. He threw both guns behind him. He turned Mundy over and opened his shirt. One wound was in his breast, close beside his heart; another was through his heart. MacGregor looked down upon him.

"The puir, mad, misguided lad!" he said, between pain-wrung lips. "Surely he was gone horn-mad with hate and wrong and revenge!"

He covered the dead man's face, and straightened the stiffening arms, and sat beside him. He looked at the low sun, the splendor of the western range. He held his hand to his own breast to stay the pulsing blood.

"And the puir lassie—she will hear this shameful tale of him! Had I killed yonder knave Hamerick, she had blamed none but me. 'Twas ill done. . . . Ay, but she's young still. She will have a cave and a fire of her own yet."

There was silence a little space and his hand slipped. Then he opened his dulling eyes:

"Hullo, Central! . . . Give me Body, please. . . . Hullo, Body! Hullo! That you, Body? . . . MacGregor's Soul speaking. I am going away. Good luck to you—good-by! . . . I don't know where."

TAPPAN'S BURRO

by ZANE GREY

I

TAPPAN gazed down upon the newly born little burro with something of pity and consternation. It was not a vigorous offspring of the redoubtable Jennie, champion of all the numberless burros he had driven in his desert-prospecting years. He could not leave it there to die. Surely it was not strong enough to follow its mother. And to kill it was beyond him.

"Poor little devil!" soliloquized Tappan. "Reckon neither Jennie nor I wanted it to be born. . . . I'll have to hole up in this camp a few days. You can never tell what a burro will do. It might fool us an' grow strong all of a sudden."

Whereupon Tappan left Jennie and her tiny, gray lop-eared baby to themselves, and leisurely set about making permanent camp. The water at this oasis was not much to his liking, but it was drinkable, and he felt he must put up with it. For the rest the oasis was desirable enough as a camping site. Desert wanderers like Tappan favored the lonely water holes. This one was up under the bold brow of the Chocolate Mountains, where rocky wall met the desert sand, and a green patch of *palo verdes* and mesquites proved the presence of water. It had a magnificent view down a many-leagued slope of desert growths, across the dark belt of green and the shining strip of red that marked the Rio Colorado, and on to the upflung Arizona land, range lifting to range until the saw-toothed peaks notched the blue sky.

Locked in the iron fastnesses of these desert mountains

was gold. Tappan, if he had any calling, was a prospector. But the lure of gold did not bind him to this wandering life any more than the freedom of it. He had never made a rich strike. About the best he could ever do was to dig enough gold to grubstake himself for another prospecting trip into some remote corner of the American Desert. Tappan knew the arid Southwest from San Diego to the Pecos River and from Picacho on the Colorado to the Tonto Basin. Few prospectors had the strength and endurance of Tappan. He was a giant in build, and at thirty-five had never yet reached the limit of his physical force.

With hammer and pick and magnifying glass Tappan scaled the bare ridges. He was not an expert in testing minerals. He knew he might easily pass by a rich vein of ore. But he did his best, sure at least that no prospector could get more than he out of the pursuit of gold. Tappan was more of a naturalist than a prospector, and more of a dreamer than either. Many were the idle moments that he sat staring down the vast reaches of the valleys, or watching some creature of the wasteland, or marveling at the vivid hues of desert flowers.

Tappan waited two weeks at this oasis for Jennie's baby burro to grow strong enough to walk. And the very day that Tappan decided to break camp he found signs of gold at the head of a wash above the oasis. Quite by chance, as he was looking for his burros, he struck his pick into a place no different from a thousand others there, and hit into a pocket of gold. He cleaned out the pocket before sunset, the richer for several thousand dollars.

"You brought me luck," said Tappan, to the little gray burro staggering around its mother. "Your name is Jenet. You're Tappan's burro, an' I reckon he'll stick to you."

Jenet belied the promise of her birth. Like a weed in fertile ground she grew. Winter and summer Tappan patrolled the sand beats from one trading post to another, and his burros traveled with him. Jenet had an especially good training. Her mother had happened to be a remarkably good burro before Tappan had bought her. And Tappan had patience; he found leisure to do things, and he had something of pride in Jenet. Whenever he happened to drop into Ehrenberg or Yuma, or any freighting station, some prospector always tried to buy Jenet. She grew as large as a medium-sized mule, and a three-hundred-pound pack was no load to discommode her.

Tappan, in common with most lonely wanderers of the desert, talked to his burro. As the years passed this habit grew, until Tappan would talk to Jenet just to hear the sound of his voice. Perhaps that was all which kept him human.

"Jenet, you're worthy of a happier life," Tappan would say, as he unpacked her after a long day's march over the barren land. "You're a ship of the desert. Here we are, with grub an' water, a hundred miles from any camp. An' what but you could have fetched me here? No horse! No mule! No man! Nothin' but a camel, an' so I call you ship of the desert. But for you an' your kind, Jenet, there'd be no prospectors, and few gold mines. Reckon the desert would be still an unknown waste. . . . You're a great beast of burden, Jenet, an' there's no one to sing your praise."

And of a golden sunrise, when Jenet was packed and ready to face the cool, sweet fragrance of the desert, Tappan was wont to say:

"Go along with you, Jenet. The mornin's fine. Look at the mountains yonder callin' us. It's only a step down there. All purple an' violet! It's the life for us, my burro, an' Tappan's as rich as if all these sands were pearls."

But sometimes, at sunset, when the way had been long and hot and rough, Tappan would bend his shaggy head over Jenet, and talk in different mood.

"Another day gone, Jenet, another journey ended—an' Tappan is only older, wearier, sicker. There's no reward for your faithfulness. I'm only a desert rat, livin' from hole to hole. No home! No face to see. . . . Some sunset, Jenet, we'll reach the end of the trail. An' Tappan's bones will bleach in the sands. An' no one will know or care!"

When Jenet was two years old she would have taken the blue ribbon in competition with all the burros of the Southwest. She was unusually large and strong, perfectly proportioned, sound in every particular, and practically tireless. But these were not the only characteristics that made prospectors envious of Tappan. Jenet had the common virtues of all good burros magnified to an unbelievable degree. Moreover, she had sense and instinct that to Tappan bordered on the supernatural.

During these years Tappan's trail crisscrossed the mineral region of the Southwest. But, as always, the rich strike held aloof. It was like the pot of gold buried at the foot of the rainbow. Jenet knew the trails and the water holes better than Tappan. She could follow a trail obliterated by drifting sand or cut out by running water. She could scent at long distance a new spring on the desert or a strange water hole. She never wandered far from camp so that Tappan had to walk far in search of her. Wild burros, the bane of most prospectors, held no charm for Jenet. And she had never yet shown any especial liking for a tame burro. This was the strangest feature of Jenet's complex character. Burros were noted for their habit of pairing off, and forming friendships for one or more comrades. These relations were permanent. But Jenet still remained fancy free.

Tappan scarcely realized how he relied upon this big, gray, serene beast of burden. Of course, when chance threw him among men of his calling he would brag about her. But he had never really appreciated Jenet. In his way Tappan was a brooding, plodding fellow, not conscious of sentiment. When he bragged about Jenet it was her good qualities upon which he dilated. But what he really liked best about her were the little things of every day.

During the earlier years of her training Jenet had been a thief. She would pretend to be asleep for hours just to get a chance to steal something out of camp. Tappan had broken this habit in its incipiency. But he never quite trusted her. Jenet was a burro.

Jenet ate anything offered her. She could fare for herself or go without. Whatever Tappan had left from his own meals was certain to be rich dessert for Jenet. Every meal time she would stand near the camp fire, with one great long ear drooping, and the other standing erect. Her expression was one of meekness, of unending patience. She would lick a tin can until it shone resplendent. On long, hard, barren trails Jenet's deportment did not vary from that where the water holes and grassy patches were many. She did not need to have grass or grain. Brittle-bush and sage were good fare for her. She could eat greasewood, a desert plant that protected itself with a sap as sticky as varnish and far more dangerous to animals. She could eat cacti. Tappan had seen her break off leaves of the prickly pear cactus, and stamp upon them with her forefeet, mashing off the thorns, so that she could consume the succulent pulp. She liked mesquite beans, and leaves of willow, and all the trailing vines of the desert. And she could subsist in an arid waste land where a man would have died in short order.

No ascent or descent was too hard or dangerous for Jenet, provided it was possible of accomplishment. She would refuse a trail that was impassable. She seemed to have an uncanny instinct both for what she could do, and what was beyond a burro. Tappan had never known her to fail on something to which she stuck persistently. Swift streams of water, always bugbears to burros, did not stop Jenet. She hated quicksand, but could be trusted to navigate it, if that were possible. When she stepped gingerly, with little inch steps, out upon thin

crust of ice or salty crust of desert sink hole, Tappan
would know that it was safe, or she would turn back.
Thunder and lightning, intense heat or bitter cold, the
sirocco sand storm of the desert, the white dust of the
alkali wastes—these were all the same to Jenet.

One August, the hottest and driest of his desert experience, Tappan found himself working a most promising
claim in the lower reaches of the Panamint Mountains
on the northern slope above Death Valley. It was a hard
country at the most favorable season; in August it was
terrible.

The Panamints were infested by various small gangs
of desperadoes—outlaw claim jumpers where opportunity afforded—and out-and-out robbers, even murderers
where they could not get the gold any other way.

Tappan had been warned not to go into this region
alone. But he never heeded any warnings. And the idea
that he would ever strike a claim or dig enough gold to
make himself an attractive target for outlaws seemed
preposterous and not worth considering. Tappan had become a wanderer now from the unbreakable habit of it.
Much to his amaze he struck a rich ledge of free gold in
a canyon of the Panamints; and he worked from daylight until dark. He forgot about the claim jumpers, until
one day he saw Jenet's long ears go up in the manner
habitual with her when she saw strange men. Tappan
watched the rest of that day, but did not catch a glimpse
of any living thing. It was a desolate place, shut in, red-
walled, hazy with heat, and brooding with an eternal
silence.

Not long after that Tappan discovered boot tracks of
several men adjacent to his camp and in an out-of-the-
way spot, which persuaded him that he was being
watched. Claim jumpers who were not going to jump his
claim in this torrid heat, but meant to let him dig the
gold and then kill him. Tappan was not the kind of man
to be afraid. He grew wrathful and stubborn. He had six

small canvas bags of gold and did not mean to lose them. Still, he was worried.

"Now, what's best to do?" he pondered. "I mustn't give it away that I'm wise. Reckon I'd better act natural. But I can't stay here longer. My claim's about worked out. An' these jumpers are smart enough to know it. . . . I've got to make a break at night. What to do?"

Tappan did not want to cache the gold, for in that case, of course, he would have to return for it. Still, he reluctantly admitted to himself that this was the best way to save it. Probably these robbers were watching him day and night. It would be most unwise to attempt escaping by traveling up over the Panamints.

"Reckon my only chance is goin' down into Death Valley," soliloquized Tappan, grimly.

The alternative thus presented was not to his liking. Crossing Death Valley at this season was always perilous, and never attempted in the heat of day. And at this particular time of intense torridity, when the day heat was unendurable and the midnight furnace gales were blowing, it was an enterprise from which even Tappan shrank. Added to this were the facts that he was too far west of the narrow part of the valley, and even if he did get across he would find himself in the most forbidding and desolate region of the Funeral Mountains.

Thus thinking and planning, Tappan went about his mining and camp tasks, trying his best to act natural. But he did not succeed. It was impossible, while expecting a shot at any moment, to act as if there was nothing on his mind. His camp lay at the bottom of a rocky slope. A tiny spring of water made verdure of grass and mesquite, welcome green in all that stark iron nakedness. His camp site was out in the open, on the bench near the spring. The gold claim that Tappan was working was not visible from any vantage point either below or above. It lay back at the head of a break in the rocky wall. It had two virtues—one that the sun never got to it, and the other that it was well hidden. Once there, Tappan knew he could not be seen. This, however, did not diminish his growing uneasiness. The solemn stillness was a menace. The heat of the day appeared to be augmenting to a degree beyond his experience. Every few moments Tappan would slip back through a narrow defile in the rocks and peep from his covert down at the camp. On the last of these occasions he saw Jenet out in the open. She stood motionless. Her long ears were erect. In an instant Tappan became strung with thrilling excitement. His keen eyes searched every approach to his camp. And at last in the gully below to the right he discovered two men crawling along from rock to rock. Jenet had seen them enter that gully and was now watching for them to appear.

Tappan's excitement gave place to a grimmer emotion. These stealthy visitors were going to hide in ambush, and kill him as he returned to camp.

"Jenet, reckon what I owe you is a whole lot," muttered Tappan. "They'd have got me sure. . . . But now—"

Tappan left his tools, and crawled out of his covert into the jumble of huge rocks toward the left of the slope. He had a six-shooter. His rifle he had left in camp. Tappan had seen only two men, but he knew there were more than that, if not actually near at hand at the moment, then surely not far away. And his chance was to worm his way like an Indian down to camp. With the rifle in his possession he would make short work of the present difficulty.

"Lucky Jenet's right in camp!" said Tappan, to himself. "It beats hell how she does things!"

Tappan was already deciding to pack and hurry away. On the moment Death Valley did not daunt him. This matter of crawling and gliding along was work unsuited to his great stature. He was too big to hide behind a little shrub or a rock. And he was not used to stepping lightly. His hobnailed boots could not be placed noiselessly upon the stones. Moreover, he could not progress without displacing little bits of weathered rock. He was sure that keen ears not too far distant could have heard him. But he kept on, making good progress around that slope to the far side of the canyon. Fortunately, he headed the gully up which his ambushers were stealing. On the other hand, this far side of the canyon afforded but little cover. The sun had gone down back of the huge red mass of the mountain. It had left the rocks so hot Tappan could not touch them with his bare hands.

He was about to stride out from his last covert and make a run for it down the rest of the slope, when, surveying the whole amphitheater below him, he espied the two men coming up out of the gully, headed toward his camp. They looked in his direction. Surely they had heard or seen him. But Tappan perceived at a glance that he was the closer to the camp. Without another moment of hesitation, he plunged from his hiding place, down the weathered slope. His giant strides set the loose rocks sliding and rattling. The men saw him. The foremost yelled to the one behind him. Then they both broke into a run. Tappan reached the level of the bench, and saw he could beat either of them into the camp. Unless he were disabled! He felt the wind of a heavy bullet before he heard it strike the rocks beyond. Then followed the boom of a Colt. One of his enemies had halted to shoot. This spurred Tappan to tremendous exertion. He flew over the rough ground, scarcely hearing the rapid shots. He could no longer see the man who was firing. But the first one was in plain sight, running hard, not yet seeing he was out of the race.

When he became aware of that he halted, and dropping on one knee, leveled his gun at the running Tappan. The distance was scarcely sixty yards. His first shot did not allow for Tappan's speed. His second kicked up the gravel in Tappan's face. Then followed three more shots in rapid succession. The man divined that Tappan had a rifle in camp. Then he steadied himself, waiting for the moment when Tappan had to slow down and halt. As

Tappan reached his camp and dove for his rifle, the robber took time for his last aim, evidently hoping to get a stationary target. But Tappan did not get up from behind his camp duffel. It had been a habit of his to pile his boxes of supplies and roll of bedding together, and cover them with a canvas. He poked his rifle over the top of this and shot the robber.

Then, leaping up, he ran forward to get sight of the second one. This man began to run along the edge of the gully. Tappan fired rapidly at him. The third shot knocked the fellow down. But he got up, and yelling, as if for succor, he ran off. Tappan got another shot before he disappeared.

"Ahuh!" grunted Tappan, grimly. His keen gaze came back to survey the fallen robber, and then went out over the bench, across the wide mouth of the canyon. Tappan thought he had better utilize time to pack instead of pursuing the fleeing man.

Reloading the rifle, he hurried out to find Jenet. She was coming in to camp.

"Shore you're a treasure, old girl!" ejaculated Tappan.

Never in his life had he packed Jenet, or any other burro, so quickly. His last act was to drink all he could hold, fill his two canteens, and make Jenet drink. Then, rifle in hand, he drove the burro out of camp, round the corner of the red wall, to the wide gateway that opened down into Death Valley.

Tappan looked back more than he looked ahead. And he had traveled down a mile or more before he began to breathe more easily. He had escaped the claim jumpers. Even if they did show up in pursuit now, they could never catch him. Tappan believed he could travel faster and farther than any men of that ilk. But they did not appear. Perhaps the crippled one had not been able to reach his comrades in time. More likely, however, the gang had no taste for a chase in that torrid heat.

Tappan slowed his stride. He was almost as wet with

sweat as if he had fallen into the spring. The great beads
rolled down his face. And there seemed to be little
streams of fire trickling down his breast. But despite this,
and his labored panting for breath, not until he halted in
the shade of a rocky wall did he realize the heat.

It was terrific. Instantly then he knew he was safe
from pursuit. But he knew also that he faced a greater
peril than that of robbers. He could fight evil men, but
he could not fight this heat.

So he rested there, regaining his breath. Already thirst
was acute. Jenet stood near by, watching him. Tappan,
with his habit of humanizing the burro, imagined that
Jenet looked serious. A moment's thought was enough
for Tappan to appreciate the gravity of his situation. He
was about to go down into the upper end of Death Valley—a part of that country unfamiliar to him. He must
cross it, and also the Funeral Mountains, at a season
when a prospector who knew the trails and water holes
would have to be forced to undertake it. Tappan had no
choice.

His rifle was too hot to hold, so he stuck it in Jenet's
pack; and, burdened only by a canteen of water, he set
out, driving the burro ahead. Once he looked back up
the wide-mouthed canyon. It appeared to smoke with
red heat veils. The silence was oppressive.

Presently he turned the last corner that obstructed
sight of Death Valley. Tappan had never been appalled
by any aspect of the desert, but it was certain that here
he halted. Back in his mountain-walled camp the sun
had passed behind the high domes, but here it still held
most of the valley in its blazing grip. Death Valley
looked a ghastly, glaring level of white, over which a
strange dull leaden haze drooped like a blanket. Ghosts
of mountain peaks appeared to show dim and vague.
There was no movement of anything. No wind! The valley was dead. Desolation reigned supreme. Tappan could
not see far toward either end of the valley. A few miles
of white glare merged at last into leaden pall. A strong

odor, not unlike sulphur, seemed to add weight to the air.

Tappan strode on, mindful that Jenet had decided opinions of her own. She did not want to go straight ahead or to right or left, but back. That was the one direction impossible for Tappan. And he had to resort to a rare measure—that of beating her. But at last Jenet accepted the inevitable and headed down into the stark and naked plain. Soon Tappan reached the margin of the zone of shade cast by the mountain and was now exposed to the sun. The difference seemed tremendous. He had been hot, oppressed, weighted. It was now as if he was burned through his clothes, and walked on red-hot sands.

When Tappan ceased to sweat and his skin became dry, he drank half a canteen of water, and slowed his stride. Inured to desert hardship as he was, he could not long stand this. Jenet did not exhibit any lessening of vigor. In truth what she showed now was an increasing nervousness. It was almost as if she scented an enemy. Tappan never before had such faith in her. Jenet was equal to this task.

With that blazing sun on his back, Tappan felt he was being pursued by a furnace. He was compelled to drink the remaining half of his first canteen of water. Sunset would save him. Two more hours of such insupportable heat would lay him prostrate.

The ghastly glare of the valley took on a reddish tinge. The heat was blinding Tappan. The time came when he walked beside Jenet with a hand on her pack, for his eyes could no longer endure the furnace glare. Even with them closed he knew when the sun sank behind the Panamints. That fire no longer followed him. And the red left his eyelids.

With the sinking of the sun the world of Death Valley changed. It smoked with heat veils. But the intolerable constant burn was gone. The change was so immense that it seemed to have brought coolness.

In the twilight—strange, ghostly, somber, silent as death—Tappan followed Jenet off the sand, down upon

the silt and borax level, to the crusty salt. Before dark
Jenet halted at a sluggish belt of fluid—acid, it appeared
to Tappan. It was not deep. And the bottom felt stable.
But Jenet refused to cross. Tappan trusted her judgment
more than his own. Jenet headed to the left and followed
the course of the strange stream.

Night intervened. A night without stars or sky or
sound, hot, breathless, charged with some intangible current! Tappan dreaded the midnight furnace winds of
Death Valley. He had never encountered them. He had
heard prospectors say that any man caught in Death
Valley when these gales blew would never get out to tell
the tale. And Jenet seemed to have something on her
mind. She was no longer a leisurely, complacent burro.
Tappan imagined Jenet seemed stern. Most assuredly she
knew now which way she wanted to travel. It was not
easy for Tappan to keep up with her, and ten paces beyond him she was out of sight.

At last Jenet headed the acid wash, and turned across
the valley into a field of broken salt crust, like the rough-
ened ice of a river that had broken and jammed, then
frozen again. Impossible was it to make even a reasonable headway. It was a zone, however, that eventually
gave way to Jenet's instinct for direction. Tappan had
long ceased to try to keep his bearings. North, south,
east, and west were all the same to him. The night was a
blank—the darkness a wall—the silence a terrible menace flung at any leaving creature. Death Valley had endured them millions of years before living creatures had
existed. It was no place for a man.

Tappan was now three hundred and more feet below
sea level, in the aftermath of a day that had registered
one hundred and forty-five degrees of heat. He knew,
when he began to lose thought and balance—when only
the primitive instincts directed his bodily machine. And
he struggled with all his will power to keep hold of his
sense of sight and feeling. He hoped to cross the lower
level before the midnight gales began to blow.

Tappan's hope was vain. According to record, once in a long season of intense heat, there came a night when the furnace winds broke their schedule, and began early. The misfortune of Tappan was that he had struck this night.

Suddenly it seemed that the air, sodden with heat, began to move. It had weight. It moved soundlessly and ponderously. But it gathered momentum. Tappan realized what was happening. The blanket of heat generated by the day was yielding to outside pressure. Something had created a movement of the hotter air that must find its way upward, to give place for the cooler air that must find its way down.

Tappan heard the first, low, distant moan of wind and it struck terror to his heart. It did not have an earthly sound. Was that a knell for him? Nothing was surer than the fact that the desert must sooner or later claim him as a victim. Grim and strong, he rebelled against the conviction.

That moan was a forerunner of others, growing louder and longer until the weird sound became continuous. Then the movement of wind was accelerated and began to carry a fine dust. Dark as the night was, it did not hide the pale sheets of dust that moved along the level plain. Tappan's feet felt the slow rise in the floor of the valley. His nose recognized the zone of borax and alkali and niter and sulphur. He had reached the pit of the valley at the time of the furnace winds.

The moan augmented to a roar, coming like a mighty storm through a forest. It was hellish—like the woeful tide of Acheron. It enveloped Tappan. And the gale bore down in tremendous volume, like a furnace blast. Tappan seemed to feel his body penetrated by a million needles of fire. He seemed to dry up. The blackness of night had a spectral, whitish cast; the gloom was a whirling medium; the valley floor was lost in a sheeted, fiercely seeping stream of silt. Deadly fumes swept by, not lingering long enough to suffocate Tappan. He would gasp

and choke—then the poison gas was gone on the gale.
But hardest to endure was the heavy body of moving
heat. Tappan grew blind, so that he had to hold to Jenet,
and stumble along. Every gasping breath was a tortured
effort. He could not bear a scarf over his face. His lungs
heaved like great leather bellows. His heart pumped like
an engine short of fuel. This was the supreme test for his
never proven endurance. And he was all but vanquished.

Tappan's senses of sight and smell and hearing failed
him. There was left only the sense of touch—a feeling of
rope and burro and ground—and an awful insulating
pressure upon all his body. His feet marked a change
from salty plain to sandy ascent and then to rocky slope.
The pressure of wind gradually lessened: the difference
in air made life possible; the feeling of being dragged
endlessly by Jenet had ceased. Tappan went his limit
and fell into oblivion.

When he came to, he was suffering bodily tortures.
Sight was dim. But he saw walls of rocks, green growths
of mesquite, tamarack, and grass. Jenet was lying down,
with her pack flopped to one side. Tappan's dead ears recovered to a strange murmuring, babbling sound. Then he
realized his deliverance. Jenet had led him across Death
Valley, up into the mountain range, straight to a spring
of running water.

Tappan crawled to the edge of the water and drank
guardedly, a little at a time. He had to quell terrific
craving to drink his fill. Then he crawled to Jenet, and
loosening the ropes of her pack, freed her from its burden. Jenet got up, apparently none the worse for her or-
deal. She gazed mildly at Tappan, as if to say: "Well, I
got you out of that hole."

Tappan returned her gaze. Were they only man and
beast, alone in the desert? She seemed magnified to Tappan, no longer a plodding, stupid burro.

"Jenet, you—saved—my life," Tappan tried to enun-
ciate. "I'll never—forget."

Tappan was struck then to a realization of Jenet's

service. He was unutterably grateful. Yet the time came when he did forget.

II

TAPPAN had a weakness common to all prospectors: Any tale of a lost gold mine would excite his interest; and well-known legends of lost mines always obsessed him.

Peg-leg Smith's lost gold mine had lured Tappan to no less than half a dozen trips into the terrible shifting-sand country of southern California. There was no water near the region said to hide this mine of fabulous wealth. Many prospectors had left their bones to bleach white in the sun, finally to be buried by the ever blowing sands. Upon the occasion of Tappan's last escape from this desolate and forbidding desert, he had promised Jenet never to undertake it again. It seemed Tappan promised the faithful burro a good many things. It had been a habit.

When Tappan had a particularly hard experience or perilous adventure, he always took a dislike to the immediate country where it had befallen him. Jenet had dragged him across Death Valley, through incredible heat and the midnight furnace winds of that strange place; and he had promised her he would never forget how she had saved his life. Nor would he ever go back to Death Valley! He made his way over the Funeral Mountains, worked down through Nevada, and crossed the Rio Colorado above Needles, and entered Arizona. He traveled leisurely, but he kept going, and headed southeast toward Globe. There he cashed one of his six bags of gold, and indulged in the luxury of a complete new outfit. Even Jenet appreciated this fact, for the old outfit would scarcely hold together.

Tappan had the other five bags of gold in his pack; and after hours of hesitation he decided he would not cash them and entrust the money to a bank. He would take care of them. For him the value of this gold amounted to a small fortune. Many plans suggested themselves to Tappan. But in the end he grew weary of them. What did he want with a ranch, or cattle, or an outfitting store, or any of the businesses he now had the means to buy? Towns soon palled on Tappan. People did not long please him. Selfish interest and greed seemed paramount everywhere. Besides, if he acquired a place to take up his time, what would become of Jenet? That question decided him. He packed the burro and once more took to the trails.

A dim, lofty, purple range called alluringly to Tappan. The Superstition Mountains! Somewhere in that purple mass hid the famous treasure called the Lost Dutchman gold mine. Tappan had heard the story often. A Dutch prospector struck gold in the Superstitions. He kept the location secret. When he ran short of money, he would disappear for a few weeks, and then return with bags of gold. Wherever his strike, it assuredly was a rich one. No one ever could trail him or get a word out of him. Time passed. A few years made him old. During this time he conceived a liking for a young man, and eventually confided to him that some day he would tell him the secret of his gold mine. He had drawn a map of the landmarks adjacent to his mine. But he was careful not to put on paper directions how to get there. It chanced that he suddenly fell ill and saw his end was near. Then he summoned the young man who had been so fortunate as to win his regard. Now this individual was a ne'er-do-well, and upon this occasion he was half drunk. The dying Dutchman produced his map, and gave it with verbal directions to the young man. Then he died. When the recipient of this fortune recovered from the effects of liquor, he could not remember all the Dutchman had told him. He tortured himself to remember names and places. But the mine was up in the Superstition Mountains. He never remembered. He never found the lost mine, though he spent his life and died trying. Thus the story passed into the legend of the Lost Dutchman.

Tappan now had his try at finding it. But for him the

shifting sands of the southern California desert or even the barren and desolate Death Valley were preferable to this Superstition Range. It was a harder country than the Pinacate of Sonora. Tappan hated cactus, and the Superstitions were full of it. Everywhere stood up the huge *sahuaro*, the giant cacti of the Arizona plateaus, tall like branchless trees, fluted and columnar, beautiful and fascinating to gaze upon, but obnoxious to prospector and burro.

One day from a north slope Tappan saw afar a wonderful country of black timber, above which zigzagged for many miles a yellow, winding rampart of rock. This he took to be the rim of the Mogollon Mesa, one of Arizona's freaks of nature. Something called Tappan. He was forever victim to yearnings for the unattainable. He was tired of heat, glare, dust, bare rock, and thorny cactus. The Lost Dutchman gold mine was a myth. Besides, he did not need any more gold.

Next morning Tappan packed Jenet and worked down off the north slopes of the Superstition Range. That night about sunset he made camp on the bank of a clear brook, with grass and wood in abundance—such a camp site as a prospector dreamed of but seldom found.

Before dark Jenet's long ears told of the advent of strangers. A man and a woman rode down the trail into Tappan's camp. They had poor horses, and led a pack animal that appeared too old and weak to bear up under even the meager pack he carried.

"Howdy," said the man.

Tappan rose from his task to his lofty height and returned the greeting. The man was middle-aged, swarthy, and rugged, a mountaineer, with something about him that Tappan instinctively distrusted. The woman was under thirty, comely in a full-blown way, with rich brown skin and glossy dark hair. She had wide-open black eyes that bent a curious possession-taking gaze upon Tappan.

"Care if we camp with you?" she inquired, and she smiled.

That smile changed Tappan's habit and conviction of a lifetime.

"No indeed. Reckon I'd like a little company," he said.

Very probably Jenet did not understand Tappan's words, but she dropped one ear, and walked out of camp to the green bank.

"Thanks, stranger," replied the woman. "That grub shore smells good." She hesitated a moment, evidently waiting to catch her companion's eye, then she continued. "My name's Madge Beam. He's my brother Jake. . . . Who might you happen to be?"

"I'm Tappan, lone prospector, as you see," replied Tappan.

"Tappan! What's your front handle?" she queried, curiously.

"Fact is, I don't remember," replied Tappan, as he brushed a huge hand through his shaggy hair.

"Ahuh? Any name's good enough."

When she dismounted, Tappan saw that she had a tall, lithe figure, garbed in rider's overalls and boots. She unsaddled her horse with the dexterity of long practice. The saddlebags she carried over to the spot the man Jake had selected to throw the pack.

Tappan heard them talking in low tones. It struck him as strange that he did not have his usual reaction to an invasion of his privacy and solitude. Tappan had thrilled under those black eyes. And now a queer sensation of the unusual rose in him. Bending over his camp-fire tasks he pondered this and that, but mostly the sense of the nearness of a woman. Like most desert men, Tappan knew little of the other sex. A few that he might have been drawn to went out of his wandering life as quickly as they had entered it. This Madge Beam took possession of his thoughts. An evidence of Tappan's preoccupation was the fact that he burned his first batch of biscuits. And Tappan felt proud of his culinary ability. He was on his knees, mixing more flour and water, when the woman spoke from right behind him.

"Tough luck you burned the first pan," she said. "But it's a good turn for your burro. That shore is a burro. Biggest I ever saw."

She picked up the burned biscuits and tossed them over to Jenet. Then she came back to Tappan's side, rather embarrassingly close.

"Tappan, I know how I'll eat, so I ought to ask you to let me help," she said, with a laugh.

"No, I don't need any," replied Tappan. "You sit down on my roll of beddin' there. Must be tired, aren't you?"

"Not so very," she returned. "That is, I'm not tired of ridin'." She spoke the second part of this reply in lower tone.

Tappan looked up from his task. The woman had washed her face, brushed her hair, and had put on a skirt —a singularly attractive change. Tappan thought her younger. She was the handsomest woman he had ever seen. The look of her made him clumsy. What eyes she had! They looked through him. Tappan returned to his task, wondering if he was right in his surmise that she wanted to be friendly.

"Jake an' I drove a bunch of cattle to Maricopa," she volunteered. "We sold 'em, an' Jake gambled away most of the money. I couldn't get what I wanted."

"Too bad! So you're ranchers. Once thought I'd like that. Fact is, down here at Globe a few weeks ago I came near buyin' some rancher out an' tryin' the game."

"You did?" Her query had a low, quick eagerness that somehow thrilled Tappan. But he did not look up.

"I'm a wanderer. I'd never do on a ranch."

"But if you had a woman?" Her laugh was subtle and gay.

"A woman! For me? Oh, Lord, no!" ejaculated Tappan, in confusion.

"Why not? Are you a woman-hater?"

"I can't say that," replied Tappan, soberly. "It's jusr —I guess—no woman would have me."

"Faint heart never won fair lady."

Tappan had no reply for that. He surely was making a mess of the second pan of biscuit dough. Manifestly the woman saw this, for with a laugh she plumped down on her knees in front of Tappan, and rolled her sleeves up over shapely brown arms.

"Poor man! Shore you need a woman. Let me show you," she said, and put her hands right down upon Tappan's. The touch gave him a strange thrill. He had to pull his hands away, and as he wiped them with his scarf he looked at her. He seemed compelled to look. She was close to him now, smiling in good nature, a little scornful of man's encroachment upon the housewifely duties of a woman. A subtle something emanated from her—a more than kindness or gayety. Tappan grasped that it was just the woman of her. And it was going to his head.

"Very well, let's see you show me," he replied, as he rose to his feet.

Just then the brother Jake strolled over, and he had a rather amused and derisive eye for his sister.

"Wal, Tappan, she's not overfond of work, but I reckon she can cook," he said.

Tappan felt greatly relieved at the approach of this brother. And he fell into conversation with him, telling something of his prospecting since leaving Globe, and listening to the man's cattle talk. By and by the woman called, "Come an' get it!" Then they sat down to eat, and, as usual with hungry wayfarers, they did not talk much until appetite was satisfied. Afterward, before the camp fire, they began to talk again, Jake being the most discursive. Tappan conceived the idea that the rancher was rather curious about him, and perhaps wanted to sell his ranch. The woman seemed more thoughtful, with her wide black eyes on the fire.

"Tappan, what way you travelin'?" finally inquired Beam.

"Can't say. I just worked down out of the Superstitions. Haven't any place in mind. Where does this road go?"

"To the Tonto Basin. Ever heard of it?"

"Yes, the name isn't new. What's in this Basin?"

The man grunted. "Tonto once was home for the Apache. It's now got a few sheep an' cattlemen, lots of rustlers. An' say, if you like to hunt bear an' deer, come along with us."

"Thanks. I don't know as I can," returned Tappan, irresolutely. He was not used to such possibilities as this suggested.

Then the woman spoke up. "It's a pretty country. Wild an' different. We live up under the rim rock. There's mineral in the canyons."

Was it that about mineral which decided Tappan or the look in her eyes?

Tappan's world of thought and feeling underwent as great a change as this Tonto Basin differed from the stark desert so long his home. The trail to the log cabin of the Beams climbed many a ridge and slope and foothill, all covered with manzanita, mescal, cedar, and juniper, at last to reach the canyons of the Rim, where lofty pines and spruces lorded it over the under forest of maples and oaks. Though the yellow Rim towered high over the site of the cabin, the altitude was still great, close to seven thousand feet above sea level.

Tappan had fallen in love with this wild wooded and canyoned country. So had Jenet. It was rather funny the way she hung around Tappan, mornings and evenings. She ate luxuriant grass and oak leaves until her sides bulged.

There did not appear to be any flat places in this landscape. Every bench was either up hill or down hill. The Beams had no garden or farm or ranch that Tappan could discover. They raised a few acres of sorghum and corn. Their log cabin was of the most primitive kind, and outfitted poorly. Madge Beam explained that this cabin was their winter abode, and that up on the Rim they had a good house and ranch. Tappan did not inquire closely into anything. If he had interrogated himself, he would have found out that the reason he did not inquire was because he feared something might remove him from the vicinity of Madge Beam. He had thought it strange the Beams avoided wayfarers they had met on the trail, and had gone round a little hamlet Tappan had espied from a hill. Madge Beam, with woman's intuition, had read his mind, and had said: "Jake doesn't get along so well with some of the villagers. An' I've no hankerin' for gun play." That explanation was sufficient for Tappan. He had lived long enough in his wandering years to appreciate that people could have reasons for being solitary.

This trip up into the Rim Rock country bade fair to become Tappan's one and only adventure of the heart. It was not alone the murmuring, clear brook of cold mountain water that enchanted him, nor the stately pines, nor the beautiful silver spruces, nor the wonder of the deep, yellow-walled canyons, so choked with verdure, and haunted by wild creatures. He dared not face his soul, and ask why this dark-eyed woman sought him more and more. Tappan lived in the moment.

He was aware that the few mountaineer neighbors who rode that way rather avoided contact with him. Tappan was not so dense that he did not perceive that the Beams preferred to keep him from outsiders. This perhaps was owing to their desire to sell Tappan the ranch and cattle. Jake offered to let it go at what he called a low figure. Tappan thought it just as well to go out into the forest and hide his bags of gold. He did not trust Jake Beam, and liked less the looks of the men who visited this wilderness ranch. Madge Beam might be related to a rustler, and the associate of rustlers, but that did not necessarily make her a bad woman. Tappan sensed that her attitude was changing, and she seemed to require his respect. At first, all she wanted was his admiration. Tappan's long unused deference for women returned to him, and when he saw that it was having some strange softening effect upon Madge Beam, he redoubled his attentions. They rode and climbed and hunted together. Tappan had pitched his camp not far from the cabin, on a shaded bank of the singing brook. Madge did not leave him much to himself. She was always coming up to his camp, on one pretext or another. Often she would bring two horses, and make Tappan ride with her. Some of these occasions, Tappan saw, occurred while visitors came to the cabin. In three weeks Madge Beam changed from the bold and careless woman who had ridden down into his camp that sunset, to a serious and appealing woman, growing more careful of her person and adornment, and manifestly bearing a burden on her mind.

October came. In the morning white frost glistened on the split-wood shingles of the cabin. The sun soon melted it, and grew warm. The afternoons were still and smoky, melancholy with the enchantment of Indian summer. Tappan hunted wild turkey and deer with Madge, and revived his boyish love of such pursuits. Madge appeared to be a woman of the woods, and had no mean skill with the rifle.

One day they were high on the Rim, with the great timbered basin at their feet. They had come up to hunt deer, but got no farther than the wonderful promontory where before they had lingered.

"Somethin' will happen to me to-day," Madge Beam said, enigmatically.

Tappan never had been much of a talker. But he could listen. The woman unburdened herself this day. She wanted freedom, happiness, a home away from this lonely country, and all the heritage of woman. She confessed it broodingly, passionately. And Tappan recognized truth when he heard it. He was ready to do all in his power for this woman and believed she knew it. But words and acts of sentiment came hard to him.

"Are you goin' to buy Jake's ranch?" she asked.

"I don't know. Is there any hurry?" returned Tappan

"I reckon not. But I think I'll settle that," she said, decisively.

"How so?"

"Well, Jake hasn't got any ranch," she answered. And added hastily, "No clear title, I mean. He's only home-steaded one hundred an' sixty acres, an' hasn't proved up on it yet. But don't you say I told you."

"Was Jake aimin' to be crooked?"

"I reckon. . . . An' I was willin' at first. But not now."

Tappan did not speak at once. He saw the woman was in one of her brooding moods. Besides, he wanted to weigh her words. How significant they were! To-day more than ever she had let down. Humility and simplicity seemed to abide with her. And her brooding boded a storm. Tappan's heart swelled in his broad breast. Was life going to dawn rosy and bright for the lonely prospector? He had money to make a home for this woman. What lay in the balance of the hour? Tappan waited, slowly realizing the charged atmosphere.

Madge's somber eyes gazed out over the great void. But, full of thought and passion as they were, they did not see the beauty of that scene. But Tappan saw it. And in some strange sense the color and wildness and sublimity seemed the expression of a new state of his heart. Under him sheered down the ragged and cracked cliffs of the Rim, yellow and gold and gray, full of caves and crevices, ledges for eagles and niches for lions, a thousand feet down to the upward edge of the long green slopes and canyons, and so on down and down into the abyss of forested ravine and ridge, rolling league on league away to the encompassing barrier of purple mountain ranges.

The thickets in the canyons called Tappan's eye back to linger there. How different from the scenes that used to be perpetually in his sight! What riot of color! The tips of the green pines, the crests of the silver spruces, waved about masses of vivid gold of aspen trees, and won-derful cerise and flaming red of maples, and crags of yel-low rock, covered with the bronze of frostbitten sumach. Here was autumn and with it the colors of Tappan's favorite season. From below breathed up the low roar of plunging brook; an eagle screeched his wild call; an elk bugled his piercing blast. From the Rim wisps of pine needles blew away on the breeze and fell into the void. A wild country, colorful, beautiful, bountiful. Tappan imagined he could quell his wandering spirit here, with this dark-eyed woman by his side. Never before had Nature so called him. Here was not the cruelty or flinty hardness of the desert. The air was keen and sweet, cold in the shade, warm in the sun. A fragrance of balsam and spruce, spiced with pine, made his breathing a thing of difficulty and delight. How for so many years had he endured vast open spaces without such eye-soothing trees as these? Tappan's back rested against a huge pine that tipped the Rim, and had stood there, stronger than the storms, for many a hundred years. The rock of the promontory was covered with soft brown mats of pine needles. A juniper tree, with its bright green foliage and lilac-colored berries, grew near the pine, and helped to form a secluded little nook, fragrant and somehow haunting. The woman's dark head was close to Tappan, as she sat with her elbows on her knees, gazing down into the basin. Tappan saw the strained tensity of her posture, the heaving of her full bosom. He wondered, while his own emotions, so long darkened, roused to the suspense of that hour.

Suddenly she flung herself into Tappan's arms. The act amazed him. It seemed to have both the passion of a woman and the shame of a girl. Before she hid her face on Tappan's breast he saw how the rich brown had paled, and then flamed.

"Tappan! . . . Take me away. . . . Take me away from here—from that life down there," she cried, in smothered voice.

"Madge, you mean take you away—and marry you?" he replied.

"Oh, yes—yes—marry me, if you love me. . . . I don't

see how you can—but you do, don't you?— Say you do."

"I reckon that's what ails me, Madge," he replied, simply.

"*Say* so, then," she burst out.

"All right, I do," said Tappan, with heavy breath. "Madge, words don't come easy for me. . . . But I think you're wonderful, an' I want you. I haven't dared hope for that, till now. I'm only a wanderer. But it'd be heaven to have you—my wife—an' make a home for you."

"Oh—Oh!" she returned, wildly, and lifted herself to cling round his neck, and to kiss him. "You give me joy. . . . Oh, Tappan, I love you. I never loved any man before. I know now. . . . An' I'm not wonderful—or good. But I love you."

The fire of her lips and the clasp of her arms worked havoc in Tappan. No woman had ever loved him, let alone embraced him. To awake suddenly to such rapture as this made him strong and rough in his response. Then all at once she seemed to collapse in his arms and to begin to weep. He feared he had offended or hurt her, and was clumsy in his contrition. Presently she replied:

"Pretty soon—I'll make you—beat me. It's your love —your honesty—that's shamed me. . . . Tappan, I was party to a trick to—sell you a worthless ranch. . . . I agreed to—try to make you love me—to fool you—cheat you. . . . But I've fallen in love with you.—An' my God, I care more for your love—your respect—than for my life. I can't go on with it. I've double-crossed Jake, an' all of them. . . . Now, am I worth lovin'? Am I worth havin'?"

"More than ever, dear," he said.

"You will take me away?"

"Anywhere—any time, the sooner the better."

She kissed him passionately, and then, disengaging herself from his arms, she knelt and gazed earnestly at him. "I've not told all. I will some day. But I swear now on my soul—I'll be what you think me."

"Madge, you needn't say all that. If you love me—it's enough. More than I ever dreamed of."

"You're a man. Oh, why didn't I meet you when I was eighteen instead of now—twenty-eight, an' all that between. . . . But enough. A new life begins here for me. We must plan."

"You make the plans an' I'll act on them."

For a moment she was tense and silent, head bowed, hands shut tight. Then she spoke:

"To-night we'll slip away. You make a light pack, that'll go on your saddle. I'll do the same. We'll hide the horses out near where the trail crosses the brook. An' we'll run off—ride out of the country."

Tappan in turn tried to think, but the whirl of his mind made any reason difficult. This dark-eyed, full-bosomed woman loved him, had surrendered herself, asked only his protection. The thing seemed marvelous. Yet she knelt there, those dark eyes on him, infinitely more appealing than ever, haunting with some mystery of sadness and fear he could not divine.

Suddenly Tappan remembered Jenet.

"I must take Jenet," he said.

That startled her. "Jenet— Who's she?"

"My burro."

"Your burro. You can't travel fast with that pack beast. We'll be trailed, an' we'll have to go fast. . . . You can't take the burro."

Then Tappan was startled. "What! Can't take Jenet?— Why, I—I couldn't get along without her."

"Nonsense. What's a burro? We must ride fast—do you hear?"

"Madge, I'm afraid I—I must take Jenet with me," he said, soberly.

"It's impossible. I can't go if you take her. I tell you I've got to get away. If you want *me* you'll have to leave your precious Jenet behind."

Tappan bowed his head to the inevitable. After all, Jenet was only a beast of burden. She would run wild on

the ridges and soon forget him and have no need of him.
Something strained in Tappan's breast. He did not see
clearly here. This woman was worth more than all else to
him.

"I'm stupid, dear," he said. "You see I never before ran
off with a beautiful woman. . . . Of course my burro
must be left behind."

Elopement, if such it could be called, was easy for them.
Tappan did not understand why Madge wanted to be so
secret about it. Was she not free? But then, he reflected,
he did not know the circumstances she feared. Besides,
he did not care. Possession of the woman was enough.

Tappan made his small pack, the weight of which was
considerable owing to his bags of gold. This he tied on his
saddle. It bothered him to leave most of his new outfit
scattered around his camp. What would Jenet think of
that? He looked for her, but for once she did not come in
at meal time. Tappan thought this was singular. He could
not remember when Jenet had been far from his camp at
sunset. Somehow Tappan was glad.

After he had his supper, he left his utensils and supplies
as they happened to be, and strode away under the trees
to the trysting-place where he was to meet Madge. To his
surprise she came before dark, and, unused as he was to
the complexity and emotional nature of a woman, he saw
that she was strangely agitated. Her face was pale. Almost
a fury burned in her black eyes. When she came up to
Tappan, and embraced him, almost fiercely, he felt that
he was about to learn more of the nature of womankind.
She thrilled him to his depths.

"Lead out the horses an' don't make any noise," she
whispered.

Tappan complied, and soon he was mounted, riding behind her on the trail. It surprised him that she headed
down country, and traveled fast. Moreover, she kept to a
trail that continually grew rougher. They came to a road,
which she crossed, and kept on through darkness and

brush so thick that Tappan could not see the least sign of
a trail. And at length anyone could have seen that Madge
had lost her bearings. She appeared to know the direction
she wanted, but traveling upon it was impossible, owing
to the increasingly cut-up and brushy ground. They had
to turn back, and seemed to be hours finding the road.
Once Tappan fancied he heard the thud of hoofs other
than those made by their own horses. Here Madge acted
strangely, and where she had been obsessed by desire to
hurry she now seemed to have grown weary. She turned
her horse south on the road. Tappan was thus enabled to
ride beside her. But they talked very little. He was satisfied with the fact of being with her on the way out of the
country. Some time in the night they reached an old log
shack by the roadside. Here Tappan suggested they halt,
and get some sleep before dawn. The morrow would
mean a long hard day.

"Yes, to-morrow will be hard," replied Madge, as she
faced Tappan in the gloom. He could see her big dark
eyes on him. Her tone was not one of a hopeful woman.
Tappan pondered over this. But he could not understand,
because he had no idea how a woman ought to act under
such circumstances. Madge Beam was a creature of moods.
Only the day before, on the ride down from the Rim, she
had told him with a laugh that she was likely to love him
madly one moment and scratch his eyes out the next. How
could he know what to make of her? Still, an uneasy feeling began to stir in Tappan.

They dismounted, and unsaddled the horses. Tappan
took his pack and put it aside. Something frightened the
horses. They bolted down the road.

"Head them off," cried the woman, hoarsely.

Even on the instant her voice sounded strained to Tappan, as if she were choked. But, realizing the absolute
necessity of catching the horses, he set off down the road
on a run. And he soon succeeded in heading off the animal
he had ridden. The other one, however, was contrary and
cunning. When Tappan would endeavor to get ahead, it

would trot briskly on. Yet it did not go so fast but what Tappan felt sure he would soon catch it. Thus walking and running, he put some distance between him and the cabin before he realized that he could not head off the wary beast. Much perturbed in mind, Tappan hurried back.

Upon reaching the cabin Tappan called to Madge. No answer! He could not see her in the gloom nor the horse he had driven back. Only silence brooded there. Tappan called again. Still no answer! Perhaps Madge had succumbed to weariness and was asleep. A search of the cabin and vicinity failed to yield any sign of her. But it disclosed the fact that Tappan's pack was gone.

Suddenly he sat down, quite overcome. He had been duped. What a fierce pang tore his heart! But it was for loss of the woman—not the gold. He was stunned, and then sick with bitter misery. Only then did Tappan realize the meaning of love and what it had done to him. The night wore on, and he sat there in the dark and cold and stillness until the gray dawn told him of the coming of day.

The light showed his saddle where he had left it. Near by lay one of Madge's gloves. Tappan's keen eye sighted a bit of paper sticking out of the glove. He picked it up. It was a leaf out of a little book he had seen her carry, and upon it was written in lead pencil:

"I am Jake's wife, not his sister. I double-crossed him an' ran off with you an' would have gone to hell for you. But Jake an' his gang suspected me. They were close on our trail. I couldn't shake them. So here I chased off the horses an' sent you after them. It was the only way I could save your life."

Tappan tracked the thieves to Globe. There he learned they had gone to Phoenix—three men and one woman. Tappan had money on his person. He bought horse and saddle, and, setting out for Phoenix, he let his passion to kill grow with the miles and hours. At Phoenix he learned

Beam had cashed the gold—twelve thousand dollars. So much of a fortune! Tappan's fury grew. The gang separated here. Beam and his wife took stage for Tucson. Tappan had no trouble in trailing their movements.

Gambling dives and inns and freighting posts and stage drivers told the story of the Beams and their ill-gotten gold. They went on to California, down into Tappan's country, to Yuma, and El Cajon, and San Diego. Here Tappan lost track of the woman. He could not find that she had left San Diego, nor any trace of her there. But Jake Beam had killed a Mexican in a brawl and had fled across the line.

Tappan gave up for the time being the chase of Beam, and bent his efforts to find the woman. He had no resentment toward Madge. He only loved her. All that winter he searched San Diego. He made of himself a peddler as a ruse to visit houses. But he never found a trace of her. In the spring he wandered back to Yuma, raking over the old clues, and so on back to Tucson and Phoenix.

This year of dream and love and passion and despair and hate made Tappan old. His great strength and endurance were not yet impaired, but something of his spirit had died out of him.

One day he remembered Jenet. "My burro!" he soliloquized. "I had forgotten her. . . . Jenet!"

Then it seemed a thousand impulses merged in one drove him to face the long road toward the Rim Rock country. To remember Jenet was to grow doubtful. Of course she would be gone. Stolen or dead or wandered off! But then who could tell what Jenet might do? Tappan was both called and driven. He was a poor wanderer again. His outfit was a pack he carried on his shoulder. But while he could walk he would keep on until he found that last camp where he had deserted Jenet.

October was coloring the canyon slopes when he reached the shadow of the great wall of yellow rock. The cabin where the Beams had lived—or had claimed they lived—was a fallen ruin, crushed by snow. Tappan saw other signs of a severe winter and heavy snowfall. No horse or cattle tracks showed in the trails.

To his amaze his camp was much as he had left it. The stone fireplace, the iron pots, appeared to be in the same places. The boxes that had held his supplies were lying here and there. And his canvas tarpaulin, little the worse for wear of the elements, lay on the ground under the pine where he had slept. If any man had visited this camp in a year he had left no sign of it.

Suddenly Tappan espied a hoof track in the dust. A small track—almost oval in shape—fresh! Tappan thrilled through all his being.

"Jenet's track, so help me God!" he murmured.

He found more of them, made that morning. And, keen now as never before on her trail, he set out to find her. The tracks led up the canyon. Tappan came out into a little grassy clearing, and there stood Jenet, as he had seen her thousands of times. She had both long ears up high. She seemed to stare out of that meek, gray face. And then one of the long ears flopped over and drooped. Such perhaps was the expression of her recognition.

Tappan strode up to her.

"Jenet—old girl—you hung round camp—waitin' for me, didn't you?" he said, huskily, and his big hands fondled her long ears.

Yes, she had waited. She, too, had grown old. She was gray. The winter of that year had been hard. What had she lived on when the snow lay so deep? There were lion scratches on her back, and scars on her legs. She had fought for her life.

"Jenet, a man can never always tell about a burro," said Tappan. "I trained you to hang round camp an' wait till I came back. . . . 'Tappan's burro,' the desert rats used to say! An' they'd laugh when I bragged how you'd stick to me where most men would quit. But brag as I did, I never knew you, Jenet. An' I left you—an' forgot. Jenet, it takes a human bein'—a man—a woman—to be faithless. An' it takes a dog or a horse or a burro to be great. . . . Beasts? I wonder now. . . . Well, old pard, we're goin' down the trail together, an' from this day on Tappan begins to pay his debt."

III

Tappan never again had the old *wanderlust* for the stark and naked desert. Something had transformed him. The green and fragrant forests, and brown-aisled, pine-matted woodlands, the craggy promontories and the great colored canyons, the cold granite water springs of the Tonto seemed vastly preferable to the heat and dust and glare and the emptiness of the waste lands. But there was more. The ghost of his strange and only love kept pace with his wandering steps, a spirit that hovered with him as his shadow. Madge Beam, whatever she had been, had showed to him the power of love to refine and ennoble. Somehow he felt closer to her here in the cliff country where his passion had been born. Somehow she seemed nearer to him here than in all those places he had tracked her.

So from a prospector searching for gold Tappan became a hunter, seeking only the means to keep soul and body together. And all he cared for was his faithful burro Jenet, and the loneliness and silence of the forest land.

He was to learn that the Tonto was a hard country in many ways, and bitterly so in winter. Down in the brakes of the basin it was mild in winter, the snow did not lie long, and ice seldom formed. But up on the Rim, where Tappan always lingered as long as possible, the storm king of the north held full sway. Fifteen feet of snow and zero weather were the rule in dead of winter.

An old native once warned Tappan: "See hyar, friend, I reckon you'd better not get caught up in the Rim Rock country in one of our big storms. Fer if you do you'll never get out."

It was a way of Tappan's to follow his inclinations, regardless of advice. He had weathered the terrible midnight storm of hot wind in Death Valley. What were snow and cold to him? Late autumn on the Rim was the most perfect and beautiful of seasons. He had seen the forest land brown and darkly green one day, and the next burdened with white snow. What a transfiguration! Then when the sun loosened the white mantling on the pines, and they had shed their burdens in drifting dust of white, and rainbowed mists of melting snow, and avalanches sliding off the branches, there would be left only the wonderful white floor of the woodland. The great rugged brown tree trunks appeared mightier and statelier in the contrast; and the green of foliage, the russet of oak leaves, the gold of the aspens, turned the forest into a world enchanting to the desert-seared eyes of this wanderer.

With Tappan the years sped by. His mind grew old faster than his body. Every season saw him lonelier. He had a feeling, a vague illusive foreshadowing that his bones, instead of bleaching on the desert sands, would mingle with the pine mats and the soft fragrant moss of the forest. The idea was pleasant to Tappan.

One afternoon he was camped in Pine Canyon, a timber-sloped gorge far back from the Rim. November was well on. The fall had been singularly open and fair, with not a single storm. A few natives happening across Tappan had remarked casually that such autumns sometimes were not to be trusted.

This late afternoon was one of Indian summer beauty and warmth. The blue haze in the canyon was not all the blue smoke from Tappan's camp fire. In a narrow park of grass not far from camp Jenet grazed peacefully with elk and deer. Wild turkeys lingered there, loath to seek their winter quarters down in the basin. Gray squirrels and red squirrels barked and frisked, and dropped the pine and spruce cones, with thud and thump, on all the slopes.

Before dark a stranger strode into Tappan's camp, a big man of middle age, whose magnificent physique impressed even Tappan. He was a rugged, bearded giant, wide-eyed and of pleasant face. He had no outfit, no horse, not even a gun.

"Lucky for me I smelled your smoke," he said. "Two days for me without grub."

"Howdy, stranger," was Tappan's greeting. "Are you lost?"

"Yes an' no. I could find my way out down over the Rim, but it's not healthy down there for me. So I'm hittin' north."

"Where's your horse an' pack?"

"I reckon they're with the gang thet took more of a fancy to them than me."

"Ahuh! You're welcome here, stranger," replied Tappan. "I'm Tappan."

"Ha! Heard of you. I'm Jess Blade, of anywhere. An' I'll say, Tappan, I was an honest man till I hit the Tonto."

His laugh was frank, for all its note of grimness. Tappan liked the man, and sensed one who would be a good friend and bad foe.

"Come an' eat. My supplies are peterin' out, but there's plenty of meat."

Blade ate, indeed, as a man starved, and did not seem to care if Tappan's supplies were low. He did not talk. After the meal he craved a pipe and tobacco. Then he smoked in silence, in a slow realizing content. The morrow had no fears for him. The flickering ruddy light from the camp fire shone on his strong face. Tappan saw in him the drifter, the drinker, the brawler, a man with good in him, but over whom evil passion or temper dominated. Presently he smoked the pipe out, and with reluctant hand knocked out the ashes and returned it to Tappan.

"I reckon I've some news thet'd interest you," he said.

"You have?" queried Tappan.

"Yes, if you're the Tappan who tried to run off with Jake Beam's wife."

"Well, I'm that Tappan. But I'd like to say I didn't know she was married."

"Shore, I know thet. So does everybody in the Tonto. You were just meat for the Beam gang. They had played the trick before. But accordin' to what I hear thet trick was the last fer Madge Beam. She never came back to this country. An' Jake Beam, when he was drunk, owned up thet she'd left him in California. Some hint at worse. Fer Jake Beam came back a harder man. Even his gang said thet."

"Is he in the Tonto now?" queried Tappan, with a thrill of fire along his veins.

"Yep, thar fer keeps," replied Blade, grimly. "Somebody shot him."

"Ahuh!" exclaimed Tappan with a deep breath of relief. There came a sudden cooling of the heat of his blood.

After that there was a long silence. Tappan dreamed of the woman who had loved him. Blade brooded over the camp fire. The wind moaned ntfully in the lofty pines on the slope. A wolf mourned as if in hunger. The stars appeared to obscure their radiance in haze.

"Reckon thet wind sounds like storm," observed Blade, presently.

"I've heard it for weeks now," replied Tappan.

"Are you a woodsman?"

"No, I'm a desert man."

"Wal, you take my hunch an' hit the trail fer low country."

This was well meant, and probably sound advice, but it alienated Tappan. He had really liked this hearty-voiced stranger. Tappan thought moodily of his slowly ingrowing mind, of the narrowness of his soul. He was past interest in his fellow men. He lived with a dream. The only living creature he loved was a lop-eared, lazy burro, growing old in contentment. Nevertheless that night Tappan shared one of his two blankets.

In the morning the gray dawn broke, and the sun rose

without its brightness of gold. There was a haze over the blue sky. Thin, swift-moving clouds scudded up out of the southwest. The wind was chill, the forest shaggy and dark, the birds and squirrels were silent.

"Wal, you'll break camp to-day," asserted Blade.

"Nope. I'll stick it out yet a while," returned Tappan.

"But, man, you might get snowed in, an' up hyar thet's serious."

"Ahuh! Well, it won't bother me. An' there's nothin' holdin' you."

"Tappan, it's four days' walk down out of this woods. If a big snow set in, how'd I make it?"

"Then you'd better go out over the Rim," suggested Tappan.

"No. I'll take my chance the other way. But are you meanin' you'd rather not have me with you? Fer you can't stay hyar."

Tappan was in a quandary.

Some instinct bade him tell the man to go. Not empty-handed, but to go. But this was selfish, and entirely unlike Tappan as he remembered himself of old. Finally he spoke:

"You re welcome to half my outfit—go or stay."

"Thet's mighty square of you, Tappan," responded the other, feelingly. "Have you a burro you'll give me?"

"No, I've only one."

"Ha! Then I'll have to stick with you till you leave."

No more was said. They had breakfast in a strange silence. The wind brooded its secret in the tree tops. Tappan's burro strolled into camp, and caught the stranger's eye.

"Wal, thet's shore a fine burro," he observed. "Never saw the like."

Tappan performed his camp tasks. And then there was nothing to do but sit around the fire. Blade evidently waited for the increasing menace of storm to rouse Tappan to decision. But the graying over of sky and the increase of wind did not affect Tappan. What did he wait for? The truth of his thoughts was that he did not like the way Jenet remained in camp. She was waiting to be packed. She knew they ought to go. Tappan yielded to a perverse devil of stubbornness. The wind brought a cold mist, then a flurry of wet snow. Tappan gathered fire-wood, a large quantity. Blade saw this and gave voice to earnest fears. But Tappan paid no heed. By nightfall sleet and snow began to fall steadily. The men fashioned a rude shack of spruce boughs, ate their supper, and went to bed early.

It worried Tappan that Jenet stayed right in camp. He lay awake a long time. The wind rose, and moaned through the forest. The sleet failed, and a soft, steady downfall of snow gradually set in. Tappan fell asleep. When he awoke it was to see a forest of white. The trees were mantled with blankets of wet snow, the ground covered two feet on a level. But the clouds appeared to be gone, the sky was blue, the storm over. The sun came up warm and bright.

"It'll all go in a day," said Tappan.

"If this was early October I'd agree with you," replied Blade. "But it's only makin' fer another storm. Can't you hear thet wind?"

Tappan only heard the whispers of his dreams. By now the snow was melting off the pines, and rainbows shone everywhere. Little patches of snow began to drop off the south branches of the pines and spruces, and then larger patches, until by mid-afternoon white streams and avalanches were falling everywhere. All of the snow, except in shaded places on the north sides of trees, went that day, and half of that on the ground. Next day it thinned out more, until Jenet was finding the grass and moss again. That afternoon the telltale thin clouds raced up out of the southwest and the wind moaned its menace.

"Tappan, let's pack an' hit it out of hyar," appealed Blade, anxiously. "I know this country. Mebbe I'm wrong, of course, but it feels like storm. Winter's comin' shore."

"Let her come," replied Tappan imperturbably.

"Say, do you want to get snowed in?" demanded Blade, out of patience.

"I might like a little spell of it, seein' it'd be new to me," replied Tappan.

"But man, if you ever get snowed in hyar you can't get out."

"That burro of mine could get me out."

"You're crazy. Thet burro couldn't go a hundred feet. What's more, you'd have to kill her an' eat her."

Tappan bent a strange gaze upon his companion, but made no reply. Blade began to pace up and down the small bare patch of ground before the camp fire. Manifestly, he was in a serious predicament. That day he seemed subtly to change, as did Tappan. Both answered to their peculiar instincts, Blade to that of self-preservation, and Tappan, to something like indifference. Tappan held fate in defiance. What more could happen to him?

Blade broke out again, in eloquent persuasion, giving proof of their peril, and from that he passed to amaze and then to strident anger. He cursed Tappan for a nature-loving idiot.

"An' I'll tell you what," he ended. "When mornin' comes I'll take some of your grub an' hit it out of hyar, storm or no storm."

But long before dawn broke that resolution of Blade's had become impracticable. Both men were awakened by a roar of storm through the forest, no longer a moan, but a marching roar, with now a crash and then a shriek of gale! By the light of the smoldering camp fire Tappan saw a whirling pall of snow, great flakes as large as feathers. Morning disclosed the setting in of a fierce mountain storm, with two feet of snow already on the ground, and the forest lost in a blur of white.

"I was wrong," called Tappan to his companion. "What's best to do now?"

"You damned fool!" yelled Blade. "We've got to keep from freezin' an' starvin' till the storm ends an' a crust comes on the snow."

For three days and three nights the blizzard continued, unabated in its fury. It took the men hours to keep a space cleared for their camp site, which Jenet shared with them. On the fourth day the storm ceased, the clouds broke away, the sun came out. And the temperature dropped to zero. Snow on the level just topped Tappan's lofty stature, and in drifts it was ten and fifteen feet deep. Winter had set in without compromise. The forest became a solemn, still, white world. But now Tappan had no time to dream. Dry firewood was hard to find under the snow. It was possible to cut down one of the dead trees on the slope, but impossible to pack sufficient wood to the camp. They had to burn green wood. Then the fashioning of snowshoes took much time. Tappan had no knowledge of such footgear. He could only help Blade. The men were encouraged by the piercing cold forming a crust on the snow. But just as they were about to pack and venture forth, the weather moderated, the crust refused to hold their weight, and another foot of snow fell.

"Why in hell didn't you kill an elk?" demanded Blade, sullenly. He had become darkly sinister. He knew the peril and he loved life. "Now we'll have to kill an' eat your precious Jenet. An' mebbe she won't furnish meat enough to last till this snow weather stops an' a good freeze'll make travelin' possible."

"Blade, you shut up about killin' an' eatin' my burro Jenet," returned Tappan, in a voice that silenced the other.

Thus instinctively these men became enemies. Blade thought only of himself. Tappan had forced upon him a menace to the life of his burro. For himself Tappan had not one thought.

Tappan's supplies ran low. All the bacon and coffee were gone. There was only a small haunch of venison, a bag of beans, a sack of flour, and a small quantity of salt left.

"If a crust freezes on the snow an' we can pack that flour, we'll get out alive," said Blade. "But we can't take the burro."

Another day of bright sunshine softened the snow on the southern exposures, and a night of piercing cold froze a crust that would bear a quick step of man.

"It's our only chance—an' damn slim at thet," declared Blade.

Tappan allowed Blade to choose the time and method, and supplies for the start to get out of the forest. They cooked all the beans and divided them in two sacks. Then they baked about five pounds of biscuits for each of them. Blade showed his cunning when he chose the small bag of salt for himself and let Tappan take the tobacco. This quantity of food and a blanket for each Blade declared to be all they could pack. They argued over the guns, and in the end Blade compromised on the rifle, agreeing to let Tappan carry that on a possible chance of killing a deer or elk. When this matter had been decided, Blade significantly began putting on his rude snowshoes, that had been constructed from pieces of Tappan's boxes and straps and burlap sacks.

"Reckon they won't last long," muttered Blade.

Meanwhile Tappan fed Jenet some biscuits and then began to strap a tarpaulin on her back.

"What you doin'?" queried Blade, suddenly.

"Gettin' Jenet ready," replied Tappan.

"Ready! For what?"

"Why, to go with us."

"Hell!" shouted Blade, and he threw up his hands in helpless rage.

Tappan felt a depth stirred within him. He lost his late taciturnity and silent aloofness fell away from him. Blade seemed on the moment no longer an enemy. He loomed as an aid to the saving of Jenet. Tappan burst into speech.

"I can't go without her. It'd never enter my head.
Jenet's mother was a good faithful burro. I saw Jenet
born way down there on the Rio Colorado. She wasn't
strong. An' I had to wait for her to be able to walk. An'
she grew up. Her mother died, an' Jenet an' me packed it
alone. She wasn't no ordinary burro. She learned all I
taught her. She was different. But I treated her same as
any burro. An' she grew with the years. Desert men said
there never was such a burro as Jenet. Called her Tappan's
burro, an' tried to borrow an' buy an' steal her. . . .
How many times in ten years Jenet has done me a good
turn I can't remember. But she saved my life. She dragged
me out of Death Valley. . . . An' then I forgot my debt.
I ran off with a woman an' left Jenet to wait as she had
been trained to wait. . . . Well, I got back in time. . . .
An' now I'll not leave her here. It may be strange to you,
Blade, me carin' this way. Jenet's only a burro. But I won't
leave her."

"Man, you talk like thet lazy lop-eared burro was a
woman," declared Blade, in disgusted astonishment.

"I don't know women, but I reckon Jenet's more faithful than most of them."

"Wal, of all the stark, starin' fools I ever run into you're
the worst."

"Fool or not, I know what I'll do," retorted Tappan.
The softer mood left him swiftly.

"Haven't you sense enough to see thet we can't travel
with your burro?" queried Blade, patiently controlling his
temper. "She has little hoofs, sharp as knives. She'll cut
through the crust. She'll break through in places. An'
we'll have to stop to haul her out—mebbe break through
ourselves. Thet would make us longer gettin' out."

"Long or short we'll take her."

Then Blade confronted Tappan as if suddenly unmask-
ing his true meaning. His patient explanation meant nothing. Under no circumstances would he ever have con-
sented to an attempt to take Jenet out of that snow-bound
wilderness. His eyes gleamed.

"We've a hard pull to get out alive. An' hard-workin' men in winter must have meat to eat."

Tappan slowly straightened up to look at the speaker. "What do you mean?"

For answer Blade jerked his hand backward and downward, and when it swung into sight again it held Tappan's worn and shining rifle. Then Blade, with deliberate force, that showed the nature of the man, worked the lever and threw a shell into the magazine. All the while his eyes were fastened on Tappan. His face seemed that of another man, evil, relentless, inevitable in his spirit to preserve his own life at any cost.

"I mean to kill your burro," he said, in voice that suited his look and manner.

"No!" cried Tappan, shocked into an instant of appeal.

"Yes, I am, an' I'll bet, by God, before we get out of hyar you'll be glad to eat some of her meat!"

That roused the slow-gathering might of Tappan's wrath.

"I'd starve to death before I'd—I'd kill that burro, let alone eat her."

"Starve an' be damned!" shouted Blade, yielding to rage.

Jenet stood right behind Tappan, in her posture of contented repose, with one long ear hanging down over her gray meek face.

"You'll have to kill me first," answered Tappan, sharply.

"I'm good fer anythin'—if you push me," returned Blade, stridently.

As he stepped aside, evidently so he could have unobstructed aim at Jenet, Tappan leaped forward and knocked up the rifle as it was discharged. The bullet sped harmlessly over Jenet. Tappan heard it thud into a tree. Blade uttered a curse. And as he lowered the rifle in sudden deadly intent, Tappan grasped the barrel with his left hand. Then, clenching his right, he struck Blade a sodden blow in the face. Only Blade's hold on the rifle prevented him from falling. Blood streamed from his nose and mouth. He bellowed in hoarse fury,

"I'll kill you—fer thet!"

Tappan opened his clenched teeth: "No, Blade—you're not man enough."

Then began a terrific struggle for possession of the rifle. Tappan beat at Blade's face with his sledge-hammer fist. But the strength of the other made it imperative that he use both hands to keep his hold on the rifle. Wrestling and pulling and jerking, the men tore round the snowy camp, scattering the camp fire, knocking down the brush shelter. Blade had surrendered to a wild frenzy. He hissed his maledictions. His was the brute lust to kill an enemy that thwarted him. But Tappan was grim and terrible in his restraint. His battle was to save Jenet. Nevertheless, there mounted in him the hot physical sensations of the savage. The contact of flesh, the smell and sight of Blade's blood, the violent action, the beastly mien of his foe changed the fight to one for its own sake. To conquer this foe, to rend him and beat him down, blow on blow!

Tappan felt instinctively that he was the stronger. Suddenly he exerted all his muscular force into one tremendous wrench. The rifle broke, leaving the steel barrel in his hands, the wooden stock in Blade's. And it was the quicker-witted Blade who used his weapon first to advantage. One swift blow knocked Tappan down. As he was about to follow it up with another, Tappan kicked his opponent's feet from under him. Blade sprawled in the snow, but was up again as quickly as Tappan. They made at each other, Tappan waiting to strike, and Blade raining blows on Tappan. These were heavy blows aimed at his head, but which he contrived to receive on his arms and the rifle barrel he brandished. For a few moments Tappan stood up under a beating that would have felled a lesser man. His own blood blinded him. Then he swung his heavy weapon. The blow broke Blade's left arm. Like a wild beast, he screamed in pain; and then, without guard,

rushed in, too furious for further caution. Tappan met
the terrible onslaught as before, and watching his chance,
again swung the rifle barrel. This time, so supreme was
the force, it battered down Blade's arm and crushed his
skull. He died on his feet—ghastly and horrible change!—
and swaying backward, he fell into the upbanked wall of
snow, and went out of sight, except for his boots, one
of which still held the crude snowshoe.

Tappan stared, slowly realizing.

"Ahuh, stranger Blade!" he ejaculated, gazing at the
hole in the snow bank where his foe had disappeared.
"You were goin' to—kill an' eat—Tappan's burro!"

Then he sighted the bloody rifle barrel, and cast it from
him. He became conscious of injuries which needed attention. But he could do little more than wash off the blood
and bind up his head. Both arms and hands were badly
bruised, and beginning to swell. But fortunately no bones
had been broken.

Tappan finished strapping the tarpaulin upon the burro;
and, taking up both his and Blade's supply of food, he
called out, "Come on, Jenet."

Which way to go! Indeed, there was no more choice
for him than there had been for Blade. Toward the Rim
the snowdrift would be deeper and impassable. Tappan
realized that the only possible chance for him was down
hill. So he led Jenet out of camp without looking back
once. What was it that had happened? He did not seem
to be the same Tappan that had dreamily tramped into
this woodland.

A deep furrow in the snow had been made by the men
packing firewood into camp. At the end of this furrow
the wall of snow stood higher than Tappan's head. To get
out on top without breaking the crust presented a prob-
lem. He lifted Jenet up, and was relieved to see that the
snow held her. But he found a different task in his own
case. Returning to camp, he gathered up several of the
long branches of spruce that had been part of the shelter,

and carrying them out he laid them against the slant of snow he had to surmount, and by their aid he got on top. The crust held him.

Elated and with revived hope, he took up Jenet's halter and started off. Walking with his rude snowshoes was awkward. He had to go slowly, and slide them along the crust. But he progressed. Jenet's little steps kept her even with him. Now and then one of her sharp hoofs cut through, but not to hinder her particularly. Right at the start Tappan observed a singular something about Jenet. Never until now had she been dependent upon him. She knew it. Her intelligence apparently told her that if she got out of this snow-bound wilderness it would be owing to the strength and reason of her master.

Tappan kept to the north side of the canyon, where the snow crust was strongest. What he must do was to work up to the top of the canyon slope, and then keeping to the ridge travel north along it, and so down out of the forest.

Travel was slow. He soon found he had to pick his way. Jenet appeared to be absolutely unable to sense either danger or safety. Her experience had been of the rock confines and the drifting sands of the desert. She walked where Tappan led her. And it seemed to Tappan that her trust in him, her reliance upon him, were pathetic.

"Well, old girl," said Tappan to her, "it's a horse of another color now—hey?"

At length he came to a wide part of the canyon, where a bench of land led to a long gradual slope, thickly studded with small pines. This appeared to be fortunate, and turned out to be so, for when Jenet broke through the crust Tappan had trees and branches to hold to while he hauled her out. The labor of climbing that slope was such that Tappan began to appreciate Blade's absolute refusal to attempt getting Jenet out. Dusk was shadowing the white aisles of the forest when Tappan ascended to a level. He had not traveled far from camp, and the fact struck a chill upon his heart.

To go on in the dark was foolhardy. So Tappan selected a thick spruce, under which there was a considerable depression in the snow, and here made preparation to spend the night. Unstrapping the tarpaulin, he spread it on the snow. All the lower branches of this giant of the forest were dead and dry. Tappan broke off many and soon had a fire. Jenet nibbled at the moss on the trunk of the spruce tree. Tappan's meal consisted of beans, biscuits, and a ball of snow, that he held over the fire to soften. He saw to it that Jenet fared as well as he. Night soon fell, strange and weirdly white in the forest, and piercingly cold. Tappan needed the fire. Gradually it melted the snow and made a hole, down to the ground. Tappan rolled up in the tarpaulin and soon fell asleep.

In three days Tappan traveled about fifteen miles, gradually descending, until the snow crust began to fail to hold Jenet. Then whatever had been his difficulties before, they were now magnified a hundredfold. As soon as the sun was up, somewhat softening the snow, Jenet began to break through. And often when Tappan began hauling her out he broke through himself. This exertion was killing even to a man of Tappan's physical prowess. The endurance to resist heat and flying dust and dragging sand seemed another kind from that needed to toil on in this snow. The endless snow-bound forest began to be hideous to Tappan. Cold, lonely, dreary, white, mournful —the kind of ghastly and ghostly winter land that had been the terror of Tappan's boyish dreams! He loved the sun—the open. This forest had deceived him. It was a wall of ice. As he toiled on, the state of his mind gradually and subtly changed in all except the fixed and absolute will to save Jenet. In some places he carried her.

The fourth night found him dangerously near the end of his stock of food. He had been generous with Jenet,

But now, considering that he had to do more work than she, he diminished her share. On the fifth day Jenet broke through the snow crust so often that Tappan realized how utterly impossible it was for her to get out of the woods by her own efforts. Therefore Tappan hit upon the plan of making her lie on the tarpaulin, so that he could drag her. The tarpaulin doubled once did not make a bad sled. All the rest of that day Tappan hauled her. And so all the rest of the next day he toiled on, hands behind him, clutching the canvas, head and shoulders bent, plodding and methodical, like a man who could not be defeated. That night he was too weary to build a fire, and too worried to eat the last of his food.

Next day Tappan was not unalive to the changing character of the forest. He had worked down out of the zone of the spruce trees; the pines had thinned out and decreased in size; oak trees began to show prominently. All these signs meant that he was getting down out of the mountain heights. But the fact, hopeful as it was, had drawbacks. The snow was still four feet deep on a level and the crust held Tappan only about half the time. Moreover, the lay of the land operated against Tappan's progress. The long, slowly descending ridge had failed. There were no more canyons, but ravines and swales were numerous. Tappan dragged on, stern, indomitable, bent to his toil.

When the crust let him down, he hung his snowshoes over Jenet's back, and wallowed through, making a lane for her to follow. Two days of such heart-breaking toil, without food or fire, broke Tappan's magnificent endurance. But not his spirit! He hauled Jenet over the snow, and through the snow, down the hills and up the slopes, through the thickets, knowing that over the next ridge, perhaps, was deliverance. Deer and elk tracks began to be numerous. Cedar and juniper trees now predominated. An occasional pine showed here and there. He was getting out of the forest land. Only such mighty and justifiable hope as that could have kept him on his feet.

He fell often, and it grew harder to rise and go on. The hour came when the crust failed altogether to hold Tappan and he had to abandon hauling Jenet. It was necessary to make a road for her. How weary, cold, horrible, the white reaches! Yard by yard Tappan made his way. He no longer sweat. He had no feeling in his feet or legs. Hunger ceased to gnaw at his vitals. His thirst he quenched with snow—soft snow now, that did not have to be crunched like ice. The pangs in his breast were terrible—cramps, constrictions, the piercing pains in his lungs, the dull ache of his overtaxed heart.

Tappan came to an opening in the cedar forest from which he could see afar. A long slope fronted him. It led down and down to open country. His desert eyes, keen as those of an eagle, made out flat country, sparsely covered with snow, and black dots that were cattle. The last slope! The last pull! Three feet of snow, except in drifts; down and down he plunged, making way for Jenet! All that day he toiled and fell and rolled down this league-long slope, wearing toward sunset to the end of his task, and likewise to the end of his will.

Now he seemed up and now down. There was no sense of cold or weariness. Only direction! Tappan still saw! The last of his horror at the monotony of white faded from his mind. Jenet was there, beginning to be able to travel for herself. The solemn close of endless day found Tappan arriving at the edge of the timbered country, where wind-bared patches of ground showed long, bleached grass. Jenet took to grazing.

As for Tappan, he fell with the tarpaulin, under a thick cedar, and with strengthless hands plucked and plucked at the canvas to spread it, so that he could cover himself. He looked again for Jenet. She was there, somehow a fading image, strangely blurred. But she was grazing. Tappan lay down, and stretched out, and slowly drew the tarpaulin over him.

A piercing cold night wind swept down from the snowy heights. It wailed in the edge of the cedars and moaned out toward the open country. Yet the night seemed silent. The stars shone white in a deep blue sky— passionless, cold, watchful eyes, looking down without pity or hope or censure. They were the eyes of Nature. Winter had locked the heights in its snowy grip. All night that winter wind blew down, colder and colder. Then dawn broke, steely, gray, with a flare in the east.

Jenet came back where she had left her master. Camp! As she had returned thousands of dawns in the long years of her service. She had grazed all night. Her sides that had been flat were now full. Jenet had weathered another vicissitude of her life. She stood for a while, in a doze, with one long ear down over her meek face. Jenet was waiting for Tappan.

But he did not stir from under the long roll of canvas. Jenet waited. The winter sun rose, in cold yellow flare. The snow glistened as with a crusting of diamonds. Some- where in the distance sounded a long-drawn, discordant bray. Jenet's ears shot up. She listened. She recognized the call of one of her kind. Instinct always prompted Jenet. Sometimes she did bray. Lifting her gray head she sent forth a clarion: *"Hee-haw hee-haw-haw—hee-haw how-e-e-e!"*

That stentorian call started the echoes. They pealed down the slope and rolled out over the open country, clear as a bugle blast, yet hideous in their discordance. But this morning Tappan did not awaken.

LAST WARNING

by WILLIAM MACLEOD RAINE

ALL day John Muir had been stringing wire for the south pasture. Dust and sand had sifted into every crease of his clothes. He was hot and tired and dirty. Yet the sweat and toil under a broiling sun had not obscured a certain gallant grace in this slender black-haired man. He sat lightly in the saddle, a figure to draw the eyes of men as well as women.

He topped a rise and rode into a park knee deep with grass and flowers. Not in a dozen years had there been such spring rains as in the past few months, and among the aspen were strewn abundantly gentian and bluebell, Indian paintbrush, fireweed, and columbine. It was a goodly spread, this mountain Eden he had homesteaded, but its beauty could not drive away the frown that furrowed his brow. Though he held legal title to the demesne, a bullet might at any hour terminate his ownership. Might and indeed probably would, unless he could bend his stubborn pride to make terms with the enemy.

Riding across the floor of the park toward his cabin in the pines was one who made him forget his fears and his weariness. Even at a distance he recognized that slender erect body. Above it was a bare head, golden in the sunset, and he knew that when he drew nearer he would see a face of lovely planes and eager sparkling eyes. She was of the house of his foe, but between them was a tie on his side at least closer than friendship.

She saw him and flung up a hand in greeting, pulling up her pony to wait for him. To see her there surprised him.

They had met at dances, once at a rodeo, and twice in town—six times in all. No word of love had they spoken, but it had been in the background of both their thoughts. Never had she been on his land since he had filed claim to it. Now she had come, he was sure, for a reason that soon would be explained, an important and not a trivial one.

He lifted the dusty sombrero from his dark head. "Welcome to Sweet Springs park," he said.

She let her gaze sweep over the grass-carpeted valley bright with flowers, across the busy brook to the gentle slope leading to the small house that nestled in the cool evergreens. "You've chosen a lovely spot for a home," she replied.

"No place is home where a man lives alone," he told her, and a moment later regretted the impulsive confession.

The girl blushed pink, from throat to cheek. "I must send you a paper I saw one of our men reading yesterday," she answered lightly. "You write to a lady, object matrimony, exchange photographs, and she comes to you sight unseen to live happily with you ever after."

His dark eyes rested on her, bitterness in them. "I would have a lot to offer her—a homestead right, a cabin, a few cattle, and a feud."

She held her bright head proudly, her brave look direct and unashamed. "Does a woman marry a man for the things he owns?" she asked.

Neither of them had meant to lay bare the hidden emotions that had leaped out, to speak of the frustrations and barriers that held them apart. But one revealing second had brushed aside their guards.

He shook his head. "A nester doesn't marry the daughter of a cattle king with whom he is at war."

In her answer there was a touch of scorn. "Not if he is humble and timid and wants above all to nurse his grudge." She gave him no time for a reply. Already she had gone too far, had said more than any modest girl might with propriety reveal. If he did not choose to follow the offered lead she could not help it. "I came because I overheard two of our men talking and what they said worried me. I don't suppose there is anything in it. There can't be. But it was disturbing. Father was away from home. So I came to you. Maybe I was silly. I caught your name and listened. One of them said it would be with you the way it was with Barry and the other added, 'Unless he lights out sudden.' When I came out from the stable and surprised them they said they had just been fooling. But I know better." She flung a sharp question at Muir. "What did they mean about Barry? I know he left suddenly."

The homesteader's smile was thin and grim. "Nobody knows for sure what happened to Barry."

Her blue startled eyes held fast to his. "Do you mean—he didn't leave?"

"He didn't take his team. The horses were found in the pasture after he was missed. He did not go by train."

"Perhaps he met with an accident."

"Or was dry-gulched. He had been warned to get out or take the consequences."

"Who warned him?"

"The fellow didn't leave his name," Muir answered dryly.

The girl felt a cold sinking at the stomach. They had turned and were riding up the slope toward the house. "Did he have an enemy?" she asked, almost in a whisper.

"He was in somebody's way." Muir spoke with stiff reserve.

On the closed door of the house a bit of yellow paper was tacked. "A message for you," she suggested, her mind still groping with the shadowy horror drawing close.

"Yes." He looked at her strangely as he slipped from the saddle to get the paper before she could read it. What he would find on that torn sheet of paper he knew.

Rose Durbin caught his swift glance and moved her horse forward to anticipate his intention. She read:

Get out, you damned rustler, before 24 hours. This
is your last warning.

There was no signature. Muir did not need one to
know who was responsible for the notice. It came from
Hank Durbin of the Bar Double S, though he had not
nailed it there himself.

"But you're not a rustler," Rose cried. "What do they
mean?"

"Even a killer needs some excuse to justify himself,"
Muir explained. "So he has trumped up this one."

"If you know who he is—"

He lifted his hands in a little gesture of hoplessness.
"Nothing I can do about it. He's protected."

"Are you going to leave?"

"No."

"Then what are you going to do?"

"I don't know."

As she looked into the lean brown boyish face, a sickness ran through her. Fear tightened her chest. She felt
the quick pounding of her heart, the terror crawling up
her spine. Swinging down from the saddle, she caught
him by the lapels of his coat and looked up into his eyes.
All the color had washed out of her cheeks and left her
ashen.

"You are not just going to stay and let them—kill
you?" she asked.

"Not if I can help it."

"This all sounds crazy," she cried. "There's a law
against murder. If you know somebody means to kill you,
it's not necessary to let him do it. Come to the Bar
Double S and stay with us until the danger is over. Father will give you a job if you want to work."

Her suggestion was as fantastic as anything else in this
impossible situation. In the first place there was no law
in this far-flung range country that would protect him
against a big outfit intent on his destruction. Nor could
he run to Hank Durbin for help against his own killer

Frenault, a man who was reported to have rubbed out eight victims, most of them for pay and from ambush. Durbin meant to hold the grass and the water holes of this district for his stock against homesteaders. The gunman was only a tool who obeyed orders.

"No," Muir told her harshly. "I have to play my own hand."

"But how? This is no time to be stubborn, John."

He did not know how. But there was in him a stiff sense of justice, of self-respect, that would not let him be driven from the property that was lawfully his. Neither argument nor pleading moved him. The girl realized at last despairingly that not even his love for her could make him alter his decision.

After she had gone Muir lit a fire, washed himself, and prepared supper. He did not want food, but he had to carry on the routine of life. Mechanically he ate, washing a few mouthfuls of bread and bacon down with coffee. His shoulders sagged wearily. In the pit of his stomach was a lump of ice. No illusions buoyed him up. Frenault would shoot him from ambush, though the gunfighter could meet him in the open with small risk. The Bar Double S warrior was a dead shot, cool, and wary. Muir had never fired a gun at a man. An emergency like this was one that preyed on his imagination. Even if he were given a chance he might be weak and unnerved at the critical moment.

He curtained the windows, bolted the door, and smoked an unsatisfying pipe. It was long before he slept. Troubled dreams disturbed his rest. Before daylight he rose, saddled a horse, and started for River Fork. There were a few loose ends of business he wanted to clear up while he could.

Rose did not mean to give up because John Muir had proved so obstinate. She found her father in the little room he used as an office. He was figuring out some costs on the back of an old envelope with the stub of a pencil.

Hank Durbin was a gross paunchy man with heavy

rounded shoulders and shapeless body. He had small gray-green eyes, sly and mocking, lit at times by an evil ironic mirth. His clothes were cheap and outworn, his boots run down at the heels. To those who knew both father and daughter it was a continuous surprise that Rose should have sprung from such a source. Of her sweet and dainty grace there was no suggestion in his thick bulky torso or his heavy-footed clumping gait.

"Somebody is planning to kill John Muir," she flung out.

Hank squinted up at her. "Who told you that?" he squeaked in a high falsetto voice that sounded strange coming from such a mountain of flesh.

"I saw a notice on the door of his cabin."

"What were you doing on his place?" Hank snapped.

"I heard two men talking, and when I couldn't find you I went to warn him."

"You keep outa this. It's none of yore business," he snarled. Swiftly he added: "What two men?"

Some instinct cautioned her to be careful. "I couldn't see who they were."

"If I find out, I'll learn the fools." He slammed a heavy fist on the table.

"I told John Muir to come and stay with us till the danger was past. He wouldn't come. You must do something about it, Father."

"So he wouldn't come." Hank tittered. "Give any reason?"

"Said he would have to play his own hand. Who is it wants to kill him?"

Durbin stroked his unshaven chin to conceal a grin. "I don't reckon anybody wants to kill him, honey. It must be some of the boys' monkey shines."

"No." She had always been afraid of something secret and sinister in him, but now she faced him resolutely, a challenge in her fear-filled eyes. "He's going to be killed unless we stop it. I know you don't like him and resent anyone homesteading your range. But you can't stand back and let him be murdered. It's too—horrible."

"I didn't invite him here to fence my water holes. He's made his own bed. If he's got a lick of sense he can still get out. I've offered to buy his spread. But he won't have it that way. I won't lift a hand for the stubborn fool."

He had come out into the open, practically admitting that what she feared was true. His little eyes glittered with malice. An appalling conviction flashed to her mind. He was the enemy who threatened John Muir's destruction. That was why John had said he was protected. Thirty Bar Double S riders fenced Hank Durbin from danger.

She drew back, as one does from a venomous reptile. A strangled sob came from her throat. She turned and ran from the room.

Rose too had an unhappy night. She rose early, in time to see her father and Frenault riding down the road that led to town. It was a relief to know that they were not traveling toward Sweet Springs park. After a hurried breakfast she had a horse saddled and set out to have another talk with John Muir. An idea was simmering in her mind. She knew he cared for her. If she could persuade him to marry her at once her father might spare her lover. Bad though he was, Rose knew he had a soft spot in his tough heart for her.

The girl found the homestead deserted. John had told her he would probably go to town to settle some accounts. Very likely he would meet her father and Frenault there. On the way home he might be waylaid. As she turned to strike the trail for River Fork she felt her heart thumping against her ribs.

John Muir knew that he was safer in River Fork than on his own land. His enemies would not dare shoot him down from ambush in the sight of men. They would have to give him a chance for his white alley. Out in the hills the law of the frontier could be ignored, since there would be no witness to prove who had violated it. Yet heavy heavy hung over the head of the homesteader. In a few hours he would be back within reach of the Bar Double S killer's rifle.

It was a day of warm and pleasant sunshine. Billowy clouds, with little white islands clinging close to their indented edges, floated lazily across the bluest possible sky. He wondered if he would see that sky tomorrow—if his eyes would not be forever closed.

He called at the office of Jim Baylor, lawyer, and made his will. Jim joked with him a little about it. Brown young riders rarely bothered about the future. From the attorney's office he went to the livery stable and settled a bill. Presently he was at a general store cleaning up what he owed there. It was while he was doing this that a lounger dropped in and mentioned casually having seen Durbin and Frenault at the Cowman's Rest.

Muir gave no sign of interest. He put the change handed him by the storekeeper in his pocket and wandered out of the building. An acquaintance passed him on the sidewalk and he nodded a greeting. But the undercurrent of his mind was busy with the implications of what he had just heard. There might still be a chance if he tried to talk Durbin into a compromise. For a full minute he hesitated, then walked down the street to the Cowman's Rest. He moved swiftly, afraid his resolution might give way if he lingered.

Durbin and Frenault were at the bar drinking. Hank caught sight of Muir in the doorway. His heavy lids narrowed, and into the gray-green eyes a cruel mirth leaped.

He called to the nester. "I hear you're leaving. Come in and have a drink with us before you go."

Muir could not draw back now. He came forward slowly setting his back teeth to choke down the fear that rose in his throat at sight of these two men together.

"I'm not leaving," he answered quietly.

"My mistake." Durbin's great midriff shook like a jelly. This was the kind of situation he enjoyed, to play cat and mouse with some poor devil he had in his power. "I heard the climate didn't agree with you."

"I'd like to talk with you, Mr. Durbin."

"Fine. Neighbors ought to have a pow-wow onct in a while. How's yore fencing going?"

"Three nights ago the wires were cut to pieces in fifty places."

Hank showed elaborate concern. "You don't say. Now who in time could have done that."

Muir moistened dry lips with his tongue. "I thought if I talked over our difficulties with you—"

"What difficulties?" the Bar Double S owner inquired blandly. "Didn't know I had any difficulties."

The homesteader went on, his voice low and pleading, "I'm running only a two-by-four spread, Mr. Durbin, and I've fenced just one water hole. That won't interfere with your stock. There's feed and water enough for both of us."

"Another glass, Mike," the cattleman told the bartender. "Mr. Muir is having a last drink with us—before leaving." Durbin turned to the nester. He too spoke low, but with a thread of suave cruelty in his spaced words. "That's where you're wrong. I had the Sweet Springs range before you ever saw this country. I aim to hold it against any two-bit drifter who tries to fence off my water holes."

"Only one, Mr. Durbin, and your cattle can get water just below my south fence."

"I don't give a tinker's damn whether it's one or twenty. I'll fight for my rights. If I let you get away with this some other guy will try it."

Mike had pushed the bottle and another glass toward Muir, but the young man paid no attention to them. "I'm not looking for trouble," he said, his forehead creased with anxious thought. "You know that, Mr. Durbin. But I have rights too. The law says . . ."

"Who the hell cares about law?" The cattleman brushed it aside with a sweep of his plump hand. "A bunch of nincompoops sit in Washington on their behinds and make laws that have no sense for a range country they have never seen and know nothing about. This is cow territory—no good for anything else. It belongs to the man who uses it first. The Sweet Springs water and grass are mine. Get that in your thick skull while there is time."

Durbin's voice was losing its smoothness and getting shrill. He pounded on the bar with his hamlike fist.

A man who had come in and ordered a bottle of beer became aware of the tensity. He had spoken to Muir and Durbin with only a scant nod of greeting. Hurriedly he drank his beer and departed without paying for it. Mike did not remind him of the obligation. His mind too was preoccupied. Maybe he had better make some excuse to beat it into the back room and escape by way of the rear door. He did not like the cold intent look Frenault held fixed on Muir.

Since the homesteader had come into the room Frenault had not spoken a word. He was slightly below middle height, tight-lipped, with a colorless face of strong bony conformation. His eyes were as cold and expressionless as those of a dead mackerel. Their wary stillness was a threat. When he changed his position, to leave his right arm freer, there was a catlike rhythm in the movement.

Muir had come in to make peace if he could, but anger at Durbin's domineering arrogance began to smolder in him. "The United States government says different," he insisted stubbornly. "I have a paper from it that tells me Sweet Springs park is mine."

"Better write to yore congressman and have him send a troop of soldiers to help you hold it," Durbin warned. "Don't go crazy with the heat, you lunkhead. I've offered to buy. Last chance, Muir."

"You didn't offer me one fourth of what my spread is worth."

"I offered you all it's worth to me. I don't give a cuss whether you accept or don't. I'll get it anyhow."

The homesteader felt a cold wind blowing over him. He was convinced that Frenault was waiting for his chief to give the word. He ought to knuckle under and give way. Not to do so was suicidal. He heard the clock on the wall ticking away the seconds between him and eternity. A chill sweat broke out on his forehead. But he could not throw up his hands and quit. He wanted to, and did not find it possible. A man could not run like a rabbit.

"I'm not going to let anybody rob me," he said thickly.

The eyes of the cattleman and his killer met. A message passed from one to the other. Without another word Durbin turned and clumped out of the building. Muir knew the showdown had come.

Before the swing doors had settled to rest somebody from outside pushed through them. He was a short thick-set man in chaps and checked shirt.

" 'Lo, Frenault," he said. "Heard you were in town and brought the twenty bucks I owe you."

The gunfighter turned his head to the newcomer. "Hand it to Mike," he said. "I'm busy right now."

Muir picked up the empty beer bottle and pressed the rim of the narrow end against the back of the desperado's neck. "Don't move," he warned.

The homesteader was surprised to find that his voice was cool and firm. Now that the moment for action had come the fear had dropped from him like a discarded coat.

Frenault stood rigid. He did not move while Muir slipped the .45 from the scabbard at the man's side.

"Goddlemighty!" the cowpuncher at the door gasped.

"Keep your hands at your sides, Frenault," Muir warned. "You may turn now."

Frenault turned, a blazing passion in his bleak eyes. His right arm moved upward swiftly. It brushed under his coat and continued to lift without stopping.

With his left hand Muir slapped down the barrel of the

revolver and at the same time fired. The bullet from Frenault's second gun crashed through the floor.

The hired killer caught at his heart. From his slack fingers the .45 clattered to the ground. He swayed, took a step forward, and plunged down beside his gun. The body twitched and lay motionless.

Muir stared down at the still huddled figure. He was amazed and shocked at what he had done. With the touch of a finger he had blasted life from a desperado of whom he had walked in terror.

The man in the doorway slapped a hand against his shiny chaps. "I never saw the beat of it," he yelped. "All his life Frenault played to get the breaks. He slips once, and—curtain, gents."

A thin film of smoke still trickled from the barrel of the revolver in Muir's hand. He fought down the sickness that ran through him and said in a low voice, "I wasn't armed."

"Not armed?" Mike looked at him in wonder. "And with a beer bottle you rubbed out the worst killer ever in this part of the country."

"If he hadn't carried two guns he might still have been alive," Muir said. "I had to do it."

The man in chaps straddled forward. "You bet you had. It was him or you, one." His eyes dropped to the body of the Bar Double S gunfighter. "No regrets. Quite a bunch of guys will breathe freer now he's gone."

There was not enough air in the room for Muir. He pushed through the swing doors and stood outside. What he wanted was to be alone in order to quiet the tumult within him.

A big man with a lumbering body was clumping up the street toward the Cowman's Rest. He pulled up abruptly, startled surprise in his little gray-green eyes. The man at the entrance to the saloon with the gun in his hand was not the one he had expected to see there. He had been hurrying back to explain to the bartender and others present how much he regretted that the homesteader had forced Frenault to kill him.

At sight of Durbin all of Muir's agitation was sloughed away. He said quietly, "We'll settle this business now."

Already a crowd was beginning to gather. From stores and offices men came running.

The cattleman lifted a fat hand in frightened protest. "Lemme explain, Muir. Don't rush this. We can fix it up all right. Whatever you say."

Durbin had been the big man in this district for twenty years. He had overridden other men's rights without compunction. It had become a tradition that nobody could safely stand up against him. A dozen men saw this legend being shattered before their eyes.

"Come here, Durbin," ordered Muir.

The ranch owner shambled reluctantly closer, terror in the fascinated eyes that clung to the grim ones dragging him forward. "Don't shoot," he begged. "You got me all wrong. We'll be good neighbors, John."

"You're through running this country," Muir told him. "Do you understand that?"

"That's all right, if you feel that way. I always was yore friend. Fact is, I was about ready to give Frenault his time."

"Some of your men burned my barn two weeks ago. You'll build me a new one."

"Sure," agreed Durbin eagerly. "If any of my boys did that, I don't know anything about it. But that's fine. I'll certainly build you a better one."

"And you'll never interfere again with any homesteader who wants to take up government land."

"Why no, I wouldn't do that. I'm a law-abiding citizen. I expect some of my boys have been a little bossy. I'll ride herd on them closer."

"Better start at once. Fork your horse and get out of town."

Durbin hesitated. He wanted to save face if he could.

His furtive glance slid round, to meet a circle of unfriendly eyes. They told him that his reign was over. Plodding across the street to the hitch rack where his horse was tied, he swung heavily to the saddle and rode away.

Through the crowd a girl pushed her way to Muir.

"You here?" he cried.

"I was afraid I would be too late." Rose was trembling from the reaction to the fear that had driven her all through her long ride.

He took both her hands in his and looked down into her eyes. "You're just in time," he told her.

HOPALONG SITS IN

by CLARENCE E. MULFORD

HOPALONG CASSIDY dismounted in front of the rough-boarded hotel, regarding it with a curious detachment which was the result of a lifetime's experience with such hybrid affairs. He knew what it would be even before he left the saddle: saloon, gambling house and hotel, to mention its characteristics in the order of their real importance.

Hopalong entered the main room and found that it ran the full length of the building. A bar paralleled one wall, card tables filled the open space; and in the inside corner near the door was a pine desk on which was a bottle of muddy ink, a corroded pen, a paper-covered notebook of the kind used in schools for compositions, and a grimy showcase holding cigars and tobaccos. Behind the desk on the wall was a short piece of board with nails driven in it, and on the nails hung a few keys.

A shiftless person with tobacco-stained lips arose from a near-by table, looking inquiringly at the newcomer.

"Got a room?" asked Hopalong.

"Yeah. Two dollars, in advance," replied the clerk.

"By the week," suggested Hopalong.

"Twelve dollars—we don't count Sundays," said the clerk with a foolish grin.

"Eat on the premises?" asked the newcomer, sliding a gold coin across the desk.

The clerk tossed the coin into the air, listened to the ring as it struck the board, tossed it into a drawer, made change and hooked a thumb over his shoulder.

"Right in yonder," he said, indicating the other half of the building. "Doors open six to eight; twelve to one; six to seven. Pay when you eat an' take what you get. Come with me an' I'll show you the room."

Hopalong obeyed, climbing the steep and economical stairs with just the faintest suggestion of a limp. As they passed down the central hall, he could see into the rooms on each side. They were all alike, even to the arrangement of the furniture. The beds all stood with their heads against the hall wall, in the same relative positions.

"Reckon this will do," he grunted, looking past the clerk into the room indicated. "Stable out back?"

"Yeah. Take yore hoss around an' talk to the stableman," said the clerk, facing around. "Dinner in about an hour."

Hopalong nodded and fell in behind his guide, found the stairs worse in descent than in ascent, and arranged for the care of his horse. When he returned to the room he dropped his blanket roll on the foot of the bed, and then looked searchingly and slowly at the canvas walls. There was nothing to be seen, and shaking his head gently, he went out and down again to wander about the town until time to enter the dining room.

After dinner he saddled his horse and rode down the wide cattle trail, going southward in hope of meeting the SV herd. This was the day it was due; but he was too old a hand to worry about a trail herd being behind time. Johnny Nelson would reach the town when he got there, and there was no reason to waste any thought about the matter. Still, he had nothing else to do, and he pushed on at an easy lope.

He, himself, had been over at Dodge City, where he had learned that Johnny Nelson had a herd on the trail and was bound north. It was a small herd of selected cattle driven by a small outfit. He had not seen Johnny for over a year, and it was too good an opportunity to let pass. For the pleasure of meeting his old friend he had written a letter to him addressed to an important mail station on the new trail, where all outfits called for mail. Some days later he had left Dodge and ridden west, and now he was on hand to welcome the SV owner.

Hopalong passed two herds as he rode, and paused to exchange words with the trail bosses. One of the herds was bound for Wyoming, and the other for Dakota. Trailing had not been very brisk so far this season, but from what the two bosses had heard it was due to pick up shortly. About mid-afternoon Hopalong turned and started back toward town, reaching the hotel soon after the dining-room doors opened.

After supper the town came to life, and as darkness fell, the street was pretty well filled with men. The greater part of the town's population was floating: punchers, gamblers and others whose occupations were not so well known.

The main room of the hotel came to life swiftly, the long bar was well lined and the small tables began to fill. The noise increased in volume and it was not long before the place was in full swing. From time to time brawls broke out in the street and made themselves heard; and once pistol shots caused heads to raise and partly stilled the room.

Hopalong sat lazily in a chair between two windows, his back to the wall, placidly engaged in watching the activities about him. More and more his eyes turned to one particular table, where a game of poker was under way, and where the rounds of drinks came in a steady procession. His curiosity was aroused, and he wondered if the situation was the old one.

To find out, he watched to see which player drank the least liquor, and he found that instead of one man doing that, there were two. To a man of Hopalong's experience along the old frontier, that suggested a very pertinent thought; and he watched more keenly now to see if he could justify it. So far as he was concerned, it was purely an impersonal matter; he knew none of the players and cared noth ing who lost in the game. As hand followed hand, and the liquor began to work, the cheating became apparent to him and threatened to become apparent to others; and he found his gorge slowly rising.

Finally one of the players, having lost his last chip and being unable to buy more, pushed back his chair and left the table, reeling toward the street door. Just then, elbowing his way from the crowd at the bar, came one of the trail bosses with whom Hopalong had talked that afternoon. The newcomer stopped behind the vacant chair and gestured toward it inquiringly.

"Shore. Set down," said one of the sober players. The others nodded their acquiescence, soberly or drunkenly as the case might be, and more drinks were ordered. The two sober men had drunk round for round with the others, and yet showed no effects from it. Hopalong flashed a glance at the bar, and nodded wisely. Very likely they were being served tea.

Hopalong pulled his chair out from the wall, tipped it back and settled down, his big hat slanting well before his eyes. He had ridden all day and was tired, and he found himself drowsing. After an interval, the length of which he did not know, he was aroused to alertness by a shouted curse; but before he could get to his feet or roll off the chair, a shot roared out, almost deafening him. There was a quick flurry at the table, a struggle, and he saw the trail boss, disarmed, being dragged and pushed toward the door. Hopalong removed his sombrero and looked at the hole near the edge of the brim. He was inserting the tip of his little finger into it when one of the players, in a hurried glance around the room, saw the action.

"Close, huh?" inquired the gambler with momentary interest, and then looked around the room again. Several men had pushed out from the crowd and stood waiting in a little group, closely watching the room. As he glimpsed these men, the gambler's face lost its trace of anxiety and he smiled coldly.

Hopalong's eyes flicked from the gambler to the watchful guards and back again, and then he turned slowly to look at the wall behind him, just back of his right ear. The bullet hole was there.

"Yeah, it was close," he said slowly, grinning grimly. "At first I reckoned mebby it might be an old one; but that hole in the wall says it ain't. Who stepped on that fool's pet corn?"

"Nobody; just too much liquor," answered the gambler. "Sometimes it makes a man ugly. Now he's busted up the game, for I shore don't care for a four-hander. Mebby you'd like to take his place?"

"I might," admitted Hopalong with no especial interest. "What you playin', an' how steep?"

"Draw, with jackpots after a full house or better," replied the gambler, looking swiftly but appraisingly at the two drunken players. They had leaned over the table again, and were not to be counted upon to make denials of any statement. "Two bits, an' two dollars; just a friendly game, to pass away the time."

"All right," replied Hopalong, thinking that friendship came rather high in Trailville, if that was the measure of a friendly game.

The gambler waved a hand, and four men stepped to the table. After a moment's argument they took the helpless players from their chairs and started them toward the front door.

Hopalong smiled, thinking that now the game was less

than four-handed. He said nothing, however, but stepped forward and dropped into one of the vacant chairs.

"We can get a couple more to take their places," Hopalong said, and nodded gently as his prophecy was fulfilled. He smiled a welcome to the two men and waited until the gambler had taken his own chair. Then Hopalong leaned forward. "You can call me Riordan," he said.

"Kitty out a white chip every game for the house," said the gambler, reaching for the cards. "We play straights between threes and flushes; no fancy combinations. A faced card on the draw can't be taken."

"You playin' for the house?" asked Hopalong needlessly. He was drawing a hand from a pocket as he spoke, and at the gambler's answering nod, he opened the hand and pushed the coins toward the other. "You got chips enough to sell me some," he said.

The game got under way, and the liquor began to arrive. Hopalong was smiling inwardly: he was well fortified to meet the conditions of this game. In the first place, he could stand an amazing amount of whisky; but he did not intend to crowd his capacity by drinking every round. In the second, poker was to him a fine art; and the more dishonest the game, the finer his art— thanks to Tex Ewalt. He always met crookedness with crookedness rather than to cause trouble, but he let the others set the pace.

He looked like a common frontier citizen, with perhaps a month's wages in his pockets, and he believed that was the reason for the moderate limit set by the gambler, who was a tinhorn, and satisfied with small pickings if he could not do better; but as a matter of fact, Hopalong was a full partner in a very prosperous northern ranch, and he could write a check for six figures and have it honored. Last, and fully as important, he was able to take care of himself in any frontier situation from cutting cards to shooting lead. He believed that he was going to thoroughly enjoy his stay in Trailville.

"On the trail?" carelessly asked the gambler as the cards were cut for the first deal.

"No," answered Hopalong, picking up the deck by diagonal corners in case the cards had been shaved. "I'm just driftin' toward home."

As the game went on it appeared that he had a bad poker weakness: every time he had a poor hand and bluffed strongly, his mouth twitched. It took some time for this to register with the others, but when it did, he found that he was very promptly called; and his displeasure in his adversaries' second sight was plain to all who watched.

Along about the middle of the game his mouth must have twitched by accident, for he raked in a pot that had been well built up and leveled up nearly all his loss. The game seesawed until midnight, when it broke up; and Hopalong found that he cashed in twenty dollars less chips than he had bought; twenty dollars' worth of seeds, from which a crop might grow. He knew that he would be a welcomed addition to any poker game in this hotel, that his weaknesses were known, and his consistent and set playing was now no secret.

He went to his room, closed the door and lighted the lamp, intending to go to bed; but the room was too hot for comfort. There was not a breath of air stirring, and as yet the coolness of the night had not overcome the heat stored up by the walls and roof during the day. He stood for a moment in indecision and then, knowing that another hour would make an appreciable difference in the temperature of the room, he turned and left it, going down to the street.

The night was dark, but star-bright, and he stood for a moment looking about him. The saloons and gambling shacks were going full blast, but they had no appeal for him. He walked toward the corner of the hotel and looked back toward the stables; and then he remembered

that he had seen a box against the side wall of the bar-
room. That was just what he wanted, and he moved
slowly along the wall, feeling his way in the deeper
shadow, found it, and seated himself with a sigh of relief,
leaning back against the wall and relaxing.

Men passed up and down the street, and human voices
rose and fell in the buildings along it. Time passed with
no attempt on Hopalong's part to keep track of it, but
by the deepening chill which comes at that altitude, he
believed that the room would now be bearable. About to
get up and make a start for the street, he heard and saw
two men lazily approach the corner of the building and
lean against it, and glance swiftly about them. From the
faint light of the front window he thought that he knew
who one of them was; and as soon as the man spoke, he
was certain of the identity.

"You know what to do," said the speaker. "I looked
'em over good. There's about two hundred head of fine,
selected cattle, four-year-olds. It'll be easy to run off
most of 'em, or mebby all of 'em. Take 'em round about
into Wolf Hollow, an' then scatter 'em to hell an' gone.
We'll round 'em up later. Don't bungle it *this* time. Get
goin'."

The two men separated, one moving swiftly to where
a horse was standing across the street. He mounted
quickly and rode away. The other moved out of sight
around the corner and disappeared, apparently into the
hotel. Three men came past the corner and paused to
argue drunkenly; and by the time they had moved on
again Hopalong knew that he had lost touch with the man
who held his interest.

The coast being clear, Hopalong moved slowly toward
the street, went into the bar-room and glanced about as
he made his way to the stairs. Reaching his room, he
closed the door behind him and listened for a few moments. During lulls in the general noise downstairs he
could hear a man snoring.

Undressing, he stretched out and gave himself over to

a period of quiet but intensive thought. He had nothing positive to go upon; the horseman had ridden off so quickly that he was gone before Hopalong could come to any decision about following him; he realized that by the time he could have saddled up the man would have been out of reach. He did not know for sure that the two men had referred to the SV herd, nor where to find it if he did know. All he could do was to wait, and to keep his ears open and his wits about him. It would be better to conceal his interest in Johnny Nelson and Johnny's cattle. As a matter of fact he had nothing but unfounded suspicions for the whole structure he was building up.

Back in Dodge City he had been well informed about Trailville and the conditions obtaining there, since a large per cent of the unholy population of Dodge had packed up and gone to the new town. The big herds no longer crossed the Arkansas near the famous old cattle town, to amble up the divide leading to the Sawlog. The present marshal of Dodge was a good friend of Hopalong's, and had been thorough in his pointers and remarks.

Hopalong had learned from him, for one thing, that a good trail herd with a small outfit would be likely to lose cattle and have a deal of trouble before it passed the new town; especially if the trail crew was further reduced in numbers by some of the men receiving time off to enjoy an evening in the town. Further than that the marshal had mentioned one man by name, Bradley, and stressed it emphatically; and only tonight Hopalong had heard that man's name called out while the poker game was under way, and had looked with assumed carelessness across the table at the player who had answered to it.

Hopalong had taken pains during the remainder of the evening to be affable to this gentleman, and to study him; he had been so affable and friendly that he even had forborne giving a hint that he knew the gentleman cheated when occasion seemed to warrant it. And this man Bradley was the man he had overheard speak just a few minutes before at the corner of the building.

Perhaps, after all, he would ride down the trail in the morning, if he knew that he was not observed doing it, and try to get in touch with Johnny, even though he did not know how far away the SV herd might be. He knew that the herd numbered about two hundred head of the best cattle to be found on four ranches; and he knew that the outfit would be small. He feared . . . Ah, hell! What was the use of letting unfounded suspicions make a fool of him, and keep him awake? He turned over on his side and went to sleep like a child.

He was the second man through the dining-room door the next morning, and soon thereafter he left town, bound down the trail, hoping that the SV herd was within a day's ride, and that he could meet it unobserved. He had not covered a dozen miles before he saw a horseman coming toward him up the trail, and something about the man seemed to be familiar. It was not long before he knew the rider to be Bradley.

The two horsemen nodded casually and pulled up, stopping almost leg to leg.

"Leavin' us, Riordan?" asked the upbound man.

"No," answered Hopalong. "The town's dead durin' daylight, an' I figgered to look over the country an' kill some time."

"There ain't nothin' down this way to see," replied the other. "Nor up the other way, neither," he added.

"Ride with you, then, as far as town," said Hopalong, deciding not to show even a single card of his hand.

They went on up the trail at a slow and easy gait, talking idly of this and that, and then Hopalong turned sidewise and asked a question with elaborate casualness.

"Who's town marshal, Bradley?" he asked.

"Slick Cunningham. Why?" asked Bradley, flashing a quick glance at his companion.

Hopalong was silent for a moment, turning the name

over in his mind; and then his expression faintly suggested relief.

"Never heard of him," he admitted, and laughed gently, his careless good nature once more restored. "Reckon, accordin' to that, he never heard of me, neither."

"Oh, Slick's all right; he minds his own business purty well," said Bradley, and grinned broadly. "Anyhow, he's out of town right now."

Continuing a purely idle conversation, they soon saw the town off on one side of the trail, and Bradley raised a hand.

"There she is," he said, pulling up. "I've got a couple of errands to do that wouldn't interest you none; so I'll quit you here, an' see you in town tonight."

"Keno," grunted Hopalong, and headed for the collection of shacks that was Trailville. He was halfway to town when he purposely lost his hat. Wheeling, he swung down to scoop it up, and took advantage of the movement to glance swiftly backward; and he was just in time to see Bradley dipping down into a hollow west of the trail. The remainder of the short ride was covered at a walk, and was a thoughtful one.

The day dragged past, suppertime came and went, and again the big room slowly filled with men. Hopalong sat in the same chair, tipped back against the wall, the bullet hole close to his head. Bradley soon came in, stopping at the bar for a few moments, and then led the same group of card players to the same table. Looking around for Hopalong, they espied him, called him by his new name of Riordan and gestured toward the table. In a few moments the game was under way.

The crowd shifted constantly, men coming and going from and to the street. There was a group bunched at the bar, close to the front door. Two men came in from the street, pushing along the far side of the group, eager to quench their thirst. One of them was Slick Cunningham, town marshal, just back from a special assignment. His name was not even as old as Trailville. He glanced through a small opening in the group to see who was in the room, and as his gaze settled on the men playing cards with Bradley, he stiffened and stepped quickly backward, covered by the group.

"Outside, George," he whispered to his companion. "Pronto! Stand just outside the door an' wait for me!"

George was mildly surprised, but he turned and sauntered to the street, stopping when he reached it.

The marshal was nowhere in sight, but he soon appeared around the corner of the building, and beckoned his friend to his side.

"I just had a good look through the window," he said hurriedly. "I knowed it was him; an' it shore is! When Bradley said he was figgerin' on takin' his pick of that SV herd I told him, an' all of you, too, that he was gettin' ready to pull a grizzly's tail. An' he is! Nelson was one of the old Bar 20 gang. . . . An' who the hell do you reckon is sittin' between Bradley an' Winters, playin' poker with 'em? Hopalong Cassidy! Hopalong Cassidy, damn his soul!"

"Thought you said he was up in Montanny?" replied George, with only casual interest.

"He was! But, great Gawd! he don't have to stay there, does he? You get word to Bradley, quick as you can. Settin' elbow to elbow with Cassidy! If that don't stink, then I don't know what does! Cassidy here in Trailville, an' Nelson's cattle comin' up the trail! I'm tellin' you that somethin's wrong!"

"You reckon he knows anything?" asked George, to whom the name of Hopalong Cassidy did not mean nearly so much as it did to his companion.

"Listen!" retorted the marshal earnestly. "Nobody on Gawd's gray earth knows how much that feller knows! I've never run up ag'in him yet when he didn't know a damn sight more than I wanted him to; an' what he don't know, he damn soon finds out. You get word to Bradley. I'm pullin' out of town, an' I'm stayin' out till this mess is all cleaned up. If Cassidy sees me, he'll know that I know him; an' if he knows that I know him, he'll know that I'll pass on the word to my friends. I'll give a hundred dollars to see him buried."

"You mean that?" asked George, with sudden interest.

Slick peered into his eyes through the gloom, and then snorted with disgust.

"Don't you be a damn fool!" he snapped. "I didn't say that I wanted to see *you* buried, did I?"

"Hell with that!" retorted George. "I'm askin' you if you really mean that as an offer; if you'll pay a hundred dollars to the man that kills him?"

"Well, I didn't reckon nobody would be fool enough to take me up," said Slick, but he suddenly leaned forward again, as a new phase of the matter struck him. "Yes, you damn fool! Yes, I will!" He pulled his hat down firmly and nodded. "My share of that herd money will come to a lot more than a hundred dollars; but if that pizen pup stays alive around here we won't steal a head, an' I won't get a cent. Yes, the offer goes; but you better get help, an' split it three ways. There's only one man in town who would have any kind of a chance, an' his name ain't George."

"I'll take care of that end of it," replied George; "an' now I'm goin' in to get word to Bradley. So long."

"So long," said Slick, and forthwith disappeared around the corner on his way to the little corral behind the marshal's office. There was a good horse in that corral, and a horse was just what he wanted at the moment.

George pushed through the group, signaled to the bartender, ordered a drink, and whispered across the counter. Placing his glass on the bar, George moved carelessly down the room, nodding to right and to left. He stopped beside the busy poker table, grunted a greeting to the men he knew, and dragged up a chair near Bradley's right elbow, where he could look at the cards in his friend's hand, and by merely raising his eyes, looked over their tops at the player on the left.

Hopalong had dropped out for that deal, and was leaning back in his chair, his eyes shaded by the brim of his hat. His placid gaze was fixed on the window opposite and he was wondering whose face it was that he had glimpsed in the little patch of light outside. The face had been well back, and the beams of light from the lamps had not revealed it well; but it was something to think about, and, having nothing else to do at the moment, he let his mind dwell on it. He did not like faces furtively peering in through lighted windows.

Bradley chuckled, pulled in the pot and tossed his cards unshown into the discard.

"Hello, George," he said, turning to smile at the man on his right.

"Hello, Bill. Won't nobody call yore hand tonight?"

"They don't call me at the right time," laughed Bradley, in rare good humor. "This seems to be my night." He looked up at the man who now stepped into his circle of vision. "What is it, Tom?"

"Bartender wants to see you, Bill. Says it's important, an' won't take more'n a minute."

"Deal me out this hand," said Bradley, pushing back his chair and following the messenger.

Hopalong let the cards lay as they fell, and when the fifth had dropped in front of him his fingers pushed them into a neat, smooth-sided book, and he watched the faces of the other players as the hands were picked up. The house gambler was in direct line with that part of the bar where Bradley had stopped, and Hopalong's gaze, lifting from the face of the player, for a moment picked out Bradley and the bartender. The latter was looking straight at him and the expression on the man's face was grim and hostile. Hopalong looked at the next player, lifted his own cards and riffled the corners to let the pips flash before his eyes.

"She's open," said the man on the dealer's left, tossing a chip into the center of the table.

"Stay," grunted Hopalong, doing likewise in his turn.

A furtive face at the window, a message for Bradley, and a suddenly hostile bartender—and Johnny's herd was small, selected, and had a small outfit with it. Suspicions, suspicions, always suspicions! He bent his head, and then raised it quickly and looked at George before that person had time to iron out his countenance. From that instant Hopalong did not like George, and determined to keep an eye on him.

Bradley returned, slapped George on the shoulder and drew up to the table, watching the play. Not once did he look at Hopalong.

When the play came around to Hopalong it had been raised twice, and that person, studying his cards intently, suddenly looked over their tops and tossed them away. Bradley's expression changed a flash too late.

"They ain't runnin' for me," growled Hopalong, glancing from Bradley to George. "Game's gettin' tiresome, but I'll try a few more hands."

"Hell!" growled Bradley, affable and smiling again. "That ain't the trouble—the game's too small to hold a feller's interest."

"Right!" quickly said the house gambler, nodding emphatically as he sensed a kill. "Too tee-totally damn small! Let's play a round of jackpots to finish this up; an' then them that don't want to play for real money can't say they was throwed out cold."

"I'll set out the round of jacks an' come in on the new game," said Hopalong, risking quick glances around the room. No one seemed to be paying any particular attention to him.

"Me, too. No, I'll give you fellers a chance," said Bradley.

"Don't need to give me no chance," said a player across from him. "I'm ready for the big game."

Hopalong saw a young man push through the crowd near the door and head straight for the table. As he made his way down the room he was the cynosure of all eyes, and a ripple of whispered comment followed him. Hopalong did not know it, but the newcomer was a killer famous for his deeds around Trailville—a man who would kill for money, who had always "got" his man, and who was a close friend of Bradley's.

"Hello, Bill," the newcomer addressed Bradley, and then dropped into the chair which George surrendered to him as if he was expected to do so; and thereupon George moved toward the bar and was lost to sight.

Bradley nodded, smiled and faced the table again, gesturing with both hands.

"Riordan, meet Jim Hawes. Jim, Riordan's a stranger here."

The two men exchanged nods, sizing each other up. Hawes saw a typical cowpuncher, past middle age; but a man whose deeds rang from one edge of the cattle country to the other; a man whose reputation would greatly enhance that of anybody who managed to kill him with a gun in an even break. His mantle of fame would rest automatically upon the shoulders of his master.

Hopalong saw a vicious-faced killer, cold, unemotional, and of almost tender years. There was a swagger in his every movement and one could easily see that he was an important individual. The young man's eyes were rather close together, and his chin receded. To Hopalong, both of these characteristics were danger marks. He had found, in his own experience, that the prognathous jaw is greatly overrated. Hawes reminded him of a weasel.

"Haven't had a game for a long time," said Hawes, speaking with almost pugnacious assurance. "Reckon I'll set in an' give her a whirl."

"She's goin' to be a real one, Jim," said the house dealer uneasily. His profession, to his way of thinking, called for a little trickery with the cards upon occasion; but with Jim Hawes in the game only an adept would dare attempt it; not so much that Hawes was capable of detecting fine work, but because he would shoot with as little compunction as a rattler strikes.

"I like 'em big; the bigger the better," boasted Hawes,

his cold eyes on Hopalong. "What you say, Riordan?" he asked, and the way he said the words made them a challenge. It appeared that his humor was not a pleasant one tonight.

"I'd rather have 'em growed up," replied Hopalong, looking him in the eyes, "*Well* growed up," amended Hopalong, his gaze unswerving.

Somewhere in the room a snicker sounded, quickly hushed as Hawes glanced toward the sound. The room had grown considerably quieter, ears functioning instead of tongues, and this, in itself, was a hint to an observing man. Hawes' gaze was back again like a flash, and he kept it set on the stranger's face while he slowly, with his left hand, drew his chair closer to the table, in the space provided for him by Bradley. He, too, sensed the quiet of the room, and a tight, knowing smile wreathed his thin lips.

"We'll make it growed up enough for you, Mister Riordan," he said, his left hand now drawing a roll of bills from a pocket. "How's five, an' twenty?" he challenged.

"Cents or dollars," curiously asked Hopalong, his face expressionless.

Hawes flushed, but checked the fighting words before they reached his teeth.

"What makes *you* reckon it might be cents?" he demanded, triumphantly.

"Just had a feelin' that it might be," calmly answered Hopalong. "Either one is a waste of time.

Bradley raised his eyebrows, regarding the speaker intently.

"Yeah?" he softly inquired. "How do you grade a growed-up game?"

"It all depends who I'm playin' with," answered Hopalong, his eyes on Hawes' tense face.

"Five an' fifty—*dollars!*" snapped the youth, showing his teeth.

"She's improvin' with every word," chuckled the house player.

"Damn near of age, anyhow," said Hopalong, nodding "Straight draw poker? Threes, straights, flushes, an' so forth? No fancy hands?"

"The same game we have been playin'," said the house player. "Jackpots after full houses, or better. That suit everybody?"

Silence gave consent, the chips were redeemed at the old figure, deftly stacked and counted by the house player, and resold at the new prices. Hopalong drew out a roll of dirty bills, peeled off two of them, and with them bought a thousand dollars' worth of chips. He placed the remainder of the roll on the table near the chips, and nodded at it.

"When that's gone, I'm busted," he said, and looked at Hawes.

"Oh, don't worry! There's mine," sneered the youth, and bought the same amount of counters. Inwardly he thrilled; in so steep a game, cheating would be a great temptation to anyone inclined that way; and a crooked play would be justification for what followed it, and would suit him as well as any other excuse.

The player who had announced that he was ready for the bigger game now raised both hands toward heaven, pushed back his chair, and motioned grandiloquently toward the table; but no one in the room cared to take his place: the game was far too steep for them, and they sensed a deadly atmosphere.

"Quittin' us, Frank?" asked Bradley, with a knowing grin.

"Cold an' positive! My money comes harder than your'n, Bradley; an' I ain't got near as much of it. No, sir! I'll get all the excitement I'll need, just settin' back an' watchin' the play."

He had been sitting on Hopalong's left, and when he withdrew from the game, he pulled his chair back from the table, and now he drew it farther out of the way. Hopalong shifted in that direction, to even up the spacing; but as he stopped, he sensed Bradley's nearness, and saw that the latter had moved after him, but too far. Bradley's impetus had carried him even closer to Hopalong than he had been before. Bradley smiled apologetically and moved back, but only for a few inches. The fleeting expression on Hawes' face revealed satisfaction, and dressed the blundering shift with intent. What intent? In Hopalong's mind there could be only one; and that one, deadly.

The game got under way, and it was different from the more or less innocent affair which had preceded it. It was different in more ways than one. In the first place there was now present a thinly veiled hostility, an atmosphere of danger. In the second, a man could bluff with more assurance; a player would think twice before he would toss in fifty dollars to call a hand when he, himself, held little. In the third, a clever card manipulator would be tempted to make use of his best mastered tricks of sleight of hand; and should any man call for a new deck, or palm the old one for a moment, it would be well to give thought to the possible substitution of a cold deck. Here was the kind of a game Hopalong could enjoy; he had cut his teeth on them, and had been given excellent instruction by a past master of the game. Tex Ewalt had pronounced him proficient.

The first few hands were more in the nature of skirmishes, for with the change in the stakes had come a change in the style of play. Hopalong's fingers were calloused, but the backs of his fingers were not; and he now bunched his cards in his left hand, face to the palm, and let the backs of the fingers of his right hand brush gently down the involved patterns, searching for pin pricks. As the cards were dealt to him, Hopalong idly pushed them about on the table, to get a different slant of lamplight on each one. If the polish had been removed by abrasives or acids the reflected light would show it.

At last came a jackpot, and it was passed three times, growing greatly in the process. The house player picked up the cards to deal, shuffling them swiftly, and ruffled them together with both hands hiding them. He pushed the deck toward Hopalong for the cut, in such a manner that if the latter chose the easier and more natural movement, he would cut with his nearest, or left, hand. If he did this, his fingers would naturally grasp the sides of the deck, and not the ends; and if the cards were trimmed, such a cut might well be costly.

As the dealer took his hand off the deck, Hopalong let his left hand reach for his cigarette; and it being thus occupied, and quite innocently so, he reached across his body with the idle right and quite naturally picked up the upper part of the deck by the ends. The dealer showed just the slightest indication of annoyance at this loss of time, and, finding Hopalong's bland gaze on the cards, forewent switching the cut, and dealt them as they lay.

Hawes opened for ten dollars. Bradley saw and raised it only five. Hopalong qualified. The dealer saw, and Hawes saw Bradley's raise, and boosted the limit. The others dropped out. Hawes showed his openers and took the pot. As the play went on, Hopalong observed a strange coincidence. The ante was five dollars; the limit, fifty. Every time that Hawes opened for ten dollars, and Bradley raised it five, or Bradley opened for ten, and Hawes raised it five, the opener thereupon boosted the limit when his time came, and very often dropped out on the next round to let the other win. Here was team work: Hawes and Bradley vs. all.

Hopalong glanced inquiringly at the house player, and caught an almost imperceptible wink directed at himself. There was no need for these two men to go into conference where teamwork was concerned; they knew how to join forces without previous agreements. And now, teamwork was called for as a matter of self-preservation.

The play went on without much action, and Hawes picked up the cards, bunching them for the deal. He was not an expert, and a dozen men in the room saw the clumsy switch, and held their breaths; but nothing violent happened. Apparently the other three players had not seen anything of interest. Bradley opened for ten dollars. Hopalong, looking at his cards, saw three kings and a pair of tens. He passed, and smiled inwardly at the dealer's poorly concealed look of amazement. The house player saw, but when both Hawes and Bradley had raised the limit in turn, he threw his hand in the discard and watched Bradley take the pot by default.

Hopalong, toying idly with his cards, now looked at them again, and swore loudly and bitterly.

"Damn fool! I thought it was two pairs . . . Will you *look* at *that?*"

Hopalong's outspread cards revealed their true worth, and the house player chuckled deep in his throat, his eyes beaming with congratulations.

"Pat king full," he said. "Well, Riordan, it can be beat."

"It can," admitted Hopalong, trying to smile. For an instant the two men looked understandingly into each other's eyes.

There was now no question about the status of this game. Both Hopalong and the house player had seen the clumsy switch; and it had been followed by a pat king full. The bars were now down and the rules were up. It was just a case of outcheating cheaters, and the devil take the less adept.

On Bradley's deal Hawes took another small pot by default, and Hopalong picked up the cards. His big hands moved swiftly, his fingers flicking almost in a blur of speed. The house player watched him, and then, curiously, against his habit, picked up each card as it fell in front of him. Seven, five, eight, and six of hearts. The fifth card seemed to intrigue him greatly: with it he would get the measure of a dexterous player's real mentality; and he hoped desperately that he would not have to play a pat hand. He sighed, picked up the card, and saw the jack of clubs. For a moment he regarded the dealer thoughtfully, and almost affectionately, and then he swiftly made up his mind. He would risk one play for the sake of knowledge. He opened for a white chip.

Hawes saw, and raised a red. Bradley stayed. Hopalong dropped out. The house player saw, and raised a blue, a true mark of confidence in a stranger's dealing ability; and almost before the chips had struck the table, Hawes saw and raised the limit. Bradley stayed, and the house player, rubbing his chin thoughtfully, evened it up, and asked for one card. He looked at it and turned it over, face up on the table. It was the four of hearts.

"Thanks," he said, nodding to Hopalong. "I needed that. It costs fifty dollars to play with me," he said to the others.

Hawes thought swiftly. As a heart, the cards would fill a flush; as a four spot, it would build up three of a kind, a straight, a full house or four of a kind. Had it been a jack he would have hesitated; but now he tried to hide his elation, and tossed in a hundred dollars to see and to raise. Bradley sighed and dropped out.

"You took two cards," murmured the house player thoughtfully. "Mebby—mebby you got another; but I doubt it. She's up ag'in."

"Once more," said Hawes, his eyes glinting.

"Well, it's my business to know a bluff when I see one," said the house player, studying his adversary. "It's my best judgment that you . . . Well, anyhow, I'll back it, Hawes, an' boost her once more."

"*Gracias!*" laughed Hawes, a little tensely. "When I went to school a four spot was a right small card. See you, an' raise ag'in."

"An' once more."

"Ag'in."

"Once more."

"Ag'in."

"An' once more," said the house player. "I allus like to play a hand like this clean to the end. They're right scarce."

Suddenly Hawes had a disturbing suspicion. Could it

be that his opponent had held four of a kind pat? He, himself, had thrown away an ace and a queen. That left two possible high fours: kings or jacks. He looked at his own cards, and decided that he had pressed them for all they were worth.

"Then show it to me!" he growled, calling.

"It's the gambler's prayer," said the house player, laying down his cards slowly and one by one. The five of hearts joined the face-up four; then the six, and then the seven. He looked calmly over the top of the last card, holding it close to his face; and then, sighing, placed it where it belonged, and dropped both hands under the edge of the table.

"Straight flush," he said calmly.

Hawes flushed and then went pale. Both of his hands were on the table, while the house player's were out of sight. He swore in his throat and started to toss his cards into the discard, but the house player checked him.

"It's a showdown, Hawes. I paid as much to see your hand as you paid to see mine. Turn 'em over."

Hawes obeyed, slamming the cards viciously, and four pleasant ten-spots lay in orderly array.

"Hard luck for a man to git a hand like that at the wrong time," said the winner.

He drew in the chips and picked up the cards. A thought passed through his mind: when playing with keen, smart men, a foolish play will often win. In such a case, two successive bluffs often pay dividends. The house player chuckled in his throat.

"Jacks to open this one," the house player—it was his deal—announced as Hopalong cut. It pleased him to see the way in which Hopalong followed the natural way to cut the deck, and lifted it by the sides; but it only showed confidence, because the dealer wanted no cut at all, and switched it perfectly as he took it up again. In what he was about to do, he would accomplish two things: he would return a favor, and also help Hawes into the situation the latter had been looking for. To make plain his own innocence in the matter, he talked while he dealt.

"The art of cuttin' cards is a fine one," he said. "You hear a lot about slick dealin', but hardly a word about slick cuttin'. That's because it's mighty rare. Why, once I knowed a feller that could cut . . . Oh, well. I'll tell that story after the hand is played."

But it so happened that the house player never told that lie.

Hawes passed. Bradley opened for ten. Hopalong stayed, and the dealer dropped out. Hawes raised it five, and Bradley tossed in a blue and a white chip, seeing, and raising the limit. Hopalong leveled up and added another blue. Hawes dropped out. Bradley studied his hand and saw. He drew two cards and Hopalong took one. The latter would have been very much surprised if he had been disappointed, for he had detected the switched cut. Bradley pushed out a blue chip, and Hopalong saw and raised another. Bradley pushed in two, and Hopalong two more. Back and forth it went, time after time.

Hawes leaned over and looked at Bradley's hand. He studied Hopalong a moment, and gave thought to the straight flush he had just had the misfortune to call. Straight flushes do not come two in a row—at least, that was so in his experience. He leaned forward, his left hand resting on his piled chips.

"Side bet, Riordan?" he inquired sneeringly.

"How much?" asked Hopalong, a little nervously.

"How much you got?" snapped Hawes.

"Plenty."

"Huh! Dollars, or *cents?*" sneered Hawes, quoting an unpleasant phrase.

"Dollars. Lemme see. Five, ten, fifteen, twenty, twenty-five, thirty, thirty-five, forty, forty-one, two, three, four, five, six—forty-six hundred, leavin' me ham an' aig money. You scared?"

"Scared hell!" snapped Hawes. He counted his own resources, found them greatly short, and looked inquiringly at Bradley. "Lend me the difference?" he asked.

Bradley nodded, and beckoned to the head bartender.

"Give Hawes what he needs, an' put a memo in the safe," he ordered.

In a few moments the game went on, the side bets lying apart from the pot. Then Bradley, grinning triumphantly, raised the limit again, certain that Riordan did not have money enough left to meet it. It was a sucker trick, but sometimes it worked.

Hopalong looked at him curiously, hesitated, went through his pockets, and then turned a worried face to his adversary.

"Anybody in the room lend me fifty dollars?" he asked, loudly; and not a voice replied. Hawes' malignant gaze had swept the crowd and held it silent. Not a man dared to comply with the request.

"Is that the way you win yore pots, Bradley?" asked Hopalong coldly.

"I've raised you. Call or quit."

Hopalong's right hand dug down into a pocket, and he laughed nastily as he dropped a fifty-dollar bill on top of the chips in the center of the table.

"What you got, tin-horn?" he asked.

"I got the gambler's second prayer," chuckled Bradley, exposing four aces, and reaching for the pot.

"But I got the first," grunted Hopalong. "Same little run of hearts that we saw before."

For a moment there was an utter silence, and then came a blur of speed from Hawes, but just the instant before it came, Bradley fell off his chair to the left, his own left arm falling across Hopalong's right forearm, blocking a draw; but other men had discovered, when too late, that Hopalong's left hand was the better of the two. The double roar seemed to bend the walls, and sent the lamp flames leaping, to flicker almost to extinction.

One went out, the other two recovered. The smoke thinned to show Hawes sliding from his chair, and Bradley on the floor where he had fallen by his own choice, with both hands straining at the Mexican spur which spiked his cheek.

The two leveled Colts held the crowd frozen in curious postures. Hands were raised high, or held out well away from belts. Hopalong backed to the wall, his left-hand gun still smoking. He felt the wall press against him, and then he nodded swiftly to the house player.

"You had a hell of a lot to say about the cut, after you switched it! Now, let's see what you know about a *draw!*" As Hopalong spoke, he shoved both guns into their sheaths, and slowly crossed his arms.

The gambler made no move, scarcely daring to breathe. He still doubted his senses.

"All right, then. Get out, an' stay out!" ordered Hopalong, and as the house player passed through the door, another man came in; a man unsteady on his feet, and covered with sweat and dust and blood.

The newcomer leaned against the bar for a moment, his gaze searching the room; and as he saw his old friend, Hopalong Cassidy, his old friend recognized him. It was Johnny Nelson.

"Hoppy!" he called, joyously.

"Johnny! What's up?"

"They rushed us in the dark, an' shot all of us up. Not seriously, but we're out of action. They got every head—near two hundred!"

Johnny Nelson's gaze wavered, rested for an instant on the open window to one side of his friend, and across the room from him; and, vague and unsteady as he was, he yielded to the gunman's instinct. His right hand dropped, and twisted up like a flash to the top of the holster, and the crash of his shot became a scream in the night outside the open window. George had lost his hundred-dollar fee—and with it, his life.

"Pullin' down on you, from the dark, Hoppy; but I got the skunk," muttered Johnny. He leaned against the bar again and took the whisky which an ingratiating bartender placed under his nose. "They got 'em all. Hoppy—near two hundred head."

Hopalong had his back to the wall again, both guns out and raised for action.

"Good kid!" he called. "I just made a trade with the fellers that stole your cattle. They can keep the steers, and we'll keep the poker winnin's I made by outcheating them two cheaters. Two hundred head at near thirty dollars apiece, kid—which gives you a bigger profit, an' saves you twelve hundred miles of trailin'. Watch the room, kid." He raised his hand. "Bartender, cash in them chips at five, ten an' fifty. *Pronto!*"

It did not take long to turn the counters into money, and Hopalong, backing past the table and toward his capable friend, picked up his winnings, jammed them into a pocket, and slowly reached the stair door.

"It's a tight corner, kid," said Hopalong crisply. "But yo're in no shape to ride. Up them stairs, in front of me." He stepped aside for his friend to pass, and then he stepped back again, his foot feeling for the first tread. His gaze flicked about the room, and he smiled thinly.

"My name's Cassidy," he said, and the smile now twisted his hard face. "My friends call me Hopalong. When I go to bed, I go to sleep. Any objections?"

The spellbound silence was broken by murmurs of surprise. Several faces showed quick friendliness, and a man in a far corner slowly got to his feet.

"An old friend of your'n is a right good friend of mine, Cassidy," he said, glancing slowly and significantly around the room. "Anybody that can't wait for daylight will taste my lead. Good night, you old hoss-thief!"

"Good night, friend," said Hopalong. The door slowly closed, and the crowd listened to the accented footsteps of a slightly lame, red-haired gentleman who made his unhurried way upward.

The man in the corner licked his lips and looked slowly around again.

"An' I meant what I said," he announced, and s~~ down to find his glass refilled.

SUNSET

by W. C. Tuttle

I

A YEAR and a half is a long time for a letter to lay in a post-office. But this one had no return address, and the postmaster felt sure that some day Cultus Collins would come back to Cuyamac. It was a simple little note, which read:

Dear Cultus:
  Our first baby, a boy, came two weeks ago, and we have named him after you.

                    Love from
                    Jack and Mary Neal

And that was the main reason why Cultus Collins was this day riding down the twisting grades, which led to Santa Carmelita. Under his left arm was a woolly elephant, the wrappings almost entirely worn away, and tied to the back of his saddle were a toy drum and a little red wagon.

Collins was several inches over six feet in height, bronzed as an Indian, with a long, gaunt face. Men said that he had the face of a gargoyle and the smile of a saint. He was long of arm, bony of wrist and big of hand. His faded shirt seemed molded to his muscular torso. His huge, bat-wing chaps were weathered and patched, as

were his belt and holster; and the big, black-handled
Colt in his holster was shiny from use.

His horse, a tall, gaunt, smoke-gray animal, with a
snakelike head, traveled with a swinging walk; a tireless,
venomous-looking brute, which Cultus called "Amigo."

They were well known along the Border, these two;
and more than once had a price been placed on the head
of Cultus Collins. To the harassed Border Patrol, piti-
fully small for the great length of Border they tried to
guard, he was a godsend; but to those outside the law he
was a distinct menace.

Now he came swinging down the twisting road to
Santa Carmelita with no thought in his mind, except to
see the only child that had ever been named after him.
He wondered if they called the baby Cultus, or Collins.
Few people ever knew that Cultus was merely a nick-
name bestowed by an Indian tribe in the Northwest. In
the Chinook jargon, an old trade language, the word *cultus* means something that is very bad.

Two Indians of that tribe had stolen a horse from Cultus, who had followed them to their village. There had
been six Indians at the trading post, when he arrived.
Knowing that two of them were guilty, but not knowing
which two, and not being able to talk their language, he
whipped all six of them and took his horse. The nick-
name had been fairly earned.

Santa Carmelita was a small Border town, more Mexican than American in architecture. The one street of the
town was crooked and dusty. Many of the houses had
balconies, which projected over the hard-trodden paths,
used instead of sidewalks.

Cultus tied Amigo to a long hitch-rack near the Mexicana Cantina, hung the woolly elephant on his saddle-
horn, and headed for the doorway. There were three
other horses at the rack. Cultus stopped short at the
doorway, staring at the tableau inside the place.

Two men were in front of the bar; the bartender was

behind the bar. Seated behind a card table, directly behind the two men at the bar, was the fourth man. The man, whose back was toward Cultus, had a gun in his right hand, the muzzle trained on the middle of the man in front of him, and this man had his hands shoulder-high, watching his captor with alert eyes. The bartender had backed against the backbar, his face registering apprehension and alarm.

Slowly the man with the gun reached back with his left hand and drew a pair of handcuffs from a hip-pocket. The man behind the table was moving slowly, reaching cautiously for his gun. Cultus' eyes narrowed. He did not know this man, but he had recognized the two men at the bar as Dave Selby, sheriff from Cuyamac, and Pat Eagan, a well-known badman.

"Let down yore hands and stick 'em out, Eagan," ordered the sheriff. Eagan's eyes flashed to the big man behind the table. Directly in front of the man behind the table was a cigar-box full of poker-chips.

Cultus saw the man draw his gun, but before he could lift it above the level of the table, Cultus drew and fired a forty-five slug square into the box of chips, which seemed to fairly explode almost in the man's face. He flung himself backwards and sideways.

The startled sheriff jerked back, taking his eyes off Eagan for a moment, and in that moment Eagan reached for his gun. Eagan was a flash with a gun, but as his hand smacked against the butt of his holstered gun, Cultus shifted his aim, shot so close to the sheriff that the bullet scored along the flare of his chaps, and smashed into Eagan's holster, knocking the gun out of his hand.

It was over in a matter of split seconds. Eagan nursing a numb hand and wrist, and the other man, sagged sideways in his chair, gun dangling against the floor. Several chips had evidently hit him full in the face, judging from a cut nose and one eye, which was rapidly swelling and turning purple.

"Yuh better handcuff that feller, Dave," drawled Cultus, and the sheriff hastened to obey. Then he turned and looked at Cultus, clinging to the arm of Eagan.

"Right out of nowhere!" he snorted. "Thanks a lot, Cultus."

"Don't mention it, Dave. Hyah, Eagan."

"Go to hell," snarled the prisoner.

"Thank yuh," smiled Cultus, and turned to the other man, who had holstered his gun and was wiping his bleeding nose.

"Jist about who are you?" asked Cultus.

"That's some more of my business," replied the man. He was a big man of middle age, with a hard face and small, monkeylike, slaty eyes.

"Is he a friend of yours, Eagan?" asked the sheriff.

"You can't put no deadwood onto him," replied the prisoner.

"I don't *think* I want him," said the sheriff. "At least, not this time."

The man evidently thought that silence was the proper thing, because he shut his thin lips and leaned back in his chair.

"How on earth did you happen here at the right time, Cultus?" asked the grateful sheriff.

"They say I do things like that," grinned Cultus.

"They're right. But you've been away so long that—well, it was kinda uncanny. What brings yuh back here, Cultus?"

"A baby," grinned Cultus. "A son was born to Jack and Mary Neal a year and a half ago. I got the letter yesterday in Cuyamac, in which they tell me they named the baby after me. Can yuh imagine that? Dave, I've got to see that kid."

"Well, I'll bet yuh have! I ain't never seen the kid myself."

"What have yuh got on our friend Eagan?"

"Oh, a little matter of murderin' a feller in Yuma six months ago. This is the first time I've sighted him since. They tell me he's been hibernatin' across the Border with a gang knowed as the Rhein outfit. This here Rhein has served twice, and they tell me he's a *mucho malo hombre*. What about it, Eagan?"

"Find out," growled the prisoner, and added, "You'll have a sweet time tryin' to convict me."

"The word of a dyin' man goes a long ways with a jury, Eagan."

"Dyin', hell! He never lived—"

The sheriff laughed softly. "I may have to subpoena you, Cultus, to testify to that slip of the tongue."

"Anythin' that's right, Dave. How about a little drink?"

"I think we've got it comin'—on me."

The sheriff turned to the man behind the table.

"Have a little drink with us, stranger?"

"Sorry, but I'm not drinkin'," he replied ungraciously.

Eagan was not particular. He managed to handle his drink with his manacled hands, but looked gloomily at himself in the fly-specked mirror.

"Well, Eagan, I reckon we better start back for Cuyamac," said the sheriff. "It's a long ride."

The man got to his feet and sauntered toward the doorway.

"You ain't goin' out—not yet," said Cultus "Don't forget that you had a gun out a while ago—and the sheriff gets a long head-start."

The man scowled thoughtfully, looked at the three men, but went back to his chair. The sheriff shook hands with Cultus, and went out with his prisoner while Cultus leaned on the bar. The man sat there, idly arranging some of the broken poker-chips, but he finally looked up at Cultus.

"I've heard that you are a great hand to not mind yore own business," he said coldly.

"So you've heard of me, eh?" smiled Cultus. "Well?"

"Yore own business don't pay yuh much, does it?"

"Plenty of satisfaction."

"That's about all that nosey folks ever git out of life."

"What's yore business?"

"Mindin' my own—mostly."

Cultus laughed at him. "Was it yore own business to shoot a sheriff in the back?"

"It jist happens that I didn't shoot him."

"Fate, I suppose. Prob'ly lucky yuh didn't. I'm touchy on folks shootin' men in the back. I figured that them chips would kinda annoy yuh enough to let yuh see the error of yore ways. After all, Pat Eagan is a bad boy."

The man fingered the chips thoughtfully. Then—

"They tell me that once upon a time a man named Gonzales put a price on yore head; and that you went into Mexico, took Gonzales away from his own gang and brought him over the line."

"Dragged him over by his own mustaches," corrected Cultus. "It was painful for Mr. Gonzales. In fact, his upper lip was still sore, when they hung him."

"And," continued the big man, "they say there is still a reward for yore scalp at a place called Mesquite."

"There was when I left down here," replied Cultus. "I never was able to find out who was goin' to pay it. They was scared I might come over and do a little collectin', like I did on Gonzales. I don't know if the reward is still open or not. I've been away a long time."

"Things got too warm for yuh down here, eh?"

"Got too dull. Every *contrabandista* in the country quit and went farmin', I guess."

"I see. About how long do yuh reckon I better stay here, in order to give the sheriff plenty of room?"

"Oh, you can go now, if yuh want to. Dave rides fast."

"Thank you very much."

"But I wouldn't ride too fast—not north."

"Yo're takin' quite a lot upon yourself, ain't yuh, Collins?"

"Well, I ain't bein' unreasonable, do yuh think?"

"No, I suppose it's all right. Well, *adiós*, Collins; I

hope to see yuh again, while yo're down here, lookin' at babies."

The man walked out, mounted a horse and went west, traveling slowly.

Cultus turned to the bartender, Felipe.

"Do yuh know that *hombre*, Felipe?"

"I don't know hees name," replied the bartender. "I'm see heem only once biffore."

"He came here with Eagan, didn't he?"

"*Sí*—weeth Eagan. Mebbe they 'ang Eagan, eh?"

"*Quien sabe?* Well, *hasta luego*, Felipe."

"*Vaya con Dios*, Senor Collins."

"Yes," smiled Cultus, as he untied Amigo. "Go with God—and you'll help plot a way to send me out on a hot bullet, Felipe."

Cultus' destination was the Running W Rancho, located about three miles east of Santa Carmelita. The Running W was owned by Dan Welch, stepfather of Jack Neal; and Jack Neal had been the foreman, when Cultus had left the Border country.

As the tall gray horse shuffled along the dusty road, several big steers came out of the brush, driven by two riders who saw Cultus and drew up to wait for him. They were Whitey Higgins and Pete Rosales, two of the Running W cowboys. Higgins was a short, chunky person, with a pock-marked face and a livid scar across one cheek. Rosales was a mixture of Mexican and Yaqui.

"Where the hell did you come from?" asked Higgins, as he spat a stream of tobacco juice past the left ear of his horse.

"Hello, Whitey," grinned Cultus. "How are you, Pete?"

"Oh, *poco bueno*," replied the grinning breed.

"What the hell yuh got there?" asked Higgins. "Toy elephant?"

"Shore. Got a drum and a wagon, too."

"*San Nicolas?*" grinned Pete.

"No Santa Claus," replied Cultus. "How's things at the Runnin' W these days?"

"Oh, we keep busy," replied Whitey. "Not a whole lot doin'. Yuh see, the price of beef went all to the devil. In fact, it wouldn't pay to ship 'em. Hides wasn't worth yankin' off the critters."

"Everythin' has been kinda quiet, I reckon."

"Shore has," replied Whitey. "Where you been all this time?"

"Wyomin' and Nevada—kinda driftin' around."

"How's things up thataway for a cow hand, Collins?"

"Not so good—unless yuh want to herd sheep."

Whitey spat disgustedly.

"Thank yuh—not for me. Anyway, it gets too cold up there."

"Een Wyoming ees w'ere they 'ave geezard," said Pete wisely. "My cousin he ees on those places and hees say that een weenter they 'ave mos' awful geezard."

"Shore," agreed Cultus soberly, fingering the woolly elephant. "Yuh see, I'm takin' these things to Jack Neal's baby. I jist found out the other day that they named the kid after me."

Pete and Whitey exchanged glances. Whitey eased himself in his saddle, spat reflectively and looked curiously at Cultus.

"You was aimin' to find the Neals at the Runnin' W?"

"Yeah—of course."

Whitey shook his head. "They ain't there."

"No?"

"Ain't been there for a year. Jack had a run-in with the Old Man, and moved his family out to that old Ramirez place. The road forks down here a ways, and his place is a couple miles north."

"Had trouble with the old man, eh?"

"Yeah—with Welch. I reckon Welch throwed him out."

"Shucks, that's too bad. How are they makin' it?"

"Not too good, I don't guess."

"I'm sorry to hear it," said Cultus slowly. They had moved in close to the slow-moving steers, and Rosales slashed at a straggler with a rope end. They were all Hereford strain, huge white-faced animals. One of them had a white mark on its right side, like a swastika, with one point missing.

They reached the fork of the road and Cultus turned north.

"Tell Welch I might run out and see him," said Cultus.

"Shore will," replied Higgins. "You goin' to be down here long?"

"*Quien sabe?*" replied Cultus. "Who knows?"

"I'll tell him," nodded Higgins, and they went on with their dozen steers.

II

Cultus found the Neals at home, and they welcomed him warmly. He could see at a glance that they were far from prosperous. It was an old rancho, almost a ruin. Mary Neal was as pretty as ever, but her smiles could not cover the brooding sadness in her eyes. Jack looked many years older, more serious. The baby boy was a jewel, with a wide grin and a gurgle for this strange man, who held him so tenderly in his muscular hands.

"We call him Collie," explained Jack. "Collins seems too darn dignified for a little feller like him."

"No matter what yuh call him—he's a dinger," grinned Cultus. "But how are the both of yuh? I ran into Whitey and Pete this side of town, and they showed me how to find this place."

"You thought we were still at the Running W?" asked Mary.

"You was there the last time I seen yuh, Mary."

She nodded wearily. "We've been here about a year, Cultus."

Cultus sat down on the porch, with the baby cooing in his arms, and asked them what had happened at the Running W.

"Kicked out," replied Jack glumly. "By rights, part of the Runnin' W belongs to me, Cultus. You see, before my mother died, Dan Welch got her to sign over her half of the property to him. She was in bad health, and I doubt if she realized what she was doin'. She didn't leave any will, because she didn't have anythin' to leave.

"I got along with Dan Welch all right for several years. I was his foreman when you was here before. Well, he got to gamblin' and drinkin', the price of beef went down—and all that. Mary and I got married, and everythin' was goin' along all right, when Welch got to hob-nobbin' around with a bunch from the other side of the line. He took a likin' for a feller named Eagan, who hung around the Runnin' W. I felt that Eagan wasn't much good—jist a driftin' gunman. But I didn't bother him, until—" Jack's jaw muscles tightened.

"Well, he got to annoyin' Mary. I wouldn't stand for that, Cultus. I didn't want to have trouble with Eagan; so I went to Welch and explained things to him. He laughed at me, and said I couldn't blame Eagan for likin' Mary's looks."

Jack drew a deep breath and began rolling a cigarette.

"Well?" queried Cultus softly.

"I hit Dan Welch square in the nose and knocked him down. Then I went down to the corral, told Eagan what I had done, and told him to rattle his hocks out of the country. Eagan reached for his gun and I shot him through the arm. They took him to a doctor at Santa Carmelita and had his arm fixed up, and he pulled out."

"And Welch kicked yuh out, eh?"

"That's right. I understand that Eagan is wanted on a murder charge."

"The sheriff got him today," said Cultus, and then told them what happened in the Mexicana Cantina.

"Good stuff!" exclaimed Jack. "But how lucky it was

that you showed up. Eagan wouldn't hesitate to kill the sheriff. But what sort of a lookin' feller was the other one?"

Cultus was able to give Jack a minute description.

"Duke Rhein!" exclaimed Jack. "That's who it was, Cultus."

"The leader of the Rhein gang, eh?"

"Just as sure as yo're alive! They say he's a snake. I saw him, when he first came here. Whitey Higgins knew him, and told me who he was. He served two terms in the pen."

"Does the law want him?" asked Cultus.

"No, I don't think they've got any deadwood on him right now."

"It seems to me," said Mary softly, "that you've done your part along the Border."

Cultus shook his head slowly. "Not until I'm unable to set on a horse and pull a trigger on the devils that bring poison into this country have I done my part."

Mary and Jack knew why Cultus was so bitter against the drug traffic. Cultus' sister, the only living relative, as far as he knew, whom Cultus had been supporting in a Los Angeles school, had contracted the drug habit; and he had found her in Yuma, a hopeless addict. Before she had died she had told him how the dope peddlers sold it among the students, building up a profitable business.

Up to that time Cultus, a wild-riding cowboy and plunging gambler, had given no thought to such things. He had sent his sister nearly all his earnings and winnings. She was the only thing on earth that he loved; and after he had heard her story and then buried her, he had lived and worked only to smash drug runners. And to "smash" them did not mean to even try to put them behind the bars

"I talked with some of the Border Patrol the other day," said Jack. "They say that the smugglers have been inactive a long time. They don't think the stuff is comin' across at all any more."

"I wish it was true," said Cultus. "But there's the Rhein gang. Yuh see, I didn't come down here to meddle with things. I jist got a hankerin' to drop down here and look around. Then I got yore letter, and I jist had to see you two—and this here tike."

"Can you stay a while?" asked Mary eagerly.

"Mary," he replied dryly, "I'm still the only boss I've got."

"We ain't got much," said Jack, "but it's yours, Cultus."

"Thank yuh, Jack; but I don't aim to burden anybody. We'll stock up the kitchen and then set around, while Mary cooks things."

Cultus poked a long finger playfully at the baby, who gurgled with delight.

"Daw-w-w-gone!" breathed Cultus. "I wish I knowed whether he's laughin' at me or with me. Anyway, he's laughin'—and I don't care a hang."

III

Three miles below the Border, and directly south of Santa Carmelita, was the Ruiz Rancho, owned by Juan Ruiz. At least, he claimed it. Ruiz had been a leader in an ill-fated revolution; so he quit public life, took over this rancho, which he had raided, and became a cattle raiser. The rancho was a picturesque old place, well isolated and also well guarded against a casual visitor.

Not long after Cultus reached the Neal place, Duke Rhein rode in, tossed his reins to a Yaqui, and strode into the main building, where he found Juan Ruiz, Tecate Charley, a Chinaman, Bill Tell and Bert Flowers playing draw-poker. Ruiz was a fat Mexican with flowing mustaches and an exalted idea of his own importance. Tecate Charley was well-known as a procurer of diamonds, a smart gambler, and a man who knew all the tricks of those men who use the Border as a source of revenue.

Tell and Flowers were gunmen, wanted on the north

side of the line. Although Rhein was leader here, none of them paid any attention to his entrance into the place. He came up to the table and watched the playing of one pot, which was won by Tecate Charley.

"That cleans me," said Tell, grinning sourly. "Where's Eagan? He owes me twenty dollars."

"Eagan is on his way to Cuyamac," said Rhein coldly. "The sheriff got him in Santa Carmelita."

"The hell he did!" exclaimed Tell. "Got him, eh? Couldn't you—"

"Wait a minute," interrupted Rhein. "Here's what happened."

In a few terse words he told of what happened in the Mexicana Cantina.

"Collins, eh?" said Tecate Charley. His English was flawless.

"The son-of-a-gun's back!" grunted Tell. "I hoped he'd never come back again. Where's that bottle, Juan? I need a drink."

"Never mind the liquor," said Rhein. "I want Collins. He's gone out to visit Jack Neal—and I want him."

"We could easy pot him over there," said Flowers. "I know that place. We could—"

"I don't want him potted; I want him alive."

"I'll pass," said Bill Tell quickly. Rhein looked at him. "Scared?" he asked sarcastically.

"Superstitious," replied Tell. "No, it's perfectly all right, Duke. Go ahead and take him alive; I'd like to see it done."

"Something must be done," said Tecate thoughtfully. "That man *is* dangerous. No, I'm not over-rating him, Duke. I was mixed up in a diamond deal that he busted up, and it cost me thirty thousand dollars. I know of several other deals that he busted up that cost fortunes— and lives were lost. He is more dangerous than a dozen men."

"I want him alive," said Rhein slowly. "Alive and well."

"He shore marked you up, Duke," said Tell. "But from the way I see it, yo're lucky he didn't shoot at you, instead of that box of chips. And I'll give yuh a little tip —don't never try to beat him on the draw."

"He's fast, is he?" growled Rhein.

"I don't know, 'cause he never drawed on me."

"Then what the hell do you know about his speed with a gun?"

"The only thing I know is that he's still alive; and the men who tried to beat him—ain't. While you're the boss of this gang you can give certain orders; but don'tcha ever order me to go over the line and take that horse-faced panther alive, 'cause I ain't goin'."

"How about you, Flowers—scared, too?" queried Rhein.

"Yeah," nodded Flowers dryly. "I ain't lost no Cultus Collins."

"Well, I'm goin' to git him," declared Rhein angrily. "No man can do what he done to me today and get away with it. I'm not scared."

"We'll have to quit operations, until he goes away," said Tecate. "We've got the greatest scheme for sending stuff across that has ever been used—but—"

"We're not goin' to quit!" snapped Rhein angrily. "The stuff goes across. Do you think I'm goin' to let one man scare *me*? I've heard all about this feller, and he's jist lucky, that's all. His luck can't hold good all the time. What do you think, Ruiz?"

The big Mexican shrugged his shoulders.

"Eet mus' 'urt like hell to be drag' by the mustache," he replied.

"I've got a fine lot of helpers," snarled Rhein angrily.

"Look at it thisaway," suggested Tell. "If he had hit *me* with that handful of poker chips, would you risk yore hide to drag him over here for me to have revenge?"

"We'll drop the personal side of it," replied Rhein. "Do you want him to kill the goose that's been layin' the golden eggs for us?"

"When he starts shootin' at my goose, I'll try to protect her," replied Tell dryly.

"Don't forget that he's responsible for Eagan bein' in
the hands of the law."

"Eagan was a fool," said Flowers. "He knew he was
wanted over there. Anyway, it makes one less on the
split."

"And one less gun for protection. What do you think
about it, Charley?"

Tecate Charley smiled thinly. He was no gunman

"I would wait a while," he said thoughtfully. "Perhaps
this man is only here for a few days. We have been
quietly successful, and our organization has worked perfectly. Forget Eagan and forget Cultus Collins. Let Collins make the first move. And if he does, I believe I have
a scheme to stop him."

"What is it?" asked Rhein anxiously.

"I'll tell you—when we need it. Who dealt that last
hand?"

IV

The next morning Jack Neal went to Santa Carmelita,
and Cultus was down at the little blacksmith shop, reset-
ting some shoes on Amigo, when a lean, hard-faced man
rode in and got off his horse. Cultus met him at the doorway and they looked keenly at each other.

"Cultus, you old *pelicano!*" exclaimed the newcomer.

"Hyah, Sims!" grunted Cultus, extending a smudged
hand. "Long time no see yuh, feller."

Jim Sims had been a member of the Border Patrol as
long as Cultus had been in that country.

"I stopped in Santa Carmelita and heard you was here.
Jack told me; so I come a-whoopin'. Dog-gone, yo're a
sight for weak eyes!"

"They named their baby after me," said Cultus, mo-
tioning toward the house. "He's shore a daisy. I'll show
yuh to him, before yuh go."

"Named him after you?"

"Yeah-a-ah. Collins Neal. They calls him Collie. Cutest little devil yuh ever seen." Cultus hitched up his belt, grinning widely. "And he acts like he thought I was all right, too."

"Too young to realize," said Sims. "Well, how have yuh been? We often set around, wonderin' how things are with yuh, and if you'll ever come back. If namin' a baby after yuh would have brought yuh back, I'd have named one of mine. I've got six now."

"Gee, that's great, Sims. Six. How's yore wife?"

"Fine. She'd like to see yuh. When are yuh comin' back to Cuyamac?"

"*Quien sabe?* How's things along that Border?"

Sims spat reflectively. "Quiet. In fact, too damn quiet. Some of the boys say I'm a calamity howler; but when things get too blamed quiet, I get suspicious. And there is more stuff than ever comin' across from Mexico."

"Comin' across down here?" asked Cultus.

"If it is, we don't know how it's done."

"What do yuh know about this Rhein gang, Sims?"

"Not much. We don't know of anythin' they're doin'. I heard about you helpin' Dave Selby capture Pat Eagan."

Cultus grinned. "I described Eagan's pardner to Jack, and he says it was Duke Rhein."

"Is that right? I've heard that Rhein is plenty salty; but I've never met the gent. Somebody said he was hangin' out at the Ruiz place down there."

"Do yuh know Ruiz?"

"No. Some of the boys know him. He's apparently runnin' a cattle ranch down there—and raisin' good stock. He sells across the line once in a while, and the boys say it's all good stuff. Welch has bought a few head lately. Lemme see-e-e."

Sims consulted a notebook.

"I've got a record here of eighty-three head that we passed for the Runnin' W. Thirty, twelve, sixteen and twenty-five head brought in at four different times."

"I've never seen a good cow in Mexico," said Cultus.

"These were all Herefords," said Sims, putting away his book.

"How's Jack and his wife gettin' along?" he asked.

Cultus shook his head. "Not too good. Oh, they ain't starvin', but they ain't doin' well. Jack and his wife are regular folks, too."

"Jack got jipped on that Runnin' W, I understand," said Sims. "I hear that Welch got Jack's mother to sign things over to him; so Jack couldn't claim any of the ranch. That's dirty work."

"I suppose Welch is doin' well enough," said Cultus.

"He seems to have plenty poker money. How long are you figurin' on stayin' down here this time, Cultus?"

"I don't know. I'd like to help Jack and his wife, but I don't know what I can do. I've got a few hundred dollars cached away; but they ain't folks yuh can give money to. Mebbe I can give a couple hundred to the kid —I dunno."

"Do you feel the same toward drug runners as yuh used to feel?" asked Sims. Cultus looked at him seriously.

"When a rattler bites yuh, Sims, you never feel charitable toward rattlers, do yuh?"

"I'm glad, Cultus; and we need yuh down here. Stay a while—but look out. They ain't forgettin' what you've done."

Cultus nodded slowly. "I'm havin' fun down here," he said. "Yuh see, I ain't never had a baby to play with before. Funny little jiggers, ain't they?"

"I'm playin' with my sixth," grinned Sims, "and it's still fun. Well, I'll try and see yuh again in a few days. I'll tell the boys on this end of the line that yo're here; so they'll know it's hands off, if they see anythin' they jist don't understand."

"Don't make it too strong," replied Cultus. "I may not last long enough to do any queer things."

After Sims rode away Cultus went up to the porch,

where Mary Neal joined him, bringing a pair of powerful binoculars.

"Jack bought these from a man about a year ago," she told Cultus. "They are too powerful for ordinary use, but if you can put them on something stationary, they are wonderful."

Cultus soon found that Mary was right. The least tremor, and the object was lost.

"If yuh can hold 'em on a cow, yuh can see the color of its eye at a mile," grinned Cultus. "But when she switches her tail, yuh dodge. I never seen a glass so powerful."

They amused themselves with the glass, until Jack came home, and that evening Cultus questioned Jack about the exact location of the Ruiz Rancho.

"You ain't figurin' on goin' down there, are yuh?" asked Jack.

"I dunno," grinned Cultus. "Sims was tellin' me that Ruiz is in the cow business."

"I guess he is, Cultus."

"How long has he had that old rancho?"

"Oh, I suppose he's been there a year and a half."

"Where did he buy his cattle?"

"I suppose he's raisin' 'em."

"Raisin' big white-faced steers in a year and a half?" Jack smoked thoughtfully.

"I never thought about that," he admitted. "I seen one bunch of twenty-five head bein' brought in for the Runnin' W—and they was big, heavy stuff. What have yuh got on yore mind, Cultus?"

"Nothin'—yet. What's the Ruiz brand?"

"Oh, it's a crazy lookin' thing; five connected circles. Them Mexicans do figure out the worst brands."

"Five connected circles, eh? What spot does he mark?"

"Right side, I think."

"Five circles," mused Cultus. "That would shore be a hard one to alter. Yuh might put a one in front, and call

it the Ten Thousand brand. Like the feller who used the
IC brand. A rustler altered it to ICU, and the rancher
changed his register to show ICU2. They say that had
the rustler stopped."

"Is there any brand that you can't alter?" asked Jack.

"There's only one I know of that yuh can't."

"What's that, Cultus?"

"The brand of Cain," replied Cultus dryly. "Yuh can
hide it, but yuh can't alter it, Jack."

V

The next morning, against the advice of Jack and
Mary, Cultus saddled Amigo, borrowed the powerful
glasses and rode toward Mexico. He did not know that a
horseman, back in the hills, saw him leave the ranch, and
followed; but Cultus was too wise in the ways of Border
outlaws to overlook anything. Once off the road he took
advantage of all the brushy cover, steering a very
crooked course, which soon baffled the man who had followed him.

For over an hour he remained hidden in a brushy canyon, watching the skyline for anyone who might be following. Then he walked and led the ghost-gray to the
mouth of the canyon. Mounting again he angled back to
high ground, where he dismounted and sprawled on a
rocky pinnacle, working the powerful glasses. Finally he
picked up a horse and rider, far down in a little valley.

Cultus chuckled softly when he saw that this man was
also using a pair of field-glasses, scanning the hills. The
man rode slowly, stopping often to look around, and he
was heading for the Ruiz Rancho. When he disappeared
around the point of a hill, Cultus mounted and rode on.

"I reckon I better move away from the Neal place,"
he told himself. "If they're watchin' the place, somethin'
might happen to hurt some of the Neal family."

Less than an hour later Cultus sprawled on an out-
cropping of rocks in the shade of a scrub-oak and trained
his glasses on the Ruiz Rancho. He could see a saddled

horse tied to the corral fence, and two men talking to-gether in the yard. As near as he could judge there were about thirty head of Hereford cattle in the corral. Cultus found a flat shelf of rock on which to rest the glasses, giving him a wonderful view of the place.

The two men entered the house, and when they appeared again there was a third man. Cultus could see by the actions of one man that he was using the glasses. Finally two of the men left the man with the glasses and went down to the corral, where they saddled another horse. They mounted and rode due north, which would take them to the left of where Cultus lay. One man carried a rifle in the crook of his arm. The man with the glasses went into the house.

Cultus tried to figure out what this move meant. One man had followed him into Mexico, and seemed greatly concerned, when he was unable to discover what had become of him. Judging from the use of a field-glass, they were still looking for him. But why were these two men leaving the rancho, he wondered?

Again he settled down behind the glasses and studied the corral. The field of vision was not very large, but it seemed as though he was standing near the cattle. Suddenly he squinted closely, and a grin parted his wide lips.

And almost at the same moment he heard a noise below him. Cautiously he moved the glasses away and peered over the rock. Just below him, not over a hundred feet away, were the two riders, dismounting in the heavy brush. They were both armed with rifles. Here was a wide cattle trail, over which they had ridden silently.

They tied their horses and examined their rifles. Cultus was unable to hear their low-voiced conversation, but he saw one of them point up toward the rocky point, where he was concealed. The other man went on, following the cattle trail, which wound up the side of the hill.

Cultus looked around and smiled grimly. One of the

men was coming up to use that rocky point as a possible place of ambush.

Cultus hunched low, gun in hand, and listened to the man who was making hard work of that steep hillside. Cultus heard him swear as his feet slipped. Then he came clawing over the edge of the rock and almost rammed his long nose against the muzzle of Cultus' gun.

"Keep right on crawlin' over," said Cultus softly, "or I'll be obliged to blow yuh right off yore perch."

Cultus moved aside and let the man have room to obey orders. Cultus took the rifle and laid it aside.

"Unbuckle yore belt and hand me one end of it," he ordered.

With both rifle and six-shooter safely aside, he looked at the man, who happened to be Bill Tell, and grinned widely. But Bill did not see any humor in the situation. In fact, it was anything but funny.

"You wasn't aimin' to trap me, was yuh, feller?" asked Cultus.

Bill took a deep breath, swallowed painfully and a tear trickled down his leathery cheek. Something had choked him a little.

"Huh-how did you git here?" he asked huskily.

"You was expectin' me, wasn't yuh?"

"Not right here. I mean—I don't even know who yuh are."

"Why, I'm the feller you follered from the Neal ranch."

"It—it wasn't me," denied Bill. "Honest t' gosh it wasn't."

"No? Well, that proves the old sayin' ain't true."

"What old sayin'?"

"That a dyin' man always tells the truth."

"A dyin' man?' Bill's voice almost squeaked. "Why, I—"

"You only think yuh ain't," said Cultus grimly.

"You ain't goin' to kill me," said Bill, but there was no

conviction in his voice. "I ain't done a thing to you. You can't prove that I wanted to hurt you."

"I ain't askin' for proof, feller. Judges and juries do that. I'm handlin' this case, yuh must remember; and the evidence says that you and yore pardner sneaked in here, hopin' to dry-gulch me if I came in sight. He's up there somewhere now, waitin' to notch a sight on me."

"What are yuh goin' to do?" asked Bill.

"That's easy to answer. I'm goin' to shoot you. When he hears the shot, he'll come down here to see who yuh hit—and I'll plug him. Duke Rhein will come out of the house to see what the two of yuh got, won't he. Shore he will; and then I'll line up some rifle sights on him, and make it unanimous."

Bill shivered slightly, although it was well over a hundred in the shade. He had heard tales of this homely cowpuncher.

"How'd yuh like to tell me a little story about how Rhein's gang sends drugs across the Border?" asked Cultus.

Bill blinked violently.

"I don't know anythin' about any drugs," he said.

Cultus grinned at him.

"Then what is the idea of tryin' to dry-gulch me? What was the idea of watchin' Neal's ranch? Yo're lyin', and you know yo're lyin'. Do yuh know where liars go when they die?"

"I'm not talkin'," declared Bill, getting a grip on his nerve.

"Yo're not, eh? Know any good prayers?"

"No."

"Prob'ly wouldn't do any good, anyway. I hardly ever shoot a man who can pray good. I had one feller pray for thirty minutes. Git yore feet out straight, will yuh. When a feller is all doubled up thataway, he kicks around like a chicken with its head off."

But Bill Tell couldn't move his legs. He grimaced from

the supreme effort, but his muscles refused to do his bidding.

"Can't do it, eh?" queried Cultus. "Gone plumb yaller. Well, I tell yuh what to do. Slide backwards off that rock, and I'll shoot yuh on the way down hill. You don't mind, do yuh? Then you can't see me pull the trigger. Go ahead; slide off."

Like a man in a trance Bill Tell tremblingly obeyed. He clung to the rock, with a deathlike grip, until Cultus rapped him sharply across the knuckles with the barrel of his gun, when he shut his eyes and collapsed, falling head-over-heels down the steep slope, and almost rolling into the two tied horses down on the trail.

Picking up the rifle and revolver, Cultus tossed them into the brush, hurried to Amigo; and before Bill Tell realized that he was still alive, Cultus was leading the gray horse along a thicket of mesquite, heading away from the Ruiz Rancho.

Bill Tell was so shaken and dazed from his rolling fall down the hill that he did not attempt to move for a minute. Back in his scrambled mind was the thought that at any moment a bullet would hit him. He blinked the dust out of his eyes, groaned hollowly, as he moved a little, and sank back to wait for the bullet, which did not come.

Finally he inched his feet around under him, dived through a cruel thicket of thorny mesquite, and went lunging, sprawling, jumping down the hill, tearing his clothing to shreds in his mad haste to save his life. He brought up with a crash against the pole corral, where he fell through between the poles and went on a mad gallop up to the ranch-house.

Juan Ruiz, Duke Rhein and Tecate Charley met him at the doorway, having seen some of his gyrations between his first stop and the corral fence. Bill's intentions were to dive through the group and get under cover, but he stumbled and fell flat in front of them.

"What in hell happened to you?" blurted out Rhein.

Bill Tell gawped at them, turned his head painfully and looked back toward the hill. He looked back at Rhein and said dumbly, "I—I found him for yuh."

"You found who for me? What are you talkin' about?"

"Cultus Collins."

"You found—where is he, Bill?"

Bill looked around at his tattered shirt, his scratched arms, felt of his bare head and then wiped a smear of blood off his nose.

"He was where I was," replied Bill, and as an after-thought, "You better send and git Bert Flowers, before that devil gits his hands on him. He said he was goin' to kill me and kill Bert, and when you come outside to see what the shootin' was all about, he was goin' to kill you."

"The hell he did!" snorted Rhein. "Why didn't he kill you?"

Bill drew a deep breath and shook his head.

Bert Flowers had noted the activity around the house; so he deserted his post to come and find out what it was all about. They took Bill into the house, gave him a big drink of tequila, after which Bill was better able to tell them what actually happened.

"Had a pair of glasses, eh?" grunted Rhein. "Spyin' on us."

"Wanted to know how we took the drugs across the line."

"He asked yuh that, eh? What else did he ask yuh?"

"He asked me if I knowed where liars went when they died."

"Didja?" asked Bert Flowers seriously.

"Well, I didn't do any arguin' with him. He said for me to put my legs out straight; so I wouldn't hop like a chicken, when the bullet hit me. Then he decided to shoot me on the run. Mebbe I was rollin' too fast for him to hit me—I dunno."

Rhein turned to Tecate Charley.

"I reckon it's time for you to frame up that scheme yuh mentioned, Charley," he said.

"And leave me out of it," said Bill Tell. "If I never git within a thousand miles of that hard-faced galoot again, it'll be too close."

"It kinda bothers me—him not shootin' you," said Flowers.

"Cultus Collins is not a murderer," declared Tecate Charley. "He didn't try to force you to tell things."

"You mean—he knows somethin'?" asked Rhein quickly, anxiously.

"I think," replied the Chinaman, "it is time to do a little planning along a new line."

VI

Cultus came out of Mexico at nearly the same spot where he had entered. He chuckled often, as he rode through the broken hills, when he thought of Rhein's gunman falling all the way down that hill. Cultus never had had any intention of shooting Bill Tell; he always gave a man an even break.

As he neared the road a big, white-faced steer went crashing out of the brush ahead of him, snorting with alarm. It was an old-timer, wary, but vicious. Cultus got close enough to see the five circles on its side, identifying it as a Ruiz animal. The five circles were more like poorly drawn ovals.

Cultus shook out his rope and tried to get near the animal. But the old steer was wise in the ways of cowboys and their ropes. It headed into heavier brush, where a rope could not be used.

Slowly Cultus followed him, working him carefully to more open country. For possibly a half-mile the angry steer avoided the rope, but finally Cultus drove him out on a flat mesa of about five acres, where the brush was low.

"I'm goin' to tie onto you if I lose my string," he told the steer, and spurred Amigo into a quick dash.

Straight across the mesa raced the steer, turning sharp at the edge of a small canyon. Amigo swung quickly, sensing the steer's turn, and the loop flashed out, dropping square around those two long horns. But before the rope tightened, the steer whirled like a flash and came back at the horse.

The tall gray swerved just in time to avoid the slashing horns, and the next moment the big steer was pitching headlong over the rim of the canyon. Luckily Cultus had dallied his rope on the horn, instead of tying-off, and he was able, in that flash, to let loose of the rope, which flipped away.

He dismounted quickly and looked into the canyon, which was about twenty-five feet deep. The steer was down there. In fact, it always would be down there. Cultus climbed down and squatted on his heels beside the dead animal, while he recovered his rope. Then he made a careful examination of the brand.

He was both amused and thoughtful, as he climbed back and got on his horse.

"Amigo," he said, as he rode away, "I've seen a lot of blotted and altered brands, but that's the slickest I ever did see. Why, that evidence down there would hang Ruiz higher'n a kite—if they could catch him on this side of the line."

Cultus rode to Santa Carmelita and tied Amigo with three Running W horses at the Mexicana hitch-rack. As he came up to the doorway, Dan Welch, Whitey Higgins and another cowboy came out.

"Hyah, Dan," said Cultus cordially.

"Oh, hello, Collins," replied the big cowman. "I heard you was in this country again. How's everythin' with you?"

"All right," replied Cultus. "I dropped down to see Jack and Mary Neal. Yuh see, they named their baby after me."

"So Whitey was sayin'. I get my news of the Neal family second-handed these days."

"I reckon yuh do."

"I suppose," said Welch, "you've only had one side of the story."

"I'm not askin' for any alibi, Dan," replied Cultus slowly. "Yuh see, it ain't any of my business."

Welch's smile had a sarcastic twist, as he said, "Do you always mind your own business, Collins?"

"Fairly close," replied Cultus. "Yuh see, sometimes my business covers quite a lot of territory."

"I see. You make it elastic for your own convenience."

Cultus looked at Welch curiously.

"You ain't tryin' to rib up an argument with me, are yuh, Dan?"

"Not at all. Only I don't like to have Jack Neal exaggerate what happened. I know him well enough to know that he would. Fact of the matter is this: too many cowpunchers and only one pretty girl."

"Yea-a-ah?"

"Jack got jealous," said Welch. "You can't blame the boys; they're human. Mary was all right about it. She didn't mind——"

At that very moment Cultus' bony right hand, backed by every ounce of his long, lean body, thudded against Dan Welch's mouth. Welch was a big man, over six feet in height, well built; but he went down like a pole-axed steer, falling half into the doorway of the cantina.

Whitey Higgins, who was close to Welch, made an instinctive grab for his gun, leaving his right side open for Cultus' left swing, which cracked against his ear, knocking him against the wall of the cantina, from where he slid to a sitting position, looking owlishly about, evidently wondering where all the bells were located. The third member of the Running W backed away. This lean-faced, hard-hitting puncher was just too fast with his hands.

Quite a crowd had gathered before either man recovered. Whitey was the first—but he stayed down. Welch finally got to his feet and spat out a tooth. Both lips were cut and swollen. Cultus stood there, stolid, emotionless. Welch had the reputation of being a fighter, and Cultus expected gun-play. Welch looked at Cultus narrowly.

"We'll finish this later," he said painfully, and went into the cantina, followed by Whitey, who made no comments at all.

"Set yore own time," replied Cultus indifferently, and went to get his horse.

"He's mad at me, Amigo," he told the gray, as they went out to the ranch. "Well, it don't matter. He acted like he wanted to kinda stir me up; so he ought to be satisfied."

"Oh, I'm so glad you're back," said Mary when Cultus reached the ranch. "Jack is down at the stable, and I know he was worried."

"It's somethin' kinda new—havin' anybody worry about me," smiled Cultus. "I was jist as safe as though I'd been home. I reckon I'm gettin' old, Mary; I keep out of trouble now. Used to be a time when I liked to fight."

Jack came up from the stable and sat down with them.

"I did feel a little worried," confessed Jack. "I happen to know how they feel toward you down there, Cultus. Did you find the Ruiz place?"

"Yeah, I found it, but I didn't go all the way."

The baby cried from its bed, and Mary went to get it.

"You've got skinned knuckles on both hands, Cultus," said Jack.

"Yeah," said Cultus softly. "I fell down on the side of a hill."

"How's the hill?" queried Jack.

"Minus a tooth or two. Sh-h-h-h."

Mary came out with the baby, and Cultus immediately forgot that he had any enemies along the Border.

"It's too danged bad that yore mother didn't live to see this baby, Jack," remarked Cultus.

"If she had lived," replied Jack sadly, "we wouldn't be here in this tumble-down shack."

"I reckon that's true. It was mostly her money and property that put Dan Welch where he is now, wasn't it?"

"He didn't have anythin'," replied Jack fiercely. "It all belonged to her."

"But in case of his death, you'd get it, wouldn't yuh?"

"In the neck. He told me one day that he had made out a will, and everythin' he owned would go to a brother of his in Ohio."

"Mebbe he was lyin'," said Cultus.

"No, he wasn't. I asked Henry Chase, his lawyer; and Chase said he had the will in his safe. He wouldn't tell me what was in it, of course. No, he fixed it so I wouldn't get a cent, Cultus."

"Chase? I remember him. Tall, long-faced person; kinda sad to look upon, ain't he?"

"Yeah. His office is across the street from the Santa Carmelita Hotel. He's the only lawyer in town. I don't see how he makes a livin'. He sleeps in a room behind his office; so I don't suppose it costs him much to live."

"I reckon Dan Welch *is* kinda mean," agreed Cultus.

"Oh, he would be nice to you," said Mary quickly.

Cultus flexed the sore knuckles of his right hand.

"Yuh never can tell about them mean fellers," he said slowly.

VII

It was raining when they awoke next morning. The summer rains were overdue, which would mean a heavy rainfall for quite a while. Jack and Cultus hitched up the wagon team and went to town to get more provisions. After a few days of heavy rains the road would be almost impassable.

Sims and another of the Border Patrol were in Santa Carmelita, and Cultus had a serious talk with Sims, who agreed with his suggestions.

"But I don't quite get the idea, Cultus," said Sims.

"Neither do I," admitted Cultus. "But there's an answer somewhere in that deal. Look for a big steer with a mark on its side, like one of them swastika things, except that the top prong is missin'. I seen two Runnin' W punchers herdin' that steer toward the ranch the day I got here. Yesterday I seen that steer in the Ruiz corral in Mexico. And don't forget that I roped and killed a Runnin' W steer that had been altered to that Five Circle, or Five Oval brand. My opinion is that the steer I killed was an old outlaw critter that they couldn't handle; so they let him go."

"Yo're the doctor," grinned Sims. "I never lost on yore diagnosis yet."

Cultus and Jack loaded the wagon and went back to the ranch. It was a cold rain, and both men looked forward to a session in front of the ranch fireplace. As they drove into the yard Jack remarked about the lack of smoke from the chimney.

"I left plenty wood for Mary," he said uneasily. "She said she was bakin' today—but there's no smoke from the kitchen."

"It does look kinda funny," admitted Cultus. "I'll un-hitch the team, while you go and see if everythin' is all right."

Jack handed the lines to Cultus and sprang off the wagon. Cultus drove down to the corral and was start-ing to unhitch the team, when Jack came running, bare-headed in the rain, his face as colorless as a sheet of paper. Cultus dropped the harness and came out to meet him. For several moments Jack could not speak. Then he said huskily, "The baby—they—"

"What about the baby?" asked Cultus. "He ain't sick—is he? Jack, why don'tcha say somethin'?"

"Gone," choked Jack. "They—they tied Mary up—and took the baby."

Cultus' jaw sagged for a moment. "They—well—c'mon."

They ran to the house, where they found Mary sitting on the edge of a bed, crying. Some of the ropes were still dangling from her.

"Brace up," choked Cultus. "Tell me what happened, Mary. We've got to know."

"I—I can't tell much," she said weakly. "I had my back to the kitchen doorway—making bread. I heard a noise, and the next thing I knew a man had both arms around me. I screamed—and then they put something over my head. There was more than one man, and they tied me all up. I—I tried to fight, Jack—but I wasn't strong enough."

"You—you couldn't fight men," said Jack weakly.

"They threw me on the bed, and I heard one of them say, 'Take one of them blankets to cover the kid.' "

"How long was this after we left?" asked Cultus.

"About fifteen minutes, I think," replied Mary.

Jack paced the length of the room, stopped at the center table, where he picked up a note. He read it quickly and handed it to Cultus. It read:

> *The baby is in safe hands. Do not report this to the law, but follow instructions which you will receive soon, and the baby will be returned safely.*

It had been printed with bold pencil capitals on wrapping paper, but was unsigned.

"Ransom, eh?" gritted Cultus.

"Ransom?" queried Jack bitterly. "How could I pay anythin'? I ain't got five dollars in money, Cultus. I've got a few head of cattle and a few head of horses—but not worth anythin'—much."

Cultus nodded toward Mary and said softly, "Talk to her, Jack; I'll unhitch and unload."

Cultus was like an old man as he went down there in the rain. He realized that these men were hitting at him. If he had stayed away this never would have happened. Now it was up to him to get that baby safely back to its mother. But how, he wondered?

He stabled the horses and made several trips to the house, carrying sacks and bundles. Then he built a fire in the fireplace and took off his muddy boots. Mary and

Jack joined him, and Mary was able now to talk calmly. She had not seen the faces of any of the men, nor could she identify any of the voices. Her wrists were raw from her frantic efforts to get loose, but she was otherwise unhurt.

"That note says we'll get further instructions," said Cultus. "All we can do is set tight, until we know what they want."

"If the baby is only safe," said Mary weakly.

"We've got their word—if that's worth anythin'," said Jack.

"I believe it is," replied Cultus. "They'll keep their word, if they get what they want."

It was about three o'clock, when an old Yaqui rode up to the house; a disreputable old buck, soaking wet. He gave Jack a sealed envelope, refused to answer any questions, and rode away. The note read:

> *Cultus Collins—if you want to save the life of the Neal baby follow these instructions—— Come to the Ruiz ranch at sunset tomorrow. If you are wearing a gun or make any attempt to bring anyone with you we will kill the baby. As soon as you have surrendered to us the baby will be returned to the Neal family. This is our price.*

Mary and Jack said nothing; they merely looked at Cultus, who calmly rolled a cigarette and lighted it from a twist of paper in the fire.

"Sunset tomorrow," he said slowly. "And this is almost sunset today."

"But you can't do that, Cultus," said Mary. "They'll kill you."

"We've got to do somethin'," choked Jack.

"Take it easy," advised Cultus. "Sunset tomorrow is quite a while away. Anyway, it's my own fault. I can't seem to mind my own business. I brought this on you folks."

"I'm goin' to town," declared Jack. "I'll get the Border

Patrol. I'll tell everybody in Santa Carmelita. It's terrible!"

"And you'll never see yore baby, if yuh do," said Cultus. "There ain't a bit of evidence as to who done the job —and they won't leave any evidence, if you start anythin'. This place is watched. They're waitin' to see what we do."

"But what *are* we goin' to do," asked Jack anxiously.

"Nothin'—now. They've got to figure that we'll do as they say. I'm sure the baby is all right. I know jist how much hell it must be for both of yuh—but we've got to take it—now."

The inaction was terrible for Mary and Jack, but Cultus insisted that it was too early for any move to be made. It rained so hard that at times the landscape was obliterated, and they kept busy taking care of the ranch-house leaks.

Darkness came early, and they sat in front of a roaring fire. Cultus hunched in a chair, chin in hands, staring at the dancing flames; but he was not looking at the fire.

Bedtime came, and Mary went wearily to her room. No word had been spoken for an hour when Cultus lifted his head and said, "Have yuh got an old pair of shoes, Jack? We wear about the same size."

"Shoes? Why do yuh want shoes?" asked Jack.

"High-heel boots are bad for walkin'."

"Where are you goin' to walk, Cultus?"

The tall cowboy made a vague gesture.

"*Quien sabe?*"

Jack found an old pair of shoes, which fitted Cultus.

"Pretty good shoes," nodded Cultus. "I ain't worn a pair for a long time."

"Do I go with yuh?" asked Jack.

"You'll stay right here, Jack. Another thing—don't worry. Tell Mary not to worry, if I don't come back— early."

"But you'll come back, won't yuh, Cultus?"

"Yea-a-ah, I think I will. Go to bed—that's what I'm goin' to do; and don't wonder what's wrong, if yuh hear me goin' out through a window about midnight. I've got a little prowlin' to do."

"Why not take a horse?" asked Jack.

"Not tonight. Unless I'm mistaken, the stable is watched. And in the mornin', I wish you'd both stay in here. Them horses can go a few extra hours without food. I want 'em to think I'm still here."

VIII

It was no summer shower that was visiting those broken hills along the Border. Every canyon was a raging flood of murky water in the pale light of morning. Leaden clouds hung low, sending the rain hissing down through the brushy hills.

Crouched in behind a tangle of mesquite on the slope of a hill near the Ruiz rancho, was Cultus Collins. He wore no hat, and the rain drizzled down his furrowed face and down the back of his neck. He was muddy to his knees, and from that point upward he was as wet as a man might get.

But he seemed impervious to discomforts as he hunched there in the mud and water watching the ranch-house. A small herd of cattle were humped together in the corral, their rumps to the storm. Smoke came from the kitchen chimney of the ranch-house, indicating that breakfast was being prepared.

A man clad in a slicker came from the house and entered the stable where he remained for several minutes before going back. Cultus looked disgustedly at his sack of soggy tobacco, and threw it aside.

"Dang fool!" he muttered. "Fall in the crick and lose m'hat in the dark. Nothin' to smoke—and blisters on m' feet."

It was fully another hour, before anyone left the house, but this time three men came. They were Rhein, Flowers and Tell, but Cultus could not recognize them. They saddled their horses, opened the corral gate, and drove the herd outside. They seemed to be talking things over, regarding the weather, and Cultus saw one of them point toward the west, where the storm seemed to be breaking away. They bunched the small herd, and started westward with them, heading for the old road, which led to Santa Carmelita.

Cultus waited until they were out of sight, and then he began cautiously working his way down toward the ranch-house. He reached the stable, where he crouched at a corner and studied the house. He saw Tecate Charley come from the kitchen with a pan of water, which he threw outside. Apparently Cultus was not expected so early, because the Chinaman did not even stop to look around.

Cultus walked to the upper corner of the stable. It was about a hundred feet to the house, and Cultus realized that he would only be visible from the one front window, the other window being blocked off by some vines over the porch. Taking that one chance, he ran across the yard and came in against the corner of the house.

Ducking low under the window on that side of the house, he went to the kitchen door, where he could hear voices. He flattened himself against the wall, trying to hear what was said. Then the doorlatch clicked and the door was opened a few inches. Cultus could see the hand that held the latch—the fat, black hand of Ruiz, who was saying:

"Sure. I'm know theese theengs damn well, Tecate. But Rhein he say he ees ver' smart man. *Quien sabe?* Personally, myselves, I'm theenk Rhein bites off more than I can chew."

With a chuckle at his own wise observations, Juan Ruiz stepped outside; and the next moment Mr. Ruiz lost all interest in whether Duke Rhein was wise or foolish, when the barrel of Cultus' six-gun clanked hard against his head.

Tecate Charley whirled around, holding a butcher knife in one hand, a joint of beef in the other, and looked into the muzzle of Cultus' gun.

"You can drop both of 'em," said Cultus coldly, and both articles thudded to the floor.

"I'm a little early," said Cultus. "Yuh better set down before yore legs let loose and drop yuh. Wait. After thinkin' it over, I guess yuh better go into the other room."

Tecate preceded him, and Cultus grunted delightedly at sight of several ropes in a corner of the room. It only required a few moments for Cultus to hogtie the China-man to a chair, after which he dragged in the unconscious Ruiz and bound him thoroughly.

Then he proceeded to search the place. Nothing was overlooked.

In Rhein's room he found a heavy box, which he carried to the main room. Tecate Charley scowled at Cultus, but said nothing. With a pointed poker from the fire-place Cultus pried the cover off the box, disclosing a tidy fortune in several kinds of drugs.

Tecate was heavily interested in that particular cargo, and he almost cried, when Cultus dumped them all into the fireplace.

"You have no right to do that," he said huskily. "That is not contraband here."

"It makes a right nice lookin' blaze," observed Cultus. "And as far as right is concerned, I ought to kill both of you."

Cultus searched around, until he had found plenty of dry clothes, after which he dressed. He took a fancy leather jacket, belonging to Ruiz, and he took one of Ruiz's big hats, which fitted him well. A yellow slicker was added to the costume, after which he went down to the stable, selected a horse and saddle, and rode away. He had no idea what time Rhein and his two cowboys would be back, but he felt sure they would be back before sundown.

No one would have recognized Cultus in that array of garments, riding a silver-mounted saddle on a beautiful black gelding, which was the pride and joy of Juan Ruiz.

Cultus had spent quite a long time at the Ruiz rancho, and it was nearly noon, when he again rode across the Border, going north.

But this time he rode straight for Dan Welch's Running W ranch. The baby was not at the Ruiz rancho, that much was certain. Cultus was on the hunt now—and he was not waiting for sundown. He could see the two-story ranch-house long before he reached it; and he saw a man on the roof. The man disappeared suddenly. Cultus drew his gun and held it inside his slicker; he was not taking a chance on having a wet holster when he would need a gun quickly.

Straight through the big arched gate he rode boldly. Whitey Higgins was on the broad porch, watching him, and Cultus smiled grimly under the broad Mexican sombrero when Whitey seemed to relax and came down the steps to meet him. Whitey recognized the horse and the hat. They were not over twenty feet apart, when Whitey recognized the man.

But it was too late to be of any advantage to the Running W cowboy, whose jaw sagged weakly, when his eyes looked into the muzzle of that big Colt gun.

"All alone here, eh?" gritted Cultus. "Don't lie, Whitey."

"I—I ain't lyin'," whispered Whitey. "My gosh! I thought—"

"Never believe what yuh see," advised Cultus. "Turn around and head for the stable."

There was not another soul in sight around the place, as Cultus drove Whitey down across the yard to the big stable where he dismounted, roped Whitey and dumped him into a manger, after gagging him as effectively as possible. Cultus was working fast now. He took the black horse past the house and tied him to a cottonwood where he could not be seen from the road or yard.

Walking swiftly he entered the house and stopped in the center of the big main room. A Mexican woman was coming down the stairs, and she stopped short at sight of him. She was a middle-aged person, the housekeeper and cook of the ranch.

"You—you look for somebody?" she asked. Then she saw the gun in his hand, and she shrank back. He came up the stairs, and she backed slowly upward, feeling for the treads with her feet.

"Yeah, I'm lookin' for somebody," he said harshly. "A baby."

"*Madre de Dios!*" she whispered. "No keel—please."

"Where's the baby?" asked Cultus, as they reached the top floor. "Don't lie to me or I'll see yuh hung for this."

"I tell," she said hoarsely. "I no take heem. In here."

Cultus saw at a glance that it was Dan Welch's room. There was his desk, a cabinet of books, pictures on the walls. But what he was more interested in was the baby, lying asleep on the bed. Cultus pointed to a chair.

"Set down there," he whispered. "And if you move, I'll shoot yuh."

"No move," she said, and slid into the chair.

On the desk was a metal dispatch box, locked with a small padlock. A heavy screw-driver in Cultus' muscular hands was as quickly effective as a key would have been. There was currency in the box, but he flung it aside, quickly sorting the papers and documents, until he selected one, folded it quickly and put it in his pocket.

He turned to the Mexican woman.

"You stay right here and keep still. If you leave the room, or start yellin' you'll get killed."

"No move," she replied. "I'm no wan' be keeled."

"Smart woman," said Cultus. He picked up the sleeping baby, wrapped in its blanket, and stepped out on the balcony, where he could look down into the main room. There was not a sound, as he came down the open stairway.

On the table, among an assortment of other things, was a new shoe-box and a bottle of black, liquid shoe polish. Cultus halted at the table, picked up the top of the cardboard box and uncorked the bottle of polish. He was going to leave a printed sign on the table--some sort of a grim joke on the Welch outfit.

Suddenly he jerked up his head and looked toward a window. Four riders were dismounting in the yard, and he saw that one of them was Duke Rhein. Cultus knew now that he had wasted too much time. There was no way out of that house by which he could reach his horse unseen. Alone, he would have accepted the long odds— but not with that baby in his arms.

Dipping a forefinger into the black fluid, he printed swiftly on the cardboard cover of that box:

YOU ARE TRAPPED

DROP YOUR GUNS

AND COME OUTSIDE.

SHERIFF.

He propped the cardboard on the table to face the kitchen entrance, as the four men started in that direction. There was a sort of a closet under the stairs, and he backed under there, carefully holding one hand over the baby's mouth to prevent an outcry. Luckily the baby was more interested in sleep than in causing any trouble, and Cultus wondered if it had been drugged.

He heard the four men come into the kitchen, and Rhein's voice called, "Where is everybody? Anybody at home?"

"That's damn funny!" snorted Bill Tell, as he partly closed the kitchen door. "I don't like it, Duke."

"Aw, there ain't anythin' wrong," rasped Rhein. "C'mon."

They walked into the main room and looked around. The light was not very good, but good enough to show them the sign on the table.

"Down!" rasped Rhein. He sprang into the kitchen, shut the door and dropped the bar into place.

"Trapped!" wailed Bill Tell. "What's the use of makin' a battle of it Duke? They've got us trapped."

"You yaller quitter!" snarled Rhein. "Do yuh want to

hang? We've always got a chance in a fight. Cover that window—one of yuh. If they git us, we'll git some of them first."

"I told yuh to let Cultus Collins alone," wailed Tell. "I told yuh we was fools to cross the line. But you know so damn much more than anybody else. Tecate said it was a fool move, didn't yuh, Tecate?"

"Shut up!" hissed Rhein. "They're closin' in."

Rhein stepped into the kitchen, close to the door, as footsteps came up close. As the latch rattled, Rhein's heavy Colt thundered, waist-high below the latch. A choking cry and a heavy thud echoed the report, and Rhein sprang back into the doorway.

"That's one of 'em, damn their souls!" he snarled.

From outside came a muffled babel of voices. All was quiet, except for the heavy breathing of the four men. Then a huge rock came crashing through a window, tearing away the curtain.

"Down!" snapped Rhein. "Save yore shells, boys; we'll need to make every shot count."

"A lot of chance we've got!" exclaimed Tell. "All they've got to do is to wait out there for us. I'm ready to quit. The law can't put any deadwood on us. We never stole the damn kid."

"It was Tecate's idea," said Flowers.

"Shut up and watch the window!" gritted Rhein.

"There's a man in the hay-window of the stable," said Flowers. "He's got a rifle."

"Let's surrender and take a chance," urged Tell. "No use buckin' about it. Rhein led us into a trap, and he'd—"

Two revolver shots crashed out, spaced about two seconds apart. Cultus was unable to see what happened, but he heard Flower's querulous voice, saying, "Damn it, Charley, Rhein shot Bill; and Bill was my bunkie. I ain't no quitter—but two of us can't git far. Kick open that door, and we'll go out with our hands in the air."

Powder smoke eddied into Cultus' hiding place. He heard the door open, and after a few moments he heard excited voices outside. No one came into the house; and in a few minutes he heard the sound of galloping horses.

Gripping his gun tightly he inched out, leaving the baby on the floor, until he had investigated. Sprawled in the middle of the floor were Duke Rhein and Bill Tell. Cultus knew that Rhein had killed Tell, because Tell wanted to quit; and Flowers had shot Rhein, because Tell had been his bunkie.

The kitchen door was wide open, and just outside, sprawled half off the steps, was Dan Welch, shot dead center by the bullet Rhein had fired through the door. There was not a horse nor cowboy in sight.

Cultus went quickly back, picked up the baby and left the house. The black horse was still there. He snorted at the bundle in Cultus' arms and tried to object; but the firm-handed cowboy was in the saddle quickly, handling the black with the practice born of long association with bad horses.

IX

The baby cried, as they went away from the ranch, cutting into the hills. The rain had ceased, but the muddy ground prevented speed.

Mary and Jack were on the little porch, watching and waiting, when Cultus came in sight. He waved the big Mexican sombrero at them and held up the bundle. Both of them fairly flew through the mud to meet him. He handed the baby down to Jack, and without a word left them and went to stable the black horse.

Cultus found them in front of the fireplace. They merely looked at him, with tears in their eyes, unable to speak. He found Jack's tobacco and papers on the table and rolled a long-delayed smoke.

"Anybody been here today?" he asked. Jack shook his head.

"If anybody asks yuh," said Cultus slowly, "'jist tell 'em that I've been here all day. What the world don't know won't hurt 'em."

It was an hour later, before Mary recovered sufficiently to cook a meal. No questions had been asked. Jack knew that if Cultus didn't want to tell what happened, there would be no use in asking questions.

They were eating supper when Sims and two more of the Border Patrol rode up. Cultus welcomed them heartily, and they came in.

"Well, what do yuh know?" asked Cultus. Sims looked at him quizzically, as he replied dryly, "I've seen a lot, but I don't know a blamed thing, Cultus. There seems to have been a battle at the Runnin' W."

"A battle?"

"Dan Welch is dead from a bullet through his own kitchen door. Duke Rhein and one of his gang are dead in the house; and the Mexican housekeeper either can't, or won't talk. We searched the house and the stables, but we can't find anybody else."

Cultus knew then that Whitey had been found and liberated.

"Kinda funny, don'tcha think, Sims?" queried Cultus.

"Too many crooks, I reckon," said Sims. "But here's what yore tip did for us, Cultus. A bunch of Ruiz cattle were brought in this mornin', and on the strength of yore advice, we held up passin' 'em. Welch was there, with one of his men, and I believe he got suspicious. Anyway, he pulled out.

"That steer with the swastika mark was in the bunch, and we got to examinin' it. Shorty Reed was the one that gave the snap away. He roped that blamed steer by the horns, snubbed him tight—and the steer lost a horn."

"Lost a horn, eh? So that was it!"

"It shore was. Cultus, them steers—six of 'em—had been dehorned for this special job. The fake horns fit perfectly, I tell yuh. Nobody could tell that they wasn't the real thing. Can yuh imagine how much dope they could send across that way? And that idea of alterin' the Runnin' W to a Five Oval connected brand. Lampblack and glue. At least, that's our guess. It made a dandy brand. Why, yuh could even see the old scab. They could take it off at the Runnin' W—and there's the original Runnin' W. And they've been doin' it for months."

Cultus laughed softly and shook his head.

"They used special marked steers," he said, "and that was their big mistake. Well, I'm glad yuh got 'em on it, Sims."

"Thanks to you—the bunch is busted up. But there will be no arrests; they've got to face a bigger judge than we've got in our courts."

"Crooks do fall out, yuh know," said Cultus.

"Tell him about what that lawyer said, Sims," suggested one of the officers.

"Oh, yes," smiled Sims. "We've had another angle to the case. You know Henry Chase, the Santa Carmelita lawyer, don't yuh, Cultus?"

"Yeah, I know who he is."

"This afternoon," continued Sims, "someone heard a lot of noise in Chase's office, and they investigated. Chase had been roped and gagged, but had managed to get his feet loose and was kicking on the furniture.

"He said that about midnight he woke up to find a masked man in the room with him. The man made him open his safe, and then tied him up. Chase had been tied and gagged all that time, and was he a mad lawyer. The stuff from his safe was all scattered over the room, but Chase said that the only thing missing, as far as he was able to determine, was the copy of Dan Welch's will. That's kinda queer—with Welch gettin' killed today. Chase said that Welch had a copy of the will at the ranch. Mebbe he has. When we searched the place we found Welch's strong box. The padlock had been wrenched off, and we examined the papers—but there wasn't any will. Whoever opened the box overlooked a big sum of money in currency."

"Kinda funny about the will," said Cultus thought-fully. "It seems to me that Jack Neal has a bigger claim to the Runnin' W than any other person on earth. I don't

know who else Welch would leave it to; so the missin'
will won't make a lot of difference."

"Not a bit," agreed Sims. "Well, boys, we better be
goin'. Thanks a lot, Cultus—until yo're better paid."

"I've been paid," said Cultus.

He stood in the doorway and watched the three men
ride away. Then he turned to see Mary and Jack looking
at him. He shut the door and came back to the fire, a
whimsical smile on his lean face.

"It's jist about sunset," he said.

ROUTINE PATROL

by JAMES B. HENDRYX

CORPORAL DOWNEY, ace of the North-West Mounted
Police non-coms in the Yukon, glanced uneasily at the
glittering, distorted sun, low-hung in the sky to the southward. There was an unfamiliar, unreal look to it; and an
unnatural feel to the dead, still air. Before him stretched
the unending windings of the river, flanked to the northward by high sparsely timbered hills, and to the southward by flat tundra and low rolling prairie, even more
sparsely timbered.

At late sunrise the wind had died and it had grown
steadily colder. For two days past his Government map
had been useless, vague dottings showing the supposed
course of the river. His working map, hand-drawn in
Dawson by a breed who had helped Stan Braddock pack
his stock of trade goods and liquor to the new camp of
Good Luck, had been doubted at Selkirk. Two men who
professed to have been to Good Luck insisted that the
breed had located the camp on the wrong branch of the
Pelly. They drew Downey a new map. Another argued
that the breed's map might be right, but doubted that any-

one could cover the ground in eight days even on the hard, wind-packed snow. An old Indian, who had trapped the country to the eastward a dozen years before, drew a crude map that coincided with neither of the others. In disgust Downey had pulled out of Selkirk, leaving those knowing ones wrangling among themselves.

The dogs slowed. Even Topek, the lead dog, was traveling listlessly, his muzzle low to the unbroken snow. Tight-curled tails had lost their gimp, and breath plumes frosted shaggy coats. Downey, himself, was conscious of a growing lassitude. He swore unconvincingly at the dogs, but the long-lashed whip remained coiled in his mittened hand, and the dogs paid no heed.

Somewhere on the heights to the left a tree exploded with the frost. Again Downey glanced across the rolling prairie toward the sun. White specks danced before his eyes—specks that resolved themselves into false suns that danced their silent mockery in the ice-green sky above the cold dead waste of snow.

In a dull, detached way, he estimated that it was one o'clock. The conclusion seemed of no importance, and of no importance seemed the slow pace of the dogs as he walked on and on behind the sled. Vaguely his mind reverted to his maps—the breed's map, and the others. He shivered with a chill not born of the cold—for he realized that, to his dulled senses, the maps, too, seemed of no importance. Pulling himself together with an effort, he cracked his whip and swore loudly at the dogs. His voice sounded curiously flat and unfamiliar, and the animals plodded on without increasing their pace, proud tails at half-cock. Downey, too, plodded on without bothering to coil his whip, the long walrus lash dragging behind him, his eyes on the unbroken snow that covered the river ice. Since leaving Selkirk he had seen no tracks. No moose, nor caribou—not even a wolf nor a fox had crossed the river. And this fact, too, seemed of no importance even though he was low on meat—for himself, and for his dogs. Tonight they would get the last of the frozen fish—then no more till Good Luck. Perhaps they would never reach Good Luck. The matter seemed of no importance beyond being a good joke on the dogs. Downey realized that he was chuckling inanely.

The lopsided, brassy sun touched the horizon and as the officer looked, the false suns leaped and danced—a dance of hideous mockery on the rim of the frozen world. "I've heard of it," he mumbled, striving to control his brain—"the white death—it comes in the strong cold—but it ain't the cold—the air goes dead, or somethin'—some of the old timers claim it's a lie—but others claim a man dies or goes crazy. . . . Well, if a man goes crazy, or dies, what the hell?" A delicious lassitude permeated his brain—a pleasant, warming numbness—and he slogged on.

The leader swung abruptly from the river and headed up a small feeder that emerged from a notch in the hills. "Hey, you, Topek! Gee, Topek, gee!" But the leader paid no slightest heed to the command, and Downey grasped the tail-rope as the superb brute threw his weight into the collar, tightening the traces. By his very strength and power he dragged his lagging team mates into a faster pace. "Whoa, Topek! Down ! Damn you—down!"

Ignoring the command, the big dog plunged on, head up, ears cocked expectantly ahead. Tightening his grip on the tail-rope, the officer followed. He glanced over his shoulder toward the southward. The brief March sun had set. No false suns danced crazily before his eyes—only long plumes of blue-green light were visible, radiating from a bright spot on the horizon to the zenith above his head. His glance shifted to Topek. Topek, the best lead dog in the police service, deserting the trail! Ignoring commands! What did it mean? Downey heard his own voice babbling foolishly: "Gone crazy—crazy with the white death—dogs and men both—they go crazy or die, if they don't camp. Or, maybe Topek knows a new trail —no one else knows this damn country—maybe Topek knows. Might as well die up one crick as another. Hi, Topek—mush!"

The high hills closed in abruptly, shutting out the weird light of the blue-green plumes. Naked rock walls rose sheer to jagged rims outlined high above against the sky. The canyon, a mere cleft in the living rock, was scarce fifty feet from wall to wall. The new snow was softer, here—protected from the sweep of the wind by the high walls. Dully Downey realized that, despite the shifty footing, and the increased drag of the sled in the softer snow, the pace was fast. Drooping tails once more curled over shaggy backs as each dog threw his weight into the collar. Gone was the languor that had marked the brief daylight hours of travel. It was as though Topek had inspired his team—was inspiring Corporal Downey, too. Slowly, but consciously, as one awakening from a horrible dream, the officer realized that the dangerous brain lethargy that had gripped him on the river was losing its hold. He shook his head to clear it of the last remnant of fogginess, and his voice rang sharp and hard through the narrow corridor as he shouted words of encouragement to the dogs.

One mile—two—and the canyon suddenly widened to a hundred yards and terminated abruptly in a dead end —a sheer rock wall at the base of which stood a grove of stunted spruce.

"Fire-wood, anyway," the officer muttered, as he glanced about him in the semi-darkness. Topek headed straight for the copse and disappeared, his team mates following, pulling the sled which came to a halt partially within the timber a few yards from where Downey stood. Rumbling, throaty growls issued from the copse, and the officer hurried forward to see the huge lead dog, his muzzle low against the door of a small pole-and-mud cabin, lips curled back to expose gleaming white fangs as growl after growl issued from the depths of the mighty chest.

Making his way around the sled, Downey was about to speak to the dog when the great brute settled back on his haunches, pointed his sharp muzzle to the sky, and howled. Loud and eerie the ululation rose until as if at a signal, each of the other six dogs of the team followed the example of their leader until the horrid cacophony rolled and reverberated in an all-engulfing hullabaloo of strident noise. Then, as suddenly as it had begun, the deafening hubbub ceased, and at a word of command, the dogs sank onto their bellies, reaching out here and there to snap up mouthfuls of snow.

For some moments the officer stood peering into the gathering darkness. A neatly piled rank of firewood, an ax standing against the wall beside the door, a pair of snowshoes hanging from a peg driven into the wall all spoke of occupancy. Yet—not a track was to be seen. No one had passed in or out of the cabin since the latest fall of snow.

Pulling the thong that raised the crude wooden latch bar, Downey pushed the door open and stepped into the absolute blackness of the room. Shaking off a mitten, he shuddered slightly as he groped in his pocket for a match —the interior seemed colder even than the outside air, seemed fraught with a deadly chill that struck to the very marrow of his bones. Closing the door, he scratched the match upon its inner surface, and as the light flared up he started back in horror at sight of the dead man who lay upon his back in the middle of the floor, his glassy, frozen eyes staring straight up into his own. The match burned Downey's fingers and he dropped it, plunging the room into darkness. Reaching for another, he scratched it and, stepping over the still form on the floor, held the flame to the wick of a candle-stub that protruded from the neck of a bottle on the rude pole table.

When the flame burned steadily, flooding the room with mellow light, Downey thrust his hand, already stiff from cold, back into his mitten, picked up the bottle and, stepping to the dead man's side, stood gazing down into the marble-white face—the face of an old man. An unkempt white mustache and a scraggly white beard somewhat stained by tobacco juice masked the lower half of his face. Thin white hair edged the brow, and as Downey stood staring in fascination into the frozen eyes, a peculiar sensation stole over him. He felt that the man wanted to speak—that behind those frozen eyeballs a spark of brain still lived—that the man had something to tell him —something of vast importance.

"Poor devil," muttered the officer, his glance shifting to the blue-black revolver that lay close beside the out-flung right hand, and back to the ugly hole in the man's right temple. "He couldn't take it no longer. The North got him .The strong cold—or maybe the white death that some claim is a lie." He turned abruptly away and re-turned the bottle to the table. "An' it'll be gettin' me, too, if I don't get a fire goin'. It's sixty below in here right now—or I miss my guess."

Stepping to the stove, he started in surprise. "Why the hell," he wondered aloud as he applied a match to the bark beneath the kindlings that showed through the open door, "would he lay his fire an' then blow his brains out without lightin' it?"

With the fire roaring in the stove Downey stepped out-side, unharnessed his dogs, tossed them a frozen salmon apiece, and carried his own grub and the remainder of his meager supply of dog food into the cabin.

The room was beginning to warm. The candle flared and flickered, having burned to the bottle neck and, rummaging on a shelf, Downey found another and lighted it. Filling his tea pail with snow, he placed it on the stove, and turned his attention to an exploration of the tiny room. He found sufficient flour, tea, sugar, and salt to last a man two months. There was also an ample supply of desiccated vegetables, and a bag of beans. A plate on the table held several good cuts of caribou steak frozen to the hardness of iron.

Beside the cheap alarm clock on the shelf from which he had taken the candle, Downey found a small box containing a number of dynamite caps, part of a box of rifle ammunition, for which there seemed to be no rifle. He found no revolver ammunition, nor any box in which such ammunition had been packed.

Beneath the pole bunk he found half a case of dynamite and a coil of fuse. Also, dozens of samples of hard rock—quartz for the most part, many of them showing flecks of free gold.

On the table, pushed back against the wall, was an Indian-tanned caribou skin from which had been cut several pieces of a uniform pattern, evidently for the purpose of fashioning the small pouches commonly used in the country as receptacles for gold dust.

In a corner, where they had been carelessly tossed, lay a pair of worn mukluks of the same size and pattern as those on the feet of the dead man. Downey noted with interest that on one of these boots dust had collected on the inside and out, while the other was nearly free from dust.

He replenished the fire, dropped a pinch of tea into the snow water, and set the plate of caribou steaks on the stove to thaw. Again he turned his attention to the dead man, and again as he stared down into the frozen eyes, the strange feeling stole over him that the man wanted to speak to him—to impart a matter of importance.

Dismissing the fancy with a frown of annoyance, the officer stooped closer. "Too bad, old timer, that you can't talk," he muttered. "Prob'ly want to tell me how you missed out on the mother lode. But—whatever it is'll have to keep a long, long time, I guess."

Examination of the wound disclosed powder marks on the surrounding skin, and its position indicated that it could easily have been inflicted by a pistol held in the man's right hand. Blood had flowed from it, trickling down just in front of the ear, and had dripped from the stained white beard, freezing as it fell, to form a tiny red pyramid, or inverted cone upon the floor. "Done it when the strong cold was on," Downey muttered, "or that blood wouldn't have froze as it dripped. But not this spell of the strong cold. He hasn't left the shack since the last snow—an' that must be a week, or more."

Picking up the revolver, he noted that it was of .41 caliber, and that it held five loaded cartridges and an empty shell. "Funny he'd shoot himself with plenty of grub on hand, an' enough giant, an' caps, an' fuse to last him quite a while," he mused aloud, as is the wont of lone men. "Might be he got just one disappointment too many. But them old timers is used to disappointments. They've got a sort of hopelessly hopeful faith that they'll hit it next week, er next month, er next year. It's what keeps em' goin'—that faith in the mother lode."

Clearing a space along the wall near the stove, Downey stooped to lift the corpse. As he raised the outflung right arm from the floor a low exclamation escaped his lips. He lowered the body, and for long moments knelt there—staring. For, gripped between the thumb and finger of that iron-hard right hand was an unlighted match! "A man can't shoot himself in the right temple with a gun held in his left hand," he murmured slowly. "An' he can't hold a gun in his right hand—when that hand is grippin' a match." His glance strayed to the face of the corpse, and he started nervously. For, as a drop of grease guttered down the length of the candle, the flame flared, and in the flickering light the frozen left eye seemed to wink knowingly. The officer grinned into the glassily staring eyes. "I get you, old timer," he said. "You sure put it acrost—what you wanted to tell me. This ain't suicide—it's murder!"

Arranging the body close against the wall, Downey turned his attention to a more minute examination of the room. An hour later he fried the caribou steaks, seated himself at the table, and devoured a hearty meal. "Things had a wrong look, in the first place," he mused. "What with a revolver, an' no extry shells for it. An' some rifle shells on the shelf, an' no rifle. An' that pair of mukluks—one all covered with dust, an' the other without no dust on it to speak of. But I guess, now, I've got the picture—

someone comes along, an' the old timer invites him in. He lays his fire, an' just as he's about to light it, the other shoves the revolver almost against his head an' pulls the trigger. Then he makes a quick search an' finds the old man's cache of gold in one of them mukluks—the one without the dust. There'd be seven pokes of it, accordin' to that caribou hide—maybe eight, ten thousand dollars. Then he beat it without lightin' the fire. He wasn't takin' no chances in bein' caught in this box canyon if someone should come along. A man can't never tell what he's goin' to run up against on one of these routine patrols."

In the morning Downey inventoried the old man's effects, lifted his body to the bunk and covered it with a blanket, requisitioned a quarter of caribou meat to augment his meager supply of dog food, and struck off down the canyon. The strong cold persisted, but the curious dead feel was gone from the air, and the dogs bent to their work with a will. Later in the day a light breeze sprang up and the temperature moderated considerably.

On the third day thereafter the outfit pulled into the camp of Good Luck, situated at the precise location the breed had indicated on his map. Stepping into Stan Braddock's saloon, Downey was greeted by Old Bettles and Camillo Bill, two sourdoughs who had thrown in with the Good Luck stampede.

"Hello, Downey!" cried Bettles, "yer jest in time to have one on me! What in hell fetches you up to Good Luck? So fer, we've got along fine without no police."

Corporal Downey winked at Camillo Bill as he filled the glass Stan Braddock spun toward him with professional accuracy. "The inspector sent me up here to see why two able-bodied men would be hangin' around a saloon in the daytime, instead of workin' their claim," he replied.

"Well, ain't a man got a right to celebrate his birthday?" grinned the oldster.

Camillo Bill laughed: "Bettles, he celebrates his birthday every month."

"Shore I do! Every month except Feb'ry. Why wouldn't I? It was a damn important day fer me. I was born on the thirtieth—so every time the thirtieth comes around, I celebrate. What I claim—a man overlooks a lot of bets if he don't celebrate his birthday only onct a year."

"Guess that's right," Downey agreed. "How's things goin'?"

"Oh, not so bad. Good Luck ain't no Bonanza nor Hunker. But she's a damn sight better'n a lot of other cricks men are stickin' to. Most of the boys is takin' out a lot better'n wages."

"Heard any complaints? Any cache robbin', or claim jumpin' goin' on?"

Stan Braddock shook his head: "Nope. Here it is damn near April, an' we've gone through the winter without no crime that anyone knows of—an I'd have heard it in here, if anythin' out of the way had be'n goin' on. Some of the boys is in here every night."

"They's be'n three deaths," supplemented Bettles, "but they was all of 'em common ones. A rock squushed one fella where it fell on him, an' the other two died of some sickness they got. There ain't no doctor in camp, but we figger it was their guts went back on 'em, er mebbe their heart. We buried 'em decent, an' saved their names an' their stuff fer the public administrator. Two of 'em didn't have much, but one done pretty well fer hisself. It's all in Stan's safe, there—he'll turn it over to you."

"How many men do you figure wintered in **Good** Luck?"

"Couple hundred wouldn't miss it far," Braddock replied.

"Mostly chechakos, I s'pose."

"Yeah," said Camillo Bill, "Good Luck's jest like all the other camps. What with the damn chechakos crowdin' into the country, it's gittin' so us old timers can't hardly git enough of us together no more fer a decent stud game."

"Speakin' of old timers," said Downey, casually, "who's the old fella that located in a box canyon about three days back down the river?"

"He must mean old Tom Whipple," Bettles opined. "This here canyon runs in from the north, an' dead ends a couple of mile up, don't it?"

"That's the one."

"Yeah, that's old Tom. He's kinda batty—like all them hard-rock men—allus huntin' the mother lode. I know'd Tom first, must be fifteen, sixteen year ago—on Birch Crick, over on the American side. He wouldn't pay no 'tention to the placer stuff in the crick beds. Stuck to the hard rock—shootin' an' peckin'—peckin' an' shootin'—pryin' a little flake gold out of his samples with the p'int of his belt knife. He passed up all the good cricks—Forty Mile—Bonanza—Hunker—Dominion. We tried to git him to quit foolin' around amongst the rocks an' git in on some of the cricks—but it wasn't no use. He was old, then—too old, I guess, to learn him new tricks. He'd look at us like we didn't have all our buttons—like he was kinda takin' pity on us, er somethin'. 'That damn stuff in the crick beds ain't nothing but float,' he'd say. 'I wouldn't fool away my time on it. It's all got to come from the mother lode. Find the mother lode—that's where the gold is,' he'd tell us. 'An' the mother lode's in the hills —not in the crick beds.'

"There can't no one claim old Tom ain't got faith. He stuck to his idee when we was pannin' out two, three dollars to the pan on Birch Crick, an' up to seven, eight dollars on Forty Mile, an' then twenty an' a hundred on Bonanza. He watched us gittin' rich right in under his nose—but he wouldn't fool with it. An' he's stickin' to the same idee yet, up on the head of that canyon."

"A damn sight more faith than sense—that's what he's got, if you ask me," opined Camillo Bill. "Gold's where you find it, whether it's in the cricks, er on the hills."

"Didn't he ever make a strike," Downey asked.

Bettles shook his head: "Nope. Jest keeps on shootin'

down rock, an' peckin' with his pick, an' pryin' with his knife. Don't cost him nothin' much to live. Never has nothin' to do with wimmin er licker—never blow'd an ounce in his life. Beans, an' tea, an' flour, an' sugar—a little chawin' terbacker, an' ca'tridges fer that old rifle of his—that's all he needs."

"But, keepin' at it long as he has, an' not spendin' no more'n what he spends, he'd be bound to have some dust cached away somewheres, wouldn't he?"

"Oh, chances is, he's got some—prob'ly enough to keep him the rest of his life, when he gits too old to fight the rocks. I doubt an' he kin show ten thousan' in dust fer God knows how many years he's worked."

"You spoke of an old rifle," said Downey. "Would you know that gun if you saw it?"

"Shore, I'd know it. So would Camillo, here, an' Moosehide Charlie, an' Swiftwater Bill. It's a Marlin. He bust the stock, one time on Birch Crick, an' we wired it up fer him with some wire we ontwisted out of a chunk of cable. But—what you so int'rested in old Tom Whipple fer?"

"Didn't own a revolver that you know of?" persisted Downey, ignoring the question. "A forty-one calibre six-gun?"

"Hell, no! What would old Tom be doin' with a revolver? He allus travelled light. I seen him 'long about Christmas. Come up here draggin' a hand-sled after a load of grub an' giant. I kidded him about not havin' no dogs, an' he claimed it cost too much to feed 'em, an' he didn't need none. Claimed he sold off all his dogs two year back, when he located where he's at. There wasn't no Good Luck then—Tom had the country all to hisself. Claimed he's right up agin the mother lode, this time, an' would never have to make another move. Told me he'd be into it, come spring, fer shore—an' then he'd show us what damn fools we was fer muckin' around in the gravel. Pore old cuss—he'll keep on huntin' the mother lode till the last day he kin stand on his legs—an' allus it'll be jest ahead of him. If he'd throw'd in on the stampedes, like we done, he could of had as much dust as the best of us—more, 'cause he's a hard worker, an' he don't never spend nothin'. It's too damn bad. A fella with faith like that ort to win."

Stan Braddock smiled, and set out a fresh bottle. "I don't look at it that way, Bettles," he said, as the glasses were filled. "A man like that wouldn't never be satisfied with placer gold—no matter how much he took out. He'd always figure he was a fool fer passin' up the mother lode. An' what good would a lot of dust do him, anyhow— livin' like he does? I'm telling you, he's a damn sight happier'n the most of us. He's got enough to keep him, an' he's got his faith—an' he'll have it till he dies. If a man knows he's goin' to be the richest man in the world next week, er next month, er next year, he's bound to be happy. What happens to him in the meantime don't matter. Ain't that so, Corporal?"

Corporal Downey nodded slowly, as he toyed with his glass on the bar: "Yes," he said, "I guess maybe yer right."

Men began to drift into the saloon, and Braddock became busy with bottles and glasses. The officer turned to Bettles: "This last snow—when did it come?"

" 'Bout a week ago. It snowed fer two days."

"An' before that you'd had a spell of the strong cold?"

"I'll tell che world we did! Worst I ever seen. She hit fifty below fer twelve days, hand runnin'." He paused and indicated a man who had just entered and was limping painfully to the bar. "There's a bird kin tell you more about it than me. It ketched him comin' in—froze all his toes an' one of his heels. He's in a hell of a shape, without no doctor in camp. Them toes had ort to come off."

"Chechako?"

"Yeah—rawer'n hell. Claims he come in over the White Pass an' split off from his pals at Selkirk, when he heard about this strike."

Corporal Downey regarded the man intently as he

hobbled to the bar and elevated a clumsily swathed foot
to the rail. He was a large man, unprepossessing and ill-
kempt, with a month's growth of beard. He called for
whiskey without inviting others to join him, and when
Braddock set out the bottle, he filled his glass to the
brim and emptied it at a gulp. He repeated the per-
formance and tossed a pouch to the bar.

"He ain't be'n able to do much work since he got here,
has he?" Downey asked. "Ain't taken out much dust?"

"Hell, no!" Camillo Bill replied. "He moved into Bill
Davis's shack—it was Bill got squushed by the rock. Me
an' Bettles went down there yesterday to see if we could
do somethin' fer him, an' the stink in there was somethin'
fierce. Them toes of his has started to rot. We offered
to cut 'em off fer him—but the damn fool wouldn't let
us. By God, if they was my toes they'd come off—if I
had to do it myself with an ax! But, that's the way with
a damn chechako. They don't know nothin'—an' never
will. He cussed the hell out of us when we told him
he'd be dead in a month with the blood pizen."

Corporal Downey watched Stan Braddock pick up
the sack the man had tossed onto the bar and shake a few
yellow flakes of gold into the scales. "Kind of queer,
ain't it?" he observed, "that a chechako jest in over the
pass, an' not in shape to take out any dust after he got
here, should be spendin' dust?"

Old Bettles looked up quickly. "Why—why—shore it
is!" he agreed.

"Damn if it ain't," said Camillo Bill. "Where would he
git it?"

"I believe," replied Downey, "that I know."

The man had turned from the bar and hobbled to a
chair on the opposite side of the room as Downey slipped
to the scales just as Braddock lifted the little pan to
transfer the gold to the till. He thrust out his hand, palm
up. "Pour it in there, Braddock. I want to have a look at
it," he ordered, and when the man complied, he returned
to where Bettles and Camillo Bill waited under one of

the big swinging lamps. Eagerly, the three examined the yellow grains, as the officer prodded them about with a forefinger. "Ever see any stuff like it?" he asked, abruptly.

"Them flakes is sort of sharp edged," ventured Camillo Bill. "They don't show no water wear."

"That," replied Downey, "is because they didn't come out of a crick bed. They was pried out of rock samples— with the point of a belt knife, maybe."

"You mean!" exclaimed Bettles, his eyes suddenly widening, "that—"

The officer silenced him with a wink, and a glance toward the chechako who sat sprawled in his chair, his eyes on his bandaged foot. "Yeah," he replied, in an undertone. "Old Tom Whipple was murdered an' robbed in his cabin in that box canyon. It happened durin' the last spell of the strong cold—there was no tracks in the new snow. Whoever done it stole Whipple's dust, an' his rifle. The three of us'll jest sift down to this chechako's shack, now. Besides Whipple's old rifle I think we'll find his dust, in caribou-hide sacks—six of 'em, besides the one the chechako's packin' on him. An' when we rip 'em apart, I think we'll find that the pieces was cut out of a hide I fetched along out of Whipple's shack. We'd ort to find some forty-one-caliber revolver ammunition, too. Forty-ones ain't common. It's the gun the murderer left to make it look like Whipple killed himself. When we find them things, I'll arrest that bird—an' I'll have enough evidence to hang him higher than hell."

"It'll be all right with me," growled Camillo Bill, as the three stepped out onto the hard-packed snow, "if we can't find no evidence whatever in his shack. Hangin's too good fer a damn cuss that would murder old Tom Whipple—which Tom had prob'ly took him in to save him from the strong cold. I'd ruther see him left here to rot from his toes clean up to his chin!"

"How come you turned off up that canyon, if there wasn't no tracks in the snow?" queried Bettles, as Downey spoke to his dogs who had lain down in the harness, wrapped snugly in their bushy tails.

"That was pure accident," the officer replied. "The air had gone dead. There was a peculiar feel to it, an' there was false suns dancin' in the sky. I felt sort of weak an' light headed—like nothin' mattered—an' I guess the dogs felt it, too. Anyhow, my lead dog turned off up this canyon, an' I couldn't head him off. Like I said—nothin' seemed to matter—one crick seemed as good as any other—so I let 'em go."

Old Bettles nodded: "The white death reachin' fer you, eh? Some claim it's a lie—that there ain't no sech thing. But don't you believe 'em, Downey. I know."

"You tellin' me?"

"Where'd you git that lead dog?" the oldster asked, after a moment's pause, his eyes on the great brute who stood alert, awaiting the word of command.

"Down in Dawson, a year ago. Best lead dog in the country. It's funny he'd leave the trail fer a side crick."

"Not so damn funny as you think," Bettles replied. "I know that dog. He's Topek. Old Tom Whipple raised him from a pup."

A SHOT IN THE DARK

by HENRY HERBERT KNIBBS

YOUNG JOE HARDESTY from the Mebbyso mine, and his Eastern friend Borden stood watching the little man with the youthful face and the bald head, rub down a steel-gray pony. The pony's name was Peanut. The little man was Charley Price. Once a year he made the rounds of the Arizona cow towns, matching Peanut against the local quarter horses. A steel-gray thunderbolt in a race,

Peanut was gentle when off the track, with a dog-like affection for his owner.

Having cleaned up a substantial sum in Bowdry, Charley Price was heading for Claybank to run his pony against the fast Claybank sorrel, Wasp.

"Better stop by at the mine on your way over," said Young Hardesty. "Bedrock'll sure be glad to see you."

Price shook his head. "Not this time. I'm pulling straight through for Claybank. I want to give Peanut a chance to rest up before I run him again. Besides—"

Young Hardesty nodded. Bowdry was a tough camp. Price, who never packed a gun, would have several hundred dollars in his money belt. By taking the seldom-traveled desert cut-off he would make fast time and run little risk of meeting anyone.

Half an hour later Young Joe Hardesty and Borden left town, facing a thirty-mile ride to the Mebbyso mine. They intended to stop overnight at the mine, and pull out for Claybank in the morning. The coming race would be the sporting event of the season.

As they passed the junction of the old desert trail and the main road they saw that recently someone, presumably from Bowdry, had ridden down the abandoned cut-off leading to Claybank. Charley Price was still in Bowdry. Moreover, the tracks were those of a much larger horse than Peanut.

"Some cowhand in a hurry to get to Claybank and lose his money," commented Young Hardesty. "A lot of Bowdry sports are goin' to back the Claybank pony, just because he was raised in Arizona. Peanut and Charley hail from Texas."

It was past midnight when Borden and Young Hardesty arrived at the Mebbyso. After a word with Bedrock about the Bowdry races, they staked their horses in the meadow above the spring, and turned in for a much-needed rest.

With Claybank in mind, Young Hardesty was up and had the breakfast fire going before Bedrock and Borden were awake. When he went up to the spring for a bucket of water he discovered that his pony, Shingles, had broken the stake rope and strayed. Young Hardesty reported the fact with considerable off-hand embellishment, and set out to track the missing pony.

He had been trailing the pony for nearly an hour, when, rounding the shoulder of a high sand ridge, his dark eyes suddenly narrowed in apprehension. His stake rope dragging, Shingles stood warming his back in the early sun. Near him stood Charley Price's pony, Peanut, saddled, and the reins hanging. Young Hardesty's gaze leaped to a huddled shape in the shadow of an upthrust rock.

Charley Price had been waylaid and shot. Before him lay his money belt. It was empty.

As Young Hardesty stood gazing down at the dead man, Borden rode round the shoulder of the ridge. "Been trailing you," he said glancing at the two ponies. "Thought maybe I could lend a hand. How does Peanut happen to be here? Where's Charley Price?"

Young Joe gestured toward the huddled shape at his feet. Borden's sun-dazed eyes focused down. His face went white. He asked who had killed Price, realizing immediately the stupidity of his question.

"He was packin' too much money," said Young Hardesty. "And no gun."   .

"Hadn't we better ride over to Grant and telephone the sheriff?" suggested Borden.

"And when Collins hears it was me found him, he'll just naturally try to tangle me up in this killin'. He's been tryin' to hang somethin' on me ever since he was elected."

"But what else can we do?"

"When Charley don't show up in Claybank, folks will say he was scared to run Peanut against the sorrel, and headed back for Texas. The fella that killed him won't tell 'em any different. That'll give us time to do a little figurin'."

"How about the pony?"

"I'll stake him up in the meadows along with Shingles. Nobody'll see him up there—for a spell, anyhow."

Borden gestured toward the body.

Young Hardesty shrugged. "We got plenty shovels at the mine. What I mean, Charley had no kinfolks in Texas. Said so himself. And the sheriff won't do nothin' about the murder except mebby send out a buckboard and haul Charley to town and bury him. Collins will know dam' well that somebody around Bowdry did the job. But he's awful good at keepin' his hands off the wild bunch. You ought to know that."

Borden was gazing at the steel-gray pony standing near the dead man. "His horse didn't leave him. Stood right here, waiting. . . ."

"That kind of got me, too," said Young Hardesty. "Peanut and Charley was pardners."

Tracks in the vicinity showed that someone had waited at the ledge of rock at the southern end of the sand ridge until Price rode down the Claybank cut-off. Evidently after the shot was fired Peanut had whirled and dashed back up the draw, stopping when his rider had fallen from the saddle. The murderer had then dismounted, walked to where Price lay, robbed him, and made for the distant Pinnacles. Recalling the tracks they had seen yesterday, Young Hardesty surmised that the murderer had come down the Bowdry-Grant road to the cut-off. Catching up the two loose horses, Young Hardesty and Borden rode back to the mine.

Bedrock, who had known Charley Price for years, was greatly upset about the murder. After pointing out that Young Hardesty ran a serious risk if he buried the body without notifying the authorities, Bedrock regretfully admitted that the sheriff would do little, if anything, to apprehend the murderer. But Bedrock disliked the idea of Young Joe mixing up in it.

"We was plannin' to go to Claybank, anyhow," said Young Hardesty. "Out of the Bowdry bunch of sports and cowhands at Claybank will be three, four that won't show up, bein' drunk, or broke, or not able to leave their jobs. But there'll be one fella that won't show up because he knows there won't be any horse race."

"Would it be possible," said Borden, "to take Peanut to Claybank and run the race ourselves?"

Surprised by the idea, Young Hardesty asked what good it would do if they ran the race.

"Matter of sentiment, with me," said Borden. "I'd like to see Peanut trim the Claybank sorrel. Besides, people are apt to forget themselves at a horse race—drink more than usual, do a lot of talking, show more of their real feelings. And the fact that Peanut is there might surprise at least one of them."

"You figure that the man we're lookin' for will be there?"

"If he thinks there's the slightest chance of ever being suspected of the murder, he's a fool if he doesn't show up in Claybank. Of course no one else knows that Charley Price was murdered. But the man himself knows. He can't get away from himself."

"Well, if we're goin'," said Young Hardesty, "we ought to pull out right soon. It's only ten miles by the cut-off, but it's mostly up and down and Peanut is a flat-country horse. He'll need plenty rest before he runs against the sorrel."

Bedrock shook his head. "Arriving in daylight would be a mistake. You don't want anybody to know Peanut is in Claybank until just before the race. It would be better to start 'long about four. That would get you to Claybank round ten or eleven, this evening."

Following a lengthy discussion as to the feasibility of the scheme they finally decided to take Peanut to Claybank and run him against the sorrel.

"Well, that's settled," said Young Hardesty. "But there's Charley, down there . . ."

Huge, white bearded, slow moving, Old Bedrock took

a shovel and a blanket, and strode down toward the desert. Charley Price and he had been close friends for a good many years.

At four that afternoon Borden and Young Hardesty got ready to leave for Claybank. Bedrock stalked into the lean-to, came out with an extra sack of tobacco and his Winchester. "I'll ride Shingles," he stated. Although neither of his companions had counted on his going along, they made no comment. Bedrock's grim attitude did not invite conversation.

Crossing the Mebbyso range, they dropped down into The Other Valley, and continuing on west across the succeeding range, arrived in Claybank about eleven that night. Bedrock hunted up an old timer, Jimmy Owens. They conferred privately. Jimmy Owens crooked his thumb and looked Bedrock in the eye. "I'll do it, by gum! I know right where you can cache that pony so that no-body but a bloodhound could find him."

Shingles and Borden's mount were put into Jimmy's corral. Peanut was stabled in the abandoned adobe next to Jimmy's house. The abandoned adobe was the last place anyone would think of as a stable for a horse.

Borden and Young Hardesty slept on Owens' veranda. Bedrock, who didn't intend to let Peanut out of his sight, borrowed a blanket and stationed himself in the adobe. From the saloon up the street came the sound of sage-brush revelry. Yet Borden and Young Hardesty slept soundly until Jimmy Owens called them to breakfast.

They spent the morning chatting with Bowdry ac-quaintances. Notably absent were four who had attended the Bowdry races. An accident accounted for the absence of one, too much liquor for the absence of another. Ac-cording to precedent the remaining absentees should have been in Claybank: Sims, a cowhand, and Jack Renter, notoriously a friend of Sheriff Collins of Bowdry.

Noon came and Charley Price failed to appear. It was rumored that Price, fearing to run his pony against the sorrel, had quietly left for Texas. The crowd began to feel that it was in for a disappointment. There would be no big race—only the preliminaries, run by no-account local ponies.

About one that afternoon, Young Hardesty appeared in the street riding his own pony, Shingles. He tied at the saloon hitch-rail. Accompanied by Borden, he strolled to the bar. A tall, rangy man eyed them sharply. It was Renter, who, Young Hardesty learned later on, had arrived in Claybank the previous day. Young Hardesty covered his surprise with a nod and a greeting. Renter, he knew, would gamble on anything from a dog fight to a national election. Young Hardesty asked him how the betting was going.

"Got any money on you?" said Renter brusquely.

"Not enough to sag my pants. But I can get some."

"Who do you pick to win the lap-and-tap?"

"The pony I'm going to ride," declared Young Hardesty.

Borden all but gasped.

"You're drunk," said Renter. "You better go and sleep it off."

Young Hardesty grinned amiably. "Did you say you was bettin' on the big race, or was you just talkin' to yourself?"

The dog-faced bartender gestured toward the doorway. "Mebby you ain't took a look at Young Joe's pony. He's what you might call The Mebbyso Special."

Stepping to the doorway, Renter sized up Young Hardesty's mount, Shingles. "Goin' to run that heifer?"

"The little bay—that's Joe's horse," said Borden obligingly. "His name is Shingles."

"Satisfied, Jack?" said Young Joe.

"Hell, yes! Satisfied you're crazy."

"So am I," declared Borden in a sprightly tone, "a hundred dollars' worth—if that interests you."

Borden seemed eager to lose money. But then, Borden

was a tenderfoot, didn't know a horse from a hitch-rail. "I'll take you on," said Renter. From a fat roll of bills he counted out a hundred dollars.

"Stick in another hundred for me," said Young Hardesty, as Borden put up his money.

Both Borden and Renter produced another hundred. The bartender was made stakeholder. "There's goin' to be a lot of soreheads around here," he said as he shoved the money into the till. "Price ain't showed up."

"Of course," said Borden, glancing at Young Hardesty, "if Charley Price doesn't show up, I suppose all bets will be called off."

"The hell they will!" Renter ordered a drink. "I put up my cash on the Claybank sorrel. I didn't say anything about what horse was to run against him."

"Neither did I." Borden's tone was mild. "I said I was backing Joe to win the race. Take it or leave it, Mr. Renter."

"You're feelin' real healthy," sneered Renter. "Mebby you'd like to raise your bet."

Borden seemed to be considering. Finally he agreed to Renter's suggestion. "All right, Mr. Renter. Three hundred, even, that Joe wins the lap-and-tap race."

Renter stripped a new hundred-dollar bill from his roll. Borden laid a similar bill on the bar. He noted, casually, that both bills were of the same series. In Bowdry, Charley Price had changed a hundred-dollar bill for Borden, giving him fives and tens, as more flexible money with which to make bets in that community. Price had put the bill in his money belt. Later, Price might have passed the hundred-dollar bill on to someone else. Still, that Renter now had it seemed interesting.

Hunting up Gimp, who owned the Claybank sorrel, Young Hardesty said that in case Charley Price didn't show up, he would like to ride against the sorrel in the big race. Taking it for granted that Young Joe was to ride the stocky pony, Shingles, Gimp and his backers considered this suggestion a joke. But word had got round that the tenderfoot, Borden, was betting heavily against the sorrel, so Gimp was only too willing to accept the proposal. It had looked as if the grand clean-up had fizzled out. Now, with a readjustment of bets, there was some easy money in sight.

The three preliminary races didn't cause much excitement. The crowd was waiting for the big event. Gimp and his backers stood in a group near the sorrel. Young Hardesty, holding Shingles, was arguing about the start. "I know you and your red-headed race pony," he was saying. "If you shoulder me in gettin' away, somebody's goin' to get knocked off a sorrel horse so quick he'll wonder who done it."

The foreman of the Claybank ranch stepped between the belligerents. They could do their arguing after the race. Centering on the dispute, the crowd did not see Bedrock coming across the flat leading Price's pony. But the foreman saw him. He stared hard at Young Joe, asked in a low voice where Price was.

"At the Mebbyso. He ain't in shape to come. I'm reppin' for him."

"You aim to ride Price's pony?"

"I sure do."

"I don't know about that."

"Well I do. Gimp and Charley agreed in Bowdry to run Peanut and the sorrel in Claybank today. I was with 'em when they ribbed it up. So was you. There was nothin' said about who was to ride either of the horses. If you think you can run a whizzer on me, you're wrong. The crowd wants to see a real horse race."

Ignoring exclamations and questions Old Bedrock shouldered his way up to Young Joe. "Here's your pony," he said handing him the reins, "all slick and ready to go." Like a monument Bedrock towered above the crowd, his pipe going, and his Winchester across his arm. He suggested that the bystanders give the boys a little more room.

Peanut knew what was coming. He was alert, his fine

ears working, but he wasn't nervous. Gimp's sorrel, however, fidgeted, stepping round with his hind end humped,
clearing the space Bedrock had asked for. The starter
stood waiting, a white stick in his hand. A laugh went up
as Young Joe pulled off his boots and thrust his stock-
inged feet into the narrow stirrups. Borden was approached by several who wanted to change or withdraw
their bets. He told them politely that he was quite satisfied as things stood. "When I took you on," he said, "I
told you I was backing Joe Hardesty to win this race. I
said nothing whatever about the horse he was to ride."

Standing near the starter, Renter was gazing fixedly at
Borden. Renter said something to the starter in a low tone.
Peanut and the Claybank sorrel lined up, the sorrel wild
to be off. Young Joe clenched his teeth. The sorrel was
fast and mean. It wouldn't be an easy job to lap him and
get away.

The sorrel shot out, a full jump ahead of Peanut. Young
Hardesty hadn't even tried to lap Gimp's horse. They
were brought back. Peanut was now on his toes. Again
both ponies leaped toward the scratch. The sorrel reared
and fought his rider. Again they were brought back.

Young Hardesty had never ridden a lap-and-tap race.
But he was familiar with the rules. The start actually
began several yards back of scratch. The two horses had
to come to the scratch with one overlapping the other
if only by a nose, or they were called back. It was a
short race. A quick start often meant more than the
actual distance. This incurred much jockeying. It was
evident that Gimp and the sorrel were trying to wear
down Price's pony and his inexperienced rider.

Again the ponies dashed for the scratch, the sorrel
obviously not lapped by Peanut. The starter called them
back. Renter stepped up to him. "Call 'em back on another
start like that and something will happen to you," he
said in a low tone.

"Don't you worry any. The boys are going to get away
to a clean start," said someone just behind Renter. He

turned to face Old Bedrock, his pipe in his mouth, his Winchester in the hollow of his arm. "Don't bother to move," said Bedrock, "I can see all right."

As the ponies came back from another false start the crowd grew restless. Those nearest the riders heard Gimp tell Young Hardesty to go to hell. Lacking the steel-gray's training, the sorrel was becoming hard to hold. When he did leave the scratch he would run as if shot out of a cannon—run blind, a danger both to himself and anyone who happened to be in the way.

A shout went up as the ponies finally got away. About three lengths from scratch. Gimp's horse suddenly plunged sideways, shouldered Peanut. Peanut went to his knees. His backers groaned. Young Hardesty felt him surge up, break into his stride again. Nose and nose the two ponies tore down the stretch, Gimp quirting the sorrel viciously. Before Young Joe realized it the race had ended. Putting all that he had into the last four or five jumps, Peanut had finished a good half length ahead.

Except for the shouting of Peanut's backers, the crowd was silent. In spite of Gimp's dirty work, the little steel-gray pony had won the race. He had stumbled to his knees, caught himself, and beaten the sorrel in a terrific sprint.

Young Hardesty led a lame horse back to the starting line. Dismounting, he handed the reins to Bedrock.

Back down the stretch came Gimp, fighting the crazy sorrel to keep him from bolting into the crowd. Suddenly Gimp swung his shot-loaded quirt and struck the sorrel between the ears. The horse staggered, but managed to keep its feet.

When Gimp dismounted, he claimed Young Joe had fouled him. Even the Claybankers laughed. Gimp turned on Young Hardesty, whose black eyes were fixed in a stare that Bedrock didn't like. The old man started toward him, but before he could get through the crowd, Young Hardesty swung his arm. The blow was so swift that some of the bystanders jumped as if they themselves had been hit. Young Hardesty had laid the butt of his own quirt across Gimp's head. Gimp lay on the ground like a heap of someone's cast-off clothes.

Gimp's friends blustered, surged round Young Hardesty. Old Bedrock pushed forward. "You hadn't ought to done it, Joe," he said calmly, "even if he did shoulder you and lame Charley's pony. But seeing as you did it, I'm glad of it."

The crowd knew Bedrock. He was slow to wrath, but hell on wheels when he got started. Ordinarily he never carried a Winchester. And partisanship or no partisanship, Gimp had got what was coming to him. There was no further argument.

Having recorded his bets in a small notebook, Borden had little difficulty in collecting his winnings. The losers, as a whole, were good sportsmen. The few exceptions either slunk away or refused outright to settle up, claiming they had bet against Shingles, not Price's pony.

The crowd began to drift toward the saloon. Many of the cowhands left town, if not actually broke, pretty badly bent. Those of the Bowdry contingent who had backed Peanut decided to celebrate. They had already taken a running start when Borden entered the bar, looking for Jack Renter. He was told that Renter had left town right after the race. Borden finally managed to get hold of the bartender, who immediately turned to the till and handed him six hundred dollars. Those who saw the transaction stared. Borden pocketed the bills, bought a round of drinks for the crowd. He wondered why Renter had left town so suddenly, and why he hadn't protested because of the substitution of Peanut for the pony he had supposed would run against the sorrel. It wasn't like Renter calmly to let three hundred go like that. Again Borden caught the bartender on the fly. "Did Renter say anything about the bet?"

"Sure. Said to hand the dough over to you. Said Price's pony won, hands down. Funny Jack didn't howl, seein' how you fellas put it over him."

"I did expect to hear a slight yelp," said Borden, "Thanks."

Borden stalked out to find Bedrock and Young Hardesty waiting. "Renter paid up," said Borden, anticipating a question. "He has left town."

"We're leavin', right now," said Young Joe. "Gimp and his crowd will be ragin' drunk this evening. Somebody might get hurt."

"I wonder," said Borden, pondering, "if Renter took the Claybank cut-off."

Bedrock shook his head. Renter had paid his bet too easily.

Peanut was lame. Grumblingly Young Hardesty walked and led him. Far out on the flats east of Claybank, Old Bedrock dismounted. He preferred, he said, to travel on foot—was used to it. Joe could ride Shingles and lead the lame pony.

Just before sunset, as they neared the foothills of the range east of The Other Valley, Bedrock called a halt. Fresh hoofprints showed that someone from the direction of Claybank had cut into the trail at this spot, apparently heading for The Other Valley. There were no other tracks going east, save their own. "Might be anybody," asserted Bedrock. "But the timber is mighty thick on the hills yonder, and it'll be dark as Jonah's pocket crossing the range."

"Renter?" said Borden .

"That's the trouble of being loaded up with suspicions. A fella gets hair-trigger before there's anything to shoot at. How come, you're packing a powerful lot of money. Mebby we better cut round the end of the mountain, and take the road. It's open country all the way."

In spite of Bedrock's precaution they were due for a surprise. On the crest of the distant range, near the edge of the timber, a man sat his horse watching the oncoming travelers. He saw them pause, apparently in debate. When they left the Claybank cut-off and struck south along the foothills, the man watching them cursed. Reining round, he rode south through the timber, paralleling their course. When they swung round the end of the mountain and struck into the Grant road, he would be there.

About eight that night, they reached the road, which ran close to the foothills through country sparsely dotted with brush and cactus. Stalking ahead of his companions in the starlight, Bedrock stopped to fill and light his pipe. As the cupped match flared, a shot crashed from the foothill brush. Bedrock dropped flat, crawled behind a rock, and spat the stem of the pipe from his mouth. The bowl had gone zipping off into space. "Not bad shooting for this kind of light," he told himself placidly. His Winchester over the top of the rock, he lay watching the brush across the road.

The pony, Peanut, had whirled at the shot, dragging Young Hardesty and Shingles round with him. In the melee, Borden's horse took fright. Finally they were brought to a stop. Down the road Old Bedrock's Winchester boomed. Sitting their trembling horses, Borden and Young Joe heard the crackling of the foothill brush, and the sound of a horse on the run.

"Thank God!" said Borden fervently.

"For what?"

"That last shot. Bedrock is all right."

"I was wonderin' about the other fella," stated Young Joe.

Rejoining Bedrock, who assured them that his health was flourishing, possibly because he had quit smoking, he explained the absence of the pipe. Borden whistled. Young Joe said nothing—stared in the direction from which the shot had come. No one with nerve enough to waylay them would light out on the dead run like that simply because one of the party had taken a shot at him in the dark. There was something queer about it. Why hadn't the unknown stayed until he had either finished the job, or got put down himself? Had he been hit by Bedrock's shot or had it stung the horse and stampeded him? Young Joe would have given his share of the race winnings for fifteen minutes of daylight. But there was nothing they could do now but push along and take a chance that the bushwhacker wouldn't try it again.

This time they traveled in a close group. Borden thought this was a mistake. In case they were fired upon again, they would afford a bigger target. Bedrock admitted it, adding that at night, a group of moving men and horses created a blurred target in which it was almost impossible to outline an individual. "More chance of hitting one of the horses than one of us," he said.

"I suppose you was firin' at the middle of the mountain," commented Young Joe.

"Not exactly, son. When I cut loose I was holding right close on something higher than the brush and not so high as a tree. But if I hit it, it was just plumb luck."

Dawn was breaking when they finally reached the desert east of the range. Unmolested they made the remaining five miles in broad daylight. Tired and glum, they ate a hasty breakfast and turned in for a much-needed sleep. Charley Price's pony had won the Claybank race. But Charley Price's murderer was still at large.

Early the following morning, Bedrock led his burro down from the meadow. He was going to Bowdry to bank their winnings, he explained, and get himself a new pipe. He was going alone. He was very definite about that. No, he did not intend to report the murder of Charley Price. That, he said, could wait.

It was obvious that Old Bedrock was on the prod. It would be best to leave him to his own devices. Young Hardesty, however, could not refrain from a parting comment. "We got Charley's pony here, which is all right with me. But it might look funny to some folks."

"It might, if they knew Charley was dead," said Bedrock. "Charley could have sold the pony to Borden. Time enough to worry when Collins starts to asking questions. And the way I figure it, he ain't going to ask any."

Bedrock was gone. Young Joe and Borden loafed a while in camp, then saddled their horses and headed for the Grant road and the spot where they had been way-laid. After considerable circling through the brush they found the tracks they were looking for. These led east along the foothills, and eventually, into the desert.

Bedrock himself did not take the Bowdry-Grant road, but headed for the Claybank cut-off which would finally take him to the road, several miles north of the mine. Reaching the cut-off he was not altogether surprised to find horse tracks also leading north. With the burro in the lead, Bedrock strode along, developing a plan which he would put into operation when he reached Bowdry. He would find out if Renter was in town, when he arrived from Claybank, and then hunt him up and ask him a few questions.

As Bedrock and the burro approached the long ridge of sand where Young Joe had discovered Charley Price, dead and robbed, the burro stopped and slanted its ears. Bedrock shifted his Winchester and stepped ahead.

Round the shoulder of the ridge stood a big bay horse, dust-caked and evidently leg weary. The horse was saddled. One rein had been broken short off at the bit. As Bedrock approached, the horse wheeled and began to walk away. In the shadow of the ledge of rock lay a man who tried to rise as Bedrock came up.

"Take it easy, Renter," said Bedrock. "Just where did I get you?"

Renter groaned, stared at the old man's placid face. "Water," he muttered.

"Hit pretty bad," said Bedrock as he held his canteen to Renter's blue lips. "Reckon you ain't got long to talk. Mebby you'd like to say something."

"Go to hell," groaned Renter.

"No. I was thinking of Charley Price."

Renter tried to draw his gun. Bedrock took it from him. "Why did you kill Charley?" he said quietly.

Renter, who knew that he was done for, shaped his mouth in a hard grin. "Like to know, wouldn't you?"

"I reckon I know. I buried Charley, right yonder.

Queer that you quit your horse right where you killed Charley. Only God Almighty can explain such things."

Renter stared up at Bedrock. Bedrock gave him more water. "Any word you want to send to your friends, Jack?"

Renter made as if to speak. Following a convulsion his body stiffened. His jaw dropped. Bedrock stood his rifle against the ledge, hung his canteen on the pack saddle, and coming back, searched the body. Renter still had considerable money in small bills. In the watch-pocket of his overalls Bedrock found a silver-cased stop watch. It had belonged to Charley Price, was engraved with his initials.

"Too sure of himself, and his friends in Bowdry," said Bedrock. "Now I always figured Jack had more brains."

Chance had anticipated Bedrock's plan. But there still remained a tag-end to tie up. Over Renter's body he laid the pack sheet, with a rock on each corner. Then he continued his journey to Bowdry.

In Bowdry the day following, Sheriff Collins was loafing in the Silver Dollar saloon when Bedrock appeared.

"Just the man I'm lookin' for," said Collins, glad of an audience. "I hear you got Price's pony at the mine—ran him in Claybank against the sorrel."

Bedrock gazed at the paunchy Collins, whose mottled face reddened.

"What I mean," continued Collins, "where is Charley Price?"

"If Renter was alive he could tell you. Trouble is, he's dead."

"Dead! What do you mean?"

"I found him, yesterday morning at the rock ledge on the Claybank cut-off. He was shot up pretty bad. I left him there. But here's what I found on him." Bedrock produced a roll of bills, matches, tobacco and cigarette papers and a jack knife.

"It wasn't your business to go through him," said the sheriff.

"Mebby so. But I feared you might miss something if you searched him."

"And that's everything you found?"

"Not quite, Collins." Bedrock laid Charley Price's stop watch on the bar. "Renter went broke on the Bowdry races. But he showed up in Claybank with five or six hundred dollars. Considerable money for a man that didn't do any work. And he had Charley's watch on him."

"So you say."

"I didn't come here to kill you," said Bedrock softly, "but I'm willing. If you want to draw any more conclusions, go ahead. But you want to draw 'em awful quick."

For a second or so Bedrock stood facing the sheriff, then, letting his Winchester sag to the hollow of his arm, turned and strode out.

When Bedrock finally returned to the Mebbyso mine he found Borden and Young Joe anxiously awaiting him. Tracking from the scene of the recent hold-up, they had discovered Renter's body under a pack cloth near the rock ledge. "That shot in the dark," began Young Joe.

Bedrock nodded. "Made another shot in the dark, in Bowdry. It hit plumb center or I reckon I wouldn't be here."

DOG EATER

by CHARLES M. RUSSELL

"A MAN that ain't never been hungry can't tell nobody what's good to eat," says Rawhide. "I've et raw sow bosom and frozen biscuit when it tasted like a Christmas dinner.

"Bill Gurd tells me he's caught one time. He's been ridin' since daybreak and ain't had a bite. It's plum dark when he hits a breed's camp. This old breed shakes hands and tells Bill he's welcome, so after strippin' his saddle and hobblin' his hoss, he steps into the shack. Being wolf hungry, he notices the old woman's cooking bannacks at the mud fire. Tired and hungry like Bill is, the warmth and the smell of grub makes this cottonwood shack that ain't much more than a windbreak, look like a palace.

" 'Tain't long till the old woman hands him a tin plate loaded with stew and bannacks with hot tea for a chaser. He don't know what kind of meat it is but he's too much of a gentleman to ask. So he don't look a gift hoss in the mouth. After he fills up, while he's smokin' the old man spreads down some blankets and Bill beds down.

"Next mornin' he gets the same for breakfast. Not being so hungry, he's more curious, but don't ask no questions. On the way out to catch his hoss he gets an answer. A little ways from the cabin, he passes a fresh dog hide pegged down on the ground. It's like seeing the hole card —it's no gamble what that stew was made of, but it was good and Bill held it.

"I knowed another fellow one time that was called 'Dog Eatin' ' Jack. I never knowed how he got his name that's hung to him, till I camp with him. This old boy is a prospector and goes gopherin' round the hills, hopin' he'll find something.

"I'm huntin' hosses one spring and ain't found nothing but tracks. I'm up on the Lodgepole in the foothills; it's sundown and my hoss has went lame. We're limping along slow when I sight a couple of hobbled cayuses in a beaver meadow. One of these hosses is wearing a Diamond G iron, the other a quarter circle block hoss. They're both old cow ponies. I soon locate their owner's camp—it's a lean-to in the edge of the timber.

"While I'm lookin' over the layout, here comes the owner. It's the Dog Eater. After we shake hands I unsaddle and stake out my tired hoss. When we're filled up on the best he's got (which is beans. bacon and frying pan bread, which is good filling for hungry men), we're sittin' smokin' and it's then I ask him if he ever lived with Injuns.

"'You're thinkin'' says he, 'about my name. It does sound like Injun, but they don't hang it on me. It happens about ten winters ago. I'm way back in the diamond range; I've throwed my hosses about ten mile out in the foothills where there's good feed and less snow. I build a lean-to, a good one, and me and my dog settles down. There's some beaver here and I got out a line of traps and figger on winterin' here. Ain't got much grub but there's lots of game in the hills and my old needle gun will get what the traps won't.

"'Snow comes early and lots of it. About three days after the storm I step on a loose boulder and sprain my ankle. This puts me plumb out; I can't more than keep my fire alive. All the time I'm running short of grub. I eat a couple of skinned beaver, I'd throwed away one day. My old dog brings in a snowshoe rabbit to camp and maybe you don't think he's welcome. I cut in two with him but, manlike, I give him the front end. That's the last we got.

"'Old Friendship (that's the dog's name) goes out every day but he don't get nothing and I know he ain't cheating—he's too holler in the flanks. After about four days of living on thoughts, Friendship starts watchin' like he's afraid. He thinks maybe I'll put him in the pot, but he sizes me up wrong. If I'd do that, I hope I choke to death.

"'The sixth day I'm sizin' him up. He's laying near the fire. He's a hound with a long meaty tail. Says I to myself, "Oxtail soup! What's the matter with dog tail?" He don't use it for nothing but sign talk but it's like cutting the hands off a dummy. But the eighth day, with hunger and pain in my ankle, I plumb locoed and I can't get that dog's tail out of my mind. So, a little before noon, I slip up on him while he's sleeping, with the ax. In a second it's all over. Friendship goes yelpin' into the woods and I am sobbin' like a kid, with his tail in my hand.

" 'The water is already boiling in the pot an' as soon as I singe the hair off it's in the pot. I turned a couple of flour sacks inside out and dropped them in and there's enough flour to thicken the soup. It's about dark. I fill up and if it weren't for thinkin', it would have been good. I could have eat it all but I held out over half for Friendship, in case he come back.

" 'It must be midnight when he pushes into the blankets with me. I take him in my arms. He's as cold as a dead snake, and while I'm holdin' him tight, I'm crying like a baby. After he warms up a little, I get up and throw some wood on the fire and call Friendship to the pot. He eats every bit of it. He don't seem to recognize it. If he does, being a dog, he forgives.

" 'We go back to the blankets. It's just breaking day when he slides out, whinin' and sniffin' the air with his ears cocked and his bloody stub wobblin'. I look the way he's pointin' and not twenty-five yards from the lean-to stands a big elk. There's a fine snow fallin'; the wind's right for us. I ain't a second gettin' my old needle gun but I'm playin' safe—I'm coming inun on him. I use my ram rod for a rest. When the old needle speaks, the bull turns over—his neck's broken. 'Tain't long till we both get to that bull and we're both eatin' raw, warm liver. I've seen Injuns do this but I never thought I was that much wolf, but it was sure good that morning.

" 'He's a big seven-point bull—old and pretty tough, but me and Friendship was looking for quantity, not quality and we got it. That meat lasted till we got out.'

" 'What became of Friendship?' says I.

" 'He died two years ago,' says Jack. 'But he died fat.' "

COURT DAY

by LUKE SHORT

THE closing arguments were finished and, after instruct-
ing the jury and watching it file out, Judge Morehead
recessed the court and went over to the Stockman's
House for a beer.

The courtroom spilled its crowd onto the hard-packed
adobe yard. A March wind that had been pelting sand
against the courtroom windows and shaking them was a
wild thing out in that thin sunlight, and the crowd of
ragged nesters hugged the sheltered east face of the
adobe building, as silent and patient in waiting as their
teams that lined the tie rails.

Ernie Manners, his worn jumper gray and paper-thin
over his thick shoulders, walked with a solid and deliberate step as far as the cast-iron watering trough by the tie
rail and sat on its edge. Beyond him across the road and
under a leafless cottonwood, the Socorro stage was waiting. It had been there since court convened this morning,
and it would leave as soon as the jury returned a verdict
and Joe Williams was either freed or put aboard it for
the journey north to Santa Fe.

Trouble had ridden Ernie Manners and gentled him,
so that his square weather-scoured face was almost impassive as he looked at the stage. To the other small
ranchers it was a token of their and Joe Williams' defeat,
soon to be made public.

Tim Bone came down the walk and stopped by Ernie
and said, "Don't look like anyone ever doubted that jury,
does it?"

"No."

"Are those Spade riders with the driver?"

"Yes. Guards," Ernie murmured.

Tim Bone laughed shortly, without humor, and fisted his hands in his hip pockets. He was a middle-aged man and wifeless, his face shaped with a strange violence that danced wicked little lights in his eyes and made his speech aggressive. "Don't look like Bill Friend had any doubts either," he observed, quietly for him.

A bailiff left the courthouse door and walked over to the Stockman's House, the crowd's murmur following him. Almost immediately, Judge Morehead came out before the others and crossed the dusty road ahead of a team, waving at the driver. The others followed. To Ernie Manners and to all those small ranchers of the San Jon basin it was a roll call of their victors.

There was young John Comer, the deputy sheriff, who walked alongside the Spade foreman, Ferd Willis, as far as the near walk, and then stopped and waited for old Bill Friend, the Spade owner, and Martha Friend, his daughter.

Comer didn't need to stop, Ernie knew. Ferd Willis knew it too. Where it would have been easy for Ferd to walk past that clot of hostile men and women, ignoring them, it was not easy to stand and face them. But it was a concession he made to John Comer's arrogance, and Ferd stood there, idly scraping a circle in the dirt with the toe of his boot, looking down at the ground to avoid the stares.

Afterward, he fell in beside Bill Friend, while Martha Friend walked along with John Comer. Of those four, only Martha tried to greet the loose rank of nester men and women watching. Ernie saw her nod occasionally, saw the womenfolk nod in return and less often a man raise a hand to his worn hat. Bill Friend looked straight ahead, erect and unbending and implacable. John Comer whistled softly, his walk slow and unconcerned and somehow wary.

When they entered the door, Ernie looked down at his hand and then wiped it on his leg.

"Maybe we ain't ready yet," Tim Bone murmured. "Maybe we better wait and see what they do to Joe."

Ernie looked up quickly and Tim's glance slid away.

"Don't be a fool," Ernie said quietly. "This'll turn out short weight for us, but don't make the mistake of tryin' to fix it that way."

"Sure," Tim said, disbelief in his voice.

The crowd broke and filed back into the courthouse. Ernie was the last one in. What happened then was news to none of them. For the crime of killing and butchering out a Spade beef with which to feed his family, Joe Williams was found guilty by a jury of townsmen and sentenced to ten years in the Santa Fe penitentiary.

Out by the iron watering trough again, Ernie saw the arrangement of these waiting men was a little different this time. If trouble was coming, it would come now, and he hated the thought of it. It was patience that saved men, patience and waiting, and he wondered if these men would wait.

When the deputy came out the door with Joe Williams, it was Comer whom Ernie watched. The crowd stirred, gauging Comer's hand. It was a good one. Joe Williams, handcuffed, walked beside him. On Joe's other side was Ferd Willis, and on the stage top across the street were three Spade riders, rifles in hand.

Comer was so sure of himself that he paused to touch a match to his cigarette, a big man with thick shoulders and a proud way of carrying his young head.

In front of Ernie, Joe Williams said to Comer, "Can I talk to Ernie a minute?"

Comer liked the risk. He nodded and signaled Ferd Willis to step aside and then coolly surveyed the courthouse yard, knowing he and poverty had these silent men whipped.

Joe Williams said to Ernie, "She's goin' over with the Littlefields, Ernie."

"She'll be all right there, fine."

"She can raise a garden. Pay for her keep."

"Sure."

"Look," Joe's face was curiously attentive. "If she runs into any hard luck, you'll know it, won't you, Ernie?"

"I'll look out for her."

"That's what I mean. Thanks."

Ernie put out his hand and Joe took it wordlessly, a little of the bitterness and desperation in him mounting to his eyes.

Ernie said, "You find someone up there that can write, Joe. Keep the letters coming. We'll take care of her."

"So long," Joe said. Comer, seeing they were finished, threw his cigarette away and stepped up to Joe's side.

Tim Bone, from behind Ernie, drawled carefully, "Joe, you break out up there and I'll hide you."

Comer's gaze whipped to Tim. "Easy," he said.

"Mind now, Joe," Tim drawled.

Comer touched Joe's arm and they stepped into the street and crossed to the stage. Seconds later it rolled out and Ernie said to Tim, "Goin' upstreet?"

"In a minute," Tim murmured. He was watching Comer and Willis, who had turned and were coming back to the walk. Slowly the crowd was breaking up, drifting toward the stores.

Ernie sat down on the watering trough again, his sober and homely face watchful. Comer passed him and stopped in front of Tim.

"Your advice is likely to get him shot," Comer observed.

"I'd liefer get shot than spend ten years in Santa Fe. So would Joe," Tim drawled.

"If the rest of your friends feel that way about it, then tell them to leave the Spade stuff alone."

"You might tell 'em yourself."

"I'll do that," Comer said quietly. "Now move on."

Tim showed no intention of moving.

"Move on, I said."

"I heard you."

Ernie's quiet voice interrupted them. "I want to talk to Tim, John."

It was a graceful exit for Comer. He nodded and walked up into the courthouse, big and confident.

"Come on," Ernie said, and Tim joined him.

Court day always brought a crowd to Warms, but today there were horses at the tie rails whose brands hadn't been seen in town since last fall. They had come to see what Bill Friend would do to one of their own people, and they had found out.

Ernie stopped in front of the Emporium and Tim said, "See you down at the saloon?"

"Later, I guess," Ernie said.

Inside, he bought a sack of groceries and some dress goods with five of his last ten dollars and later, when nobody was looking, he left them in Littlefield's buckboard and went on downstreet.

Deputy Sheriff John Comer was talking to Martha Friend in front of the express office as Ernie hit the sidewalk, heading toward them. For a brief second, Ernie contemplated turning around, and then he gave it up. But he didn't want to see Martha after today's happenings.

Before Comer had come he had seen something of Martha, taken her to dances, and once he had taken her to the Fourth of July barbecue out on Tuesday Creek. But when old Bill Friend made it plain that Ernie was no different than any other range-stealing nester, Ernie quit seeing her.

Martha saw him first, and the surprise on her face was pleasant, Ernie saw. She smiled quickly, bent her arm at the elbow, raised her hand and wiggled her fingers in a wave to him. Ernie felt a flush of pleasure. He touched his hat, not intending to stop.

"Ernie," Comer called.

Ernie paused now, wheeled and walked over to them.

Martha put out her hand and smiled again and said, "You're almost a stranger now, Ernie."

"It's a long ride from the San Jon, Martha. How've you been?"

She said fine and Ernie saw she was lying. Behind the welcome in her eyes lay a sadness that Ernie had seen once before, on the night when she listened to him and her father argue whose was the rightful side in the division of the San Jon basin range.

He wanted to say more, but there was nothing he could say without bringing in today's trial, so he looked up at Comer.

"I've got a favor to ask, Ernie." It was more like a command, and Ernie studied the man's face. It was not a kind face, not cruel either, only hard and lean and determined, almost humorless.

"I'd like to have you move your boys out of town before dark," Comer went on.

"My boys?" Ernie echoed.

"Yes. All the small outfits lined up against Spade."

Ernie watched him until he was finished and then looked at Martha. Her eyes avoided his, and he returned his attention to Comer. "Why me?"

"You're the only level head in the crowd," Comer said. "They'll listen to you."

"Not when I talk that kind of foolishness," Ernie said quietly.

Comer rubbed a finger along his lower lip and said just as quietly, "It's not foolishness, Ernie. I mean it. They've got to be out of town at sundown."

"Why?"

"Spade is here in town and there'll be trouble."

"Ever think of movin' Spade?" Ernie murmured.

Comer looked thoughtfully at him and then shrugged "All right. Don't bother."

Ernie's temper was crowding him and he knew it and didn't care. "How long you been here, Comer? Four months, isn't it?"

"Five."

"You aren't a Basin man," Ernie went on slowly. "When old Sheriff Baily died Bill Friend saw a chance to buy his own law. One way or another, every commissioner on that county board was in debt to Bill, so they voted with him. They voted to bring a man in from outside and they got you." He paused. "Begin to understand?"

"No."

"You were appointed, Comer, not elected. You're not our man. We'll take somethin' like happened today. It may take us five years to swallow it clean, but we will. Just don't crowd your luck until you know us, that's all."

He looked at Martha and touched his hat and left them.

The wind sent a rising sheet of grit against Budrow's saddle shop across the street. It caromed off the false front and raked the Spade ponies tied in front of Prince's Keno Parlor and Saloon.

Ernie walked past them and beyond Grant Avenue, toward Dick Mobely's Gem Saloon, his tramp deliberate as always. His anger had already dried up, and in its place was a deep knowledge of defeat. If he carried Comer's word to the men down there at the Gem, all his work, all those patient hours of reasoning with them, would be canceled. Men, even men ground to the ways of poverty, would take only so much. He had nursed their pride along with his own, had reasoned them into taking the long view in the face of the knowledge that Joe Williams would doubtless be convicted. They would be angry now, but he could swing them to his side again —but not if he carried the red flag of Comer's word to them.

They were all here, clotted at the bar or sitting in chairs hauled over from the poker tables. There was no drinking, for drinking took money and they had none.

The talk didn't stop as they made way for Ernie. He packed his pipe and then dragged up a chair to the edge of the circle. Ed Horstmann, from out on Tuesday Creek, was speculating on just how much nerve it took for Comer to bring Joe Williams out to the stage in front of the crowd. Miles Overbeck regretted that they hadn't made a try for Comer, and Tim Bone laughed.

"Hell, it takes just one bullet," he said quietly, looking at them. "Just one bullet." When he came to Ernie, his glance passed him quickly.

"Maybe that's what we ought to do," Ed said. "Draw straws, maybe, or cut cards for him. Anyway, have a try at him. Or somethin'."

Ernie said, "You do, Ed, and you'll see your kids carrying this fight."

Ed laughed. "The oldest is only six."

"That's what I mean."

Ed looked over at him and opened his mouth to speak. Tim Bone put a word in before him. "It's either that or pull stakes for most of us, Ernie. You too."

"There's an election coming," Ernie pointed out, as he had done before.

"Next fall," Miles Overbeck said. "Hell I ain't even got alfalfa to boil up for grub. Bill Friend sent a rider out last week while I was away, to stake my well for a homestead. The corner come right on the floor of my shack and damned if he didn't tip over my stove to drive his stake. I can't even drink."

"I know," Ernie said.

"You don't know," Tim said harshly. "If you did, Ernie, then why you arguin'?"

Ernie shifted in his chair. They were willing to listen to him; they always were. "You feel that way about it, pull up into the San Jon and live off the country till election time," he said. "Don't sell your places; don't give Bill Friend a claim; just pull out and wait."

"The other way's easier," Miles said.

"You know how it's comin' out," Ernie said slowly, repeating the old argument. "Why don't you wait? We'll vote Comer out next fall. After that, we'll give Bill

Friend enough water and range for his needs and then it's done. But go at it with guns and he'll drive the lot of us over the mountains for good."

Tim Bone said, "Hell!" and walked out.

Max Troutman said, "Ernie, why you figure to play it that way? You was never afraid of a fight."

Ernie knocked his pipe out on his heel and pocketed it and then looked up at Max. He was back in the groove of the old argument, and he recited it as if it were new.

"We start pickin' and choosin' the laws we like and we ain't got any laws at all." He watched Ed Horstmann's face, which was eager to believe. "We got votes. We're Americans. And we elect our sheriffs by votes. If we can hang on this summer, we can vote Comer out—legal. And we'll vote in a fair man in his place. After that, Bill Friend will pull in his horns and leave us alone. But if we let Comer crowd us into gunplay, we're done." He looked at their faces. "What's the matter? Ain't you got the guts to starve a little for your places?"

Ed Horstmann said, "You're damn' right," and the argument started anew. Ernie knew how it would go. After an hour of talk Miles Overbeck would rise and say to Horstmann, "You goin' home, Ed?" and the meeting would break up. Safely, Ernie hoped, looking out under the swing doors to see how long the shadows were.

It worked out that way. Miles was on his feet, waiting only for a break in the talk to speak to Ed when Marty Beshears walked in. He came straight to the chairs and something in his face made Max Troutman cease talking. They all looked over at Marty.

"I just saw Comer," Marty announced, his eyes hot, his voice contained. "He's givin' us till sundown to clear out of town."

Nobody spoke for a minute. Ernie found them watching him, but he kept silent. There are times you can advise men, and there are times you can't.

"Well?" Marty said.

"Is that so?" Ed drawled. He tilted back his chair,

turned his head and spat into the sawdust. Then he stood up. "I'm goin' up to Prince's and watch the games for a couple of hours."

A voice from the door, a cool commanding voice, said, "I don't think so."

It was Comer. He had both thumbs in the top of his wide leather gun belt. Ernie felt his stomach coil hotly. The fool! The whole sorry mess would blow up in their faces now. Comer would be killed and so would a couple of others and the war would come out in the open. Ernie opened his mouth and saw it was no use and shut it again.

Ed Horstmann said quietly, "Stand over, Marty, and let him open the ball."

Ernie slid off his chair toward the wall, his hand falling to his side.

It was then that Tim Bone shouldered through the batwing doors. He had a gun in his hand and he came to a full stop some five feet inside the door, gun leveled at Comer, and said, "Hold it!"

Comer watched Ed Horstmann for a full three seconds, and then swung around to face Tim Bone. There was something in his face that told Ernie he knew he had made a mistake, and that he wasn't backing down.

"That's right," Tim drawled. "Turn around and take it in the belly."

"I said you're leavin' town by sundown," Comer said quietly. "Now get out of my way."

Tim Bone only said, "I don't reckon."

Comer didn't move. His iron bluff had failed, and a kind of panic crawled up into his face and was smothered. He shuttled his glance to Marty Beshears and got no help, and it was then he knew he might as well make his try for what it was worth, which was exactly nothing.

Ernie said sharply, "Tim, wait!"

Even as he spoke, he walked forward, knocking over a chair in his haste. He swung his body in between Comer and Tim and flipped both Comer's guns onto the floor.

Then he reached up and took Comer's badge between his fingers and roughly ripped it off his shirt, taking a triangle of cloth with it. He grabbed Comer's upper arm and swung him roughly into a chair facing a table, and before Tim Bone could protest he turned to Dick Mobely behind the bar. "Paper and pen, Dick."

He got them and put them before Comer. Nobody else had moved. Ed Horstmann had his gun unlimbered now and was scowling.

"That's for your resignation," Ernie said swiftly, pointing to the paper. "Write it out to Bill Friend. When you're through with that, write another to him and tell him to move Spade out of town right now!"

Comer picked up the pen, twisted the wad of inky paper from the ink bottle, dipped his pen and wrote in quiet haste.

When Comer had signed his name, Ernie ripped the sheets off the tablet, wheeled, and said to Tim Bone on his way out, "Just wait a minute, Tim. Just one minute."

Bill Friend was in the Stockman's House lobby talking with Judge Morehead over in a corner. Ernie walked straight to him, tossed Comer's badge in his lap and shoved the papers at him.

Bill Friend's tired face was wary. He took out his spectacles; then, sensing the urgency in Ernie's manner, he forgot to put them on. Holding the papers at arm's length, he read the first one. Without comment he turned to the second.

His eyes were hard and speculative. "Where is Comer now?"

"Down at the Gem with a gun to his ear," Ernie said quickly. "All you got to do to get him murdered is sit there and ask me questions."

Bill Friend scrubbed his mouth with the back of his hand.

"Murdered?" Judge Morehead murmured.

Ernie didn't even look at him. He was watching Bill.

He said, bitterly, "Ain't you rubbed it in enough for one day, Bill?"

Bill Friend didn't look at him. His glance roved the lobby, settled, and he called, "Ferd."

When Ferd Willis came over, Bill Friend said, "Get the boys together and go on out. Now."

Ferd looked at Ernie and grunted and went out. Ernie turned his back to Bill Friend and followed Willis as far as Prince's, where Ferd turned in. Dust was settling rapidly and the wind was dying.

At the Gem, Comer was still sitting in his chair. He had peeled a sheet of paper from the tablet and it lay torn in small pieces on the table top. Sweat runneled his cheekbones; he looked hard at the table.

Ernie stopped in front of him and he looked up.

"You're through," Ernie said mildly. "As soon as Spade gets moved out of town you better get your horse and ride out in the other direction."

He looked around for a chair and hauled it up to the table and sat down across from Comer, hearing the scrape of leather as Ed Horstmann holstered his gun.

"Damn you," Ernie said mildly, putting his elbows on the table, "I don't mind jumpin' on a man when he's down. Not on you anyway. If you don't clear this country by tonight you'll walk into a bushwhack inside another twenty-four hours."

He rose and walked to the door and stood in it a minute, his gaze directed upstreet. Tim Bone watched him, his gun sagging a little.

Ernie turned his head and said, "All right, get out."

Comer rose and walked past Tim without looking at him, his boot scuffing one of his own guns on the floor as he went. He passed Ernie and turned upstreet, his walk a little less hurried.

Ernie felt a little sick with the slackened tension. He let the door swing to and walked over to the hitch rail, placing both hands on it and hanging his head. The sudden explosion of voices from the inside welled out, and he turned away. There was a chance now. It had taken that threat of violence to crack Bill Friend. He had made a concession in moving Spade out of town, and if he could make one he would make more.

The court-day crowd had left town. Blank spaces gaped at the tie rails, and the street was quiet.

Ernie found himself walking toward the Stockman's House, and checked himself. He was ravenously hungry, but the meal at the hotel cost a half dollar. Too much. He fingered the coins in his pocket and then turned back and went into the Palace Café.

He was alone, and glad of it. Thinking back on this day, there was some order to it, some hope come out of it. If Comer would leave, if it was in the man to see wisdom, then there was something to work with and build on.

Finished, he stepped out of the Palace and paused on its step, reaching for his pipe. A rider passed, his face turned toward Ernie, the muffled clopping of his horse's hoofs in the thick dust the only sound. It was Ferd Willis, and he turned his head quickly, without speaking. Someone cursed a horse down the street.

Ernie stepped down onto the boardwalk. From across the street in the darkened doorway of the express office, someone called, "Ernie!"

Ernie stopped, half-turned. Ferd Willis pulled up his horse and looked over his shoulder, for something in this voice was urgent and angry.

John Comer swung under the hitch rack and stepped out into the street. "Make your brag again, Ernie," Comer taunted, walking forward.

Ernie didn't move. He watched Comer as he came to a stop in the middle of the street, and he wondered at the savage anger in the man's voice.

"You heard it," Ernie said quietly.

"I thought I did," Comer said. He reached down and pulled out his gun, and Ernie heard the distinct click of its cock. A wild haste seemed to be pushing Comer. He shot as the upswinging arc of his gun was only half completed, and the bullet smacked against the boardwalk, shaking it. His second shot was higher, and it slapped into the glass front of the store. The whole pane collapsed, jangling to the boardwalk.

Ernie reached down and brought out his gun, his breath held, and swung it up, moving smoothly. When the sight caught the light shirt of Comer, he fired. Comer shot once more, his slug rapping hollowly on the false front of the building, and in the same motion he sat down in the road. He put both hands to his chest and gagged, and then tried to get up and fell on his side, later rolling on his face.

Ernie walked over to him. Ferd Willis put his horse around and walked it back. Someone from Prince's ran up and then knelt by Comer, and by that time there were two more men there.

Ernie looked up at Ferd Willis. "What's your story, Ferd?" he asked quietly. Tim Bone, breathing hard, stepped over to Ernie's side.

"There's no question," Ferd Willis said quietly, without fear. "Comer tried to get you."

Ernie's glance shuttled to the low porch of the Stockman's House. A cluster of men stood on the steps, among them Bill Friend and Martha.

"Maybe you better tell Bill that right now," Ernie said. "Come along."

Ferd Willis put his horse in at the tie rail, and Ernie joined him. There were others now following.

Ernie stopped on the walk, and suddenly remembered he had his gun still in his hand. He holstered it, listening to Ferd Willis' steady voice. When Ferd was finished, Bill Friend said nothing, looking out at the people gathering in the road. Both he and Martha were facing Ernie, so that their faces were shadowed from the light behind them. It made a little golden halo around Martha's head as it touched her hair.

"Yes," Bill Friend murmured.

Tim Bone said quietly, "There's one of your deputies, Bill. How many more we got to fight?"

"None," Martha Friend said firmly. She put her hand on her father's arm and he looked at her in a tired way and did not speak.

Martha said to them, looking at Ernie, "This never would have worked and we all know it. It's an election you want, isn't it? For sheriff?"

"Yes, ma'am," Tim Bone answered.

"And the commissioners can set a date for it?"

"Any time," Max Troutman said.

"Then they will," Martha said. She looked up at her father. "Can you give them your word for that, Dad?"

Old Bill Friend never looked more weary. He watched Ferd Willis for several seconds, his eyes speculative, and then shifted his gaze to Ernie. "Yes, I can promise that." He turned and walked inside.

Those on the steps, all except Martha, walked out in the street to look at Comer, leaving Ernie to face her.

She stepped down to the walk, watching the men clot around the spot on the road, and her face was grave. Then she looked up at Ernie. "It's been a long wait, hasn't it?"

"Long enough," Ernie said.

Martha was silent a moment, and then she said, "Do you remember how it used to be, Ernie—before all this started?"

Ernie nodded, mute.

Martha put a hand on his arm, and smiled fleetingly. "It's been lonesome for me too, Ernie."

Ernie watched her closely. He parted his lips to ask, "But what about Comer?" and then remembered that figure out in the road. Martha shook her head slightly, as if she understood what he was about to ask and was forbidding him to ask it.

"Good night, Ernie," she said, and went quickly up the steps.

Ernie Manners thought he could see an end to patience, then. He put on his hat and went out into the road, steeling himself against the questions he would be asked. There would be an end to them, too, some day, because there was an end to everything a man hated to face but faced anyway. He had learned that again from her.

STAGE TO LORDSBURG

by ERNEST HAYCOX

THIS was one of those years in the Territory when Apache smoke signals spiraled up from the stony mountain summits and many a ranch house lay as a square of blackened ashes on the ground and the departure of a stage from Tonto was the beginning of an adventure that had no certain happy ending. . . .

The stage and its six horses waited in front of Weilner's store on the north side of Tonto's square. Happy Stuart was on the box, the ribbons between his fingers and one foot teetering on the brake. John Strang rode shotgun guard and an escort of ten cavalrymen waited behind the coach, half asleep in their saddles.

At four-thirty in the morning this high air was quite cold, though the sun had begun to flush the sky eastward. A small crowd stood in the square, presenting their final messages to the passengers now entering the coach. There was a girl going down to marry an infantry officer, a whisky drummer from Kansas City, an Englishman all length and bony corners and bearing with him an enormous sporting rifle, a gambler, a solid-shouldered cattleman on his way to New Mexico and a slim blond man upon whom both Happy Stuart and the shotgun guard placed a narrow-eyed interest.

This seemed all until the blond man drew back from

the coach door; and then a girl known commonly throughout the Territory as Henriette came quietly from the crowd. She was small and quiet, with a touch of paleness in her cheeks and her quiet dark eyes lifted at the blond man's unexpected courtesy, showing a faint surprise. There was this small moment of delay and then the girl caught up her dress and stepped into the coach.

Men in the crowd were smiling but the blond one turned, his motion like the swift cut of a knife, and his sharp-bright attention covered that group until the smiling quit. He was quite tall, hollow-flanked, and definitely stamped by the guns slung low on his hips. But it wasn't the guns alone; something in his face, so watchful and so smooth, also showed his trade. Afterwards he got into the coach and slammed the door.

Happy Stuart kicked off the brakes and yelled, "Hi!" Tonto's people were calling out their last farewells as the six horses broke into a trot and the stage lunged on its fore and aft springs. It rolled from town with dust dripping off its wheels like water, the cavalrymen trotting briskly behind. So they tipped down the long grade, bound on a journey no stage had attempted during the last forty-five days. Out below in the desert's distance stood the relay stations they hoped to reach and pass. Between lay a country swept empty by the quick raids of Geronimo's men.

The Englishman, the gambler and the blond man sat jammed together in the forward seat, riding backward to the course of the stage. The drummer and the cattleman occupied the uncomfortable middle bench; the two women shared the rear seat. The cattleman faced Henriette, his knees almost touching her. He had one arm hooked over the door's window sill to steady himself. A huge gold nugget slid gently back and forth along the watch chain slung across his wide chest and a chunk of black hair lay below his hat. His eyes considered Henriette, reading something in the girl that caused him to show her a deliberate smile. Henriette dropped her glance to the gloved tips of her fingers, cheeks unstirred.

They were all strangers packed closely together, with nothing in common save a destination. Yet the cattle- man's smile and the boldness of his glance was something as audible as speech, noted by everyone except the Eng- lishman who sat bolt upright in his corner, covered by a stony indifference. The army girl, tall and calmly pretty, threw a quick side glance at Henriette and afterwards looked away with a touch of color. The gambler saw this interchange of glances and showed the cattleman an irri- tated attention. The whisky drummer's eyes narrowed a little and some inward cynicism made a faint change on his lips. He removed his hat to show a bald head already beginning to sweat; his cigar smoke turned the coach cloudy and ashes kept dropping on his vest.

The blond man had observed Henriette's glance drop from the cattleman, and something bright disturbed his observant eyes; he tipped his hat well over his face and watched her—not boldly but as though he were puzzled. Once her glance lifted and touched him. But he had been on guard against that and was quick to look away.

The army girl coughed gently behind her hand, where- upon the gambler tapped the whisky drummer on the shoulder. "Get rid of that." The drummer appeared star- tled. He grumbled, "Beg pardon," and tossed the smoke through the window.

All this while the coach went tearing down the cease- less turns of the mountain road, slamming through the road ruts, whining at the curves, rocking interminably on its fore-and-aft springs. Occasionally the strident yell of Happy Stuart washed back. "Hi, Nellie! By God—!" The whisky drummer braced himself against the door and closed his eyes.

Three hours from Tonto the road, making a last round sweep, let them down into the flat desert. Here the stage stopped and the men got out to stretch. The gambler spoke to the army girl, gently: "Perhaps you would find my seat more comfortable." The army girl said, "Thank you," and changed over. The cavalry sergeant rode up to the stage, speaking to Happy Stuart.

"We'll be goin' back now—and good luck to you."

The men piled in, the gambler taking the place beside Henriette. The blond man drew his long legs together to give the army girl more room, and watched Henriette's face with a quick, quiet care. A hard sun beat fully on the coach and dust began to whip up like fire smoke. Without escort they rolled across a flat earth broken only by cacti standing against a dazzling light. In the far distance, behind a blue heat haze, lay the faint suggestion of mountains.

The cattleman reached up and tugged at the ends of his mustache and smiled again at Henriette. The army girl spoke to the blond man. "How far is it to the noon station?" The blond man said courteously: "Twenty miles." The gambler watched the army girl, something somber on his thin face, as though the run of her voice reminded him of things long forgotten.

The miles fell behind and the smell of alkali dust got thicker. Henriette rested against the corner of the coach, her eyes dropped to the tips of her gloves. She made an enigmatic, disinterested shape there; she seemed past stirring, beyond laughter. She was young, yet she had a knowledge that placed the cattleman and the gambler and the drummer and the army girl in their exact places, and she knew why the gambler had offered the army girl his seat. The army girl was in one world and she was in another, as everyone in the coach understood. It had no effect on her, for this was a distinction she had learned long ago. Only the blond man broke through her indifference. His name was Malpais Bill and she could see the wildness in the corners of his eyes and in the long crease of his lips; it was a stamp that would never come off. Yet something flowed out of him toward her that was different than the predatory curiosity of other men, something quietly gallant, quietly gentle.

Upon the box Happy Stuart pointed to the hazy outline two miles away. "Injuns ain't burned that anyhow." The sun was directly overhead, turning the light of the world a cruel brass-yellow. The crooked crack of a dry wash opened across the two deep ruts that made this road. Johnny Strang shifted the gun in his lap. "What's Malpais Bill ridin' with us for?"

"I guess I wouldn't ask him," returned Happy Stuart and studied the wash with a quick eye. The road fell into it roughly and he got a tighter grip on the reins and yelled: "Hang on! Hi, Nelly! God damn you, hi!" The six horses plunged down the rough side of the wash and for a moment the coach stood alone, high and lonely on the break, and then went reeling over the rim. It struck the gravel with a roar, the front wheels bouncing and the back wheels skewing around. The horses faltered but Happy Stuart cursed at his leaders and got them into a run again. The horses lunged up the far side of the wash two and two, their muscles bunching and the soft dirt flying in yellow clouds. The front wheels struck solidly and something cracked like a pistol shot as the stage rose out of the wash, teetered crosswise and then fell ponderously on its side, splintering the coach panels.

Johnny Strang jumped clear. Happy Stuart hung to the handrail with one hand and hauled on the reins with the other; and stood up while the passengers crawled through the upper door. All the men, except the whisky drummer, put their shoulders to the coach and heaved it upright again. The whisky drummer stood strangely in the bright sunlight, shaking his head dumbly while the others climbed back in. Happy Stuart said, "All right, brother, git aboard."

The drummer climbed in slowly and the stage ran on. There was a low, gray 'dobe relay station squatted on the desert dead ahead with a scatter of corrals about it and a flag hanging limp on a crooked pole. Men came out of the 'dobe's dark interior and stood in the shade of the porch gallery. Happy Stuart rolled up and stopped. He said to a lanky man: "Hi, Mack. Where's the God damned Injuns?"

The passengers were filing into the 'dobe's dining room. The lanky one drawled: "You'll see 'em before to-morrow night." Hostlers came up to change horses.

The little dining room was cool after the coach, cool and still. A fat Mexican woman ran in and out with the food platters. Happy Stuart said: "Ten minutes," and brushed the alkali dust from his mouth and fell to eating.

The long-jawed Mack said: "Catlin's ranch burned last night. Was a troop of cavalry around here yesterday. Came and went. You'll git to the Gap tonight all right but I do' know about the mountains beyond. A little trouble?"

"A little," said Happy briefly, and rose. This was the end of rest. The passengers followed, with the whisky drummer straggling at the rear, reaching deeply for wind. The coach rolled away again, Mack's voice pursuing them. "Hit it a lick, Happy, if you see any dust rollin' out of the east."

Heat had condensed in the coach and the little wind fanned up by the run of the horses was stifling to the lungs; the desert floor projected its white glitter endlessly away until lost in the smoky haze. The cattleman's knees bumped Henriette gently and he kept watching her, a celluloid toothpick drooped between his lips. Happy Stuart's voice ran back, profane and urgent, keeping the speed of the coach constant through the ruts. The whisky drummer's eyes were round and strained and his mouth was open and all the color had gone out of his face. The gambler observed this without expression and without care; and once the cattleman, feeling the sag of the whisky drummer's shoulder, shoved him away. The Englishman sat bolt upright, staring at the passing desert unemotionally. The army girl spoke to Malpais Bill: "What is the next stop?"

"Gap Creek."

"Will we meet soldiers there?"

He said: "I expect we'll have an escort over the hills into Lordsburg."

And at four o'clock of this furnace-hot afternoon the whisky drummer made a feeble gesture with one hand and fell forward into the gambler's lap.

The cattleman shrugged his shoulders and put a head through the window, calling up to Happy Stuart. "Wait a minute." When the stage stopped everybody climbed out and the blond man helped the gambler lay the whisky drummer in the sweltering patch of shade created by the coach. Neither Happy Stuart nor the shotgun guard bothered to get down. The whisky drummer's lips moved a little but nobody said anything and nobody knew what to do—until Henriette stepped forward.

She dropped to the ground, lifting the whisky drummer's shoulders and head against her breasts. He opened his eyes and there was something in them that they all could see, like relief and ease, like gratefulness. She murmured: "You are all right," gently, and her smile was soft and pleasant, turning her lips maternal. There was this wisdom in her, this knowledge of the fears that men concealed behind their manners, the deep hungers that rode them so savagely, and the loneliness that drove them to women of her kind. She repeated, "You are all right," and watched this whisky drummer's eyes lose the wildness of what he knew.

The army girl's face showed shock. The gambler and the cattleman looked down at the whisky drummer quite impersonally. The blond man watched Henriette through lids half closed, but the bright flare of a powerful interest broke the severe lines of his cheeks. He held a cigarette between his fingers; he had forgotten it.

Happy Stuart said: "We can't stay here."

The gambler bent down to catch the whisky drummer

under the arms. Henriette rose and said, "Bring him to me," and got into the coach. The blond man and the gambler lifted the drummer through the door so that he was lying along the back seat, cushioned on Henriette's lap. They all got in and the coach rolled on. The drummer groaned a little, whispering: "Thanks—thanks." And the blond man, searching Henriette's face for every shred of expression, drew a gusty breath.

They went on like this, the big wheels pounding the ruts of the road while a lowering sun blazed through the coach windows. The mountain bulwarks began to march nearer, more definite in the blue fog. The cattleman's eyes were small and brilliant and touched Henriette personally, but the gambler bent toward Henriette to say: "If you are tired—."

"No," she said. "No. He's dead."

The army girl stifled a small cry. The gambler bent nearer the whisky drummer, and then they were all looking at Henriette; even the Englishman stared at her for a moment, faint curiosity in his eyes. She was remotely smiling, her lips broad and soft. She held the drummer's head with both her hands and continued to hold him like that until, at the swift fall of dusk, they rolled across the last of the desert floor and drew up before Gap Station.

The cattleman kicked open the door and stepped out, grunting as his stiff legs touched the ground. The gambler pulled the drummer up so that Henriette could leave. They all came out, their bones tired from the shaking. Happy Stuart climbed from the box, his face a gray mask of alkali and his eyes bloodshot. He said: "Who's dead?" and looked into the coach. People sauntered from the station yard, walking with the indolence of twilight. Happy Stuart said, "Well, he won't worry about tomorrow," and turned away.

A short man with a tremendous stomach shuffled through the dusk. He said: "Wasn't sure you'd try to git through yet, Happy."

"Where's the soldiers for tomorrow?"

"Other side of the mountains. Everybody's chased out. What ain't forted up here was sent into Lordsburg. You men will bunk in the barn. I'll make out for the ladies somehow." He looked at the army girl and appraised Henriette instantly. His eyes slid on to Malpais Bill standing in the background and recognition stirred him then and made his voice careful. "Hello, Bill. Whut brings you this way?"

Malpais Bill's cigarette glowed in the gathering dusk and Henriette caught the brief image of his face, serene and watchful. Malpais Bill's tone was easy, it was soft. "Just the trip."

They were moving on toward the frame house whose corners seemed to extend indefinitely into a series of attached sheds. Lights glimmered in the windows and men moved around the place, idly talking. The unhitched horses went away at a trot. The tall girl walked into the station's big room, to face a soldier in a disheveled uniform.

He said: "Miss Robertson? Lieutenant Hauser was to have met you here. He is at Lordsburg. He was wounded in a brush with the Apaches last night."

The tall army girl stood very still. She said: "Badly?"

"Well," said the soldier, "yes."

The fat man came in, drawing deeply for wind. "Too bad—too bad. Ladies, I'll show you the rooms, such as I got."

Henriette's dove-colored dress blended with the background shadows. She was watching the tall army girl's face whiten. But there was a strength in the army girl, a fortitude that made her think of the soldier. For she said quietly, "You must have had a bad trip."

"Nothing—nothing at all," said the soldier and left the room. The gambler was here, his thin face turning to the army girl with an odd expression, as though he were remembering painful things. Malpais Bill had halted in the doorway, studying the softness and the humility of Henriette's cheeks. Afterwards both women followed the fat host of Gap Station along a narrow hall to their quarters.

Malpais Bill wheeled out and stood indolently against the wall of this desert station, his glance quick and watchful in the way it touched all the men loitering along the yard, his ears weighing all the night-softened voices. Heat died from the earth and a definite chill rolled down the mountain hulking so high behind the house. The soldier was in his saddle, murmuring drowsily to Happy Stuart.

"Well, Lordsburg is a long ways off and the dam' mountains are squirmin' with Apaches. You won't have any cavalry escort tomorrow. The troops are all in the field."

Malpais Bill listened to the hoofbeats of the soldier's horse fade out, remembering the loneliness of a man in those dark mountain passes, and went back to the saloon at the end of the station. This was a low-ceilinged shed with a dirt floor and whitewashed walls that once had been part of a stable. Three men stood under a lantern in the middle of this little place, the light of the lantern palely shining in the rounds of their eyes as they watched him. At the far end of the bar the cattleman and the gambler drank in taciturn silence. Malpais Bill took his whisky when the bottle came, and noted the barkeep's obscure glance. Gap's host put in his head and wheezed, "Second table," and the other men in here began to move out. The barkeep's words rubbed together, one tone above a whisper. "Better not ride into Lordsburg. Plummer and Shanley are there."

Malpais Bill's lips were stretched to the long edge of laughter and there was a shine like wildness in his eyes. He said, "Thanks, friend," and went into the dining room.

When he came back to the yard night lay wild and deep across the desert and the moonlight was a frozen silver that touched but could not dissolve the world's incredible blackness. The girl Henriette walked along the Tonto road, swaying gently in the vague shadows. He went that way, the click of his heels on the hard earth bringing her around.

Her face was clear and strange and incurious in the night, as though she waited for something to come, and knew what it would be. But he said: "Apaches like to crawl down next to a settlement and wait for strays."

She was indifferent, unafraid. Her voice was cool, and he could hear the faint loneliness in it, the fatalism that made her words so even. "There's a wind coming up, so soft and good."

He took off his hat, long legs braced and his eyes quick and puzzled in their watchfulness. His blond hair glowed in the fugitive light.

She said in a deep breath. "Why do you do that?"

His lips were restless and the sing and rush of strong feeling was like a current of quick wind around him. It was that unruly. "You have folks in Lordsburg?"

She spoke in a direct, patient way as though explaining something he should have known without asking. "I run a house in Lordsburg."

"No," he said, "it wasn't what I asked."

"My folks are dead—I think. There was a massacre in the Superstition Mountains when I was very young."

He stood with his head bowed, his mind reaching back to fill in that gap of her life. There was a hardness and a rawness to this land and little sympathy for the weak. She had survived, and had paid for her survival and looked at him now in a silent way that offered no explanations or apologies for whatever had been; she was still a pretty girl, with the tragic patience of all the past years in her eyes, in the inexpressiveness of her lips.

He said: "Over in the Tonto Basin is a fine land. Piece of a ranch of mine there yet—with a house half built."

"If that's your country why are you here?"

His lips laughed and the rashness in him glowed hot again and he seemed to grow taller in the moonlight. "A debt to collect."

"That's why you're going to Lordsburg? You will never get through collecting those kind of debts. Everybody in the Territory knows you. Once you were just a rancher. Then you tried to wipe out a grudge and then there was a bigger one to wipe out—and the debt kept growing and more men are waiting to kill you. Some day a man will. Run away from the debts."

His bright smile kept constant, which made her shoulders lift in resignation. "No," she murmured, "You won't run." He could see the sweetness of her lips and the way her eyes were sad for him; he could see in them the patience he had never learned.

He said: "We'd better go back," and turned her with his arm. They went across the yard in silence, hearing the undertone of men's drawling talk roll out of the shadows, seeing the glow of men's pipes in the dark corners. Malpais Bill stopped and watched her go through the station door; she turned to look at him once more, her eyes dark and her lips softly sober, and then passed down the narrow corridor to her own quarters. Beyond her window, in the yard, a man was murmuring to another man: "Plummer and Shanley are in Lordsburg. Malpais Bill knows it." Through the thin partition of the adjoining room she heard the army girl crying with a suppressed, uncontrollable regularity. Henriette stared at the dark wall, her shoulders and head bowed; and afterwards returned to the hall and knocked on the army girl's door and went in.

Six fresh horses fiddled in front of the coach and the fat host of Gap Station came across the yard swinging a lantern against the dead, bitter black. All the passengers filed sleep-dulled and miserable from the house. Johnny Strang slammed the express box in the boot and Happy Stuart said: "All right, folks," gruffly.

The passengers climbed in. The cattleman came by and Malpais Bill drawled: "Take the corner spot, mister," and got in, closing the door. The Gap host grumbled: "If they don't jump you on the long grade you'll be all right. You're safe when you get to Al Shrieber's ranch." Happy's bronze voice shocked the black stillness and the coach lurched forward, its leather springs squealing.

They rode for an hour in this complete darkness, chilled and uncomfortable and half asleep, feeling the coach drag on a heavy-climbing grade. Gray dawn cracked through, followed by a sunless light rushing all across the flat desert now far below. The road looped from one barren shoulder to another and at sun-up they had reached the first bench and were slamming full speed along a boulder-strewn flat. The cattleman sat in the forward corner, the left corner of his mouth swollen and crushed, and when Henriette saw that her glance slid to Malpais Bill's knuckles. The army girl had her eyes closed, her shoulders pressing against the Englishman who remained bolt-upright with the sporting gun between his knees. Beside Henriette the gambler seemed to sleep, and on the middle bench Malpais Bill watched the land go by with a thin vigilance.

At ten they were rising again, with juniper and scrub pine showing on the slopes and the desert below them filling with the powdered haze of another hot day. By noon they reached the summit of the range and swung to follow its narrow rock-ribbed meadows. The gambler, long motionless, shifted his feet and caught the army girl's eyes.

"Shrieber's is directly ahead. We are past the worst of it."

The blond man looked around at the gambler, making no comment; and it was then that Henriette caught the smell of smoke in the windless air. Happy Stuart was cursing once more and the brake blocks began to squall. Looking through the angled vista of the window panel

Henriette saw a clay and rock chimney standing up like a gaunt skeleton against the day's light. The house that had been there was a black square on the ground, smoke still rising from pieces that had not been completely burnt.

The stage stopped and all the men were instantly out. An iron stove squatted on the earth, with one section of pipe stuck upright to it. Fire licked lazily along the collapsed fragments of what had been a trunk. Beyond the location of the house, at the foot of a corral, lay two nude figures grotesquely bald, with deliberate knife-slashes marking their bodies. Happy Stuart went over there and had his look; and came back.

"Shriebers. Well—."

Malpais Bill said: "This morning about daylight." He looked at the gambler, at the cattleman, at the Englishman who showed no emotion. "Get back in the coach." He climbed to the coach's top, flattening himself full length there. Happy Stuart and Strang took their places again. The horses broke into a run.

The gambler said to the army girl: "You're pretty safe between those two fellows." He hauled a .44 from a back pocket and laid it over his lap. He considered Henriette more carefully than before, his taciturnity breaking. He said: "How old are you?"

Her shoulders rose and fell, which was the only answer. But the gambler said, gently, "Young enough to be my daughter. It is a rotten world. When I call to you, lie down on the floor."

The Englishman had pulled the rifle from between his knees and laid it across the sill of the window on his side. The cattleman swept back the skirt of his coat to clear the holster of his gun.

The little flinty summit meadows grew narrower, with shoulders of gray rock closing in upon the road. The coach wheels slammed against the stony ruts and bounced high and fell again with a flat jar which the springs could not soften. Happy Stuart's howl ran steadily above this rattle and rush; fine dust turned all things gray.

Henriette sat with her eyes pinned to the gloved tips of her fingers, remembering the tall shape of Malpais Bill cut against the moonlight of Gap Station. He had smiled at her as a man might smile at any desirable woman, with the sweep and swing of laughter in his voice; and his eyes had been gentle. The gambler spoke very quietly and she didn't hear him until his fingers gripped her arm. He said again, not raising his voice: "Get down."

Henriette dropped to her knees, hearing gunfire blast through the rush and run of the coach. Happy Stuart ceased to yell and the army girl's eyes were round and dark, yet showing no fright. The walls of the canyon had tapered off. Looking upward through the window on the gambler's side, Henriette saw the weaving figure of an Apache warrior reel nakedly on a calico pony and rush by with a rifle risen and pointed in his bony elbows. The gambler took a cool aim; the stockman fired and aimed again. The Englishman's sporting rifle blasted heavy echoes through the coach, hurting her ears, and the smell of powder got rank and bitter. The blond man's boots scraped the coach top and round small holes began to dimple the paneling as the Apache's bullets struck. An Indian came boldly abreast the coach and made a target that couldn't be missed. The cattleman dropped him with one shot. The coach hubs screamed as its wheels slewed around the sharp ruts and the whole heavy superstructure bounced high in the air. Then they were rushing down-grade.

The gambler said, quietly, "You had better take this," handing Henriette his gun. He leaned against the door, with his small hands gripping the sill. Pallor loosened his cheeks. He said, to the army girl: "Be sure to keep between those gentlemen," and looked at her with a way that was desperate and forlorn, and dropped his head to the window's sill.

Henriette saw the bluff rise up and close in like a yellow wall. They were rolling down the mountain without brake. Gunfire fell off and the crying of the Indians faded back. Coming up from her knees then she saw the desert's flat surface far below, with the angular pattern of Lordsburg vaguely on the far borders of the heat fog. There was no more firing and Happy Stuart's voice lifted again and the brakes were screaming on the wheels, and going off, and screaming again. The Englishman stared out of the window sullenly, the army girl seemed in a deep desperate dream; the cattleman's face was shining with a strange sweat. Henriette reached over to pull the gambler up, but he had an unnatural weight to him and slid into the far corner. She saw that he was dead.

At five o'clock that long afternoon the stage threaded Lordsburg's narrow streets of 'dobe and frame houses, came upon the center square and stopped before a crowd of people gathered in the smoky heat. The passengers crawled out stiffly. A Mexican boy ran up to see the dead gambler and began to yell his news in shrill Mexican. Malpais Bill climbed off the top, but Happy Stuart sat back on his seat and stared taciturnly at the crowd. Henriette noticed then that the shotgun messenger was gone.

A gray man in a sleezy white suit called up to Happy. "Well, you got through."

Happy Stuart said: "Yeah. We got through."

An officer stepped through the crowd, smiling at the army girl. He took her arm and said, "Miss Robertson, I believe. Lieutenant Hauser is quite all right. I will get your luggage."

The army girl was crying then, definitely. They were all standing around, bone-weary and shaken. Malpais Bill remained by the wheel of the coach, his cheeks hard against the sunlight and his eyes riveted on a pair of men standing under the board awning of an adjoining store. Henriette observed the manner of their waiting and knew why they were here. The blond man's eyes, she noticed, were very blue and flame burned brilliantly in them. The army girl turned to Henriette, tears still in her eyes. She murmured: "If there is anything I can ever do for you . . ."

But Henriette stepped back, shaking her head. This was Lordsburg and everybody knew her place except the army girl. Henriette said formally, "Good-bye," noting how still and expectant the two men under the awning remained. She swung toward the blond man and said, "Would you carry my valise?"

Malpais Bill looked at her, laughter remote in his eyes, and reached into the luggage pile and got her battered valise. He was still smiling as he went beside her, through the crowd and past the two waiting men. But when they turned into an anonymous and dusty little side street of the town, where the houses all sat shoulder to shoulder without grace or dignity, he had turned sober. He said: "I am obliged to you. But I'll have to go back there."

They were in front of a house no different from its neighbors; they had stopped at its door. She could see his eyes travel this street and comprehend its meaning and the kind of traffic it bore. But he was saying in that gentle, melody-making tone:

"I have watched you for two days." He stopped, searching his mind to find the thing he wanted to say. It came out swiftly. "God made you a woman. The Tonto is a pretty country."

Her answer was quite barren of feeling. "No. I am known all through the Territory. But I can remember that you asked me."

He said: "No other reason?" She didn't answer but something in her eyes pulled his face together. He took off his hat and it seemed to her he was looking through this hot day to that far-off country and seeing it fresh and desirable. He murmured: "A man can escape nothing. I have this chore to do. But I will be back."

He went along the narrow street, made a quick square turn at the end of it, and disappeared. Heat rolled like a heavy wave over Lordsburg's housetops and the smell of dust was very sharp. She lifted her valise, and dropped it and stood like that, mute and grave before the door of her dismal house. She was remembering how tall he had been against the moonlight at Gap Station.

There were four swift shots beating furiously along the sultry quiet, and a shout, and afterwards a longer and longer silence. She put one hand against the door to steady herself, and knew that those shots marked the end of a man, and the end of a hope. He would never come back; he would never stand over her in the moonlight with the long gentle smile on his lips and with the swing of life in his casual tone. She was thinking of all that humbly and with the patience life had beat into her. . . .

She was thinking of all that when she heard the strike of boots on the street's packed earth; and turned to see him, high and square in the muddy sunlight, coming toward her with his smile.

WINE ON THE DESERT

by MAX BRAND

THERE was no hurry, except for the thirst, like clotted salt, in the back of his throat, and Durante rode on slowly, rather enjoying the last moments of dryness before he reached the cold water in Tony's house. There was really no hurry at all. He had almost twenty-four hours' head start, for they would not find his dead man until this morning. After that, there would be perhaps several hours of delay before the sheriff gathered a sufficient posse and started on his trail. Or perhaps the sheriff would be fool enough to come alone.

Durante had been able to see the wheel and fan of

Tony's windmill for more than an hour, but he could not make out the ten acres of the vineyard until he had topped the last rise, for the vines had been planted in a hollow. The lowness of the ground, Tony used to say, accounted for the water that gathered in the well during the wet season. The rains sank through the desert sand, through the gravels beneath, and gathered in a bowl of clay hardpan far below.

In the middle of the rainless season the well ran dry but, long before that, Tony had every drop of the water pumped up into a score of tanks made of cheap corrugated iron. Slender pipe lines carried the water from the tanks to the vines and from time to time let them sip enough life to keep them until the winter darkened overhead suddenly, one November day, and the rain came down, and all the earth made a great hushing sound as it drank. Durante had heard that whisper of drinking when he was here before; but he never had seen the place in the middle of the long drought.

The windmill looked like a sacred emblem to Durante, and the twenty stodgy, tar-painted tanks blessed his eyes; but a heavy sweat broke out at once from his body. For the air of the hollow, unstirred by wind, was hot and still as a bowl of soup. A reddish soup. The vines were powdered with thin red dust, also. They were wretched, dying things to look at, for the grapes had been gathered, the new wine had been made, and now the leaves hung in ragged tatters.

Durante rode up to the squat adobe house and right through the entrance into the patio. A flowering vine clothed three sides of the little court. Durante did not know the name of the plant, but it had large white blossoms with golden hearts that poured sweetness on the air. Durante hated the sweetness. It made him more thirsty.

He threw the reins of his mule and strode into the house. The water cooler stood in the hall outside the kitchen. There were two jars made of a porous stone, very ancient things, and the liquid which distilled through the pores kept the contents cool. The jar on the left held water; that on the right contained wine. There was a big tin dipper hanging on a peg beside each jar. Durante tossed off the cover of the vase on the left and plunged it in until the delicious coolness closed well above his wrist.

"Hey, Tony," he called. Out of his dusty throat the cry was a mere groaning. He drank and called again, clearly, "Tony!"

A voice pealed from the distance.

Durante, pouring down the second dipper of water, smelled the alkali dust which had shaken off his own clothes. It seemed to him that heat was radiating like light from his clothes, from his body, and the cool dimness of the house was soaking it up. He heard the wooden leg of Tony bumping on the ground, and Durante grinned; then Tony came in with that hitch and sideswing with which he accommodated the stiffness of his artificial leg. His brown face shone with sweat as though a special ray of light were focused on it.

"Ah, Dick!" he said. "Good old Dick! . . . How long since you came last! . . . Wouldn't Julia be glad! Wouldn't she be glad!"

"Ain't she here?" asked Durante, jerking his head suddenly away from the dripping dipper.

"She's away at Nogalez," said Tony. "It gets so hot. I said, 'You go up to Nogalez, Julia, where the wind don't forget to blow.' She cried, but I made her go."

"Did she cry?" asked Durante.

"Julia . . . that's a good girl," said Tony.

"Yeah. You bet she's good," said Durante. He put the dipper quickly to his lips but did not swallow for a moment; he was grinning too widely. Afterward he said: "You wouldn't throw some water into that mule of mine, would you, Tony?"

Tony went out with his wooden leg clumping loud on the wooden floor, softly in the patio dust. Durante found the hammock in the corner of the patio. He lay down in it and watched the color of sunset flush the mists of desert dust that rose to the zenith. The water was soaking through his body; hunger began, and then the rattling of pans in the kitchen and the cheerful cry of Tony's voice:

"What you want, Dick? I got some pork. You don't want pork. I'll make you some good Mexican beans. Hot. Ah ha, I know that old Dick. I have plenty of good wine for you, Dick. Tortillas. Even Julia can't make tortillas like me. . . . And what about a nice young rabbit?"

"All blowed full of buckshot?" growled Durante.

"No, no. I kill them with the rifle."

"You kill rabbits with a rifle?" repeated Durante, with a quick interest.

"It's the only gun I have," said Tony. "If I catch them in the sights, they are dead. . . . A wooden leg cannot walk very far. . . . I must kill them quick. You see? They come close to the house about sunrise and flop their ears. I shoot through the head."

"Yeah? Yeah?" muttered Durante. "Through the head?" He relaxed, scowling. He passed his hand over his face, over his head.

Then Tony began to bring the food out into the patio and lay it on a small wooden table; a lantern hanging against the wall of the house included the table in a dim half circle of light. They sat there and ate. Tony had scrubbed himself for the meal. His hair was soaked in water and sleeked back over his round skull. A man in the desert might be willing to pay five dollars for as much water as went to the soaking of that hair.

Everything was good. Tony knew how to cook, and he knew how to keep the glasses filled with his wine.

"This is old wine. This is my father's wine. Eleven years old," said Tony. "You look at the light through it. You see that brown in the red? That's the soft that time puts in good wine, my father always said."

"What killed your father?" asked Durante.

Tony lifted his hand as though he were listening or as though he were pointing out a thought.

"The desert killed him. I found his mule. It was dead, too. There was a leak in the canteen. My father was only five miles away when the buzzards showed him to me."

"Five miles? Just an hour. . . . Good Lord!" said Durante. He stared with big eyes. "Just dropped down and died?" he asked.

"No," said Tony. "When you die of thirst, you always die just one way. . . . First you tear off your shirt, then your undershirt. That's to be cooler. . . . And the sun comes and cooks your bare skin. . . . And then you think . . . there is water everywhere, if you dig down far enough. You begin to dig. The dust comes up your nose. You start screaming. You break your nails in the sand. You wear the flesh off the tips of your fingers, to the bone." He took a quick swallow of wine.

"Without you seen a man die of thirst, how d'you know they start to screaming?" asked Durante.

"They got a screaming look when you find them," said Tony. "Take some more wine. The desert never can get to you here. My father showed me the way to keep the desert away from the hollow. We live pretty good here? No?"

"Yeah," said Durante, loosening his shirt collar. "Yeah, pretty good."

Afterward he slept well in the hammock until the report of a rifle waked him and he saw the color of dawn in the sky. It was such a great, round bowl that for a moment he felt as though he were above, looking down into it.

He got up and saw Tony coming in holding a rabbit by the ears, the rifle in his other hand.

"You see?" said Tony. "Breakfast came and called on us!" He laughed.

Durante examined the rabbit with care. It was nice and

fat and it had been shot through the head. Through the middle of the head. Such a shudder went down the back of Durante that he washed gingerly before breakfast; he felt that his blood was cooled for the entire day.

It was a good breakfast, too, with flapjacks and stewed rabbit with green peppers, and a quart of strong coffee. Before they had finished, the sun struck through the east window and started them sweating.

"Gimme a look at that rifle of yours, Tony, will you?" Durante asked.

"You take a look at my rifle, but don't you steal the luck that's in it," laughed Tony. He brought the fifteen-shot Winchester.

"Loaded right to the brim?" asked Durante.

"I always load it full the minute I get back home," said Tony.

"Tony, come outside with me," commanded Durante.

They went out from the house. The sun turned the sweat of Durante to hot water and then dried his skin so that his clothes felt transparent.

"Tony, I gotta be damn mean." said Durante. "Stand right there where I can see you. Don't try to get close. . . . Now listen. . . . The sheriff's gunna be along this trail some time to-day, looking for me. He'll load up himself and all his gang with water out of your tanks. Then he'll follow my sign across the desert. Get me? He'll follow if he finds water on the place. But he's not gunna find water."

"What you done, poor Dick?" said Tony. "Now look. . . . I could hide you in the old wine cellar where nobody . . ."

"The sheriff's not gunna find any water," said Durante. "It's gunna be like this."

He put the rifle to his shoulder, aimed, fired. The shot struck the base of the nearest tank, ranging down through the bottom. A semicircle of darkness began to stain the soil near the edge of the iron wall.

Tony fell on his knees. "No, no, Dick! Good Dick!" he said. "Look! All the vineyard. It will die. It will turn into old, dead wood, Dick . . ."

"Shut your face," said Durante. "Now I've started, I kinda like the job."

Tony fell on his face and put his hands over his ears. Durante drilled a bullet hole through the tanks, one after another. Afterward, he leaned on the rifle.

"Take my canteen and go in and fill it with water out of the cooling jar," he said. "Snap into it, Tony!"

Tony got up. He raised the canteen, and looked around him, not at the tanks from which the water was pouring so that the noise of the earth drinking was audible, but at the rows of his vineyard. Then he went into the house.

Durante mounted his mule. He shifted the rifle to his left hand and drew out the heavy Colt from its holster. Tony came dragging back to him, his head down. Durante watched Tony with a careful revolver but he gave up the canteen without lifting his eyes.

"The trouble with you, Tony," said Durante, "is you're yellow. I'd of fought a tribe of wildcats with my bare hands, before I'd let 'em do what I'm doin' to you. But you sit back and take it."

Tony did not seem to hear. He stretched out his hands to the vines.

"Ah, my God," said Tony. "Will you let them all die?"

Durante shrugged his shoulders. He shook the canteen to make sure that it was full. It was so brimming that there was hardly room for the liquid to make a sloshing sound. Then he turned the mule and kicked it into a dog-trot.

Half a mile from the house of Tony, he threw the empty rifle to the ground. There was no sense packing that useless weight, and Tony with his peg leg would hardly come this far.

Durante looked back, a mile or so later, and saw the little image of Tony picking up the rifle from the dust, then staring earnestly after his guest. Durante remembered the neat little hole clipped through the head of the rabbit. Wherever he went, his trail never could return again to the vineyard in the desert. But then, commencing to picture to himself the arrival of the sweating sheriff and his posse at the house of Tony, Durante laughed heartily.

The sheriff's posse could get plenty of wine, of course, but without water a man could not hope to make the desert voyage, even with a mule or a horse to help him on the way. Durante patted the full, rounding side of his canteen. He might even now begin with the first sip but it was a luxury to postpone pleasure until desire became greater.

He raised his eyes along the trail. Close by, it was merely dotted with occasional bones, but distance joined the dots into an unbroken chalk line which wavered with a strange leisure across the Apache Desert, pointing toward the cool blue promise of the mountains. The next morning he would be among them.

A coyote whisked out of a gully and ran like a gray puff of dust on the wind. His tongue hung out like a little red rag from the side of his mouth; and suddenly Durante was dry to the marrow. He uncorked and lifted his canteen. It had a slightly sour smell; perhaps the sacking which covered it had grown a trifle old. And then he poured a great mouthful of lukewarm liquid. He had swallowed it before his senses could give him warning.

It was wine!

He looked first of all toward the mountains. They were as calmly blue, as distant as when he had started that morning. Twenty-four hours not on water, but on wine!

"I deserve it," said Durante. "I trusted him to fill the canteen. . . . I deserve it. Curse him!" With a mighty resolution, he quieted the panic in his soul. He would not touch the stuff until noon. Then he would take one discreet sip. He would win through.

Hours went by. He looked at his watch and found it was only ten o'clock. And he had thought that it was on the verge of noon! He uncorked the wine and drank freely and, corking the canteen, felt almost as though he needed a drink of water more than before. He sloshed the contents of the canteen. Already it was horribly light.

Once, he turned the mule and considered the return trip; but he could remember the head of the rabbit too clearly, drilled right through the center. The vineyard, the rows of old twisted, gnarled little trunks with the bark peeling off . . . every vine was to Tony like a human life. And Durante had condemned them all to death!

He faced the blue of the mountains again. His heart raced in his breast with terror. Perhaps it was fear and not the suction of that dry and deadly air that made his tongue cleave to the roof of his mouth.

The day grew old. Nausea began to work in his stomach, nausea alternating with sharp pains. When he looked down, he saw that there was blood on his boots. He had been spurring the mule until the red ran down from its flanks. It went with a curious stagger, like a rocking horse with a broken rocker; and Durante grew aware that he had been keeping the mule at a gallop for a long time. He pulled it to a halt. It stood with wide-braced legs. Its head was down. When he leaned from the saddle, he saw that its mouth was open.

"It's gunna die," said Durante. "It's gunna die . . . what a fool I been. . . ."

The mule did not die until after sunset. Durante left everything except his revolver. He packed the weight of that for an hour and discarded it, in turn. His knees were growing weak. When he looked up at the stars they shone white and clear for a moment only, and then whirled into little racing circles and scrawls of red.

He lay down. He kept his eyes closed and waited for the shaking to go out of his body, but it would not stop.

And every breath of darkness was like an inhalation of black dust.

He got up and went on, staggering. Sometimes he found himself running.

Before you die of thirst, you go mad. He kept remembering that. His tongue had swollen big. Before it choked him, if he lanced it with his knife the blood would help him; he would be able to swallow. Then he remembered that the taste of blood is salty.

Once, in his boyhood, he had ridden through a pass with his father and they had looked down on the sapphire of a mountain lake, a hundred thousand million tons of water as cold as snow. . . .

When he looked up, now, there were no stars; and this frightened him terribly. He never had seen a desert night so dark. His eyes were failing, he was being blinded. When the morning came, he would not be able to see the mountains, and he would walk around and around in a circle until he dropped and died.

No stars, no wind; the air as still as the waters of a stale pool, and he in the dregs at the bottom. . . .

He seized his shirt at the throat and tore it away so that it hung in two rags from his hips.

He could see the earth only well enough to stumble on the rocks. But there were no stars in the heavens. He was blind: he had no more hope than a rat in a well. Ah, but Italian devils know how to put poison in wine that will steal all the senses or any one of them: and Tony had chosen to blind Durante.

He heard a sound like water. It was the swishing of the soft deep sand through which he was treading; sand so soft that a man could dig it away with his bare hands. . . .

Afterward, after many hours, out of the blind face of that sky the rain began to fall. It made first a whispering and then a delicate murmur like voices conversing, but after that, just at the dawn, it roared like the hoofs of ten thousand charging horses. Even through that thundering confusion the big birds with naked heads and red, raw necks found their way down to one place in the Apache Desert.

THE INDIAN WELL

by WALTER VAN TILBURG CLARK

IN this dead land the only allegiance was to sun. Even night was not strong enough to resist; earth stretched gratefully when night came, but had no hope that day would not return. Such living things as hoarded a little juice at their cores were secret about it, and only the most ephemeral existences, the air at dawn and sunset, the amethyst shadows in the mountains, had any freedom. The Indian Well alone, of lesser creations, was in constant revolt. Sooner or later all minor breathing rebels came to its stone basin under the spring in the cliff, and from its overflow grew a tiny meadow delta and two columns of willows and aspens, holding a tiny front against the valley. The pictograph of a starving, ancient journey, cut in rock above the basin, a sun-warped shack on the south wing of the canyon, and an abandoned mine above it, were the only tokens of man's participation in the well's cycles, each of which was an epitome of centuries, and perhaps of the wars of the universe.

The day before Jim Suttler came up, in the early spring, to take his part in one cycle, was a busy day. The sun was merely lucid after four days of broken showers, and, under the separate cloud shadows sliding down the mountain and into the valley, the canyon was alive. A rattler emerged partially from a hole in the mound on which the cabin stood, and having gorged in the darkness, rested with his head on a stone. A road-runner, stepping long

and always about to sprint, came down the morning side
of the mound, and his eye, quick to perceive the difference between the live and the inanimate of the same color,
discovered the coffin-shaped head on the stone. At once
he broke into a reaching sprint, his neck and tail stretched
level, his beak agape with expectation. But his shadow
arrived a step before him. The rattler recoiled, his head
scarred by the sharp beak but his eye intact. The road-
runner said nothing, but peered warily into the hole without stretching his neck, then walked off stiffly, leaning
forward again as if about to run. When he had gone
twenty feet he turned, balanced for an instant, and
charged back, checking abruptly just short of the hole.
The snake remained withdrawn. The road-runner paraded
briefly before the hole, talking to himself, and then ran
angrily up to the spring, where he drank at the overflow,
sipping and stretching his neck, lifting his feet one at a
time, ready to go into immediate action. The road-
runner lived a dangerous and exciting life.

In the upper canyon the cliff swallows, making short
harp notes, dipped and shot between the new mud under
the aspens and their high community on the forehead of
the cliff. Electrical bluebirds appeared to dart the length
of the canyon at each low flight, turned up tilting. Lizards
made unexpected flights and stops on the rocks, and when
they stopped did rapid push-ups, like men exercising on a
floor. They were variably pugnacious and timid.

Two of them arrived simultaneously upon a rock below
the road-runner. One of them immediately skittered to a
rock two feet off, and they faced each other, exercising.
A small hawk coming down over the mountain, but
shadowless under a cloud, saw the lizards. Having overfled
the difficult target, he dropped to the canyon mouth
swiftly and banked back into the wind. His trajectory
was cleared of swallows, but one of them, fluttering
hastily up, dropped a pellet of mud between the lizards.
The one who had retreated disappeared. The other flattened for an instant, then sprang and charged. The road-

runner was on him as he struck the pellet, and galloped down the canyon in great, tense strides, on his toes, the lizard lashing the air from his beak. The hawk swooped at the road-runner, thought better of it, and rose against the wind to the head of the canyon, where he turned back and coasted over the desert, his shadow a little behind him and farther and farther below.

The swallows became the voice of the canyon again, but in moments when they were all silent, the lovely smaller sounds emerged, their own feathering, the liquid overflow, the snapping and clicking of insects, a touch of wind in the new aspens. Under these lay still more delicate tones, erasing, in the most silent seconds, the difference between eye and ear, a white cloud shadow passing under the water of the well, a dark cloud shadow on the cliff, the aspen patterns on the stones. Silentest of all were the rocks, the lost on the canyon floor, and the strong, thinking cliffs. The swallows began again.

At noon a red and white cow with one new calf, shining and curled, came slowly up from the desert, stopping often to let the calf rest. At each stop the calf would try vigorously to feed, but the cow would go on. When they reached the well the cow drank slowly for a long time; then she continued to wrinkle the water with her muzzle, drinking a little and blowing, as if she found it hard to leave. The calf worked under her with spasmodic nudgings. When she was done playing with the water, she nosed and licked him out from under her and up to the well. He shied from the surprising coolness and she put him back. When he stayed, she drank again. He put his nose into the water too, and bucked up as if bitten. He returned, got water up his nostrils and took three jumps away. The cow was content and moved off toward the canyon wall, tonguing grass tufts from among the rocks. Against the cliff she rubbed gently and continuously with a mild voluptuous look, occasionally lapping her nose with a serpent tongue. The loose winter shag came off in tufts on the rock. The calf lost her, became panicked and made desperate noises which stopped prematurely, and when he discovered her, complicated her toilet. Finally she led him down to the meadow where, moving slowly, they both fed until he was full and went to sleep in a ball in the sun. At sunset they returned to the well, where the cow drank again and gave him a second lesson. After this they went back into the brush and northward into the dusk. The cow's size and relative immunity to sudden death left an aftermath of peace, rendered gently humorous by the calf.

Also at sunset, there was a resurgence of life among the swallows. The thin golden air at the cliff tops, in which there were now no clouds so that the eastern mountains and the valley were flooded with unbroken light, was full of their cries and quick maneuvers among a dancing myriad of insects. The direct sun gave them, when they perched in rows upon the cliff, a dramatic significance like that of men upon an immensely higher promontory. As dusk rose out of the canyon, while the eastern peaks were still lighted, the swallows gradually became silent. At twilight, the air was full of velvet, swooping bats.

In the night jack-rabbits multiplied spontaneously out of the brush of the valley, drank in the rivulet, their noses and great ears continuously searching the dark, electrical air, and played in fits and starts on the meadow, the many young ones hopping like rubber, or made thumping love among the aspens and the willows.

A coyote came down canyon on his belly and lay in the brush with his nose between his paws. He took a young rabbit in a quiet spring and snap, and went into the brush again to eat it. At the slight rending of his meal the meadow cleared of leaping shadows and lay empty in the starlight. The rabbits, however, encouraged by new-comers, returned soon, and the coyote killed again and went off heavily, the jack's great hind legs dragging.

In the dry-wash below the meadow an old coyote, without family, profited by the second panic, which came over him. He ate what his loose teeth could tear, leaving the open remnant in the sand, drank at the basin and, carefully circling the meadow, disappeared into the dry wilderness.

Shortly before dawn, when the stars had lost luster and there was no sound in the canyon but the rivulet and the faint, separate clickings of mice in the gravel, nine antelope in loose file, with three silently flagging fawns, came on trigger toe up the meadow and drank at the well, heads often up, muzzles dripping, broad ears turning. In the meadow they grazed and the fawns nursed. When there was as much gray as darkness in the air, and new wind in the canyon, they departed, the file weaving into the brush, merging into the desert, to nothing, and the swallows resumed the talkative day shift.

Jim Suttler and his burro came up into the meadow a little after noon, very slowly, though there was only a spring-fever warmth. Suttler walked pigeon-toed, like an old climber, but carefully and stiffly, not with the loose walk natural to such a long-legged man. He stopped in the middle of the meadow, took off his old black sombrero, and stared up at the veil of water shining over the edge of the basin.

"We're none too early, Jenny," he said to the burro.

The burro had felt water for miles, but could show no excitement. She stood with her head down and her four legs spread unnaturally, as if to postpone a collapse. Her pack reared higher than Suttler's head, and was hung with casks, pans, canteens, a pick, two shovels, a crowbar, and a rifle in a sheath. Suttler had the cautious uncertainty of his trade. His other burro had died two days before in the mountains east of Beatty, and Jenny and he bore its load.

Suttler shifted his old six-shooter from his rump to his thigh, and studied the well, the meadow, the cabin and the mouth of the mine as if he might choose not to stay. He was not a cinema prospector. If he looked like one of the probably mistaken conceptions of Christ, with his red beard and red hair to his shoulders, it was because he had been away from barbers and without spare water for shaving. He was unlike Christ in some other ways.

"It's kinda run down," he told Jenny, "but we'll take it."

He put his sombrero back on, let his pack fall slowly to the ground, showing the sweat patch in his bleached brown shirt, and began to unload Jenny carefully, like a collector handling rare vases, and put everything into one neat pile.

"Now," he said, "we'll have a drink." His tongue and lips were so swollen that the words were unclear, but he spoke casually, like a club-man sealing a minor deal. One learns to do business slowly with deserts and mountains. He picked up a bucket and started for the well. At the upper edge of the meadow he looked back. Jenny was still standing with her head down and her legs apart. He did not particularly notice her extreme thinness, for he had seen it coming on gradually. He was thinner himself, and tall, and so round-shouldered that when he stood his straightest he seemed to be peering ahead with his chin out.

"Come on, you old fool," he said. "It's off you now."

Jenny came, stumbling in the rocks above the meadow, and stopping often as if to decide why this annoyance recurred. When she became interested, Suttler would not let her get to the basin, but for ten minutes gave her water from his cupped hands, a few licks at a time. Then he drove her off and she stood in the shade of the canyon wall watching him. He began on his thirst in the same way, a gulp at a time, resting between gulps. After ten gulps he sat on a rock by the spring and looked up at the meadow and the big desert, and might have been considering the courses of the water through his body, but noticed also the antelope tracks in the mud.

After a time he drank another half dozen gulps, gave Jenny half a pail full, and drove her down to the meadow, where he spread a dirty blanket in the striped sun and shadow under the willows. He sat on the edge of the blanket, rolled a cigarette and smoked it while he watched Jenny. When she began to graze with her rump to the canyon, he flicked his cigarette onto the grass, rolled over with his back to the sun and slept until it became chilly after sunset. Then he woke, ate a can of beans, threw the can into the willows and led Jenny up to the well, where they drank together from the basin for a long time. While she resumed her grazing, he took another blanket and his rifle from the pile, removed his heel-worn boots, stood his rifle against a fork, and rolling up in both blankets, slept again.

In the night many rabbits played in the meadow in spite of the strong sweat and tobacco smell of Jim Suttler lying under the willows, but the antelope, when they came in the dead dark before dawn, were nervous, drank less, and did not graze but minced quickly back across the meadow and began to run at the head of the dry wash. Jenny slept with her head hanging, and did not hear them come or go.

Suttler woke lazy and still red-eyed, and spent the morning drinking at the well, eating and dozing on his blanket. In the afternoon, slowly, a few things at a time, he carried his pile to the cabin. He had a bachelor's obsession with order, though he did not mind dirt, and puttered until sundown, making a brush bed and arranging his gear. Much of this time, however, was spent studying the records on the cabin walls of the recent human life of the well. He had to be careful, because among the still legible names and dates, after Frank Davis, 1893, Willard Harbinger, 1893, London, England, John Mason, June 13, 1887, Bucksport, Maine, Mathew Kenling, from Glasgow, 1891, Penelope and Martin Reave, God Guide Us, 1885, was written Frank Hayward, 1492, feeling my age. There were other wits too. John Barr had written, Giv it back to the injuns, and Kenneth Thatcher, two years later, had written under that, Pity the noble redskin, while another man, whose second name was Evans, had written what was already a familiar libel, since it was not strictly true, Fifty miles from water. a hundred miles from wood, a million miles from God, three feet from hell. Someone unnamed had felt differently, saying, God is kind. We may make it now. Shot an antelope here July 10, 188— and the last number blurred. Arthur Smith, 1881, had recorded, Here berried my beloved wife Semantha, age 22, and my soul. God let me keep the child. J.M. said cryptically, Good luck, John, and Bill said, Ralph, if you come this way, am trying to get to Los Angeles. B. Westover said he had recovered from his wound there in 1884, and Galt said, enigmatically and without date, Bart and Miller burned to death in the Yellow Jacket. I don't care now. There were poets too, of both parties. What could still be read of Byron Cotter's verses, written in 1902, said,

> . . . . here alone
> *Each shining dawn I greet,*
> *The Lord's wind on my forehead*
> *And where he set his feet*
> *One mark of heel remaining*
> *Each day filled up anew,*
> *To keep my soul from burning,*
> *With clear, celestial dew.*
> *Here in His Grace abiding*
> *The mortal years and few*
> *I shall* . . .

but you can't tell what he intended, while J. A. had printed,

> *My brother came out in '49*
> *I came in '51*
> *At first we thought we liked it fine*
> *But now, by God, we're done.*

Suttler studied these records without smiling, like someone reading a funny paper, and finally, with a heavy blue pencil, registered, Jim and Jenny Suttler, damn dried out, March — and paused, but had no way of discovering the day — 1940.

In the evening he sat on the steps watching the swallows in the golden upper canyon turn bats in the dusk, and thought about the antelope. He had seen the new tracks also, and it alarmed him a little that the antelope could have passed twice in the dark without waking him.

Before false dawn he was lying in the willows with his carbine at ready. Rabbits ran from the meadow when he came down, and after that there was no movement. He wanted to smoke. When he did see them at the lower edge of the meadow, he was startled, yet made no quick movement, but slowly pivoted to cover them. They made poor targets in that light and backed by the pale desert, appearing and disappearing before his eyes. He couldn't keep any one of them steadily visible, and decided to wait until they made contrast against the meadow. But his presence was strong. One of the antelope advanced onto the green, but then threw its head up, spun, and ran back past the flank of the herd, which swung after him. Suttler rose quickly and raised the rifle, but let it down without firing. He could hear the light rattle of their flight in the wash, but had only a belief that he could see them. He had few cartridges, and the ponderous echo under the cliffs would scare them off for weeks.

His energies, however, were awakened by the frustrated hunt. While there was still more light than heat in the canyon, he climbed to the abandoned mine tunnel at the top of the alluvial wing of the cliff. He looked at the broken rock in the dump, kicked up its pack with a boot toe, and went into the tunnel, peering closely at its sides, in places black with old smoke smudges. At the back he struck two matches and looked at the jagged dead end and the fragments on the floor, then returned to the shallow beginning of a side tunnel. At the second match here he knelt quickly, scrutinized a portion of the rock, and when the match went out at once lit another. He lit six matches, and pulled at the rock with his hand. It was firm.

"The poor chump," he said aloud.

He got a loose rock from the tunnel and hammered at the projection with it. It came finally, and he carried it into the sun on the dump.

"Yessir," he said aloud, after a minute.

He knocked his sample into three pieces and examined each minutely.

"Yessir, yessir," he said with malicious glee, and, grinning at the tunnel, "the poor chump."

Then he looked again at the dump, like the mound before a gigantic gopher hole. "Still, that's a lot of digging," he said.

He put sample chips into his shirt pocket, keeping a small black, heavy one that had fallen neatly from a hole like a borer's, to play with in his hand. After trouble he found the claim pile on the side hill south of the tunnel, its top rocks tumbled into the shale. Under the remaining rocks he found what he wanted, a ragged piece of yellowed paper between two boards. The writing was in pencil, and not diplomatic. "I hearby clame this hole damn side hill as far as I can dig in. I am a good shot. Keep off. John Barr, April 11, 1897."

Jim Suttler grinned. "Tough guy, eh?" he said.

He made a small ceremony of burning the paper upon a stone from the cairn. The black tinsel of ash blew off and broke into flakes.

"O.K., John Barr?" he asked.

"O.K., Suttler," he answered himself.

In blue pencil, on soiled paper from his pocket, he slowly printed, "Becus of the lamented desease of the late clamant, John Barr, I now clame these diggins for myself and partner Jenny. I can shoot too." And wrote, rather than printed, "James T. Suttler, March—" and paused.

"Make it an even month," he said, and wrote, "11, 1940." Underneath he wrote, "Jenny Suttler, her mark," and drew a skull with long ears.

"There," he said, and folded the paper, put it between the two boards, and rebuilt the cairn into a neat pyramid above it.

In high spirit he was driven to cleanliness. With scissors, soap, and razor he climbed to the spring. Jenny was there, drinking.

"When you're done," he said, and lifted her head, pulled her ears and scratched her.

"Maybe we've got something here, Jenny," he said.

Jenny observed him soberly and returned to the meadow.

"She doesn't believe me," he said, and began to perfect himself. He sheared off his red tresses in long hanks, then cut closer, and went over yet a third time, until there remained a brush, of varying density, of stiff red bristles, through which his scalp shone whitely. He sheared the beard likewise, then knelt to the well for mirror and shaved painfully. He also shaved his neck and about his ears. He arose younger and less impressive, with jaws as pale as his scalp, so that his sunburn was a red domino. He burned tresses and beard ceremoniously upon a sage bush, and announced, "It is spring."

He began to empty the pockets of his shirt and breeches onto a flat stone, yelling, "In the spring a young man's fancy," to a kind of tune, and paused, struck by the facts.

"Oh yeah?" he said. "Fat chance."

"Fat," he repeated with obscene consideration. "Oh, well," he said, and finished piling upon the rock note-books, pencil stubs, cartridges, tobacco, knife, stump pipe, matches, chalk, samples, and three wrinkled photographs. One of the photographs he observed at length before weighting it down with a .45 cartridge. It showed a round, blonde girl with a big smile on a stupid face, in a patterned calico house dress in front of a blossoming rhododendron bush.

He added to this deposit his belt and holster with the big .45.

Then he stripped himself, washed and rinsed his garments in the spring, and spread them upon stones and brush, and carefully arranged four flat stones into a platform beside the trough. Standing there he scooped water over himself, gasping, made it a lather, and at last, face and copper bristles also foaming, gropingly entered the basin and submerged, flooding the water over in a thin and soapy sheet. His head emerged at once. "My God," he whispered. He remained under, however, till he was soapless, and goose pimpled as a file, he climbed out cautiously onto the rock platform and performed a dance of small, revolving patterns with a great deal of up and down.

At one point in his dance he observed the pictograph journey upon the cliff, and danced nearer to examine it.

"Ignorant," he pronounced. "Like a little kid," he said.

He was intrigued, however, by some more recent records, names smoke and cut upon the lower rock. One of these, in script, like a gigantic handwriting deeply cut, said ALVAREZ BLANCO DE TOLEDO, Anno Di 1624. A very neat, upright cross was chiseled beneath it.

Suttler grinned. "Oh yeah?" he asked, with his head upon one side. "Nuts," he said, looking at it squarely.

But it inspired him, and with his jack-knife he began scraping beneath the possibly Spanish inscription. His knife, however, made scratches, not incisions. He completed a bad Jim and Jenny and quit, saying, "I should kill myself over a phoney wap."

Thereafter, for weeks, while the canyon became increasingly like a furnace in the daytime and the rocks stayed warm at night, he drove his tunnel farther into the gully, making a heap of ore to be worked, and occasionally adding a peculiarly heavy pebble to the others in his small leather bag with a draw string. He and Jenny thrived upon this fixed and well-watered life. The hollows disappeared from his face and he became less stringy, while Jenny grew round, her battleship-gray pelt even lustrous and its black markings distinct and ornamental. The burro found time from her grazing to come to the cabin door in the evenings and attend solemnly to Suttler playing with his samples and explaining their future.

"Then, old lady," Suttler said, "you will carry only small children, one at a time, for never more than half an hour. You will have a bedroom with French windows and a mattress, and I will paint your feet gold.

"The children," he said, "will probably be red-headed, but maybe blonde. Anyway, they will be beautiful.

"After we've had a holiday, of course," he added. "For one hundred and thirty-three nights," he said dreamily. "Also," he said, "just one hundred and thirty-three quarts. I'm no drunken bum.

"For you, though," he said, "for one hundred and thirty-three nights a quiet hotel with other old ladies. I should drag my own mother in the gutter." He pulled her head down by the ears and kissed her loudly upon the nose. They were very happy together.

Nor did they greatly alter most of the life of the canyon. The antelope did not return, it is true, the rabbits were fewer and less playful because he sometimes snared them for meat, the little, clean mice and desert rats avoided the cabin they had used, and the road-runner did not come in daylight after Suttler, for fun, narrowly missed him with a piece of ore from the tunnel mouth. Suttler's violence was disproportionate perhaps, when he used his .45 to blow apart a creamy rat who did invade the cabin, but the loss was insignificant to the pattern of the well, and more than compensated when he one day caught the rattler extended at the foot of the dump in a drunken stupor from rare young rabbit, and before it could recoil held it aloft by the tail and snapped its head off, leaving the heavy body to turn slowly for a long time among the rocks. The dominant voices went undisturbed, save when he sang badly at his work or said beautiful things to Jenny in a loud voice.

There were, however, two more noticeable changes, one of which, at least, was important to Suttler himself. The first was the execution of the range cow's calf in the late fall, when he began to suggest a bull. Suttler felt a little guilty about this because the calf might have belonged to somebody, because the cow remained near the meadow bawling for two nights, and because the calf had come to meet the gun with more curiosity than challenge. But when he had the flayed carcass hung in the mine tunnel in a wet canvas, the sensation of providence overcame any qualms.

The other change was more serious. It occurred at the beginning of such winter as the well had, when there was sometimes a light rime on the rocks at dawn, and the aspens held only a few yellow leaves. Suttler thought often of leaving. The nights were cold, the fresh meat was eaten, his hopes had diminished as he still found only occasional nuggets, and his dreams of women, if less violent, were more nostalgic. The canyon held him with a feeling he would have called lonesome but at home, yet he probably would have gone except for this second change.

In the higher mountains to the west, where there was already snow, and at dawn a green winter sky, hunger stirred a buried memory in a cougar. He had twice killed antelope at the well, and felt there had been time enough again. He came down from the dwarfed trees and crossed the narrow valley under the stars, sometimes stopping abruptly to stare intently about, like a house-cat in a strange room. After each stop he would at once resume a quick, noiseless trot. From the top of the mountain above the spring he came down very slowly on his belly, but there was nothing at the well. He relaxed, and leaning on the rim of the basin, drank, listening between laps. His nose was clean with fasting, and he knew of the man in the cabin and Jenny in the meadow, but they were strange, not what he remembered about the place. But neither had his past made him fearful. It was only his habitual hunting caution which made him go down into the willows carefully, and lie there head up, watching Jenny, but still waiting for antelope, which he had killed before near dawn. The strange smells were confusing and therefore irritating. After an hour he rose and went silently to the cabin, from which the strangest smell came strongly, a carnivorous smell which did not arouse appetite, but made him bristle nervously. The tobacco in it was like pins in his nostrils. He circled the cabin, stopping frequently. At the open door the scent was violent. He stood with his front paws up on the step, moving his head in serpent motions, the end of his heavy tail furling and unfurling constantly. In a dream Suttler turned over without waking, and muttered. The cougar crouched, his eyes intent, his ruff lifting. Then he swung away from the door again and lay in the willows, but where he could watch the cabin also.

When the sky was alarmingly pale and the antelope had not come, he crawled a few feet at a time, behind the willows, to a point nearer Jenny. There he crouched, working his hind legs slowly under him until he was set, and sprang, raced the three or four jumps to the drowsy burro, and struck. The beginning of her mortal scream was severed, but having made an imperfect leap, and from no height, the cat did not at once break her neck, but drove her to earth, where her small hooves churned futilely in the sod, and chewed and worried until she lay still.

Jim Suttler was nearly awakened by the fragment of scream, but heard nothing after it, and sank again.

The cat wrestled Jenny's body into the willows, fed with uncertain relish, drank long at the well, and went slowly over the crest, stopping often to look back. In spite of the light and the beginning talk of the swallows, the old coyote also fed and was gone before Suttler woke.

When Suttler found Jenny, many double columns of regimented ants were already at work, streaming in and out of the interior and mounting like bridge workers upon the ribs. Suttler stood and looked down. He desired to hold the small muzzle in the hollow of his hand, feeling that this familiar gesture would get through to Jenny, but couldn't bring himself to it because of what had happened to that side of her head. He squatted and lifted one hoof on its stiff leg and held that. Ants emerged hurriedly from the fetlock, their lines of communication broken. Two of them made disorganized excursions on the back of his hand. He rose, shook them off, and stood staring again. He didn't say anything because he spoke easily only when cheerful or excited, but a determination was beginning in him. He followed the drag to the spot torn by the small hoofs. Among the willows again, he found the tracks of both the cougar and the coyote, and the cat's tracks again at the well and by the cabin doorstep. He left Jenny in the willows with a canvas over her during the day, and did not eat.

At sunset he sat on the doorstep, cleaning his rifle and oiling it until he could spring the lever almost without sound. He filled the clip, pressed it home, and sat with the gun across his knees until dark, when he put on his sheepskin, stuffed a scarf into the pocket, and went down to Jenny. He removed the canvas from her, rolled it up and held it under his arm.

"I'm sorry, old woman," he said. "Just tonight."

There was a little cold wind in the willows. It rattled the upper branches lightly.

Suttler selected a spot thirty yards down wind, from which he could see Jenny, spread the canvas and lay down upon it, facing toward her. After an hour he was afraid of falling asleep and sat up against a willow clump. He sat there all night. A little after midnight the old coyote came into the dry-wash below him. At the top of the wash he sat down, and when the mingled scents gave him a clear picture of the strategy, let his tongue loll out, looked at the stars for a moment with his mouth silently open, rose and trotted into the desert.

At the beginning of daylight the younger coyote trotted in from the north, and turned up toward the spring, but saw Jenny. He sat down and looked at her for a long time. Then he moved to the west and sat down again. In the wind was only winter, and the water, and faintly the acrid bat dung in the cliffs. He completed the circle, but not widely enough, walking slowly through the willows, down the edge of the meadow and in again not ten yards in front of the following muzzle of the carbine. Like Jenny, he felt his danger too late. The heavy slug caught him at the base of the skull in the middle of the first jump, so that it was amazingly accelerated for a fraction of a second. The coyote began it alive, and ended it quite dead, but with a tense muscular movement conceived which resulted in a grotesque final leap and twist of the hind-quarters alone, leaving them propped high against a willow clump while the head was half buried in the sand, red welling up along the lips of the distended jaws. The cottony underpelt of the tail and rump stirred gleefully in the wind.

When Suttler kicked the body and it did not move, he suddenly dropped his gun, grasped it by the upright hind legs, and hurled it out into the sage-brush. His face appeared slightly insane with fury for that instant. Then he picked up his gun and went back to the cabin, where he ate, and drank half of one of his last three bottles of whiskey.

In the middle of the morning he came down with his pick and shovel, dragged Jenny's much-lightened body down into the dry-wash, and dug in the rock and sand for two hours. When she was covered, he erected a small cairn of stone, like the claim post, above her.

"If it takes a year," he said, and licked the salt sweat on his lips.

That day he finished the half bottle and drank all of a second one, and became very drunk, so that he fell asleep during his vigil in the willows, sprawled wide on the dry turf and snoring. He was not disturbed. There was a difference in his smell after that day which prevented even the rabbits from coming into the meadow. He waited five nights in the willows. Then he transferred his watch to a niche in the cliff, across from and just below the spring.

All winter, while the day wind blew long veils of dust across the desert, regularly repeated, like waves or the smoke of line artillery fire, and the rocks shrank under the cold glitter of night, he did not miss a watch. He learned to go to sleep at sundown, wake within a few minutes of midnight, go up to his post, and become at once clear headed and watchful. He talked to himself in the mine and the cabin, but never in the niche. His supplies ran low, and he ate less, but would not risk a startling shot. He rationed his tobacco, and when it was gone worked up to a vomiting sickness every three days for nine days, but did not miss a night in the niche. All winter he did not remove his clothes, bathe, shave, cut his hair or sing. He worked the dead mine only to be busy, and became thin again, with sunken eyes which yet were not the eyes he had come with the spring before. It was April, his food almost gone, when he got his chance.

There was a half moon that night, which made the canyon walls black, and occasionally gleamed on wrinkles of the overflow. The cat came down so quietly that Suttler did not see him until he was beside the basin. The animal was suspicious. He took the wind, and twice started to drink, and didn't, but crouched. On Suttler's face there was a set grin which exposed his teeth.

"Not even a drink, you bastard," he thought.

The cat drank a little though, and dropped again, softly, trying to get the scent from the meadow. Suttler drew slowly upon his soul in the trigger. When it gave, the report was magnified impressively in the canyon. The cougar sprang straight into the air and screamed outrageously. The back of Suttler's neck was cold and his hand trembled, but he shucked the lever and fired again. This shot ricocheted from the basin and whined away thinly. The first, however, had struck near enough. The cat began to scramble rapidly on the loose stone, at first without voice, then screaming repeatedly. It doubled upon itself, snarling and chewing in a small furious circle, fell and began to throw itself in short, leaping spasms upon the stones, struck across the rim of the tank and lay half in the water, its head and shoulders raised in one corner and resting against the cliff. Suttler could hear it breathing hoarsely and snarling very faintly. The soprano chorus of swallows gradually became silent.

Suttler had risen to fire again, but lowered the carbine and advanced, stopping at every step to peer intently and listen for the hoarse breathing, which continued. Even when he was within five feet of the tank the cougar did not move, except to gasp so that the water again splashed from the basin. Suttler was calmed by the certainty of accomplishment. He drew the heavy revolver from his holster, aimed carefully at the rattling head, and fired again. The canyon boomed, and the east responded faintly and a little behind, but Suttler did not hear them, for the cat thrashed heavily in the tank, splashing him as with a bucket, and then lay still on its side over the edge, its muzzle and forepaws hanging. The water was settling quietly in the tank, but Suttler stirred it again, shooting five more times with great deliberation into the heavy body, which did not move except at the impact of the slugs.

The rest of the night, even after the moon was gone, he worked fiercely, slitting and tearing with his knife. In the morning, under the swallows, he dragged the marbled carcass, still bleeding a little in places, onto the rocks on the side away from the spring, and dropped it. Dragging the ragged hide by the neck, he went unsteadily down the canyon to the cabin, where he slept like a drunkard, although his whiskey had been gone for two months.

In the afternoon, with dreaming eyes, he bore the pelt to Jenny's grave, took down the stones with his hands, shoveled the earth from her, covered her with the skin, and again with earth and the cairn.

He looked at this monument. "There," he said.

That night, for the first time since her death, he slept through.

In the morning, at the well, he repeated the cleansing

ritual of a year before, save that they were rags he stretched to dry, even to the dance upon the rock platform while drying. Squatting naked and clean, shaven and clipped, he looked for a long time at the grinning countenance, now very dirty, of the plump girl in front of the blossoming rhododendrons, and in the resumption of his dance he made singing noises accompanied by the words, "Spring, spring, beautiful spring." He was a starved but revived and volatile spirit. An hour later he went south, his boot soles held on by canvas strips, and did not once look back.

The disturbed life of the spring resumed. In the second night the rabbits loved in the willows, and at the end of the week the rats played in the cabin again. The old coyote and a vulture cleaned the cougar, and his bones fell apart in the shale. The road-runner came up one day, tentatively, and in front of the tunnel snatched up a horned toad and ran with it around the corner, but no farther. After a month the antelope returned. The well brimmed, and in the gentle sunlight the new aspen leaves made a tiny music of shadows.

TO FIND A PLACE

By Robert Easton

On a Saturday morning in September a man drove a small out-of-date coupé along a county road bordering some yellow California hills. The road humped slightly every so often where the slopes had washed and fanned off into a long plain, flat as a pan, that ran away westward toward salt marshes and a bay. The name of the man doesn't matter—call him "I" if you like. But he was young, a stranger in these parts, and looking for his first job.

It was a few minutes before one o'clock when I

caught the scent of many animals, mixed with the pleasant
and exciting smell of sea wind over the summer ground,
and topped the last hump in the road and saw the
feed-yards of the El Dorado Investment Company, and
all its thirteen thousand white-faced cattle cooped in pens
like city blocks that spread away for miles clear to the
river and the yellow fields bordering it.

At a sign with a great hand pointing, I turned and drove
to a small box of a building that said: OFFICE, and here
I inquired of a sleepy bookkeeper when Mr. Archibald
Jacks, the foreman, could be expected. The answer was
one o'clock, at the barn, and the barn was over there two
hundred yards where all the cattle began.

While the bookkeeper was talking, I let my eye wander
a little—since this was the office of the largest enterprise
of its kind in western America, I wanted to have a look—
and on the panel of an inner door I saw "T. S. Ordway,
Private." I thought about it as I drove away. T. S.
Ordway was a name known to most people west of the
Rockies. He didn't raise cattle; he manufactured them.
He turned beef into dollars as fast as Henry Ford turned
cars off the assembly line. Three months in his yards and
the heifer yearlings that had come so poor, so cheap, were
shipped away as sleek as seals with half their added pounds
clear profit. And he had steers, too, and canner cows and
baloney bulls and anything that wore horns and a hide.
He didn't care. "Give me the cattle ninety days," he used
to say, "and I'll not have to brand 'em. They'll take the
look o' the El." by which he meant his brand was the
Rocking EL and his cattle stuffed so hard with good white
fat that butchers who knew never bothered coming to
see the animals they wanted; they simply telephoned and
said, "Tom, I need a load of heifers to average eight-
seventy-five," just as you would order so many pairs of
shoes from a catalogue.

So I went along into that wilderness of boards and
cattle where everything was strange, and stopped, and
left the car and stood beside a fence not too near the

door of the barn nor yet too far away, but just between —about the place I thought correct for a young man who didn't have a job but hoped to get one.

Trucks were going by—big semi-trailers full of hay, partitioned in the middle like orange boxes. They sang past me down the road and I saw the flash of the sun-and-wind-burned faces with whom I was to work; and my own face got red and my clothes didn't fit and the chromium on my old coupé, which I had taken such scrupulous care of these past five years, looked as bright and silly as French doors on a barn. Trucks and more trucks passed, flat-beds, Diesels—every kind, in pairs, in convoys disappearing toward some secret destination in the heart of Thomas Ordway's city, where the warehouses and mill rose like castles of galvanized iron, and a gigantic pit for beet-pulp, wide as a stadium, filled the air with a sour, sticky smell. An arm of the river, a man-made slough, reached in here, and barges were tied close against a dock and giant cranes moved over them, nodding and whirling as they bit and lifted and spat away the pulp to empty the barges and fill the pit.

From everywhere there rose the sounds of action— of belts and wheels, frictions, grindings, loadings and liftings and all the business of a morning—till even the air you breathed was busy and I could see the sweat of working men soak through their shirts between the shoulder blades. Still no foreman came. If anyone had handed me a hoe and said: "Here, go to work!" I would have considered myself far richer than T. S. Ordway.

About then somebody did come, a man in a dusty pick-up who stopped his little truck five steps away and slumped immediately behind the wheel and began picking his teeth with a match. He had a short face, brown and wrinkled as a nut, sharp as a rodent's, and he wore an ancient cattleman's hat. He stuck both thumbs under the bib of his overalls and stared at the horizon while the match worked itself across his mouth and back again.

"You Mr. Jacks?" I asked.

"Part of the time," said the man, looking far away.
His attention veered slightly to the southwest. He began
singing in a flat nasal voice: "O Susanna, don't you cry
for me . . ." but broke off suddenly and said, looking
due south, "You the new man?"

I said I was.

Archibald Jacks hummed another bar.

"They's-a-boy-inside-the-barn-'ll-show-ye-what-to-
do," he popped out all together and at the same time was
stricken into action, dropped his song, spat out his match,
started his pick-up, and drove away.

In the doorway of the barn I met a little man all in blue
denim, so bowlegged you could have put a half-grown
hog between his knees and never got his blue jeans dirty.

"Howdy," said the little man. He led a saddled horse
and he leveled at me a pair of eyes like two revolvers.

I said "Howdy" quickly, the first time I remember
ever using the word, and somehow it sounded like an
echo to "Hands-up!"

Yet the little man was not unfriendly. He had heard
of me; he would show me my horse. "Barb's a gentle
horse," he said, leading the way down the barn, behind
the mangers. "Pretty good cowhorse, too, for this part
of the country." He pointed to a chunky sorrel with
white stockings. "Looks more like the ponies we had
back home."

"Where·was that?" I asked.

"Utah," said the little man. "Guess Utah was the last
one I had. Say, what do they call you?"

I told him my name and the little man put his hand
out and said, "Mine's Dynamite."

"Danny?" I said.

"No," he said, quite seriously, "*Dynamite*." He was
adjusting a stirrup for me. "Never did give a damn for
twisted stirrup leathers," he said. "Never did see 'em
till I come to Californy. Or Oregon. Guess Oregon was
first. . . . I'd rode for this feller quite some time, Charlie

Devers, Ringbolt Charlie, we called him. I'd noticed once before his leathers was twisted but I just figured, you know, that they'd *got* twisted and he'd straighten 'em when he had the chance. So one day we was riding for White River to do something—I forget what just now, to see a feller who had horses or something. . . . Anyhow, we'd got us down the road a spell and broke our ponies to a lope and I noticed them leathers o' Charlie's still was twisted. 'Hey,' I hollers, 'your leathers!' Charlie, he cranes first over this side, then over that, and looks and gets darker in the face with looking, till I knowed his thunder was a-gonner roll. 'Twisted?' he says. 'Boy, *you're* telling *me* them leathers is twisted? Now what the hell is the matter with you? How do you think leathers orter be?' Oh, he'd got kindy flusterated, took him clear to White River to cool out; and then I explained how back home all the leathers was hung straight. See, he'd never heard o' my way and I'd never heard of his'n, but I guess that's the way it is in life—they's a heap of things a feller never hears about till he travels and meets other folk but his own."

Dynamite made a little boy's grin. He had animal teeth, very white and sharp. "That's how you'll be here," he said, slapping the rump of Barb, the chunky sorrel, "meetin' other folk but your own. So let's start now and get acquainted."

He led the way outside.

Dynamite rode a ragged bay that was the very meaning of the word nag, all head and hind-end, and when he was aboard he showed me how his stirrups hung freely so that he could rake a bronc with his spurs from its ears to its hips. Then he took off down an asphalt road, where Barb and I got just three feet of clearance from the whining trucks, like any other vehicle, and finally we turned into a side alley between mangers lined with cattle, where the feeding heads made a solid row of white almost within touching of my stirrup. The Herefords hardly raised an eye to watch us pass. This, said Dyna-

mite, was because a feed-truck had just dumped its load
He said ten of them took all day to feed the yards, that
each lot of cattle was given a number and a pen when it
came in, and thereafter was never moved until ready to
cut and ship, that a good heifer might gain three pounds
a day while a steer put on two, but she-stuff brought a
cent less per pound because they had more waste to
them. "Take these ladies here, 364's; we're shipping on
'em now. See that roan by the water trough, how the fat
fits tight along her back and covers her hip bones and
makes them like pads aside her tail? See that satchel
down in front between her legs? That's what you eat
when you eat boiled brisket. . . . Now lookie her alongside these here ones over here, 369's; they just come in
last week. Both are long yearlings, both good Hereford,
but these on this side is just a-commencin' to eat. See the
bellies on 'em? If a critter don't belly-down thataway
first, she won't never get fat."

Dynamite pointed out the different brands, all famous
through the West, the Open-A-Bar, the SQ, Double
Slash, and 3C—each speaking for a country and a people
like the flags of ships met in a harbor. One came from
Stovepipe out of Amarillo, one from west Texas, one
from Oklahoma prairie and the plains of Oregon. Each
stood for its great name—Pecos, Rio Grande, Houston,
and Tombstone—for running irons, dust and leather, and
range fires by the rim-rock. "They'd take a lot of tellin',
them brands," said Dynamite, "but to make it easy old
T. S. Ordway put 'em in a pen and just called 'em
369's."

The cattle ate an evil-smelling mash that had something like gold dust scattered over it. I asked what this
might be and Dynamite said the mash was pulp left
from the processing of sugar beets and the dust was dry-
feed from the El Dorado's mill, where oat and barley
hay were chopped with vetch and alfalfa and mixed with
grain and milo maize, cottonseed cake, molasses, bone
meal rich in phosphorus, and one or two other ingredi-

ents that made the best meal a cow critter ever ate and
that laid the fat on thick and hard and white as cream.
The exact proportion only T. S. Ordway knew. It was
his discovery, his secret, and on it he had built his El
Dorado. "He ain't no cattleman, hell . . . he's a busi-
nessman. Why, all of this place ain't no more than a
drawer in his desk. He owns ranches from here to Mexico, banks, buildings in Los Angeles and San Francisco—
everything a man can own. But he knows land best. It
was land brought him here." Dynamite swept the western horizon with his arm. "Twenty thousand acres of the
richest land in America. Sure, it was under water, half of
it, when he come. Give him credit. He done her, he made
her, and she's all his."

I looked into the wind that filled my eyes with
Thomas Ordway's golden feed, whipped from the mangers, and saw it coming on the yellow fields up from salt
marshes and the bay.

"Some panoramic, eh?" said Dynamite.

In the sunlight the sloughs wound through the reeds
like threads of silver. Gulls and water-birds were dark
motes floating high, shining white suddenly when they
tipped against the sun. Beyond them the river spread to
make a bay and far in the distance was again compressed
by hills. I let my eye follow the compass round. South
across the water was a fringe of little towns so far away
their houses looked like pebbles on the opposite shore.
Eastward along the yards low harvest hills unfolded to
the river, with here and there a flock of sheep like a cluster of gray aphids. Northward for many miles the great
alluvial plain rose gradually until it met the hills from
which it had come; and, everywhere beyond, more hills
rolled northward as far as a man might see, holding in
their hollows clumps of unpainted farm buildings that
looked as if they were dying there slowly, like bits of
wood in the trough of the sea. And all of these hills were
such a color of gold and had in them such a marvelous
grace of line that when you looked steadily they seemed

to move, as though they might have flowed once from the same source and instantly been stilled.

"She's big, is El Dorado," said Dynamite, "and famous; but she has her faults like the rest of us. Some things you'll like, some not. Jacks, he's a good boss; the work ain't hard; the fellers of the best. But you'll wonder at seven working days a week and nights when they need you to unload cattle, and three bucks for a day. But we have a good time. We got to. . . . You will, too, when you're 'quainted around. Go up to Bird Town payday, come to our dances— Say, we're having one tonight and you can come. Ever square-dance? All we need's a fiddle and a bare floor, none o' this here fox-trot shilly-shally."

A truck that looked like a cigar box high on a frame was coming down the alley spewing beet-pulp out one side and leaving just enough room for a very thin horse to pass if he had steady nerves. Perched on a rear platform was a man who regulated the speed of unloading and called to the cattle in the pens who followed him bucking and bawling with delight. I followed Dynamite and threw my reins away, let old Barb take me past the truck with nearly an inch to spare between my right knee and the steel frame. Dynamite was already in conversation with the man on the rear platform whose name was Whitey and who, all the time he talked, was kicking a lever with his foot and poking at the pulp with a big feed-fork and interrupting himself now and then to cry out something in a high voice nobody could understand but which meant that the driver was to move on. Dynamite and I came slowly behind.

"Goin' to the dance?"

"Shore 'nuff."

"You wasn't to the last one."

"Shore was."

"Like hell."

"*Shore* I was; I'd go to a dance even if there was nobody there but me."

"I can believe it."

"No, I didn't go. Did you?"

"Yeah."

"How come?"

"Well, I figured you wasn't a-gonna be there."

"Oh, scairt, eh?"

And so it went for a hundred yards down the alley, until the pulp was all gone into the manger and Whitey gave a final cry and a wave to us and was whisked away for another load.

Whitey talked funny—not straight Western like Dynamite nor fully Southern, but something in between. For instance, he pronounced "wrench" and "ranch" exactly alike.

I asked where fellows came from who talked like that.

"Arkansas," said Dynamite. "Ain't you never heard a Arkansawyer talk? Well, you will. That's what we got here, along with the Okies and Missourians, and some from Texas. But you can tell a Arkansawyer. Mostly he's long and thin, red-cheeked and full of big old lies. Great hands to talk, they are, and to throw stones, and every one that's rode a horse says he's a cowboy. Like Jacks— he's one; but he ain't no cowboy. He's just a Arkansas farm boy growed up into a good job, and fat cattle is all he knows. Okies, they's different. We ain't got many that's gen-u-ine but one bunch lives up to Bird Town that I'll show ye, a whole county of 'em, Grandad, old Mammy, Pap and Ma, married boys and their kids—all junked together in one room. You couldn't miss 'em. They all got long manes and that drawed-up look, and wear them Okie caps like they was a-gonna drive a train some place."

I said California people didn't care much for Okies. "There's been a lot of hard words said about them and a lot written."

"Well," said Dynamite, "I tell you . . . I-tell-you-how-it-is. Take a sack of beans out of the field—any kind, pink, white, no matter—and pour 'em in a kettle and see how the foul stuff always comes on top—the straws and little stones. Same way with people. Pour your state into mine and it's the foul stuff shows up most, but the good beans is underneath there just the same, only a feller don't see 'em right away. Shucks sakes, we all got poor white trash—Utah, California, New York City—all of us. 'T ain't nothing to git flusterated over. . . . These folk here, they's good beans, not trash. Maybe they had a place back home but the dust got it, or maybe they got brothers and sisters'n enough back there to care for the old folks and they has to git out and rustle for theirselves. . . . Sure," said Dynamite, and then his eye wandered quickly and he shouted, "Hey you, Will Ragan, what kind of janitor's work are ye up to this day?"

A man bending over a water-trough in one of the pens straightened up slowly and revealed a shaggy Irish face on which three days' growth of beard lay like a heavy frost. "The work o' lazy cowboys is what I'm up to this day," said William Ragan, folding his hands across the top of a broom he had been using to clean the trough and getting ready to enjoy himself.

"Now lookie here, lookie here! . . . I'll not have no talkin' smart on such a day!" said Dynamite, and they both laughed and laughed. "Say, what did ye think of the fight?" Dynamite meant the prizefight of the night before in which a Pittsburgh Irishman had nearly whipped Joe Louis.

"Oh, aye," said William, "and it's well enough, I guess. Or else the Irish would be a-thinkin' themselves better than the niggers." And again he roared and slapped his thigh and poked Dynamite's horse in the flank with his broom handle, and there was three minutes' general rampage before Dynamite and I could go on.

We passed a construction crew repairing an alley, and Dynamite got his little boy's grin ready for each man and a word launched with the full vigor of his name:

"Hi Fred, hi Jingle. . . . Not doin' much, eh, Joe?" And to a man named Tex leaning on a shovel: "*Care*-ful! Easy there, Tex, or ye're a-gonner bust that handle!" He called them all the WPA and cursed them, and they loved it.

Then for a while Dynamite had nothing to say, so he sang a song:

> O send me a letter,
> Send it by mail.
> Send it in care *of*
> The Birmingham jail.
> > The Birmingham jail, love.
> > The Birmingham jail. . . .
> > The Birmingham jail. . . .
> > Pining for you, love. . . .

On a space of level ground we passed a haystack three hundred feet long and thirty high where a crane unloaded semi-trailers of hay. The trucks drove alongside the stack; the crane swung over, dangling a cable to which the driver hooked both ends of a net made of wire that lined the compartments of the truck and onto which the hay had been loaded. Five seconds later a parcel weighing several tons was delivered on the stack just as freight is loaded on a ship, there to be spread around by three men with pitchforks. "Old Ordway figured it," said Dynamite. "They tell how he come down here one afternoon and seen a dozen guys pitching hay and a dozen more trying to catch what the wind didn't blow away, and then he set and went to thinkin' and next Tuesday-week he bought the Company another crane and a hundred yards of wire cable and let a dozen men go down the road."

So we made our rounds until we came to the scale-house by the mill where the men like to sit for a smoke in the shade, or go inside the little iron shack and read the *True Detectives* Gene, the weighmaster, keeps piled there under his scale. By four o'clock it's time for talk-

ing; so the boys were ready on the bench when Dynamite and I came around. Then they shut up like clams
and looked at the earth and the sky and somehow managed to see everything there was about me before I'd got
within a hundred yards.

Dynamite sailed right in. "Jody," he said to a thin
little man with glasses and a great big country hat of
straw, "don't pay no 'tention to them other guys but just
give me a plain answer: when do we run our race?"

"Any time suits me," said Jody, making marks on the
ground with the used end of a match.

"Okay then," said Dynamite, "tomorry. We'll run tomorry instead of going to church. We'll measure out one
hundred yards of the road this side o' Bird Town."

"You want to make a man work Sunday?" said Jody.

"*Chicken!*" said a young man who lounged out of the
scalehouse and was able to keep both hands in his pockets by nudging the screen with one elbow and letting it
slam shut behind. "Jody, he's made ye a play. Auntie or
throw in your hand." Jaydee Jones, raised on Arkansas
corn fritters, ham and hominy, had at one time or other
taken something dark inside him that came out now on
his face and made every word he said funny, with a
sting. Not looking anywhere in particular, he sauntered
over to Dynamite and began combing his horse's mane
with the fingers of one hand. He asked if there was a
dance that night, if Lear had paid Dynamite the two
bucks. Then Jaydee's face got serious with thought.
"Say," he said, "did you hear about that 'lectrician over
at Vista City?"

"What about him?" said Dynamite.

"Dead," said Jaydee.

"Yeah?" said Dynamite.

For a minute, then another minute and another that
was all.

"How did it happen?" I asked.

Jaydee said quickly, "Oh, he set down on a fruit cake
and a currant ran up his laig."

The only sound was a muffled rubbing of the gears inside the mill. Jaydee sauntered back and leaned against the wall of the scalehouse and called for somebody inside named Pringle to bring him out the Climax Plug.

"Well," Dynamite said to me, "the hell with these guys. We got important business to attend to. Let's get outa here."

We rode away and when I saw Dynamite watching me, I grinned for the little cowboy and said, "I was cut too green, wasn't I? Bet if you'd stick me in the ground, I'd grow."

"Aw shucks," said Dynamite. "You ate horse, sure. But we all got to sometimes. Now you'll know Jaydee— he's kindy thataway."

We rode the alley toward the barn, watching for leaky troughs or boards off gates, dead animals, or any of those casual changes the laws of chance occurrence bring wherever a species is gathered. We found only Jacks, sitting in his pick-up by the barn as though he just happened to be there, sucking a match and looking at the horizon. In a voice so confidential it would have served to announce the merger of six companies he told Dynamite the cattle trucks would be in at eleven.

When he had gone, Dynamite swore all around the compass. "Never knew it to fail, *never* did. Cattle, cattle every day in the week and if a feller wants to dance Saturday night and have a little fun, it's nothing doing, it's *cattle*. Jesus Christ. I quit."

He stormed into the barn.

He was still saying "To hell with 'em; I quit," when the ponies were bedded-down and I was driving toward the buildings of the main ranch. "Lemme out here," said Dynamite as we passed a quadrangle of galvanized iron garages, the place the feed-trucks stayed all night.

"You're not going to the bunkhouse?" I asked.

"Me? Hell no. What would I want with a bunkhouse. I got one o' my own up to Bird Town. Wife and four kids in it." Dynamite lifted himself out, then reached for his lunch-bucket. "I'll call for ye at eleven," he said, still angry, and walked away.

To reach the bunkhouse of the El Dorado Investment Company, you passed a kind of used-car lot where no vehicle built within the last ten years, with any paint, upholstery, unbroken window, or any kind of operating decency, was exhibited. The bunkhouse itself was two old farmhouses sewn together with some sketchy carpentering. There were in all about a dozen bare rooms—six beds in the front one and so on back. Over a kind of closet by the door someone had smeared "Bull Cook" in red paint. I knocked here and an old man came out and pointed to a bed in the corner beside what once had been a chiffonier. "Give the mattress a once-over," he said, handing me the fly-spray. "Washroom's out back. The Widder Ellen, we call it, is that house by the cypress tree."

I worked over the mattress, then dumped my blankets on the bed and took a towel and went to find the washroom. Men coming from work lined the sink. There were gray basins and hot and cold running water. In the confusion it was easy to come and go and I would have moved unnoticed but for the electrician who had sat upon the fruit cake. I read knowledge of this unhappy story in every face and fled away indoors, devoured by a thousand eyes. I spent the time till supper lying on my bed because there was no place to sit except a bench and table in the middle of the room, where a man might expect to sit when he had worked for the El Dorado at least a year and never asked questions out of turn.

The occupants of the other beds came in. You would find them repeated over and over in any bunkhouse of the West, men of indefinite age, the old Jaspers who drive the Chevies and Model-A Fords, who lift the picks and build the fences, whose only home is four bare walls and a bare floor.

The supper bell rang before it was time to light two

bulbs that hung on cords from the ceiling. Nobody had said a word.

I followed behind the men, under cypress trees where the wind touched mournfully, into the cookhouse where all the others found seats. The long table was set with white oilcloth and heavy white plates and dishes heaping with food. Through an open door was the kitchen; the cook stood over his black stove, and rows of pots and spoons and knives hung each from its nail. In the doorway lounged a great gob of a man who wore a sailor's hat and nothing over his undershirt and pants but an apron. He smiled stupidly at everyone, his teeth protruding, and when I told him I was a new hand, said, "Sure, sure!" and laid one greasy paw across my back and pointed with the other to the end of the table.

There were boiled spuds and fat red beans that would keep a man going all day long, and pale string beans that really were strung, and also meat done country style, to the color and texture of gray leather. At intervals along the table stood those mysterious clumps of sauces, bottles that are never used or cleared away but stand forever fixed to the tables of American ranches—a sort of nucleus around which meals are built.

I carefully did not ask for things beyond my reach for fear of drawing attention, but the men were too busy to look at me. Along the table the double row of bodies bent and went to eating with a deadly earnest, hunched forward, no two alike yet all the same, each scarred and twisted, grown crooked from the roots, too long for its trunk or too short for its head, here missing a thumb, here an eye; yet all of them had grown in spite of every difficulty, like tough cedar trees from a rock.

Except for the Arkansawyers, the eaters were silent. But these were so altogether friendly they just couldn't stand to see a bite go down alone; it had to have a word for company, or maybe two. And if three were needed and your mouth was full of potatoes, that didn't matter

—it just showed what a good man could do with the English language. "Jody," said Jaydee Jones, "pass me the Mussolini."

Jody handed over a platter of red spaghetti.

"You backed out today," said Jaydee. "Jody, you got feather-legged."

"Aw, you're just a-talkin' now," said Jody.

"Diney offered ye the chance; ye wouldn't run."

"Let's me and *you* run," said Jody.

"Me run again you? Why man," said Jaydee, "I'd tromp you to death in fifty yards."

"Let's make it a hundred then," said Jody. "I sure wanta live till payday."

"Hell, I run down a deer once't," went on Jaydee.

"That's nothing," Jody said. "Look at Roy there; he run down a Arkansas woman."

Everybody did look at Roy who got about the color of the spaghetti.

"Sure," said Jaydee, "and ever since he ain't been able to buy her a pair of shoes."

The fat waiter wanted to be friends. While everybody still was laughing at Roy, he called from the doorway to Jaydee, "Jaydee, hey Jaydee! . . . Let's you and me go to Sacramento this Saturday. I know a couple of dolls up there on G Street." Most of all the fat waiter wanted to be acquainted with a man named Sandy, who sat back-toward him on the near side of the table. Whenever possible, he stood close to Sandy, watching him dumbly like an affectionate dog. He brought freshly filled platters with "Here Sandy, try this. . . . Here Sandy, this'll put lead in your pencil." When Sandy talked about wild parties with the man next to him, the fat waiter eagerly broke in, "Did you ever throw a whing-ding in Chicago?" But Sandy kept on talking and after a while the waiter had to make his own answer, grinning at the air: "Boy, I sure did in '36. I *sure* threw a hummer there!"

After supper the men stacked their dishes and left them on the table by the kitchen door. Nobody smoked until he got outside and then within ten steps every man seemed to have rolled and lit a Bull Durham. They went in groups of three or four, laughing, swearing, tripping each other, ragging Jody about his foot-race and Roy about his Arkansas woman; and at intervals between them walked a solitary figure, a stranger, an habitual grouch, a pervert, a Mexican, or some other outcast— each desiring in his heart nothing so much as to be included in these rough words and coarse laughter.

Someone had switched the lights on in the bunkhouse and lit a fire in the wood stove. The bare bulbs brought to completion the bare walls, ceiling, floors, and faces of the men and made them into a little world of barrenness sealed by the night. They lay upon their beds, heads on folded hands, and stared at the ceiling until time to go to bed. Though it was hot and the place filled quickly with tobacco smoke, nobody opened a window. Nobody said a word.

I slept. The next I knew, Dynamite was standing over me, saying, "Come along, cowboy."

Outside it was bright starlight. The wind had risen and darkness had released into it ten thousand new and exciting smells, each like a thought of voyages and adventure, and now it rose again and beat above us wildly through the trees like water on a lonely shore.

Dynamite's car was a 1926 Packard Sedan, a monster-vehicle, the kind wealthy ladies keep forever in their retinue, pensioned like faithful servants. But here the lady died too soon. Dynamite paid seventy-five dollars for the car, he said, and told how it came in handy as nursery for his children and as a truck for hauling wood or hogs or calves that were born in the yards and taken home. It had no glass in the rear door, no rear seat, no upholstery that a child or a hog had not stained and scented permanently, but wonderful to say—and this Dynamite pointed out immediately—the vases inside the rear doors that once a liveried chauffeur had filled with jasmine and gardenias, were still unbroken, and in one of them were tucked brown shreds of flowers, poppies, placed there last spring by one of Dynamite's little girls.

Dynamite parked beside the barn, scrunched down and kicked his feet up on the dashboard, and told me to get in back if I liked, because the trucks might be an hour or they might be five. Reluctantly I did so, climbing over from the front seat into I-could-not-see-what perils, and finally making myself almost comfortable between an old tire and a wad of gunny sacks that served as rear seat.

For a time nothing was said. The wind brought a cold mist up from the marshes that shut out the stars and set the fog-horns moaning on the river. Across the road cattle stirred in their pens, coughing now and then, and the wind beside us made a lonely, lonely sound through the cracks in the barn.

"Oh, I hate this place!" said Dynamite. "Sometimes I hate it more than ever I did man or woman. Funny a feller can git so riled at just a place. But Jesus, seven days a week is wearisome, very wearisome. Last time I had off was in May to go to a rodeo—one day I took."

Again he was quiet; then flared up, "I and the wife had hell tonight. . . . Got home from work, nobody there, no bath, no supper, chickens into the tomatoes, back door open. Pretty soon, here they come, the whole dang chivaree and the dog, trailing in off the hill like a herd a-comin' to water. 'What the hell is it now?' I says to her. . . . I was mad anyway, see, 'bout not gettin' to the dance. Well, it was the sow. 'The sow *this*, the sow *that, the sow got restless so we let her out.* . . .' Well, the sow's gonna farrer, that's why she's restless, and I told that woman a thousand times not to let her out 'cause she'll hide her pigs sure as hell's fire, and we'll have fed her six months for nothing. So I was mad and we went round and round. Me and the wife don't get along, anyway. Never did."

"You're from Utah," I said. "I thought people there had lots of wives and were always happy."

"No more, they don't, least not in public; but I knew old Mormons back in the Bookcliffs that by God never knowed they'd joined the United States. They done her the old way still—wives, kids, the whole shebang. Oh, Mormons is good people. Take an outlaw traveling through their country—they'll always help him, never squeal on him."

"You're a Mormon?"

"Oh, kind of, I guess—kind of a Jack-Mormon. That was wher I worked for one on Tennessee Crick out o' Rock City—old Josiah Bean. . . . Bear of a worker, old Joey was, and a devil of a good man with stallions. Had dozens of 'em. Some he'd caught wild out of the hills and some he'd raised, but they all was gentle when he come around. He taught me a lot about stallions. 'Never let 'em get away with nothin',' he says, 'A stallion's not like a gelding that'll try ye once and quit; he's cocky. He fig-ures if you win today, maybe he'll win tomorry, and he'll keep a-trying ye and keep a-trying.' I seen old Joey lead a black maverick stud through a barn full of mares, and if old stud cocked an ear or made so much as a whicker under his breath, Joey'd turn and just kick the stuffin' outa him right under the belly where it hurts, and then he'd turn around and lead that stud back and forth two or three times more just to show him. Great guy, old Joey. . . . Used to talk the Mormon religion to me. I was just a snot of a kid then and I guess he figured he'd get me early and lead me in the blessed way. I'd sit there on a bale of hay and let my eyes get big as saucers when he'd talk about God and Hellfire. . . . Pretend to take it all, you know, but Joey had a little daughter sixteen years old, Letticia, Letticia Bean, that I took to more'n ever I did his preaching. I never could go that stuff about turn yer other cheek when a guy slaps ye on this one. . . . Could you?"

I said I'd found it hard to go sometimes.

"And that stuff about Hellfire, how when a feller goes to Hell and gets to burnin' he don't never burn up, just stays there forever and burns and burns. I can't see it. I can't see how any Lord Jesus is gonna be that cruel. Why take even these here gangsters, John Dillingers and people, you wouldn't want to treat them that way, would ye? And tell *me* that just ordinary folks like you and me that does a sin or two is a-gonna burn and burn! *I* can't see it. . . . You got religion?"

"Kind of," I said. "My grandfather was a minister."

"Catholic?"

"No, Episcopal."

"A what?"

I explained about the Episcopal Church.

"My granddaddy was a Baptist," said Dynamite. "That's pretty near the same as a Christian, ain't it?"

I agreed and Dynamite continued: "I had an Aunt Olga that was great on the Catholic Church—what I mean she was for it strong! Used to say she'd give God Almighty anything she had and I reckon she would. Uncle Willie was different. He was off somewheres most of the time, though he always did send money home, and every year or two he'd come back himself and Olga would have another baby—nineteen she totaled. But she thought the world of Uncle Willie. Said she'd rather live with him in a dugout than with any other man in a castle, and that's about what she done. . . . Oh, that Uncle Willie was a great feller to hunt! One time I remember, he went to Canada and sent Aunt Olga home a moose, just the head of it, ye know. . . . Oh, I guess this here God-business is all right if ye like it, I just don't care for it myself."

I was sleeping again when Dynamite sang out, "Here they be!" and I heard the guttural roar of the Diesel and saw the dark hull of truck-and-trailer turning toward the barn, cutting the fog with powerful searchlights and decorated fore and aft like a ship with red and yellow clearance lights. The monster shifted gears and roared on by to find the chute.

Dynamite was there before it, signaling the driver

with his flashlight as the door came opposite the chute. Then he took the bull-board, a small beam four feet long and several inches wide fitted with iron cross-pieces at the end, and dropped it in the narrow gap between the chute and the truck. Then he undid and lifted out the door and wired it to the side of the chute. From inside came the stench of cattle. They were seen dimly, stowed like sacks in the darkness. They did not try to come out.

Dynamite climbed the top of the truck. The driver was standing by a headlight looking at his watch.

"Hey there below!" shouted Dynamite.

"Hey there above!" shouted the driver. "Is that you, Powder Keg?"

"And who else might it be, will ye tell me that? And while ye are at it, tell me where ye've been this past hour and a half?"

"Whadya mean 'Where have I been?' I been traveling, boy, traveling! Since eight o'clock this morning I've had my nose to that old concrete."

"Oh, don't hand me them stale pertaters. I know you guys—stop here for a steak, stop there for a beer, stop in Modesto to see my gal. . . ."

While he was talking, Dynamite kicked at the heads of the cattle nearest the door, and now he turned on them his full attention in words that lashed like cuts of rawhide. "Hyar, hyar ye sons of bitches! Outside!"

But the cattle were afraid of the open door.

"Shine your light in the chute," commanded Dynamite, and when this was done, the cattle went right out. They were small cattle, yearlings, poor and weak. "Where did ye get *these* things?" said Dynamite.

"Oh, down the line there five hundred miles. . . . Havermeyers, isn't it? I got it on my book. First trip ever I made to that place."

"Bad road?"

"Bad road! . . . No road at all. Blue cracked a drive shaft coming out and Dolly—no telling when Dolly'll be here."

"Never knew it to fail," said Dynamite.

The driver pulled ahead, the trailer was unloaded, and Dynamite and I took the cattle down the alley a hundred yards to the scales, Dynamite explaining that by order of the State Railroad Commission, which being a *railroad* commission naturally had it in for trucks, all cattle-trucks must weigh their loads immediately on reaching their destination, while for the railroads this was not true. "It's the old railroad graft, is what it is. They got their commission, see? And the trucks ain't got the chance of a snowball in hell."

The scales was a galvanized iron building at the end of the alley. You pushed the cattle clear down and then closed a gate which held them in the alley till you could go around and open the scale door and push the critters in, one draft at a time. Dynamite went ahead inside and lit an electric bulb, and I could hear him slapping the iron markers on the bar until they came in balance. "We'll take 'em half-and-half," the cowboy called, coming back, and we advanced together in the darkness and let the shapes of yearlings swirl around us toward the light until Dynamite leaped out, shouting terribly, which drove back half the bunch and sent the others nearly out the end of the scales. He slammed the heavy door just in time to stem the backwash of cattle and I followed him into the region of the electric bulb, which was nothing but a dirt floor and a box that housed the weighing mechanism and a board that jutted from the wall and evidently served as desk, for there were two old notebooks on it and a pencil.

"Ye can count 'em off," said Dynamite, bending over and tapping the markers and saying, "Whoa, cattle, whoa, cattle," in a voice designed to keep the tangled, swirling, bawling mass of cattle on the scale from destroying itself. I looked at the yearlings through a crack between two boards. The yellow light striped them weirdly. They didn't look at all poor or weak, and I wondered how any man on earth would be able to count them when that door came open.

"Okay!" sang Dynamite.

I opened the door wide.

Nothing happened. Then one animal put a foot out; then it took a step; then an avalanche of cattle rattled out over the boards like stones rolling down a mountain.

"How many?" said Dynamite.

"Dunno," I said.

"Didn't think ye would," said Dynamite. "But that's okay; that's all right. Next time stand out front a little and they'll not go so fast."

"Yeah, that's all right," I said. "That's hell, that's *suicide!*"

Dynamite laughed and laughed.

The truck had rolled down opposite the scales and stopped, its great cylinders idling hoarsely, getting their breath after five hundred miles. The driver, known as "Done Movin', the Laziest Man in the World," helped weigh the second draft.

"Not bad," said Dynamite. "Not bad for a city bred."

"Listen, small man, I was punching cows before you was born," replied Done Movin', and stuck Dynamite affectionately with a pencil. He was a grinning man, fat, with bad teeth and he wore brown whipcord trousers and khaki shirt and a chauffeur's cap on the back of his head with three Union buttons pinned to it.

Dynamite assailed him once more: "How'd you happen to git here first? Most times you piddle in 'long about the middle of next week." And they insulted each other back and forth while Dynamite weighed the cattle and I waited by the door, wondering what it might be to stand in front of 14,228 pounds of terror-stricken beef.

Dynamite gave his okay.

I had the sudden inspiration not to open the door very wide and then the cattle might pour out thinly like anything else. I cracked the door a few feet. A yearling

nosed out suspiciously, another followed, and another
was three and then ten thousand yearlings hit the door
and the door hit me and I went down against the fence
and stayed there while the side of my head took fire
slowly and the stars went round and round.

Dynamite poked his face out. "Hey, cowboy? All
right?" Then he saw me and began to laugh. Done
Movin' came and the moment he saw me his face brightened and he joined Dynamite in a truly hearty laugh.
"Don't never stand *behind* a door thataway," said Dynamite. "You'll get killed. Open the thing wide and stand
out front where they can see ye."

As I came back inside the scales, holding my head in
a handkerchief, Done Movin' was reminded of a story:
"Like the other day I had my racks off and went to hauling grain. So I had a flat right in front of that asylum
there in Napa and got my tools out and went to work.
D'rectly this guy come along, decent enough, 'bout fifty
I'd say, could have been anybody's daddy, and he starts
a-axing questions. Axed me what I done and I told him.
Axed me how much I had on and I could tell him to a
pound, 31,180 'cause I'd just weighed-in at the Bridge.
'Thirty-one thousand,' he says, just as polite, and 'Thank
you,' and he walks away. Well, I changed my tire and
drove along and was gettin' in towards Napa when I
heard the siren. 'Say,' the copper tells me, 'you run over
a guy back there.' He's kindy severe. 'Nossir,' I says, 'I
never run over nobody; not that I know of.' 'You come
along with me,' he says. So we turn around together and
go back, nine mile, maybe ten, and we get to the asylum
and right there in front is the feller who'd been axing me
them questions. He's kind of down and out, fact is he's
plastered to the pavement like a postage stamp. . . . A
looney, see? He'd been trying to do it a long time, and
when he did get loose he axed me all them questions so
polite and then just walked around between the truck
and trailer and laid down."

"Well, I'll be goddamned," said Dynamite.

"Yessir," said Done Movin', "that's what happened. Here," he said, "sign my ticket. I gotta be in Reno this time tomorrow." He held out a bill of lading and Dynamite signed it and kept the carbon duplicate. "Moller oughta be here any time. He was right behind me at the river, but the drawbridge got him."

"Good old Commodore," said Dynamite. "That'll make him ornerier 'n buckskin. He sure hates not to be first."

"Well, take it easy, boys!" said Done Movin' and was on his way.

We stood outside the scales and watched the big Diesel pull away into the mist, heard it shift for the slope by the beet-pulp pit, and shift again for the level of the county road, and go away up into the hills till only an echo came back faintly, like the baying of a hound.

"One gone," said Dynamite. "One gone and a dozen to go. We may as well get back to sleep."

He spoke of Moller who would bring the next truck in. They called him "Commodore" because he told everybody what to do and they laughed at him because he had no authority. He'd kill himself to get in first; never stopped for a beer and a sandwich, only for fuel. And once in a while, when he telephoned home to get his orders as all drivers did, and the dispatcher gave him orders for the others, too, he had his reward.

We heard another Diesel roar and the sound of heavy gears working on the turn beyond the barn. The Commodore was coming.

This time Dynamite left me alone and went away to fix the gates in the alley and balance the scales. In the darkness, my head still burning, I watched the Commodore roll up slowly and put the door of his truck even with the chute on the first try—a pretty good piece of work for after midnight. The engine idled down, the Commodore got out and stopped before the headlights to look at his watch, and next moment he stood beside me on the dark strip of footboard that runs along a cattle chute, just the outline of him against the fog.

"Well, you made her," I said.

"Yeah," said the Commodore, sympathetic as stone. "Where's Dynamite?"

"Down the line."

"Anyone ahead of me?"

"One," I said.

"Who was it, Henry?"

"A guy named Done Movin'."

"Well, that's Henry, ain't it? . . . I seen him at the Bridge."

I was trying to get the door open but couldn't because the Commodore had done such a good job of pulling up to the chute he had wedged it. "Here," said the Commodore, "lemme show ya." He jumped down and wrenched and tore the door away and counted the cattle carefully as they came off, twenty-four head, somehow managing always to keep his back to me, as though maybe I had shown myself a member of some inferior race, unworthy of a clear front view.

Ten minutes later a first draft was on the scales, but still no Commodore appeared. "Okay!" yelled Dynamite, and I remembered my job was to count cattle without being killed. Dynamite had said stand out in front. Dynamite had laughed loudly and long. The misgiving went through me like a sudden pain that Dynamite and Jaydee Jones were one of a kind. "Okay, okay!" sang Dynamite, "what's holdin' up the dee-tail?"

I barely put a finger on the latch. The heavy door leapt open and swung back and somehow there I was alone, just I, squarely in the black mouth of the scales, from where there came a bawling and a seething and a splintering of redwood, as though all hell were in there ready to break loose. But it didn't. Not an animal offered to move. My blood was running better and I took a step backward. A thin stream of yearlings trickled by. I counted them easily. When the stream became too large, I stepped forward, thinning it. If the yearlings ran too thin, I stepped backward and their flow increased. There was nothing to it.

"Twenty-four head!" I yelled.

"That's what I got," boomed the voice of the Commodore like a grenade exploding in the little shed; yet it was meant for me—a hard kind of compliment. The Commodore explained to Dynamite why he had come late: "So when I got back from Phoenix, I told 'em I wasn't ready to go—I'd been out a hundred hours then—but they said, 'Now listen here, T. S. Ordway wants these cattle; and whose name is wrote bigger around here, his or yours?' That's what the dispatcher said. So I gassed up and hit the road. I was the last one into Havermeyers, last one loaded out. I lent a hand to all the other guys; not one of 'em stayed to help me. But I know that Strawberry cut-off, see, where she hits the ridge this side of Nelson's Corner, so I took a left on 88 and saved two hours and came in flying clear to the River Bridge, leading *all* the way. And there I had to stop and fuel and while the hose was in the tank I seen Henry's Number 4 go by, but I'd have caught him even yet if the goddamned drawbridge hadn't stopped me." As he thought of what this bridge had done, the lines in the face of the Commodore grew deeper still, like iron bands cutting into wood. He asked no sympathy; he gave the facts. He was a Prussian and he punished himself and his machine of rubber, steel, and Diesel oil with concrete miles, as he would have punished all flesh and blood until it submitted, or became steel. "If anyone wants me," he said as he was leaving, "I'll be at the Princess Hotel in Sacramento."

The Diesel roared full-throated; the air brakes sighed; the Commodore became an echo fading in the night.

Now trucks came rapidly—two at a time, three, four —and their snoring in the line before the barn, their many-colored twinkling lights and shouts and horns made the yard look like an estuary filled with ships, or a great river anchorage with vessels waiting for the tide. In the darkness men became voices. I swore and kicked and sweated over the dank and stinking beds of trucks with comrades I never saw—Oklahoma Dutch, plain Swedish, Spanish, the lingo of Portugee Bill who owned a pool hall in Tulare and ran a bookie business on the side. These men lived quickly and were gone, yet I had known them better than if I'd seen them face to face all day.

A stubby Irishman named Kelly had a spell of trouble. His cattle would not unload. He tried them in Ulster, in South Orange, in Brooklyn, and the best of Frisco cussing, but they wouldn't move. "Goddamn," he said, breathless on the rafters that hold the open bed of a truck apart, "come out ye sons-of-bitches, it's Kelly talkin'." And they came.

So the hours were used up. At three o'clock the wind blew the fog away and let us see the stars men know who work by night—late stars, somehow brighter and better than the ones you see around ten o'clock when most people go to bed. They splattered through the sky from north to south, dusty and brown, like somebody had run there with a bucket and spilled them. They looked down and they knew who worked and who didn't and who owns the world when everything lies quiet. A truck had just pulled away. Dynamite and I stood still in the alley and the voice of the wind came rising through the boards and rails reminding us that man is very small and the earth by night is very long and lonely.

We had good luck when the last three loads came in together, even Blue with the broken shaft; but these drivers, nineteen hours on the road, would not go home. They stood around the headlights of the first big Moreland Diesel, bills of lading signed, nothing to hold them but their cigarettes and talk of what had happened in the day: "It was just where the Grapevine hits concrete and makes four lanes, takes off steep there beyond Bakersfield ten mile. So Kelly had her flying high and wide, comin' off in over-drive, you know, with me a-chasin'. Right there was where he blowed 'er. Sure thought he was gone. . . . Took her to the fourth lane and met a tanker coming up, so he took her back and she hit the ditch with her right three and dug a furry and a cloud of dust you could see by the moon. And his load got shiftin' and the frames picked up the sway and he cut a wiggle like a snake down U.S. 44. Oh, I tell you, watching him was misery. I sweat cold. I wished the bastard would spill and put me out of pain, but he never—the crazy Irishman. I'd have jumped or prayed or done something sensible, but not him—not Kelly. He rode her through and brought her out the end a-weavin' in that traffic like a maiden through the daisy-chain. . . ."

A deputy dispatcher had come along, red-haired, clean, and young American as football and corduroy trousers. He told the others where to go. "Potts," he said, "you beat it to Eureka; lay over there. Call in tomorrow, Fresno Operator 13, and she'll tell you where to go. Blue, you get that propeller-shaft to the warehouse and after breakfast—that's six o'clock for you, that ain't very long now—you take Henley's Number 9 and meet Joe Streets at Appleton, the junction there, and he'll give you his load for the city and you take 'em right on in. He has to be at Winnemuca this time Monday to haul sheep and he's been out three days. Charlie, I don't care what the hell you do. You might even go to bed somewheres, but make damn sure it's alone!"

Minute after minute they lingered, stretching this longest hardest day until somebody mentioned steak, and the idea grew and finally it was agreed they should meet at a certain diner at a certain red neon sign where Highway 18 cuts the Danvers Slough. So they got in and gunned their motors till the sleeping yards roared back the sound, and with a shout and a touch of the horn they were gone off homeward in the night. We stood alone and listened for them shifting on familiar slopes and turns, and heard them baying far along the valley till at last no sound came back.

The job was done.

Day came rapidly as I crossed the silent quadrangle of garages and heard Dynamite's old Packard labor home. I entered the washroom to clean myself and have a drink —the night's work had dried me out—and there at the sink was Jaydee Jones washing with a bar of bright red soap.

I put my lips under a faucet and took a drink.

Jaydee rubbed his face hard with his towel. "B'lieve I've took the pleurisy," he said, rubbing his chest and shoulder vigorously. "Got *such* a pain." And he made circles in the air with his shoulder and right arm. I knew there was nothing in the world the matter with Jaydee, that Jaydee knew this and knew I knew it. Once burned and twice wary, I washed my hands and said nothing.

"That old bunkhouse," went on Jaydee. "That damned old *thing!* Why there's a westerly gale across't my cot I'd be proud to see Columbus have."

I suggested a compress of hot towels.

"Reckon so?" said Jaydee. "Dunno about hot towels. Had a little cousin Sally to git a lung blistered by a hot towel her mammy give her. . . . Oh, I reckon I *could* heat one just a little. But I kind o' hate to, thinkin' about what it done to Sally Mae. Git yore cattle in?"

"Yeah," I said. "We got 'em. Took us all night but we finally got 'em."

"You stayed with her, eh?" said Jaydee, looking out at me for the first time from under his towel. "W-e-l-l, my old daddy used to tell me what I done by night was worth twice what I could do by day, providin' I weren't caught at it."

Jaydee's dark expression never changed, but he didn't bother to go on rubbing with the towel. I began to wash. When Jaydee saw I had no soap, he said, "Here y'are. Use mine," and flipped me the bright red bar.

Afterwards I went indoors and sat on the edge of my bed and began unlacing two shoes that suddenly felt made of lead, not leather. I didn't want to sleep. I wanted to go back outside and talk longer with Jaydee; but some cranes that had been roosting in the cypress trees flew away, making harsh cries, and I watched them go across the field, trailing each other through the early light.

I lay down then and fell asleep, knowing, without bothering to care just why, that the El Dorado Investment Company had room for me.

MODERN LIBRARY GIANTS

A series of sturdily bound and handsomely printed, full-sized library editions of books formerly available only in expensive sets. These volumes contain from 600 to 1,400 pages each.

THE MODERN LIBRARY GIANTS REPRESENT A SELECTION OF THE WORLD'S GREATEST BOOKS

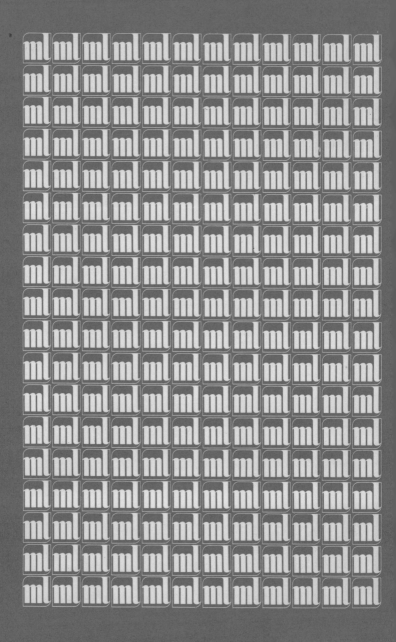